THE FLORENTINE

TOM TROTT

My thanks go to

Julia Crouch
SJ Watson
My wife
My parents
Jill Arnold
Phoenix Kiernan
Ann Horne
J.R. Riedel
Bekah Bosler
...and anyone else I've forgotten

PROLOGUE

The Package

There was a fly trapped in the fluorescent, but otherwise the corridor was silent, and he hadn't seen a soul on his way up. He rapped three sharp knocks on her door and listened, opening himself up to every sound. A car blasting out a steady thump of music sped past on the street below. A fire escape door slammed somewhere in the scratching wind circling the building. The distant rumble of the protestors swelled and died like an ocean wave. And all the time, the fluorescent buzzed and popped behind his ear. A horrible, desperate sound as the fly slowly cooked. Every few seconds its black dot would smack against the frosted plastic. Did it know, he wondered. Did it understand its situation? Any more than *she* did?

He focussed in on the sounds inside her apartment, training taking over. Floorboards creaked. Experience told him he was being studied through the spyhole. Boards creaked again, and a minute later three locks were undone, but not the chain, and the apartment door opened just a crack.

'Good evening, Miss.'

'Can I help you?'

He smiled. 'I require a few minutes of your time.'

'Who are you?'

He pulled his ID from his suit pocket. 'We share a common employer.'

She read it carefully. He saw her eyes widen as she read his name.

'Perhaps we could talk inside.'

She shut the door to undo the chain, then opened it wide, stepping back as though afraid she might catch something from him. He stepped into a studio apartment separated with screens into kitchen, bedroom, and living space.

He shut the door behind him. 'I apologise for calling on you so late, Miss. You *are* Miss Dolly Lightfoot, correct?'

She nodded.

'You already know my name.'

'Do I?'

'My ID.'

She nodded. 'Solomon Cabrera.'

'You've heard of me?'

His hands stayed by his side, but his eyes groped around the apartment, pulling books from the shelves, fondling pictures on the wall, leaving finger smears on the empty fish tank that took up half the dining table.

She folded her arms. 'Is there a problem?'

'I noticed a lot of street food sellers on my walk up the block,' he said, peering out the window. 'It's so nice to live in the beating heart of a city, don't you think? So many of the people I visit live in characterless suburbs, no identity to them. Designed that way, of course. Inoffensive, I suppose, but I'm not sure why that's anything to strive for.'

2

'Well, I can't afford to live in those places.'

'No fish?' he said, pointing to the empty tank.

'How can I help you?'

'I hope I'm not interrupting anything, I don't want to mess with your evening plans.'

'No plans tonight.'

She was still in her work suit, but she had swapped her smart shoes for trainers.

'Not going out anywhere?'

'With the protests?'

He nodded.

'How can I help you?' she repeated.

'There has been something of an incident this evening.' He stared at two Hong Kong action movie posters that dominated the longest wall, framing her television. To the left, *Last Hurrah for Chivalry*, to the right, *A Better Tomorrow*. 'I must say, you have a distinctive style.'

'This stuff was here when I moved in. What kind of incident?'

'Even the fish tank?'

'No, not the fish tank.'

'But no fish?'

She stumbled. A flash of panic in her eyes?

'It would be better if we sat down,' he said.

She attempted a smile. 'In that case, maybe you'd like a coffee?'

He froze, staring at an empty beer bottle on her windowsill. 'Is that a Pacifico?'

'Yes. I've got two more in the fridge. You want one?'

'Yes, please. You'll have one too?'

'The coffee's already made.'

She disappeared behind the screen into the kitchenette. Bottles clinked as she opened and closed the fridge. A filter jug clicked in and out of its slot. She returned with a cup of black coffee and a perfectly chilled brown bottle of Pacifico Clara.

They took the two seats at the table and sampled their drinks.

'Are you a Dolores? Or a Dorothy?'

'Just Dolly.'

'Named after the singer?'

'My mom just liked the name.'

'Just Dolly,' he repeated. 'I was named after the wise king, you know him?'

'The one who cut the baby in half.'

He smiled. 'Threatened to, yes. The judgement of Solomon.'

'From the Old Testament.'

'Yes.' He took a deep draught of the Pacifico, holding it in his mouth before swallowing, savouring the flavour like a fine cigar. 'How did you manage to get Mexican beer?'

'There's an American shop up by the peak. A friend recommended it. A lot of Agency staff get bits there. Mexican beer, Canadian whisky.'

'I'd love to meet this friend of yours.'

She straightened in her seat.

'Pacifico is brewed in Sinaloa.' He sniffed the open neck of the bottle. He could smell the barley fields swaying in the wind. 'Same state I was born in. Drinking it always takes me back to my father's house. When you're an immigrant it's difficult to feel at home anywhere, but maybe it's why I'm suited to this life. I imagine you find it more difficult.'

4

Her bitten fingernails scratched at the freckles on her milk-white arms.

'I imagine a small-town upbringing. Main Street USA. Jobs at the auto parts store. *Jenny's Grits and Grill.* Maybe a drug store with a soda fountain. Montana?'

'Idaho.'

'Most people never leave the state. Maybe a once-in-a-lifetime trip to New York or Washington. Small-town people with small-town ambitions, and yet here you are. Hong Kong, the other side of the world. How are you settling in?'

'I've been here three years.'

On the floor by the sofa was a taped-up box labelled *"knick-knacks"*. She caught him looking at it.

'You said something about an incident.'

He sighed. 'Yes. I could talk about *cerveza* all night, but that's not why I'm here.'

He took another sip, then pulled a notebook from his jacket pocket and laid it neatly on the table.

She waited.

'Agent Lightfoot, are you aware of a group who call themselves the Network?'

'No. I don't work in Ops, I'm just a technician.'

'I know.' He consulted the notebook. 'You work in the furnace. How do you like your job, Agent Lightfoot?'

'It's fine.'

'You know why they call it the furnace?'

'Because it's a furnace?'

He smiled. 'Yes, that's right. Before you were wiping hard drives, the Agency's deepest, darkest secrets had to be burned. Boxes of papers would be taken down to the basement and your predecessors would throw them into the furnace. Back then, if you touched the walls near the centre of the station you could feel the heat from the chimney. That's when you knew the Agency had something to hide, when its pants were on fire.'

'You were talking about the Network.'

He nodded. 'Yes. They are a particularly pernicious and persistent irritant. Sure, the Agency faces threats like this all the time, from foreign governments and from so-called American citizens, but they do have one distinguishing feature. Stop me if any of this jogs your memory.'

'Please continue.'

'I thought you might know a little about them.'

Her eyes narrowed. 'Why?'

'You applied for a job in my office, didn't you?'

Her shoulders relaxed. 'A couple of years ago. How could you possibly remember that?'

'Well, you have a very memorable name.'

'Maybe if you'd given me the job I *would* know about them.'

He laughed. *Touché.* 'You were a very promising candidate. You're obviously intelligent. You just don't have the experience... *yet.*'

He expected some reaction to that, for her to be flattered, but she didn't say or do anything.

'The Network claim to be a resistance *inside* the Agency,' he continued, 'exposing its dirty deeds as though it's somehow possible to protect our American countrymen while upholding the morals of a Sunday school. They organise mainly on the dark web, in forums. And of course, most of them are morbidly obese keyboard warriors who lie about their activities to feed the same craving for importance that all conspiracy theorists share. Ever since Snowden we've had to contend with a lot of these groups, but the Network appear to be a more virulent strain of treachery. And of course,' his voice dropped to a conspiratorial whisper, 'there is always the fear that, like Snowden, they are in fact *inside the gates*.'

There was a low rumble, sirens in the distance. She looked over to the window, to the neon-lit streets. They shared a brief glance. There was a flash of concern in her eyes.

'The protestors are getting closer,' he whispered. 'They're certainly passionate. Who can blame them? They want their God-given right to democracy. But that business at the airport yesterday?' He shook his head. 'The government will be out for blood tonight.'

She said nothing.

He smiled at her. 'Of course, there are those who would say the Network are a pro-democracy movement of their own. That's certainly how they'd see it. Fighting for truth, justice, and the American way. How do you figure it, Agent Lightfoot?

Nothing again.

'Dare you say the dreaded name?'

'I do think Snowden was well-intentioned.'

'I agree with you there. I don't think there's any doubt about that. Like a lot of people, though, I lost all respect for him the moment he fled to Russia. Worst decision he ever made, obliterated his entire narrative of being a patriot. A true patriot would have accepted the consequences of his actions, the judgement of his own country's courts. If you commit a political crime you don't flee, you accept imprisonment as one of the costs, so that you'll be there when the tide turns. Like

Lenin. Or Suu Kyi.'

She raised her eyebrows.

'Interesting touchpoints for our discussion, I know. I should have said Mandela.'

'You said there had been an incident.'

'Yes. *"Incident"* is a polite way of putting it. There's been a theft, Agent Lightfoot. Someone working with the Network has smuggled sensitive data out of the station tonight. A technician, we believe.'

'What kind of sensitive data?'

He smiled. 'That's a good question. We do not know. We simply know the theft *has* occurred.'

'And so you're speaking to everyone who works at the station?'

He shook his head. 'This is strictly unofficial. You can see I'm taking no notes.'

'Every technician, then?'

'Can you think of any technicians who, perhaps, were acting unusually today?'

She shook her head. 'I see very few people. I'm the only person working in the furnace at the moment.'

'Maybe someone you've seen over the last week or so?'

She said nothing.

'Any suspicions you have, no matter how small, will be very much appreciated, personally, by me. And will be treated with the utmost confidentiality.'

'Really, I haven't noticed anything.'

'I take it you've not noticed any strangers hanging around. Maybe someone very politely asked you to swipe them into the building because they went out for lunch and left their keycard in the office.'

'They wouldn't be able to leave without their

keycard. And I wouldn't do anything like that.'

'Of course not, I wasn't suggesting otherwise. I just want you to be honest with me if there has been a seemingly harmless but out-of-the-ordinary event today.'

She shook her head.

'Maybe over the last week? You can be honest with me. I promise you won't get in trouble.'

'No. There's nothing I can think of.'

'That's unexpected,' he remarked.

'Why? Has someone else said something?'

'We both know there is no one else, Agent Lightfoot. It's just that most often the perpetrator of this type of crime tries to invent a plausible alternative theory in an attempt to persuade the person investigating.'

'Excuse me?'

He didn't answer, he just shook his head. *Disappointed*, it said.

She sipped her coffee.

'You see, Agent Lightfoot, I knew it was you before you did it.'

She put down her coffee. 'Please explain.'

'No matter what impression your friends in the Network may have given you, we know all about them. We are professionals.'

He downed the end of his beer.

'You see, it's my job—*as you know*—to know you better than you know yourself. In your personnel file and your private communications there are patterns of behaviour I've seen a thousand times before. I knew you would betray our country, and therefore the only sensible course of action was to manage when and how.

A controlled descent. It was me who recommended your demotion to the furnace. For two reasons. First, to increase your personal anger at the Agency and therefore accelerate your rate of betrayal. And second, to bring you into constant contact with top secret material.'

'You said you didn't know what was stolen.'

'That's because every hard drive you were tasked with destroying is accounted for. We've also been monitoring the furnace computer and your personal devices and are certain beyond all doubt that you haven't copied any data onto an external drive. There's no network access in the furnace, so you can't have transferred the files out of the building electronically.'

She was frowning like a petulant kid. 'And so...? How did I do it?'

He smiled. 'It's a mystery. But I know you've done it.'

'How do you know that?'

'I know because I've been in this apartment before.'

Her eyes flashed up to his.

'I've been in here more than once. There was one embarrassing moment when you came home early because of a dental appointment. I had to spend twenty minutes behind your shower curtain—'

'You were saying?'

His smile dropped. 'I looked through your cupboards. Meals for one, fish tank on the dining table. Not a social creature. I looked through your drawers. No interest in becoming a social creature. You can tell a lot about a woman from her underwear, don't you think?'

She didn't flinch. He could feel the hatred rising

off her now, but he didn't care. They all hated him. They hated him because he was right.

'I even smelled your pillow. And I smelled exactly what I expected to: weakness. That's why I know you're going to tell me how you did it.'

'You didn't tell me how you knew.'

'The departure of a senior officer would be an obvious opportunity for you, knowing as you would that their hard drive would be delivered to you the next day. I arranged for the deputy station chief to be reassigned. Temporarily.'

'You still haven't told me how you knew.'

He knocked on the empty tank. The glass gave a hollow *thunk*.

'I knew because of your fish. Because four days ago you gave them to your downstairs neighbour's nephew.'

Her head turned slightly, towards the window. The neon lights reflected in her eyes, hiding her thoughts.

'Oops,' she said.

She smiled to herself. He saw a flurry of emotions pass over her face like dappled shade. Then she looked back at him.

'They were just innocent fish, I didn't want them to die for something *I* had done.'

The sounds of the protests had changed in quality. No longer a low rumble, they could make out chanting, and car horns blaring.

She smiled sweetly now, pushing her chair back to get up.

'I'd like some more coffee, are you sure you won't have some?'

'In a minute.'

He gripped her hand to stop her getting up, his hairy fingers binding her wrist like a manacle.

'You're not Lenin. You're not Aung San Suu Kyi. And you're sure as shit not Nelson Mandela. You're not even Snowden, honey. You're nobody.'

'What happens now?'

He was impressed by her calm. Her voice was level, she didn't fight against his grip, although she couldn't look him in the eye.

'You tell me what you stole, how you got it out of the station, and where the package is now. You tell me how you were planning to get it to your contact in the Network. Then you have a choice.'

'What choice?'

'We replace the sensitive material with a convincing fake, you deliver it to your contact, as planned, and going forward you continue your relationship with the Network, as our asset.'

Her tongue curled in her mouth, her jaw tense.

'You did want to work for me.'

Now she tried to pull her hand away, but he held tight.

'Or... we take you into custody tonight, and we continue our plan with not only fake material, but a fake Dolly Lightfoot too. You will be renditioned to a prison not on US soil, where you will wait for a trial that will never come. You will survive in a dark hole, with no view of the outside world, for the rest of your life.'

She had been taller than he imagined, much taller than him, but in every other way she was small. He could see the fear taking root behind her eyes. That fear was his gift. This was his favourite part of the job.

Especially with women.

'Our asset will take your place as far as the Network and the Agency are concerned, but pretty soon you will fade from existence. Your family will never know what happened to you. The Agency will not allow you to be declared dead, your family will not even receive that closure. They will not receive any life insurance or pension. Has anything you've heard about me given you a reason to doubt anything I'm saying?'

She swallowed.

He could see an internal struggle. Neither side had won yet. It surprised him. She needed one more push.

'Your mother will never know if you died alone, unknown, in some Hong Kong backstreet, calling for her.'

He could see her resolve had withered. They all gave in eventually.

'I really need some more coffee,' she said, not daring to look him in the eye.

He released her. 'Go.'

She got up, disappearing behind the screen to the kitchenette.

He listened to the chanting of the protesters. It was distinct now, he could make out words, not that he understood them. A television came on through the wall, her neighbour checking the news. Two cars sped down the street below, wheels spinning on the wet tarmac. Her neighbour yelled into his phone, his voice rising in pitch. He was calling a friend or family member, Cabrera assumed, checking they were safe.

Then he looked down at the scratched and bubbled surface of the cheap table. She had left her cup. He looked down at it with growing concern, but she returned a moment later with the filter jug. He was looking right at her when she threw the coffee in his face.

* * *

Dolly Lightfoot hadn't been prepared for quite so much screaming. An electric jolt of panic convulsed her. Instinctively, she swung the jug at the side of his head. It was heavy insulated metal, he crashed to the floor like a toppled glass cabinet.

She snatched his pistol out of its holster, aiming it at the door. The only sounds were the protestors getting closer and next door's television blaring the applause of a gameshow. No footsteps rushing down the corridor, no agents breaking down the door. She could taste the panic in the back of her throat now, it had the green acidic tang of bile.

Her downstairs neighbours thrust a broom against their ceiling. She snapped back to the present and ran to the bathroom. She lifted the lid of the cistern and dropped the pistol inside, then returned to the living room. Cabrera hadn't moved, he was out cold.

From the back of the sofa she dug out the padded envelope she had addressed and sealed only a minute before he knocked on her door. Then she went to the spyhole. No one there. He couldn't really have come alone. She looked down at the street, there was a black Chevy idling.

The protestors rounded the corner at the end of the block. A large man climbed out of the Chevy's passenger-side door and ran for her building whilst the car pulled away to avoid the crowd. The panic struck her again like a punch in the stomach. It almost floored her, but she had to push against it, had to move. She threw on her jacket, grabbed her backpack. Cradling the envelope in her arms, she gave one last look at the figure lying sprawled in a pool of coffee, turned, and marched into the corridor.

Empty in both directions. She hurried to the stairs. A pair of heavy male footsteps were clattering up the floors. They were coming for her. Without looking down, she pulled herself up the stairs taking two at a time. She burst into the corridor above hers and ran to the opposite end of the building. Then she entered the other stairwell and leapt down the six flights three steps at a time, *four steps at a time*, the impact jolting up through her knees, until she reached the street.

Her heart was kicking against her ribs. She had to catch her breath. A mist had risen off the bay and the air was thick with the tastes of salt, diesel, and cooking oil. She jogged down the street and around the corner, out of the protestors' path. She followed two young women into the road, stumbled at the last minute. Siren screaming, blue lights stabbing at the darkness. *A police van!* The driver slammed on the brakes too late, the women were knocked to the kerb. More bodies swarmed the van, two men in bandanas smashed the windscreen with the poles of their placards whilst the driver threw the van into reverse. She couldn't watch, couldn't help the women, she had to keep moving.

She barged her way through a stream of people fighting towards the MTR, they wanted anything to be off the streets. Her destination was only a couple of roads away now. She started to run, *so close.*

On the next street a police officer was beating a shrunken old man with his baton. The old man's white shirt was ragged and brown with dirt from the pavement, his arms were over his bald head as he tried to shelter from the blows. Another officer held back a heavyset woman in a pink apron as she screamed at them to stop. Dolly Lightfoot stayed on the other side of the road, reducing her pace to a quick march. The air was shaking with the steady drilling of helicopters. A taxi sped down the road, spraying her with milky gutter water. She wiped the envelope, then her face, and kept marching.

She could see the old "pillar box" at the next intersection, it's traditional British shape and *ER* insignia a colonial relic. Like all of them, its royal red had been drowned in the green of Hongkong Post. When she was ten metres away a man's hand grabbed her arm to stop her. She twisted free and ran forward, feeling the explosion without seeing it.

Dolly Lightfoot was thrown to the ground like a rag doll. Streams of paper fluttered down from a dust cloud, falling like confetti. She was lying in the street on her backpack, the tall buildings spinning round her. A chorus of startled car alarms whooped, honked, and shrieked. Her ears were warm and sticky, and there was a high electric whine inside her head.

She was helped to her feet by the same man who had tried to stop her. Shards of glass were falling from the surrounding buildings like great snakes sloughing off their skin. The colonial pillar box was black and unpeeled like a banana.

With horror she realised her hands were empty.

The ground was blanketed with charred letters and fragments of parcels. She staggered forwards, kicking and scattering letters as she walked. Someone tapped her on the shoulder, she batted them away. They tapped again, she ignored it. Finally, they grabbed her arm and spun her around to face them.

'What!?' she screamed, barely hearing herself.

A young student protestor in wire-rimmed glasses was holding the package, proffering it. She snatched it and ran. No time for thanks.

She was running, but she didn't know where she was going. Where was the next mailbox? She hadn't bothered to research an alternative. She knew there was one outside the fish market but travelling that far was a huge risk. Why couldn't she think of any others? Surely there must be one nearby. But where? She felt the panic rising again. She stumbled, it felt like she had stepped into wet concrete. She would go to the fish market, it was the only guarantee she had.

At the next MTR station, she barged her way down the underground steps to the platform and ran for a train that was closing its doors. She was too late, slamming her hand on the train as it moved off.

The two-minute wait was agony. Anxiety clouded her thoughts, blurring sound and vision like wearing a goldfish bowl. What would happen if the protestors somehow blocked a station or a train ahead? Would they get stuck in the tunnel, waiting for hours?

A rush of wind announced the next train. She waited, toes dancing in her shoes, as a stream of late commuters emptied onto the platform, then she jumped on and found somewhere she could grip one of the upright poles.

There was the familiar beep and the doors closed. The train trundled out of the station, bumping and rattling down the tunnel. She gripped the package tighter, hearing the bubble wrap squeak. It was only four stops to the fish market, a ten-minute ride. No one could possibly know where she was going, right?

She looked up to confirm the four stops, and terror gripped her like a cold hand on the back of her neck. She had run north to the mailbox, but the fish market was south. The next station was the one right next to her building. The light was already building, revealing the concrete curve of the tunnel, then the station whooshed into existence.

The train jerked to a stop. Doors opened. Two people from her carriage fought their way off, three more fought their way on. She tried to hide behind them but she was at least a foot taller than everyone else.

She moved from the pole to one of the handles swinging above her head. Closer to the door, better opportunity to run. Movement caught her eye. Everyone looked up. Dolly Lightfoot clamped her hand to her mouth, stifling her howl of fear.

Cabrera! Running down the steps to the platform. It couldn't be! His face was a violent red from the scalding coffee. Two more agents flanked him.

She found herself whispering, *'Please, please, please!'*

Eyes shut, she could hear their heavy footsteps smacking on the resin floor, thundering towards the train. She almost cried when the beep came and the doors rolled shut. Cabrera's meaty palm slammed on the window, jolting her eyes open. Their eyes locked. She tried to keep her chin up, meeting his gaze as the train moved off.

There was murder in his eyes.

The train left him behind and soon they were in the dark tunnel to the next station. She was shaking now, fizzing with adrenaline. There were two stops left, she told herself, barely able to hear her thoughts above the gnashing of the wheels on the rails. There was no way he could get there before her.

The train emerged from the tunnel into chaos. The platform of the next station was filled with protestors. When the doors opened, they flooded in. There were too many of them, cramming into the carriage, knocking her off-balance and crushing her against the opposite doors. Then she saw police with raised batons charge down the steps onto the platform. Whistles blew and the train was swarmed with uniforms. They tried to drag the protestors from the train, others tried to stop them. People were sprawled half-out the doors. An officer wearing a peaked cap was marching up the platform to the front of the train. They were not going to be moving for minutes, at least. Then the gentle rumble of the engine died, cut off at the orders of the officer. They weren't going anywhere. It only took her a heartbeat to decide.

Dolly Lightfoot darted from the train, stepping over the protestors and squeezing past the police, all ignoring the *gweilo*. She powered up the steps to the street and looked in the direction the tracks were heading. The fish market was that way.

The streets were a warzone. A melee of police and protestors, burning cars, trampled banners. She moved into the side streets, but they curved, sending her off course. She tried to adjust, but she was lost already. Knowing the fish market was by the bay, she turned down a long run of steps between buildings, heading downhill, passing through a layer of mist that clung to her eyelashes and stung her eyeballs.

There was a desperate whine of moped engines, and a swarm of them shot down the steps, a person on the back of each wielding a flopping, broken placard. She squeezed herself up against the wall. The mopeds were followed by two police motorcycles. One of the mopeds took a step wrong and bucked its riders. One of the police motorcyclists hit the tumbling moped and was launched from his steed, the motorcycle crashing end-over-end, the officer rolling, all elbows and knees, his white helmet flew loose and bounced down the steps like a football. Police set upon the thrown protestors. A mob set upon the thrown officer.

She could see the bay ahead, beyond the bottom of the endless steps. She left them, hoping to find a path or a road running parallel. She found herself on a pedestrian bridge above just such a road. There was no way down. She froze. There, below the bridge, on the pavement, was a green Hongkong Post box.

She could jump. If she broke an ankle or a leg she could hop to it. If she broke both legs she could crawl. But she might break her back. She had no choice, she had to risk it. She gripped the railings and looked over. It was two storeys at least, onto cold wet concrete.

No choice.

She swung her leg over the railings.

A muscular hand snatched her arm, yanking her away. Her feet back on the ground, she stared into the blistered red face of Solomon Cabrera.

'You were really going to do it,' he panted.

He snatched the padded envelope from her hand.

'What is it you have in here?'

'I don't even know.'

Her eyes burned. He really didn't understand her at all.

She noticed then how quiet the bridge was. The civilians had scattered like birds from a tree. Behind her, a battalion of protestors stood marshalled, ready to charge. Looking past Cabrera, to the other end, she could see police forming ranks. *Armed* police. They were about to be at the centre of a flashpoint.

'Don't even think about it, or I'll throw you from this bridge.'

'That was the idea, idiot.'

He had a new gun in his holster. She went for it, got it as high as his chest. He dropped the envelope. In that moment two shots rang out. They went through Solomon Cabrera and into Dolly Lightfoot. They fell away from each other, onto the bridge's rough concrete.

She choked, gasping for air. She was drowning. Someone was pouring ice water into her stomach. Police officers stood over her, then they were overrun with protestors.

The world turned fuzzy. *This was it.* She lifted her head up, looked around her as best she could. Cabrera's hands were still. He wasn't moving at all. The package was nowhere to be seen. She rested her head back down, knowing it would be for the last time, and turned her head to face the edge of the bridge, towards the bay, her cheek on the concrete. She wanted one last look at the sea. She could smell it. *So close.*

She saw the small brown square on the pavement

all that distance below, just metres from the mailbox.

So close.

A woman tripped over it.

Please...

The woman picked it up in frustration. She studied its unusual address, the big special airmail stamps.

Please, Dolly Lightfoot begged overhead, silent as an angel.

The woman's head looked up to the green post box. She started towards it.

Hurry!

The woman held the envelope in the slot for a moment, then finally, she pushed it in.

Dolly Lightfoot felt her life drain away as hands moved her body. Whoever it was would have seen a queer smile cross her lip as she had one final thought.

The package was in transit.

PART I

Il Americano

ONE

C ain held the glass up to the midday sun, watching it turn the deep crimson into a glowing ruby. He did this every time, even though it was always the same, because it was always Casa Di Matera. The restaurant kept a bottle on the shelf just for him. Several restaurants did this. Cain rotated through them all, taking his lunch at one and then dinner at another, within a few days he was back again.

Vittoria, the proprietor, watched him from the shadowy bar, pausing as she thumbed through the receipts on the spike. It struck her that, not counting herself, "Il Americano" had been here the longest. The waiters never stayed long, the chefs had changed too, but he always came back. And yet she knew nothing about the man. An American expat, what more was there to know? He was always polite, tipped more than his smart-but-well-worn clothes would lead you to expect. There was no hiding his age, surely around sixty, but his hair was thick and most of it still rusty-brown, even if his temples were pure white. He was a broad man, barrel-chested, and yet his stomach was stiff and flat. He had not yet gone to seed. Not someone Vittoria herself would find attractive, but someone she would happily set up on a date with a friend. If... she knew anything about him. She went back to tallying the receipts.

Cain finished his lunch of crostini di fegatini and left the restaurant with a tip of the hat to her.

The market traders would say they knew Il Americano well, which really meant they saw him often. He never took liberties with the number of samples he tasted, always smiled gratefully, and never haggled about the price. And for this last reason they always gave him the best.

Marco, the oldest of the olive sellers, ladled brined Gaeta olives into a pot. Cain had paid for two ladles-worth, and Marco made sure to heap the ladle each time. Again, Cain tipped his hat.

The old men who played chess in the piazza would say they knew him best of all. Sure, they barely said a word to him, but on the chessboard, they would say, there was no hiding yourself. Il Americano was a man who planned ahead, who never played a move without thinking it through. Not a fast player, but that meant he was good. In chess it was the ones who took their time you had to watch out for. When, through careful tactics, he arrived at an opportunity, he would be ruthless. And yet, he wasn't a hustler. He always played his best game, whether it was for money or just for sport, and he would always shake your hand afterwards.

But not today. When one of them asked Cain for a game he politely declined and continued eating his olives. Today he was just here to watch.

His landlady would have good words to say about him too, if he ever required a reference. He always paid his rent on time and accepted her annual rises without argument, which was far more than she could say for the rest of her tenants, she was sure. He would even help her change lightbulbs and hang Christmas decorations, or anything else that required standing on a ladder, and never wanted anything for it. He *must* be a Catholic, she was certain. Of course, she didn't know him as "Il Americano", she knew him as Signore Cramer (an alias), but she had heard the other tenants use the nickname.

'*Buongiorno,*' she said as he passed her on the stairs.

And, as always, he replied with a polite tip of the hat.

Someone's phone was ringing as he slipped the key in his door. An old-fashioned phone with a real bell in it. Wait, that was *his* phone.

'*Pronto,*' he answered absently, throwing his hat onto the bed.

'Cain?'

He sat down on the chair. It creaked. 'Jo?'

'He lives! It's great to hear your voice, old sport.'

'Likewise.'

'How *are* you?'

'Er... fine,' Cain replied, still discombobulated. Without seeing Jo in the flesh it was hard to believe he was really speaking to him.

'How long has it been?'

'Nine years.'

'Too long. *Nine years ago.* We drank some awful coffee, I remember *that*. Where were we?'

'Gare d'Alger.'

'Algiers. *Of course.*' Jo's voice lost some of its boyish enthusiasm. 'That was a difficult one,' he said

26

with his usual understatement.

'How are *you?*' Cain asked.

'Pending greatness, as always. How's Florence?'

'Quiet now. In October the last of the tourists go home.'

'And what do they think of you, when they realise you're not a tourist?'

'Very little, I imagine.'

There was a chuckle on the line.

Cain filled the crackling vacuum that followed. 'How did you get this number?'

'You're not upset, I hope?'

'No, of course not, just curious.'

'Please...' There was another chuckle. 'Do you even have to ask?'

'You're still with the old firm then?'

'Of course. I'm a lifer, you know that. How's retirement?'

'Peaceful. Just the way I like it.'

'What do you do all day?'

'I eat in restaurants. I go for walks. Go to galleries. They have concerts here in the summer evenings. One endless vacation. Sometimes I go for a drive out in the country, find some small village, explore. Then I eat in different restaurants. And drink wine.'

'That's a lot of restaurants.'

'That was always the plan: find the best restaurants in Italy and never eat anywhere else.'

'Not missing the excitement then?'

Cain detected the note in his voice. He knew why he was calling, knew what he was really asking. This wasn't a friendly catch-up.

'Sometimes,' he replied.

'Still living off your nest egg?'

'Surviving.'

'How is it?'

Cain looked around at his tiny one-room apartment, at the dust that had built up since he'd started cleaning it himself. It danced in the golden light through the shutters, settled on his shaving mirror and the bedframe.

'There are still a few bits of shell to pick over.'

Cain heard Jo's throaty chuckle down the line. 'Then this call couldn't have come at a better time. I may have a solution to both your problems. A temporary one, mind.'

'One last job?'

'Who's saying "last"?'

Cain smiled. 'I'm retired, Jo.'

'At least hear me out.'

Cain said nothing.

'For old times' sake?'

Cain still didn't say anything. It was pointless. Jo was the sort of person who would keep on until he had said his piece. Only then would he let him say no.

'It's local, so you can use your own car. Just one of your drives into the country. About a hundred kilometres south of Florence, to a beautiful big house overlooking a vineyard. I'm sure your hosts will give you a slap-up meal. Maybe not restaurant quality, but fine home cooking. Then at twenty-three hundred hours you receive a package and deliver payment. The hosts will have all the details, you're just the courier. You take the package back to Florence with you and await collection from one of my team. Your fee is ten thousand, I'm sorry I couldn't make it more.'

Cain tapped on the telephone table with his fingers. 'What's the package?'

'Sorry, old sport, need-to-know only.'

'How much are you paying for it?'

'I can't tell you that either.'

'That makes it very difficult to know what precautions to take.'

'It'll be a walk in the park, I promise.'

Cain sighed. This was Jo, but still he didn't like it when people made promises they couldn't keep.

'What have you got to lose?'

'Same as always, my life.'

There was another chuckle.

Cain sighed again. People still in the game always assumed you wanted any excuse to get back in. They couldn't understand how you could feel any different, but that was why they were still in the game and you were out.

'It's good to hear from you, Jo,' he started.

'No, don't say that.'

'*It really is.* And I'm flattered you would still think of me. But when I retired, I meant it. So, regretfully, I must decline. No, is my answer.'

There was static on the line, popping and clicking.

'That puts me in rather an awkward position, old sport.'

'You'll find someone else.'

'By tonight?'

'Tonight?' Cain was stunned. 'Someone let you down?'

'You see, I've already told them you'll do it.'

Cain huffed.

'I vouched for you.'

'You shouldn't have done that, Jo.'

'I'm sorry, old sport.' *But what's done is done,* his tone said.

Cain gave a deep sigh as he waited for him to say more, watching the dust that he was breathing in every moment. But no more came.

'How do I get the details?'

'They're waiting for you at a private bank, four streets away from the Accademia.'

'You don't seem to have left me much choice.'

'I'll owe you. How does ten thousand euros sound? And dinner on me when I collect the package myself.'

Cain didn't answer.

'Do you need me to give you the address?'

'No. I know the one you mean.'

'Thank you, Cain. I owe you.'

A click. The call was over. He put the receiver down.

He stared at the phone for some minutes whilst he considered his next move. But Jo wouldn't call again, he wasn't the type.

Like a sudden shower on a clear day, his past had returned, and although the rain had stopped for now, there were dark clouds dotting the horizon. And he didn't like it. He didn't like it at all.

TWO

The first thing Cain did was check on his car. He went to the lockup, pulled off the dust cover and kicked the tyres. He checked the oil, topped it up, checked the tyre pressures and topped them up. Then it was the turn of the coolant and washer fluid. He fired it up and listened to the engine, checking for misfires. He took care of the thing and it had never let him down. The second thing he did was clean and oil his gun.

'What's the name, please?' the woman behind the bank desk asked him.

'Cain.'

'One moment, please.'

He glanced around at the manicured yucca plants and the heavy wooden door frame that concealed the metal detector.

'Yes, I can see you here,' she said, 'please take a seat.'

He smiled at her. 'Out of interest, when was the appointment made?'

The receptionist took a moment to understand. 'I'm sorry, sir, I don't have that information available.'

Was that true? Or did they have a policy to never answer questions like that.

'Never mind.'

He settled into a white Eames chair. There was no name on the reception desk, nothing on the outside of the building either. No brochures on the coffee table. And all their security systems were hidden. If you didn't know what business they were in then you had no business knowing.

There were, however, copies of *The Economist*, *Newsweek*, and *Time*. He picked up an *Economist* and flicked to the obituaries.

An elderly man in rimless glasses opened the only visible door, revealing its six-inch thickness.

Cain stood up.

'*Signore Cain?*'

'Yes.'

'This way, please.'

He was led into a windowless room with a large lacquered table under bright spotlights. On the table was a black briefcase and a brown envelope. In the envelope was a printed sheet of directions to drive from Florence to somewhere near Montepulciano. "Arrive by 8 o'clock!" was scrawled on the bottom in blue pen.

'Do you know the code for the briefcase?' he asked.

'*No, Signore.*'

Cain nodded. 'Thank you.'

'Is there anything you would like destroyed?'

'No, thank you, I'll do it myself.'

He didn't like carrying the briefcase through the streets. He didn't like the idea of leaving it in his apartment either. It was four o'clock now, he had made the drive to Montepulciano before and it was two hours at the worst. Still, he thought it better to get out on the country roads.

He returned to his old Mercedes soft-top and stashed the briefcase under the passenger seat. Then he eased it out of the lockup and into the narrow Oltrarno streets, winding his way south. Within thirty seconds he was zipping down tree-lined avenues, dappled shade flickering like a zoetrope. After a minute, although he didn't know it, he had left the city he loved most for the last time.

*   *   *

The instructions said to follow the E35, but knowing the route Cain decided to stick to the little country roads and avoid the autostrada. It made it so much easier to know if you were being followed. No one showed up in his mirror more than twice, and there were long stretches where there was nothing behind him at all. He relaxed into the drive. As he zipped through Chianti territory, endless vineyards to his left and right, he looked at his battered old Speedmaster watch. He was making good time, *too good*, so he eased it down, took the road even-less-travelled, and enjoyed the cruise.

A few miles later he found a perfect dirt straight. He floored the Mercedes and got it up to 145kph, kicking up a trail of cocoa-coloured dust two miles long. Then he skidded to a stop and snatched a bunch of buxom purple grapes from one of the vines, feeling like a naughty child.

He set off again through the Tuscan countryside, chewing on the grapes and spitting the seeds and skins out into the descending twilight. The sky was burning red, then the sun finally dipped below the hills, and when the black curtain was drawn the roads were plunged into the sort of utter darkness that you forget exists when you live in the world of city lights. The beams of his headlights illuminated nothing more than dirt tracks and wooden fences, so using the trusty compass he had fixed to the dashboard he found his way back to the autostrada.

It was 7:25pm when he took the exit for Montepulciano, continuing south through a small village called Acquaviva. Then the dark countryside again, and he reached the final instruction. There was a hand painted sign with a picture of some grapes, an arrow pointing ahead, and "3km". Just past the sign he had to take a left, up a steep hillside track, and drive to the end of the road.

Five minutes later, climbing the snaking road, a rolling valley opened up below that caught the moonlight like ruched black velvet. He was climbing the hill that overlooked that view, the highest point for miles, and nearing the end of the journey. He passed a row of small cottages, then the dirt road flattened out on the ridge of the hill and a great house was revealed in front of him as though he had turned the page of a pop-up book. He slowed his speed and crawled, not disrespectfully slowly, towards it.

As he approached, the road was bordered by cypress trees, but through the gaps he could see a traditional Tuscan villa lit like a beacon. Square, sandstone, two-storeys, with a terracotta roof and small shuttered windows.

He crunched onto the gravel courtyard, stopping in the centre. The Mercedes burbled. Then, when he was satisfied, he turned to face back down the road, and killed the engine.

There were three other cars in the courtyard, a new Maserati saloon and two vintage Alfa Romeo coupés. And yet... the place was silent. The night air was chill, but smelled sweet like an orchard. There were no cicadas, no birds, just the occasional swoosh of the wind in the cypress trees.

He waited in the car for five minutes, but no one came out to greet him.

So, he got out and put the soft-top up, then he retrieved the briefcase from beneath the passenger seat, and his revolver from the glove compartment. With the gun tucked away in a shoulder holster under his arm, and the briefcase by his side, he entered through the front door.

THREE

The entrance hall was grand. And it was dark. Two storeys, with blurs of dark wood furniture against the walls, and the *clink-clonk* of a pendulum clock. The style was traditional Tuscan, stone rough enough to graze yourself, desiccated wood with open veins, unchanged possibly for centuries. A great wooden staircase led up the middle to a balcony, there were six doors off the balcony, all closed. Off the ground floor there were four open doorways, all dark except one. Footsteps scratched on the flagstones.

Cain turned to the lit doorway just as a young man appeared in it, sifting thoughtfully through a stack of white envelopes. He was dressed in a black suit with a blood red tie, and his oil-black hair was slicked back neatly. He looked up from the envelopes and froze.

'Mr Cain?'

'Yes.'

'*Prego*. Welcome to our house.'

He marched over and shook Cain's hand.

'Santino. Call me Tino.'

'*Piacere*.'

Tino checked his Armani watch. 'You made it before eight o'clock, my father will be so pleased. There is a room upstairs you can use to freshen up, first on the left, the briefcase will be quite safe in there. Dinner is at nine o'clock. Oh, please,' he touched Cain's arm, 'no guns at dinner.'

Cain nodded. 'Thank you. It's very quiet.'

'Yes.'

'Are the other guests in their rooms?'

'What other guests?'

Cain drummed on the leather of the briefcase.

'Oh, they will not be arriving before the...' he searched for the word.

'Exchange?' Cain offered.

'Yes.'

'Then the dinner...?'

'Will be just you and the family.'

'I see.' He looked around at the quiet, dark house. 'Where are the family now?'

A wry smile curled Tino's lips. 'Making preparations.'

Cain nodded. 'And where is the dining room?'

'My apologies, it is here,' he pointed to one of the dark doorways that led towards the back of the house. 'My father is so excited to have a fellow gastronome to dinner.'

Cain smiled a little suspiciously.

His guest room was spartan in design, but appointed like a luxury hotel. There was an adjoining bathroom with bottles of expensive toiletries arranged around the sink, and on the writing table there was a bottle of his favourite wine, Casa Di Matera.

He picked it up. It unsettled him. It suggested a lot of questions. How much had Jo told them about him? How did Jo know he drank Casa Di Matera? How had they had time today, living in the middle of nowhere, to

37

go down to Montepulciano and buy a bottle? Of course, a big house like this could easily have a bottle in their cellar.

He put it back down and checked his watch. 8:05pm. He took the opportunity to shower, leaving the briefcase and his revolver on the writing table with the bottle. There was no point hiding either of them. When he had showered off the dust of the road, he smelled the three Eau du Parfum's that had been placed by the sink, choosing his favourite. He even ran a little scented "product" through his hair. He buttoned up his shirt, then he went to the little shuttered window and flung it open, leaning out to drink in the revitalising night air. Every bush, tree, and hill were cast of the same iron black, but the royal blue sky was touched with brushstrokes of cloud and speckles of stars. It held the flat disc of the moon like a compact mirror.

He smelled cigar smoke. Beneath his window he could see the bald pate of an old man sitting in a chair, smoking, and drinking a glass of wine. Next to him, an empty chair.

Cain pulled on his jacket and left the room, crossing the balcony and descending the stairs with light feet. The entrance hall was still empty, the doorways still dark. He slipped out the front door onto the gravel of the courtyard.

The same three cars were there alongside the Mercedes. There were no other footsteps crunching on the gravel. The outside of the house was lit up, but beyond the bubble of light the world was absolute darkness. The cottages he had passed on the way up the road were out of sight. He knew Montepulciano was somewhere to the north-east, if he walked a few hundred metres along the ridge of the hill then maybe he would see it, but from here there was nothing.

He followed the gravel around the left of the house. All the windows were dark. On his left the path was bordered with cypress trees, and beyond them steep hillside stretched down into nothingness. When he turned the next corner the lights were off, and he could just make out the old man sitting in the gloom. There had been insects swirling around the other lights, and maybe that was why he chose to sit in the dark.

'*Buonasera.*'

'*Buonasera,*' the old man croaked, not getting up, not even turning to look at him.

He wandered over and took a seat in the spare chair. The old man said nothing to him.

Cain stared into the darkness, wondering what the man was seeing. Maybe he was just guarding his land. Owning so much felt alien to Cain. Since he was eighteen he hadn't owned more than he could pack in a kit bag. The army drilled it into him. When he left, he had kept the habit. He had no doubt he owed his life to it. The habit, then long engrained, had carried on into his retirement. The urge to buy and own things had withered on the vine. He rented his apartment, borrowed books from the library, owned three changes of clothes at a time, a toothbrush, a watch, a gun. Not that he would ever inventory it in such a way, it was a habit, not a rule. The only exception was his Mercedes, but that was justified.

Over long, drawn-out minutes, his eyes adjusted, and he began to make out shapes. There were rows of vines flowing down the hillside to the bottom of the valley, and in the valley were the jutting silhouettes of steel buildings and the apparatus of a modern winery. *Grapes, of course.* That was the sweet smell that was all around them.

Cain picked up the bottle standing by the man's chair leg. It was unlabelled.

'May I?' Cain asked in Italian.

'Be my guest,' the man croaked.

He smelled it, drinking in the aroma. It smelled wonderful, and yet... familiar.

'This is Casa Di Matera,' he said.

'*Si.*'

He held the unlabelled bottle. The shape and colour were correct. He thought back to the bottle in his room, to the bottles kept in restaurants across Florence. On the label was a Tuscan villa embossed in gold, bordered on each side by black cypress trees.

'*This* is Casa Di Matera.'

'*Si.*'

Cain beamed. 'You make my favourite wine,' he said.

'No,' the man replied sharply, 'my son.'

Cain could see the man's face now, could make him out. He was not quite bald, a cloud of hair hovered above his scalp. His face was threaded with grey stubble, his skin brown and mottled, hanging off his skull, carved with a thousand lines. It was a face that had seen a lot of pain. The eyes were milky, and Cain realised that he was blind.

He held out a twisted hand and Cain guided it to his face. The crooked fingers traced the contours of his cheekbones, felt the curls of his hair.

'You are not my son.'

'No.'

40

'Policeman,' the man said in English.

'No, no. Just a guest.'

'Yes, yes. Policeman.'

Cain didn't argue.

'Here,' he reached for a wooden box by his other chair leg, took out a cigar and clipped the end.

'Thank you,' Cain said, taking it.

A lighter flame erupted. Cain leaned the end of the cigar into the flickering orange tongue. The lighter snapped shut. Darkness.

'You are here to arrest me?'

'Should I be?'

The man didn't reply, he just frowned and shifted in his seat.

'No, I'm not here to arrest you.'

'My son?'

'No.'

'My son is innocent. He is a very good boy. Very nice man.'

'I'm glad to hear it.'

The man was still frowning. 'You come for my grandson?'

'I'm not here to arrest anyone. I'm not police.'

The man said nothing for a while, staring once again into the darkness, smelling the night air, feeling its caress on his face.

'Not policeman?' he asked.

'No.'

'Who are you?'

'My name is Cain.'

'But... who are you?'

Cain smiled wistfully, and there was just a trace of bitterness in his answer.

'Just another old man.'

The older man returned to his wine, not saying anything more to him. That was ok. Cain just sat with him, sharing the night watch.

FOUR

Out in the darkness his name was being called. It was called two more times before he remembered where he was. Then a fourth time, and he knew it was coming from above him. Had he been asleep? Or just absorbed in his own thoughts? He couldn't remember being so distant, so disconnected from the moment, for a long time. He looked up. Tino was leaning out of his window.

'It is time for dinner, Mr Cain.'

The old man was snoring.

'Don't worry about him, the servants will get him in.'

Cain wandered around the outside and back in the front doors. The doorway to the dining room was now the only one lit.

Flagstone floor, open fireplace, great wooden table, the dining room was as rustic as the rest of the house. And yet, each wall held a large piece of black and white photography, all of the winery, and they gave the place a slightly corporate air like a tasting room. There were no family photos, no ornaments, just like the bedroom they had given him. He supposed he was being given the same corporate hospitality they gave the big wine buyers.

As he entered, a man with a moustache like a dustpan brush beamed at him and opened his arms wide.

'*Signore Cain*, it is a pleasure to welcome you. My name is Gaspare Di Matera. Call me Gaspare, please.'

'Just call me Cain,' he said, holding his hand out to shake.

The handshake gave them an opportunity to size each other up. A similar age, perhaps, but very different men. Cain's body was broad, his movements powerful. Gaspare was lithe, his movements graceful. Both took care of their appearance, but although Gaspare's hair was clearly dyed to match his black moustache, Cain's rusty-brown curls didn't hide his white temples. And the last obvious difference: Gaspare's clothes were pin sharp, Cain's merely smart-casual.

'You have an incredible home,' Cain said.

'Thank you.'

Gaspare had a drink in his hand. Tino was also standing, but without a drink, and three other men of such striking similarity to Tino that they could only be his brothers.

'These are my sons,' Gaspare confirmed, 'Santino, you have already met, we call him "Tino". This is Valentino, Fortino, and Cristino.'

They all shook his hand.

'*Buonasera*,' Cain said to each.

'Please, please, we will take our seats. Would you like a Negroni?'

'I was hoping to have some of your excellent wine.' Cain said in perfect Italian. 'I couldn't believe it just now when I was speaking to your father. I drink it every day.'

'What do you mean?'

'I mean I drink it every day. It's my absolute favourite. I never order anything else if I can get it, and I won't eat in a restaurant twice if they don't have it.'

'Well, this is fantastic. We must give you some bottles to take home.'

'That's very kind of you.'

'Angelo!'

A gruff, wiry-haired man in a stained polo shirt opened a wooden door in the corner, exposing the room to sounds of cooking and crockery being laid.

'*Si?*'

'Put a case of the Riserva in the boot of Signore Cain's car.'

'A case?' Cain protested, 'I can't let you, that's too kind.'

'Nonsense! Two cases, Angelo!'

Cain couldn't help smiling. 'He'll need the key.'

'That won't bother a man like Angelo.'

Cain wasn't sure how to take that. Despite his host's warm words and beaming smile, he had the distinct impression that the man was wary of him, even scared.

'But, please, you must have a Negroni, it is made using our own vermouth.'

'I didn't know you made vermouth.'

'We don't sell it. You won't get it anywhere else.'

'In that case, how can I refuse?'

'Wonderful. Marie!'

Another servant appeared, in an apron, drying her hands with a towel.

'*Si, Signore?*'

'Another Negroni, for our guest.'

'*Si, Signore.*'

'You don't like them?' Cain asked Tino, who was drinking water and shuffling through paperwork.

'Tino does not drink,' Gaspare answered for him, 'that is why he does the books. Tino, please, no papers at the dinner table.'

'This has to be done.'

'*Not tonight.*'

Tino sighed and placed the papers on a sideboard behind his chair.

'You live in Florence, Mr Cain?' Fortino asked.

'Just Cain, please.'

'Beautiful city,' Gaspare said, 'much nicer than Venice.'

'But not as romantic.'

'Romance is where you make it, wouldn't you agree?'

Cain smiled. 'I suppose you're right. I confess I've never been much of a romantic.' He addressed the sons: 'Are you all involved in the winery?'

They all nodded.

'Valentino helps me with the general running of the company, making the big decisions. Fortino deals with all our sales, stockists, international buyers. And Cristino manages the running of the vineyard. Do you have any children?'

Marie appeared with Cain's Negroni.

He took a sip. 'Delicious.'

'I will instruct Angelo to give you a bottle of the vermouth too. *Two bottles.*'

'You're too kind. It really is delicious though.'

'*Prego.*'

'You obviously use your own wine, but what do

you use to fortify it?'

'We distil a grape spirit.'

'What do you use for the botanicals?'

Gaspare listed them on his fingers. 'Liquorice, angelica, pomelo...' He thought hard, trying to remember. 'Lavender.'

'Not lavender anymore,' Cristino corrected him.

Gaspare frowned. 'It is Cristino's project.'

Cristino got his fingers ready to list them accurately. 'Liquorice, angelica, pomelo, cardamom, vanilla, and Citrus myrtifolia.'

'Citrus myrtifolia?'

'Myrtle-leaved orange,' Cristino tried to explain, 'it is... you know it... used in chinotto.'

'In Campari, right?'

All five of them gave a sudden intake of breath, as though Cain had just said Macbeth in a theatre.

'Please, do not say that name here,' Cristino said jovially as they all broke into smiles.

'I apologise,' Cain said merrily. 'Why don't you sell it?'

'I would like to.'

'It is not ready yet,' Gaspare said, 'these things take time.'

Marie laid the table with two large platters of cold meats, cheeses, and crostini. Then two large bowls of salad. They helped themselves.

'What part of America are you from, Mr Cain?' asked Valentino, clearly the eldest son. He was dressed entirely in black except for a red flower in his buttonhole and had the air of a toreador.

Cain smiled sheepishly. 'Montreal.'

They all laughed.

'I bet people make that mistake a lot,' Fortino said. Slouched back in his chair, swirling his wine, he was the relaxed one.

'All the time. Although your brother is technically correct, I am an American, just not from the United States.'

'You speak Italian like a native,' Gaspare said. 'Your parents were Italian?'

'No, just Canadian.'

'But your heritage, you must have some Italian in you?'

'Ukrainian mostly. A little bit of English.'

'Catholic, at least?'

He smiled. 'Jewish. By birth.'

'You could have fooled me.'

'For a while, perhaps.'

Gaspare smiled. 'Smooth, Cain, that's what you are. Very polite. You save my blushes, you save my son's blushes...'

'Well, it pays to be polite in my line of work.'

'In all lines of work, wouldn't you say?'

Cain nodded, crostini crunching between his teeth.

'This is what I've always tried to teach my sons.'

'Be like wine,' they chorused, laughing amongst themselves.

Gaspare frowned.

'What does that mean?' Cain asked.

'Smooth...' Fortino said.

'Full-bodied...' Valentino continued.

'And improve with age,' Gaspare finished with a laugh.

Cain laughed merrily. 'Well,' he raised his glass,

'here's to that.'

They all raised their glasses.

The next course was a traditional Tuscan pappardelle alla lepre.

'The hare are shot on our land,' Gaspare said proudly.

'What *is* your line of work, Cain?' Tino asked, deliberately looking down at his food as though the answer didn't really interest him.

'It was a figure of speech, I'm retired.'

'You must tell me about your pretty little car,' Gaspare started merrily.

'Excuse me,' Tino butted in, 'but it was not a figure of speech.'

'Tino!' his father chided lovingly, 'don't be so rude to our guest.'

'He's right,' Cristino said, defending his brother.

'He is right,' Cain agreed.

'So...?' Tino pressed, 'what is it you do?'

'Tonight, I'm a courier.'

'And you find it pays to be polite... as a courier?'

Cain smiled. They were all very smart, but Tino's eyes were the keenest.

He shrugged. 'You could say I'm—' he stopped, corrected himself, 'I *was*... paid to have a cool head.'

'That's the sort of thing that sounds like an answer, but doesn't really tell us anything, isn't it?' Cristino remarked.

'I apologise for my sons' rudeness,' Gaspare said.

'That's quite ok, they're...' He smiled. 'They're looking out for you.'

'If a stranger walks into your house carrying a gun,' Cristino said, 'it's wise to know as much as possible about them, wouldn't you say?'

'Absolutely. But I don't know what else I can tell you.'

'Give us some examples, some references.'

'I can't do that.'

'But you've been in this kind of situation before?'

He shrugged. 'Every situation is different.'

'This kind of exchange though.'

He nodded. 'Yes.'

'Many times?'

Cain hesitated, then answered, 'Yes.'

'If you're retired,' Tino asked, 'then tonight is...?'

'A favour.'

Tino nodded.

'Marie!' Gaspare called, 'Bring the steaks and wine!'

Marie arrived with the most enormous amount of bistecca di Fiorentina Cain had ever seen. On a great silver platter, heaps of the stuff cut into thin strips to reveal the luminous pink meat, sprinkled liberally with salt and rosemary, and drizzled with olive oil.

As they loaded their plates, Gaspare poured Cain the most incredible glass of Casa Di Matera he had ever tasted. His host had relaxed now, and the conversation was able to flow more easily.

'I always assumed Casa Di Matera was produced near Matera,' Cain said. 'Foolishly, perhaps.'

'We chose the Di Matera name to reflect our humble origins. We're not ashamed of them, and we should never forget them. My father, Giuseppe, who you met, clawed his way out of that stone hell long before the forced relocations, did anything he could to take care of the family, to take care of me and my brother.

It was some time before my wife and I were able to buy this place and start the vineyard, but ultimately it's thanks to my father, and now the family takes care of him.'

Cain nodded respectfully. 'Where is your wife?'

The proud smile faded from Gaspare's face. 'She is no longer with us.'

'I'm very sorry.'

Gaspare batted his hand. 'It was a long time ago. She died when Tino was only...?'

'Three,' Tino answered.

'She left me to be both father and mother to these boys.'

'Eugh,' Valentino said, 'I hate it when you put it that way.'

'It's true, I had to teach you to be soft as well as hard. Don't you agree, Cain, that boys learn so much from their mothers?'

'Of course.'

'Not least, they teach them to respect women.'

'Well, hopefully they learn to respect all people from their mother and their father.'

'Absolutely, you're right. But so often their fathers only teach them how to be angry. It is their mother that teaches them how to be kind. That was the way in my family, for sure. And after my mother died all I had to teach me were memories. I was lucky, I was the older one. My brother was not so lucky, not so many memories.' He sipped his wine. 'First my mother, and then the boys' mother. We are a household of six men. How I wish I could have had a daughter.'

'Instead you have Tino,' Cristino joked through a mouthful of steak.

Tino glared at him.

It was obvious they had all heard their father's laments on this subject before.

'None of you are married?' Cain asked.

'No,' Gaspare answered for them.

'Girlfriends?'

They all nodded, except Tino.

'No wives, no grandchildren,' Gaspare grumbled.

'You mentioned a brother, does he also work in the family business?'

He saw a cheeky, conspiratorial look pass between the sons.

'We don't talk about him.'

He tried to top up Cain's wine, but Cain held his hand over the glass.

'Best to stay sharp for tonight.'

'You're quite right. This favour you're doing tonight, it's for Maltby?'

Cain hesitated. 'Yes.'

'You are an old friend of his.'

He nodded.

'Then perhaps you can tell us what tonight is all about?'

'I was hoping you'd know.'

Gaspare returned his scrutinising look.

'What's the package?' Cain asked him.

'We don't know, we only know the couriers,' Gaspare answered, still meeting his gaze.

'Who are they?'

He turned his nose up. 'Croatian jackals. They'll smuggle anything across the Adriatic for a price.'

'How did you get involved?'

'It took some persuading.'

Cain waited for the proper answer.

'We have... a family connection. What's in the briefcase?'

'From the weight, I'd say about fifty thousand euros.'

'You haven't checked?'

'I don't know the combination.'

Gaspare frowned. 'Your friend is playing this very close to the chest. It's disrespectful. You can tell him I said that.'

The meal was finished with a zuccotto, eaten in silence. Afterwards Cain turned to his host.

'Gaspare, I have to say that I think that is the best meal I have ever had.'

A big smile bloomed beneath his thick moustache. 'I will tell Marie, she will be so pleased. Oh my god, Marie. Marie!'

She appeared.

'*Si, Signore?*'

'You and Angelo had best get home. Leave the dishes until tomorrow.'

'Si, Signore, I will just leave these to soak.'

'Now, Marie, quickly. Where is my father?'

'In his room, Signore, in bed.'

'Good, good. You and Angelo get home, now.'

She disappeared.

'Which does she drive,' Cain asked, 'the Maserati or one of the Alfas?'

Gaspare smiled. 'They live in the cottages you passed, with the rest of the staff.'

Cain nodded. Then he froze, smiling with a sudden realisation and understanding.

'Giuseppe. Matera.' *A family connection...*

Gaspare nodded, anticipating.

'Your father is Giuseppe Gallo.'

'Yes.'

"The butcher of Matera," Cain thought, but didn't say.

Gaspare nodded again, as though reading his mind.

'Tonight we step back into a world I thought we'd left behind,' he said, checking his watch. 'It's gone ten, we'd better get ready.'

FIVE

'What's the plan?' Cain asked.

'If you don't turn up the hill you carry on for three kilometres until you come to the winery. Those are the instructions they have been given,' Gaspare explained.

They stepped into the hall. The four sons were buzzing about like bees from flower to flower, closing shutters, locking windows, opening doors, turning on lights, dousing candles.

'Valentino will meet them and walk them up to the house through the vines. He'll bring them through the glass doors into the back room.'

'Show me.'

Gaspare led Cain into a large back room with a dining table and no chairs. At the other end of the room glass doors opened onto the garden. At the end of the garden the vines started.

'How long is the walk?'

'Ten minutes. Valentino will have a flashlight to lead him through the vines, so we will see them coming the whole time.'

Cain nodded.

'The rest of us will be waiting for them in here.'

'Armed?'

'Yes, we have a couple of pistols and a couple of shotguns.'

'Do your boys know how to use them?'

'The shotguns, yes.'

Cain nodded. 'It's a good plan, I like it.'

'*Grazie*.'

'Do you mind if I modify it a bit?'

'Be my guest.'

'I want you, me, and Tino in here. Tino has one of the pistols, and give the other one to Valentino.'

Gaspare nodded.

'Have you got holsters?'

'No, err...'

'Tell Valentino to put the pistol in his jacket pocket and to keep his hand on it until they show themselves. The idea isn't to use it, just that they know he's got it.'

Gaspare nodded.

'Then I want Fortino and Cristino round the sides of the house with the shotguns, ready to come in through the back doors on my signal. They'll see them when they come up the garden, but that's good, we want that. When they get in here, I'll run the show. Understood?'

'I'll tell them now.' He went to leave.

Cain gently touched his arm. 'I don't like to order you around in your own house, but these things have to be done, you understand?'

'I quite understand, my friend.'

They shook hands.

Gaspare was a good man, Cain thought, and he hoped that after tonight they could become real friends.

He went up to his room and collected the briefcase. He tried the latches with the combination as it was. No luck. He picked up the revolver and removed it from the holster, checked it was still loaded, and put it in his waistband behind his back.

He neatened up his hair and straightened his collar, then left the bathroom to head back downstairs. He paused when he passed the writing table and picked up the bottle.

Gaspare raised his eyebrows when he saw him carrying it down the stairs.

'A gesture of goodwill,' he explained.

Gaspare nodded approvingly. 'Valentino is on his way down.'

'Good. Will he let us know when they arrive?'

'No, there is no phone signal here.'

'You must communicate somehow across the estate, the winery?'

'The winery use walkie-talkies, I didn't think to bring them up to the house.'

'Well, there's nothing that can be done about it now.'

He checked his watch as he marched to the back room. 10:32pm.

Tino was standing in the room, a pistol resting apprehensively in his hands. He looked at Cain with unhidden concern.

Cain took the pistol from him, a Beretta semi-automatic, and put it on the table with the bottle.

'Take off your jacket,' he said.

Tino obeyed.

Cain took the shoulder holster from his pocket and helped the young man put it on. Then he held

Tino's jacket as he slipped back into it. Lastly, he took the Beretta and placed it snugly into the holster under Tino's armpit.

He patted him on the shoulder. 'Leave your jacket open and your hands by your sides. Not in your pockets, just by your sides. Don't reach for it. Don't even think about using it. The idea isn't to use it, the idea is just that they know you've got it.'

He was sweating. 'Are you expecting trouble?'

'No. But I always prepare for it.'

Tino smiled nervously.

'Your father described them as "jackals", that's all I need to know. They're here because they want the money, if they think they're dealing with professionals they'll behave themselves.'

Tino nodded.

'So don't lose your head.'

Tino nodded again.

'Will we see the headlights from up here as they approach the winery?'

'Yes, we should do.'

'Go tell your brothers to give us a signal when they see them.'

He left by the open glass doors.

Gaspare reappeared. 'Are we all right?'

'We're set.'

He was pushing his jaw out, his bottom row of teeth clawing at the bristles of his moustache. A nervous tick.

'Gaspare?' Cain asked gently.

'Yes?'

'How did you get involved in this?'

He gave him a sideways look, but Cain's command

over the situation compelled him to answer.

'The road to running the winery as our sole enterprise was a long one, as was the process of extricating ourselves from my father's organisation. During that time, my father's organisation would sometimes do jobs for Maltby.'

Cain scoffed, trying not to sound too disrespectful. 'The mafia used to do jobs for the CIA?'

'Please, the mafia are Sicilians. We are Lucanian.'

'I'm still confused—'

Gaspare's face became harder. 'I don't think we need to discuss that now. When my father parted ways with the organisation they did not part as friends. Even as he is now, on death's door, there are those that would take great pleasure in killing him. They like to believe that the organisation always gets its man. Every day he lives he proves them wrong. Not to mention the fact that if my father's connection to the winery was revealed it would be catastrophic for the business.'

Cain frowned, not sure what he was hearing. 'Are you saying Jo threatened you with this?'

'It was heavily implied. What did he threaten *you* with?'

Cain didn't answer. 'It's eleven o'clock,' he said, looking at his Speedmaster. 'They should be arriving now.'

Tino returned through the glass doors.

'No headlights?' Cain asked.

'Not yet.'

'You think they're not coming?' Gaspare asked, almost hopeful.

'Or they're late,' Tino said.

Or they don't want us to see them coming, Cain

thought. He didn't see any need to share this thought with the two of them.

'Look sharp,' he said, 'if everything goes to plan they'll be up here in a few minutes. Just sit tight.'

The minutes crawled by. The sounds of the night crept in through the open doors on the cool breeze. The whistle of a scops owl, the watcher, and its distant response.

'Gaspare,' Cain whispered, 'why on earth would a CIA taskforce leader require the... "skills" of an organised crime syndicate?'

'Your friend did—sorry, *does*—dirty work. I imagine it came in useful to acquire the services of people who will do anything for the right price. What your government does all over the world.'

Cain frowned.

'As it has tonight,' Gaspare added.

'That's not why I'm here.'

'I was talking about the Croats.'

There was a shout from outside. They all snapped to attention. They could see a group of men emerging from the vines at the end of the garden. Valentino was at the front of them, his hands on his head. It was obvious he had a gun in his back.

Gaspare and Tino both started, wanting instinctively to run to him. Cain held up a quelling hand, then neatly held his hands behind his back, the right one resting on his gun.

SIX

Valentino was marched into the room, a gun in his spine. He had a nasty bruise forming across one side of his face and a cut above his eye. Cain had been pistol-whipped enough times to recognise the effect.

The gunman's eyes darted wildly, just like a jackal's, and he squinted as he entered the room. He took in Cain and Gaspare, then shoved Valentino forward so that Tino had to catch him.

'Are you all right?' he asked.

Valentino nodded.

Cain kept his eyes on the man. He was in his late twenties with lank hair and a patchy moustache. Either side of his nose there were red teeth marks. Old scars, Cain thought. The man met his gaze with amusement.

Two other men, also young, had entered behind the first. One had a sawn-off shotgun, the other an Uzi. They were wearing black turtlenecks that only just hid their tattoos. And on their feet, heavy military boots.

The first man was wearing brown loafers, and his pupils hadn't contracted when he stepped into the light. *Cocaine.* He was pacing back and forth like a guard dog behind a chain link fence.

'The little shit tried to jump us,' he spat, using his pistol to gesture at Valentino.

'No he didn't,' Cain replied.

'Are you calling me a liar, old man?' he snarled, now pointing his gun at Cain.

'Your money is in the briefcase.'

'What's the combination?'

'You know the combination.'

'Are you trying to be funny, old man? Give us the fucking combination!'

Cain didn't respond.

The man's manic eyes drilled into his, then a yellow smile cracked across his face. 'You're a cool one. Roko, open it.'

The man with the shotgun went for the briefcase.

'Wait,' Cain commanded.

Roko stopped, glancing between him and the first man. 'Luka?'

'Where's the package?' Cain asked.

Luka brushed his greasy hair out of his eyes, then he snorted, and sucked his teeth. He barked something in Croatian. Feet shuffled outside and a person was marched into the room, hands bound behind their back, a bag over their head. Despite the dirty, loose clothes, and the fact they were taller than any of the Croatians, Cain could tell it was a young woman. There was another start from Gaspare and Tino, and now Valentino too, but they had the good sense to look to Cain before they did anything.

Luka took custody of her, then he kicked her in the back of the legs so that she collapsed to her knees, landing hard on the stone floor. There was a muffled groan from beneath the bag.

'What is this?' Cain asked.

'The package. What is *that* supposed to be?' He gestured to the bottle.

'A gift. For the trouble of having to walk up the hill.'

Luka snatched it up from the table. He read the label and shrugged.

'Now,' Cain said, 'you can take your money and leave.'

Roko turned the left dial of the briefcase and popped the latch. Then he turned the right dial.

Luka slammed the bottle down on the briefcase, holding it shut. 'It's not enough,' he said.

'Excuse me?'

'You heard me, old man. I said, "it's not enough".'

'Come on, Luka,' Roko said.

'Silence!' he screamed. Then he turned back to Cain, pointing with his gun. 'This bitch has been double-trouble, so I want double-pay, or I'll blow her head off right here.'

He pulled Valentino's Beretta from his pocket and held it to the woman's head with his left hand, the gun in his right still pointed at Cain. She felt the muzzle and started quaking. Tino snatched his pistol from its holster and pointed it at Luka with trembling hands. Fortino and Cristino were at the back doors now, the muzzles of their shotguns just breaking into the light.

Cain looked at the man's bitten nose, at his wide pupils, and kept his voice calm and level.

'You made a deal,' he said.

'Double the money, old man!'

'I only have what's in the briefcase.'

'Then you'd better get on the phone to your boss.'

'I don't have a number for him. And as a matter of fact I don't have a phone.'

'The house has a phone.'

'I assume so, but I already told you I don't have a number for him.'

'Then you'd better pull one out of your asshole!'

Cain just stared at him, saw him consider the possibility that he was telling the truth. Finally, with a grimace, he accepted it.

'Then you'd better make it up with whatever you have in the house. Cash. Jewellery. Let's start with your watches.'

'We're not going to do that.'

'Luka, your father!' Roko pleaded.

Luka pistol-whipped him, knocking him to the floor. 'I said *"silence!"* I'm in charge of this.'

The Uzi-wielding Croatian at the rear exclaimed when he spotted Fortino and Cristino, turning to aim at them. Roko jumped up and joined him, aiming his sawn-off at Fortino. The fourth man was aiming his pistol calmly at Tino's head. He blew him a taunting kiss.

'Look at you,' Luka said to Cain, 'standing there with your hands behind your back like a fucking butler. Well, buttle off and get me whatever's in the safe.'

'You made a deal, Luka.'

The use of his name focussed his attention.

'What is your word worth?'

He scoffed.

'What is your father's word worth?'

He twisted the gun that was aimed at Cain, as though he was twisting a knife, warning him not to push it.

'We can all still leave here with what we came for.'

'Old man, do yourself a favour and shut your mouth. I'm going to start with this baby-faced faggot over here.' He pointed the gun in his right hand at Tino. 'I'm going to count to three, if he doesn't drop his gun I'm going to blow this bitch's brains all over the floor and still walk out with my money.'

'I'm begging you, Luka, don't do this.'

His yellow teeth flashed another smile. 'Begging, huh? Why don't you get on your knees, crawl over here, and suck my cock!? Maybe then I'll consider it.'

'Luka—'

'One.'

'Tino, put the gun down.'

* * *

Terrified, Tino did as Cain said, gently crouching down to place the Beretta on the stone floor.

'Kick it over!'

He looked at Cain, who nodded. He gave it a gentle push with his foot and it went halfway to Luka.

'Now the shotgun twins outside.'

'Fortino, Cristino,' Cain called, 'put the shotguns down on the floor and go back around the side of the house.'

Tino felt a pang of envy as he watched them disappear.

Luka narrowed his eyes slightly. 'Good. Now I feel more relaxed.'

'Now it's your turn.'

'What?'

'You can point your gun at me, I don't care, but take the other one away from her head.'

Luka laughed. 'You're wrong, old man, it's *your* turn. You're going to take me to the safe.'

'I already told you, I'm not going to do that.'

The Croatians all tightened their grip on their weapons. Tino stared at the fat black pistol the fourth man was pointing at his head. Somehow, the barrel looked as wide as his face, and he imagined the devastating, flesh-shredding effect the bullet would have, like a cannonball through a curtain.

'I will blow this bitch's brains out, old man!'

Tino was on the verge of a breakdown now, he felt madness pouring into his mind like blood into water. It was supposed to be simple, it wasn't supposed to be like this.

He and Valentino were holding hands like children. He kept looking to his father. He wanted his father to take command, to take Luka to the safe and offer them everything they had. But when he imagined it he had visions of Luka executing them all, or leaving them tied up in the main hall, flames licking their way towards them.

He and Valentino took a step back against the wall, no longer participants, just spectators. His father's eyes darted between Cain and Luka. Cain's eyes were locked.

This Luka, whoever he was, whoever his father was, was a psychopath. Tino shuddered. *A man who liked to hurt others. Lived to kill. Took pleasure—*

'One,' Luka said.

'You're making a mistake,' Cain said calmly.

'Two!'

Tino stared at Luka's hand holding the pistol to the woman's trembling head.

'It's up to you, Luka,' Cain said, 'you decide how this goes. You're the one making the choice.'

'*Three!*'

SEVEN

Four shots rang out. Deafening in the stone room. Cain had drawn his revolver and punched a bullet into each of the Croatians. Smoke billowed from the end of his gun as he hovered it between the four of them, waiting for them to fall, wondering which of them would need the fifth bullet. Roko fell first, crumpling onto his side. The man with the Uzi fell to his knees, then onto his face. The fourth man stepped backwards and tripped out the glass doors. He didn't get up again. Cain trained his gun onto Luka, the last man standing. He staggered a single step, then fell sideways, smashing his head on the table on the way down.

Fortino and Cristino arrived breathless at the back doors. They saw the carnage, saw that everyone else was ok, and slumped to the floor with relief. Valentino was leaning on the wall. Gaspare was clutching the table to stay upright. Tino started to heave, but he held it in.

Cain checked on the Croatians one at a time, giving each of them a kick. They were dead, no doubt about it. He de-cocked his gun and put it back in his waistband.

'That went about as well as it could've gone,' was

his only comment.

He took Valentino's Beretta from Luka's hand and placed it on the table.

Valentino was gently touching his bruised face, checking the cut above his eye.

'I need some ice,' he said to no one in particular, wandering out of the room.

Returned to his senses, Tino stood up straight and went to pull the bag off the woman's head.

'Not yet,' Cain said, stopping him. 'I'll take her with me as planned. There's no need for her to know where she was or who she was with. I'm going to need my holster back.'

Tino threw off his jacket, fought with the holster like it was strangling him. When it was finally off he hurried out into the night air. Cain slipped it on and put his gun back where it belonged.

Gaspare had returned to his senses too. He just looked at Cain.

'Will Marie and Angelo have heard the shots?' Cain asked.

'No, I don't think so. *Maybe.*'

'If they ask, just tell them you were shooting at a fox or something.'

Gaspare nodded. His eyes were keen now, focused. 'Go, Cain,' he said.

'I don't want to leave you with this kind of mess.'

'The mess was already here, you were the one that got us out of it.'

Cain said nothing.

'You saved my sons' lives, I have no doubt of that.' He held his hand out to shake, which Cain did.

'What will you do?'

'I presume their car is still down by the winery, so a car accident would seem apposite. There are plenty of steep drops on these country roads.'

Cain sighed.

'Don't worry, it's in our blood. We'll remove the bullets, and the car will have burnt to a shell. There will be nothing to tie them to us. What should we do about the money?'

Cain gave half a smile. 'Keep it.'

'I suppose really it should be in the wreckage.'

'A suitcase full of money will only draw unnecessary attention. And since you won't be able to take the car too far with four dead bodies in it, that attention may be drawn onto you.'

'Won't your friend want it back?'

'I don't think there's any need for him to know about this. As far as he's concerned, it *was* in the wreckage. Its absence can always be explained by light-fingered police.'

He went to the woman and untied her hands. She flexed them and rubbed her wrists, but kept them close to her body. With a hand under her arm, he helped her up to her feet. He led her into the entrance hall and towards the main doors. She felt out blindly with her other arm.

'Cain,' Gaspare called.

He stopped.

The four sons gathered around their father, forming a tableau of masculinity. Valentino had poured himself a drink and was holding the iced glass to his face.

'I hope to see you again one day, under better circumstances. Perhaps you could come to dinner

70

again.'

'I'd like that very much.'

'Just turn up.'

Cain nodded. Then he turned and exited through the main doors.

He and the woman crunched across the gravel to the Mercedes. He sat her in the passenger seat, clipped in her seat belt, and walked around to the driver's side. As he crawled the car out of the courtyard onto the dirt track, he took one last look at the house in his rear-view mirror. Then he planted his foot firmly on the accelerator and sped off into the darkness.

PART II

Birds of Passage

EIGHT

The Mercedes scrambled down the dirt road, past the cottages. Cain waited until they were halfway down the hill before he reached over and removed the bag from the woman's head. Underneath it she was wearing ear defenders and blacked-out goggles. Cain reached over and gently prised the ear defenders half-off.

'You can take all that stuff off now.'

She peeled off the ear defenders and put them in her lap, then did the same with the goggles, moving at the speed you might move when backing away from a gorilla. She sat upright, her head facing forward the whole time, but her eyes were searching the car.

Cain took quick snapshot glances at her. She was around thirty, short blonde hair, pale, underfed. He waited for a couple of minutes, but she didn't say anything. At last, she moved her head, looking out over the black velvet hills.

'Are you all right?' he asked.

She said nothing.

'Do you speak English?'

Nothing.

'I just want to know you're all right.'

Zilch.

He focussed on navigating a tricky corner before he tried again.

'Nothing delicious was ever steamed.'

A slight tilt of the head. *Something.*

'I have this theory,' he continued, 'nothing delicious was ever steamed. Fried, yes. Pan fried, deep fried. Roasted, baked, broiled, sure. But not steamed.'

Still nada.

'Name something. I bet you can't.'

'Gyoza,' she croaked.

'What are they?'

No answer.

'Are they those Japanese dumplings? Yeah, they're not bad with plenty of soy sauce.'

She didn't argue.

'Now that I know you can talk, mind giving me one word on how you're doing?'

'Thirsty.'

'There's a bottle of water in the glove compartment. It'll be warm, and I've drunk out of it, but if you don't mind that, you're welcome to it.'

She opened the glove compartment and reached for the metal bottle, unscrewing it and taking huge gulps. When she put it back she lingered for a second on the road maps.

'The only thing I've got to eat in there are mints, but they might be worth it for the sugar.'

She popped one in her mouth then shut the compartment.

'Better?'

She nodded, then shivered.

'There's a blanket under the seat if you want it.'

She felt for it, found it, and tucked it around her.

'So...' she croaked, 'we're in Italy.'

'Yes.'

'And who are you?'

She was American, he could tell that much.

'Call me Cain.'

'Is that a first name or a last name?'

'More of a nickname. What's yours?'

She didn't answer.

The Mercedes' chassis groaned as they bumped and thumped their way down the rough road. All that could be seen behind them was the cloud of dust they were kicking up, lit red by the rear lights.

'Cain, do we have to drive so fast?'

'I'm trying to put some distance between us and where we've just been.'

'And where's that?'

'That, I don't want to tell you.'

She sighed. 'So you *are* one of them.'

'What does that mean?'

'You haven't rescued me.'

'I think that's a matter of opinion.'

They reached the bottom of the hill, bouncing onto the tarmacked road heading away from the winery. He put his foot down even further. The car roared. Cain was looking ahead, and the only light in the car was the feeble glow of the dials, but he could tell she was giving him a death stare.

She cleared her throat. 'What would you do if I jumped out of this car right now?'

'Probably call an ambulance. But if you want to pull a stunt like that I'd wait until we're in a town because at the moment it's just you and me out here.'

There was silence for a minute.

'What happened back there?' she asked. 'Even through the mufflers I could still recognise gunshots.'

'I can't tell you that either.'

'Great,' she drawled.

They hit a bump in the road. She clutched her stomach and winced.

'Are you ok?'

'Not really, I was shot. Twice.'

'Recently?'

'A week. Two months. I don't know.'

Cain frowned. 'Who the hell are you?'

'I don't see why I should tell you.'

'I don't see what you have to lose.'

She huffed. 'My name is Dolly.'

'Dolly?'

'Yeah, go ahead, laugh. Everyone does.'

'I think it's a perfectly fine name, I just wanted to make sure I had it right.'

'Where are you taking me?'

'Florence.'

'How romantic.'

He saw her eyes flick to the compass on the dashboard.

He smirked. 'We're just outside Montepulciano, we should be there in about ninety minutes. What do you do?'

'*What do I do?* What is this, a cocktail party?'

'What I am trying to ascertain, by polite means, is why on earth you're being smuggled across borders like a trunk full of moonshine.'

'Where are you from? You're not American.'

'Oh, I've lived just about everywhere.'

She frowned.

'What is it you've done?' he asked.

She chuckled a little manically. 'Now that's a different question.'

'Are you going to answer it?'

'I don't see why I should, if I'm not going to get anything in return.'

'What do you want? I've already given you my water and blanket.'

'Answers.'

'I'd like some of them too.'

'You should know, you're the one trafficking me.'

'Well, I don't. As a matter of fact, I didn't even know I was transporting a person. I thought I was transporting a package. But I guess that was just a generic term.'

'If you don't like it you could just drop me off in the nearest town and drive away.'

He didn't reply.

'Well, how about it? Am I your prisoner or not?'

'Right now, you're my cargo.'

'A person isn't cargo.'

'Normally, I would agree with you. I've escorted plenty of people to safety before, but none of them against their wishes.'

'Is that where you're taking me? To safety?'

'Relatively speaking, I think that's a certainty.'

She was silent for a minute. Cain turned the car off the tarmac and onto another dirt road, deciding to avoid the autostrada entirely and go back the way he came.

'And you don't know who I am?' she asked.

He didn't answer. He didn't need to.

'It seems we can reach a deal then.'

'How do you figure that?'

'You know what I want to know. I know what you want to know. Quid pro quo.'

He smiled. 'As much as I like the idea, I don't think I can agree to that.'

'Why not?'

'Because I don't think you'll like the answers you'll get.'

'Fine, I'll go first. If you give me satisfactory answers, I'll give you some in return. How does that sound?'

They sped along a dirt track between vineyards.

'Fine. I'll take you at your word.'

'Where have we just been?'

He sighed. 'I already said I don't want to tell you that.'

'The quid pro quo wouldn't be worth anything if it only concerned things you wanted to tell.'

'Where we've been has nothing to do with any of this, trust me. The only reason I don't want to tell you is because they shouldn't have been involved in the first place. It was—' he stopped himself.

'It was what?'

'Cruel.'

'Who hired you?'

'That, I *really* can't tell you.'

'You probably don't even know. Are they NSA?'

'No.'

'CIA?'

'Someone I trust.'

'But they lied to you.'

'They omitted to tell me the full truth. In my line

of work that's nothing unusual.'

'And what is your line of work?'

'This sort of thing.'

'Who did you collect me from?'

'Croatian smugglers.'

'Know anything more about them than that?'

'No.'

'And what happens when we get to Florence?'

'We wait for you to be collected.'

'By who?'

'I don't know.'

There was pause, filled only with the roar of the engine.

'And how do you feel about all this?'

'I don't know.'

He could feel her studying his profile. He kept his eyes on the road. She was silent for a long minute.

'Well, I guess that's it, I can't think of anything more for now. And I guess you've been honest, at least... honestly unhelpful. So, ask away.'

'What is it you did?'

'What, no foreplay?'

He said nothing.

She sighed. 'I'm an NSA technician. Hong Kong station. Long story short, I learned a few things I didn't like, decided the world should know about them.'

'You did a Snowden?'

'Kinda.'

'What did you do, send it to WikiLeaks?'

'Very funny.'

'What was it you learned?'

'I can't tell you that.'

'That's funny.'

'What?'

'It seems funny to decide the world should know about something and yet not want to tell me what it is.'

'I'm not telling you because you're one of them.'

'I've already told you I don't work for the NSA.'

'I don't care, either way you're taking me to them, so you are one of *them*.'

'If I was one of them, wouldn't I already know?'

'That *is* funny.'

'Why?'

'They don't know what I stole.'

'How can they not know?'

'Because I'm very clever.'

'Fine. I'm a little confused here, when were you shot?'

She scoffed. *'Shot while trying to escape.'*

'That can't be right.'

'Why not?'

'Because if that was true you'd already be in NSA custody. Why on earth would they be using Croatian smugglers to transport you?'

She didn't answer, he seemed to have stumped her.

'What happened after you were shot?'

'I don't know. I thought I was dying. When I woke up I was in an ambulance, but they knocked me out again. I woke up in a small room, then the back of a van, then a warehouse. When I woke up they would give me food and water, the rest of the time they kept me on a drip. The languages changed, the faces. Once they had all this kit,' she gestured to the ear defenders and goggles, 'they stopped drugging me. And now I'm here.'

'What did you steal? A file? A report?'

She snorted derisively. 'Don't worry, someday soon you'll read about it.'

She glanced down at the wing mirror, into the darkness behind them. There was a tiny dot of light in it. But they hadn't passed any lights, not out here.

'They've been following us for about a mile,' Cain said.

'A motorbike?'

He nodded. 'That's what that low rumble is, it's a different note to the car engine.'

'Who are they?'

He didn't answer.

When the road became twistier they would lose sight of the single headlight, but when the road straightened out or they rose higher they would spot it again.

'Maybe we should get on the freeway?'

'What are you worried about? This could be your rescuer.'

They continued along dirt tracks until they crested a small bank and joined a tarmacked road. After three gentle corners it stretched out into a long straight that was raised just above the rows of vines, making them look like paddy fields. The motorcycle's engine began to roar and there were flashing blue lights behind them. *A police bike.* It was close now. It tucked itself neatly behind them and the siren gave a single chirrup.

Cain frowned, thinking fast. The siren chirruped again and he flicked on his indicator, slowing down gently until the Mercedes rolled to a stop at the side of road. He undid his seatbelt and popped the door catch.

'What are you doing?'

He didn't answer.

The motorcycle stopped twenty metres behind them. Cain could tell from the slight shift of its beam that the rider had put down the kickstand. He stared keenly into the wing mirror. He couldn't see the rider, his vision was blinded by the beam of the headlamp and the flashing blues.

When he killed the Mercedes engine he heard soft footsteps. Instinctively, he put the car into reverse, activating the white reversing light. In that moment he got his first glimpse of the rider's legs, of the dark blue trousers so dark they're practically black, of the red carabinieri stripe down the side, and the man's boots.

Cain trusted his instinct. He span out the open door, drew his gun, and fired.

NINE

That morning, Emilio Russo had dressed in his carabinieri uniform, including his dark blue trousers with the red stripe, not knowing that he would die performing a routine traffic stop.

He slipped into his boots and picked up his gold-rimmed Gucci sunglasses, prepared for a day on the roads. He had wanted to be a motorcycle cop since the age of seven when his uncle Roberto had given him a pedal bike painted with the carabinieri colours. At that age he had loved nothing more than cycling the country paths. Then, at fifteen, he loved nothing more than terrorising the country roads on a souped-up Piaggio Beverly. He lost his virginity thanks to that bike.

Everyone knew he was going to be a motorcycle cop one day, and so when he reached the right age he simply showed up for work. It really was that simple. He had loved it. He still did.

This week there was a new ordinance for them to tackle the number of people speeding on the twisting country lanes. Last week a man driving back from the Val d'Orcia to Arezzo hit a cow going a hundred kilometres an hour. The cow was the only fatality, but the local carabinieri chief was now determined to catch a lot of speeders, preferably tourists, in order to demonstrate their dedication to keeping these middle-of-nowhere villages safe. They were the only law out here.

Russo would wait by the long straights, sometimes hidden out of sight between the rows of vines. A sneaky tactic, he knew, but he wanted to catch people not deter them. Out in the villages people weren't too fussy about how you did things. It was like being a sheriff in the wild west, and with his gun on his hip and his steed between his legs, Russo often imagined himself as Gary Cooper, Shane, or his favourite, The Man with No Name. He was the one good man standing between order and chaos.

That morning, chaos took the shape of two speeders and one person driving without insurance. Both the speeders were locals. One was a farmer transporting livestock, the other was a grandmother on her way to the hospital who claimed she couldn't read the dials with her driving glasses on. He gave the farmer the appropriate fine and let the grandmother off with a warning, telling her to get bifocals.

The driving without insurance was a funny one. It was a case of listening to that instinct you come to trust in any job if you've been doing it long enough. Something about the model of the car, the state it was in, the split-second glimpse of the driver. He could tell whenever people tried to get away from him without *looking* like they were trying to get away. The young man was decent enough about it, it seemed like something he knew was coming. This guy was a tourist, from Dubai, so he said, and he had a UAE passport and a UAE driving license, but when Russo ran the plates the car was registered to his name. That meant he was a resident. He told the guy that if he had been a resident for more than a year he needed an Italian driving license to drive in Italy, and he did not have one. It was something people tried to put off for as long as possible. It was a nuisance, but it was a real offense. "Offense" was a good word for it, Russo thought. If you want to live in the country you've got to play by the rules, that was the way he saw it. Anything else was disrespectful.

After that he stopped by his mother's apartment. He was permitted an hour break and he often took the opportunity to drop in and see her. If he let her know in advance, then she would have a lunch ready for him. Today it was a simple tomato and bean bruschetta. She was exceedingly proud to have a son in the carabinieri and swelled with smug pride whenever her neighbours noticed his Ducati on the street.

After lunch he went back to his patrol, and it was just as he was cresting a hill outside of Montefollonico that a dark grey G-Wagen appeared in the middle of the road, speeding towards him, forcing him to slam on his brakes and swerve. They even had the cheek to honk him.

He span around on his front wheel like a stunt performer, fired up his blues, and chased after them. He wailed his siren, but they wouldn't pull over. He flashed his headlamp but still they wouldn't. They didn't stop until they turned onto a dead end and ran up against a farm gate. He was tempted to block their escape with his bike, but they would probably just reverse over it. So he waited. He just waited.

The G-Wagen's engine burbled, pinging and popping. The car had Italian plates, but he had never seen a G-Wagen on the roads around here before, no one could afford one, and anyone with enough money would buy something Italian. Was it stolen? Probably just driving without the right papers, but you never knew. That was why you carried a gun.

Russo could wait all day, so he lit a cigarette. His bike purred, warm between his legs.

Finally, the driver killed the engine.

Russo flicked away the cigarette. He kicked down his kickstand and sauntered up to the driver's side door, his hand resting on his pistol. He rapped on the window. He wore a heavy gold ring just for the noise it made against car windows. When the tinted glass came down, he was greeted with the head and shoulders of a frumpy forty-something woman with unstyled hair and no makeup. Unmistakably Germanic.

'Afternoon, Officer,' she said in bad Italian.

Russo had been expecting some hot-head, not this. The passenger seat and the back seats were empty. He relaxed, dropping his hand off his gun.

'Why didn't you pull over when I flashed you?'

'I thought you just wanted to get past me.'

They always had an excuse.

'Then why didn't you pull over to let me pass?'

'There was nowhere to pull over, and every time I turned off the road you followed me.'

He sighed. 'Do you know why you've been pulled over?'

'No.'

'You almost caused a collision because you were driving in the middle of the road.'

'No, I don't think so.'

'Yes, you did. Let me see your license.'

'I don't have it with me, Officer.'

Did she slur?

'Are you lying to me?'

'No, Officer.' She slurred again.

She had that look of someone holding themself together.

'Because if you're lying to me, I will find out. I have to check your car now to make sure you've got the required documents and equipment onboard the vehicle. So if I find a license that you've claimed you do not have on you then that's not going to be good for you. Have you been drinking today?'

'No,' she said, brushing her hair behind her ear and licking her lips.

She was giving some kind of performance.

'Step out of the car, please.'

'Is that really necessary? I'll pay the fine.'

'Yes it is. Just step out of the car now.'

With a sigh, she undid her seat belt, and stepped out. She started walking away from the car.

'Where are you going?'

'It's muddy here.'

He marched after her into long grass.

'Stop!' he barked.

'I told you, it's muddy.'

'I don't care,' he said, catching up to her.

'I do...'

He grabbed her arm, span her round to face him.

'...we don't want to get mud on your uniform.'

A car door opened. He span back to the G-Wagen, hand reaching for his gun. A blinding pain in the back of his skull! He was knocked forward by the blow. Then a white-hot pain around his throat.

He clawed at his neck. She was garrotting him, it felt like a red-hot cheese wire. Every desperate instinct in his flesh was riling against the agony. He staggered and kicked as her weight pulled him down to the ground, his legs dancing in the long grass. Through it all he could see the blurry shape of a man marching towards him from the back of the car.

'Not with that! Not with that, my treasure!' the man was saying in German. 'He will bleed.'

'This isn't my first time.'

As he lay there twitching, eyes rolling into the back of his head, he was distinctly aware of the two of them sharing a passionate kiss, even as the woman continued to garrotte him.

Then, suddenly, she released him. And if anything, the pain was worse. Then the man shifted both his knees onto Russo's shoulders, pinning him down, and his hot sweaty fingers closed around Russo's neck.

The pressure in his head built until he thought it would burst through his eyes. The world turned pink, then red, and closed like an iris around the man's grinning face.

TEN

The gunshot was just a crack in the midnight air. The man in the carabinieri uniform hit the dirt. Cain was crouched by the car, his revolver still poised. He hadn't reloaded it since shooting the Croatians, it was empty now, but the man didn't know that.

'Drop the gun!' Cain commanded.

'What are you doing!?' Dolly screamed.

'Stay in the car!' he barked at her.

She undid her seat belt and climbed out.

The man in the carabinieri uniform, now lying in the dirt, had already let go of the pistol, it was just lying half in his hand. He flicked his wrist and it rattled down near his shoes. Cain had caught him in the stomach. He'd live if he got the proper attention.

Dolly was standing by the back wheel.

'You shot him!?'

'I said "stay in the car".'

'We have to call an ambulance.'

'We will, as soon as we know who he is and why he was following us.'

'What do you mean? He's a police officer!'

'No, he's not. Carabinieri wear boots.'

'He *is* wearing boots!'

'No, they wear high boots when they're riding motorcycles, up to their knees, not army boots like those. And look how tight it all is, that uniform's not his.'

He stood up from the side of the car and stalked towards the man, revolver poised. The air held the prickling metal tang of exhaust fumes. Vines rustled like grass skirts. The man's chest was rising and falling steadily. His stubbled face was pale, sweating, but he looked calm, all things considered. You might think he got shot every day. *And twice on Saturdays.*

This whimsical thought was still passing through Cain's mind when his revolver exploded in his hand.

ELEVEN

The phone rang at 8:02 Central European Time, in a small town in Germany, in the kitchen of Moritz and Mila Fischer. Mila was just trying to convince the youngest of their two sons to eat some peanut butter on toast. Baby Oskar, restrained in his highchair, saw the interruption as the perfect opportunity to knock it out of her hand.

She snatched up the phone. '*Hallo?*'

'Hello.' The caller was English. 'Is this the bakery on Annaberger Strasse?'

'No, you have the wrong number.'

'I'm very sorry.'

'That's quite all right, it happens all the time.'

'Do you think they'll be open if I call them now?'

'I don't think they open for another twenty minutes.'

'Twenty minutes. Much obliged.'

'You're welcome, have a good day.'

She hung up the phone just as her husband appeared with their other son, Tobias, dressed in his school tie and blazer. They were throwing a lacrosse ball back and forth between them. Moritz threw it to Tobias one last time and told him to put it in his school bag

92

now.

'Who was that?' he asked Mila.

'Wrong number.'

'Dry cleaners?'

'Bakery.'

He nodded. 'Should I take this one to school, or do you want to?'

'You'd better do it.'

He nodded. 'What do you want, Tobi, toast or cereal?'

Ten minutes later he was pulling out of the driveway in their dark grey G-Wagen, Tobias in the passenger seat.

Mila wagged her finger at baby Oskar, strapped into his highchair.

'You stay there. And don't repeat anything you hear.'

He stared at her dumbly, fidgeting against his restraints.

'In ten minutes you're going to wish you hadn't knocked that toast out of mummy's hand.'

She left Oskar in the kitchen and opened the door to the basement. She didn't bother with the light, there was enough spilling down from the open door to highlight the important landmarks. Amongst the bicycles, camping gear, tools, and tins of paint, there was a dusty rolltop desk.

She opened the fuse box and took out the tiny brass key, then she went to the desk and unlocked it. When she opened the desk she was greeted by a green Bakelite telephone, notepad, and biro. The phone line disappeared out of a hole drilled through the back of the desk, into the wall, but before that it travelled through an old brass switch box. Mila flicked the switch to the down position and waited. The telephone was silent.

When the twenty minutes were up, she picked up the receiver.

'*Hallo, Annaberger Bäckerei,*' she chirped.

'The phone was ringing for two minutes,' the English voice said.

'Then you were two minutes early, sir, we've only just opened.'

The voice grumbled.

'Are you calling regarding catering services, sir?'

'Yes, I have a big event happening and I want to make sure it goes as planned.'

'I see, sir, and you'd like us to do the catering?'

'Well, if everything goes to plan then I won't need you, I'm planning to do the baking myself, but I'm a very thorough chap, and as I said it's a big event, so I can't afford to have my guests underfed, if you get my meaning.'

'I think I do.'

'Do you deliver?'

'Of course, we can deliver anywhere in Europe.'

'Excellent.'

'When is your event?'

'Tomorrow.'

'Tomorrow? That's very short notice, sir.'

'I know, I apologise. Will it be a problem?'

'No problem.'

Mila picked up the biro that was next to the telephone and held it poised above the notepad.

'How many guests are we talking about?'

'Twelve. Although there are one or two that I absolutely have to keep happy, the others I don't care about quite as much.'

'Is it one or two, sir?'

'Two.'

'I see,' she said, 'well, we have a wonderful selection platter of cakes and pastries that we can do for your two VIP guests, but it is quite expensive. We charge one hundred euros per person for that service, and you understand that is a charge for our hard work preparing them, whether our services are needed or not.'

'I quite understand.'

'But we would do our best to make those platters stretch as far as possible across all twelve guests so that we keep everyone happy if we can.'

'Marvellous. I don't want anyone to leave still hungry.'

'And the delivery address, is that in Germany?'

'Italy.'

'North or south?'

'Tuscany.'

'And what time would you need them by, sir?'

'It's at a friend's house, so he and his family will already be there. That's six of them. One of the VIP guests will be arriving to help set up from eight o'clock. He'll be arriving alone.'

'I understand.'

'The main event starts at eleven, which is when the other five guests will arrive, including the other VIP.'

'And yourself, sir?'

'I will not be attending.'

'We understand. There is a bank here in Bonn that we use, they also accept documents, so if you could send the money and the guest list, with any dietary requirements, to them. The address is—'

'I know the one you mean,' he cut in.

'*Wunderbar.*'

There was a thoughtful silence on the line, hidden behind the crackles and pops of a scrambler.

'Is there anything else you'd like to ask, sir?'

'Yes,' he hesitated, 'what do you do about leftovers?'

'Leftovers? If you're looking for a cleaning service, sir, we can recommend one.'

'No, that's not what I meant.'

'I'm sorry, sir, I must have misunderstood.'

'One of the guests, one of the VIPs, is a woman, could her leftovers be delivered to me?'

'Leftovers, sir? Cold. Delivered?' She frowned. 'We may be able to do that.'

'Well, if there's a way to get those leftovers to me still hot then I would prefer that.'

'Hot leftovers? I'm not sure I understand you, sir. You do understand that we are a bakery, not a delivery service, if that's what you're looking for I could recommend someone.'

'I understand, but it's a short drive, not far at all.'

She opened her mouth to speak but hesitated.

He pounced. 'I would pay you a bonus, of course. Another fifty euros. The rest of the leftovers you may dispose of as you see fit.'

She thought for a moment, frowned, then shrugged. 'We will do everything we can to meet your requests.'

'Thank you, I'll send the money right away.'

'What is the address for the leftovers, sir?'

'I'll send that over with the money.'

'Very well, I think I understand all your special

requirements. Should I put a name on the account, sir, in case you require our services again?'

'Yes…' There was a pause. 'Tourmaline.'

'Well, Mr Tourmaline, we look forward to doing business with you.'

She hung up.

Oskar was on the verge of bawling when she returned to the kitchen. She picked the peanut butter toast off the floor and blew on it before offering it to him. He snatched it and began to suck on it merrily, switching instantly from near tears to googly smiles.

She saw the G-Wagen reversing into the driveway and soon Moritz was in the kitchen giving her inquiring eyebrows.

'Well, my treasure?' he asked.

'We'd better take this one to your mother's.'

TWELVE

The exact point of Cain's Smith & Wesson Model 10 revolver that the sniper's bullet struck was at the top of the cylinder where it meets the frame. He was extremely lucky that he had no more bullets to fire, if the cylinder had contained anything more than empty shells the impact would have ignited any unfired shells and the cylinder would have exploded, taking much of Cain's hand and most of his fingers with it. As it happened, the steel frame sheared into several pieces of jagged metal, breaking across hinges and joins, slashing its way out of Cain's hand. All he saw hit the ground was the wooden grip, as he dropped to his knees, clutching at his cut hand, which was also mildly burned from the friction. He made no more noise than a sharp intake of breath.

With a howl of pain, the man on the floor reached down and regained his pistol, levelling it at Cain's chest. Their eyes locked. Cain knew he was at the man's mercy.

He looked out into the darkness of the vineyards, hoping to spot the shooter. He could see the silver roof of an SUV glinting just above the vines. The vines were rustling like pom-poms, someone was hurrying towards the road. Dolly was behind him, staring dumbfounded at the man on the floor, whose other hand was clutching his stomach, blood oozing out between his fingers.

The sniper emerged from the vines and up the bank onto the road. A middle-aged woman dressed in black combat gear with night-vision goggles perched on her head and a rifle as tall as her body. She placed the rifle on the ground and drew a pistol, a boxy Heckler & Koch. Dolly recoiled. The man flicked his aim onto her.

'Not her, Treasure!' the woman shouted in German.

She rushed to his side.

'Treasure,' she whispered to him, examining his wound.

'Make sure to keep pressure on it,' Cain said in perfect German. It was an obvious thing to say, but he had to establish early that he didn't want the man to die.

The woman turned her pistol on Cain, her desperate breath fluttering her ginger hair. 'You,' she said in English, her eyes locked on him. 'Girl.'

Dolly snapped to attention.

'There is a Mercedes G-Class fifty metres in the direction from which I came. The keys are in the ignition, drive it here onto the road. If you drive away, I will kill your friend.'

'I'll go,' Cain volunteered.

'No!' the woman snapped. 'Her.'

Dolly stared for a few more moments, then turned and walked in a daze to the edge of the road, disappearing down the bank. Cain watched her blonde head disappear into the vines and then looked back at the woman. Her gun, and eyes, were still on him.

'What kind of bullets do you use? Standard hollow points?'

'Jacketed. He should have an exit wound in his lower back. Both wounds need to be bandaged.'

'We have everything we need in the truck.'

'He needs a doctor.'

She scoffed.

'We can keep him alive long enough to get to a doctor,' he said earnestly, 'I've done it before. But he needs a doctor. He needs a hospital.'

They waited for a minute in silence, staring at each other. He didn't know what she saw in his lines, in hers he saw a hard woman, someone who could be coldly, dispassionately cruel.

Still no sound of Dolly starting the G-Wagen engine.

'Listen, if she doesn't come back, I can drive you to a hospital in my car.'

'If she doesn't come back, I'll kill you and take your car.'

'You should've sent me.'

'There are other weapons in the truck, you would have armed yourself and come back to kill us.'

'She might do the same.'

'No. She's weak. She won't risk her friend's life.'

'She's not my friend.'

'We'll see.'

From the darkness, the gentle rumble of the G-Wagen engine igniting. Then came the glow of the headlights, and finally the sounds of first gear and trampled vines. The headlights worked their way diagonally towards the road, mounting the bank with a roar of the engine and almost tipping over on the slope.

When the big SUV was flat on the road, twenty metres ahead of them, it lingered motionless. Cain and the woman shared a glance. Then the reversing light came on and the G-Wagen backed up to within two metres of the three of them clustered on the tarmac.

Dolly jumped down from the driver's seat and walked to the back of the G-Wagen. The woman flicked her gun onto her, making her jump, but Dolly was unarmed. The woman laid the man's head back on the tarmac, then crawled backwards until she could stand five metres away.

'You,' she pointed the gun at Dolly, 'there is a medical kit in the trunk, get it. If you touch any of the weapons I will kill you.'

Dolly gingerly opened the G-Wagen's swinging rear door. There were two black holdalls and a smaller red bag.

'The red bag.'

Dolly reached into the back.

'Give it to *him*.'

Dolly handed the bag to Cain.

'You, bandage him.'

Cain nodded and knelt down by the man. He opened the kit and took a quick inventory, laying it out on the road. Chest seal, decompression needle, combat tourniquet, none it useful for a stomach wound.

'Hurry up,' she barked.

He frowned at her. 'I'm going to do the best job I can, but I'm not a doctor.'

The woman bit her lip.

'Dolly, I'm going to need your help.'

She nodded, squatting down next to him.

'I guess you'd better get him on his side and lift up his top so we can see both wounds,' he instructed.

She helped the man roll over into something

resembling the recovery position. Then she pulled up his top. He had a tiny entry wound just above and to the right of his belly button, there was a golf ball exit wound in his lower back.

'It doesn't look like it's hit any bones,' Cain said. 'That's good. Get the water from my car.'

The woman didn't complain as Dolly hurried off into the darkness.

'I really need more light.'

'There's a flashlight in the trunk.'

'Can *you* get it?'

With a huff she went and retrieved the torch, offering it to him.

'Point it at the wound,' he said, 'you can do it from over there if you want.'

She stepped back and flicked on the beam.

Dolly returned with the bottle.

'Clean both wounds, then use this,' he passed her a clotting sponge, 'on whichever wound is bleeding fastest. Probably the exit wound. Here, wear these gloves.'

There was a penlight in the pack, he flicked it on and held it with his mouth whilst he examined the rest of the kit. Smelling salts. Gauze. Scissors. Tape. Rescue blanket. CPR microshield. Iodine prep pads. There was blood on everything already. It was on his hands. Dolly's were smeared too.

'Here,' he said, passing her two prep pads, 'wipe each wound with one of these.'

He opened a third one and cleaned his cut hand. It stung like a bastard.

'No,' the woman snapped at him, 'you can wait.'

'My hands have to be sterile too,' he replied

calmly, winding some gauze around his injured right.

Tipping out the remainder of the red bag, he found what he was looking for: surgical pads and an emergency pressure bandage. He passed Dolly a dressing pad.

'Put this on the entry wound, let me know if it's a sticky one or if you need tape.'

She opened the pad and gently pressed it to the wound. 'It's an adhesive one,' she said calmly.

'Good. Now we've got to get him sitting up so we can apply this one.'

Dolly helped the injured man to sit up.

'My treasure,' he wailed in German.

'Don't worry, Treasure!' the woman replied, a wavering note in her voice.

Cain ripped open the sterile packaging of the emergency bandage and applied the pad to the exit wound, then he wrapped it tightly around the man's chest, through the plastic cleat, then back the other way to apply pressure. He wound it once more around the man's stomach until the bandage was used up and clipped in. It neatly covered both wounds.

Some of the panic had left the woman's face, she seemed impressed by Cain's work.

'He's going to need to drink at least a litre of water to stabilise his blood pressure, otherwise he'll pass out.'

The woman ignored this pronouncement.

'You two, carefully, help him into the back of the truck.'

'My treasure,' the man pleaded.

'Quiet, Treasure. Rest.'

Cain and Dolly placed their hands under the man's armpits and got him to his feet. Then they helped him take the step up into the back seat, where he slid along to the other side and lay panting in the corner.

'Now, you two,' the woman said, 'get in.' She gestured with her pistol.

'Listen,' Cain started.

'Get in!'

'Listen,' he said again, with more authority this time but with his hands out and open. 'I shot him, I understand why you have to take me with you. I don't like it, but I understand it. She had nothing to do with it, let her go. She's not my friend, she's my prisoner. She doesn't have a phone, she can't call the police. You can shoot out the tyres on my car and on the bike, it will take her hours to reach the nearest village on foot. And you'll have one less person to worry about.'

'One more word,' she said, 'and I'll shoot her in the foot just to watch her dance.'

Cain sighed, and turned to get in the back.

'Stop!'

He did.

'Get in the front. You can drive, I will direct you.'

Cain climbed into the driver's seat and began familiarising himself with the storks and centre console. Dolly was ushered into the middle back seat and the woman climbed in next to her. Cain clipped in his seat belt. The woman raised her eyebrow at him.

He smiled. 'Safety first.'

He started the engine. The inside lights faded down to darkness.

'There's a hospital in Perugia,' he said.

'Just drive,' she growled.

THIRTEEN

The bodies of the Croatians were a bitch to drag. Even downhill, even with a rope tied around their shoulders. Luka's loafers kept slipping off and eventually Valentino got tired of putting them back on his lifeless feet and held them under his arm as he dragged. Each of the four sons dragged one Croatian, all in single file, each watching the body in front to make sure nothing fell out of their pockets. By the time they reached the bottom of the vineyard they could see the lights from their father's Alfa Romeo, idling next to the Croatian's black Audi. Valentino flashed his torch beam twice. The Alfa's headlights flashed three times in response. The coast was clear.

At least they had been spared the worst job. Gaspare had imagined using tweezers to remove bullets from soft flesh, and he had no idea how that was going to go. He wasn't sure he was up to it. The squelching, and the possibility of having to feel around inside with his fingers. Mercifully, whatever bullets Cain had used had gone right through the four of them, lodging in the walls.

The four sons dragged the bodies as far as the Audi and dumped them. They stretched their arms, flexing their hands, and arched their backs.

'How did I end up with the heavy one?' Fortino moaned.

The others weren't in the mood for jokes.

This was the dirt car park of the winery. There were the two pickup trucks they used to reach the furthest fields, and beyond them the hulking silhouettes of the corrugated steel buildings that housed the vats and barrels.

'You didn't drop anything?' Gaspare asked, standing haloed in the Alfa's headlights.

'No,' Cristino said, 'I was the last in the line, there was nothing.'

'How do you know? Do the inventory.'

They all sighed.

'Come on, quick! Check their pockets.'

They knelt down and examined the bodies, taking out wallets, keys, phones, and putting them back.

'All here.'

'Ditto.'

'Same.'

'Shit!' Cristino grunted.

'What?'

'This guy had some coins, I think.'

'You took an inventory.'

He nodded. 'They were there, definitely.'

'You have to find them.'

Valentino looked from his brother to his father. 'They're just coins, Papà.'

'I don't care! This is serious. Nothing can be missed.'

'I'll find them,' Cristino reassured him.

'Good. Now put them in the Audi. Which one had the key?'

'Mine,' Tino said.

'Put him in the back for now, we'll have to move him when we get there.'

The four sons struggled to heave the four Croatians into the car, but eventually they had them strapped in, heads lolling forward like dolls.

'Tino, you follow in the Alfa. The rest of you go back to the house and clean that room. Walls, floor, ceiling. Every item, every window. Pick the bullets out of the walls. Then clean it all again just to be sure. If we finish before the sun comes up, then we haven't done a good enough job. And find those coins!' He stabbed a finger at Cristino, then climbed into the driver's seat of the Audi.

Valentino watched Tino climb into the Alfa as the other two turned and trudged up the hill, torches pointed at the ground. Going off with his father to stage the accident should have been *his* job. He was the one his father was grooming to run the company, but deep down he knew that Tino was his favourite. The irony never ceased to amuse him about his winemaking, Catholic, "when will you boys get married?" father: his favourite son was a gay teetotaller.

Tino took the car out of neutral and followed the Audi as his father crawled it around in a gentle circle, out of the gate, and began to drive steadily down the dirt road. The Alfa's tyres crunched over the stones, its racing suspension sending jolts up Tino's spine. He knew where his father was going. There was a certain corner he had warned the boys about ever since they were little. As you climbed to the top of the hill and put your foot down the road suddenly levelled out and there it was, a sharp left with no wall, no crash barrier. When Valentino had turned thirteen and was allowed to drive the trucks around the vineyard their father had taken the four of them up there. He made them all sit on the edge of the cliff.

'Look down,' he told them.

Tino clutched Fortino's arm.

'If you fall from this height you will die.'

Their legs dangled in open air. A hundred feet below them a stream rippled over pewter rocks like jagged teeth.

'If any of you come up here, I will give you up for adoption. Do you understand?'

Tino had wanted nothing more than to get away from there, back down the hill. Years later, when he had started driving for real, his father mentioned that place again.

'Why that corner, Papà? I've never heard of anyone crashing up there. The accidents around here are always some drunk colliding with a tractor.'

His father looked away, finished his glass of wine. 'There is a local legend,' he whispered, 'some of the old hands will be able to tell you it. They say that if you stand at that spot in a full moon and look straight down into the stream you will see your loved ones who have passed over. The legend says that people lean out further to see them better, or try to climb down to them, and fall to their death.'

Tino had done nothing but stare at his father's profile, not wanting to break the spell.

'When your mother died I went up there to kill myself. It seemed only fitting. I stood on the edge of the cliff and I looked down and saw...'

'What?'

'I thought I saw a young boy, your age at the time, playing in the stream. If anything, I had expected to see your mother, but it was a moonless night. When I looked again...'

'Yes?'

'There was only darkness. I couldn't even see the water. Just darkness. It scared me. And I realised then what I had behind me, back down the road.'

'What?'

'The four of you, sleeping in your beds. And in front of me, down *there*...'

Tino slammed on the breaks, the Audi had stopped.

Nothing happened. The Audi just sat there in the middle of the road. What was his father doing? *Oh, God!* Was one of the Croatians still alive somehow? Did the Audi not have enough fuel to get up the hill? Was his father hurt in some way?

A goat wandered out from in front. It trotted up a rocky incline. He laughed, or cried, he wasn't sure, as the Audi set off again.

They were climbing now. He turned off his lights, following close behind the Audi's taillights as they crawled up the twisting road. Tino took a fleeting glance out of his window at the black countryside, and just then the moon emerged from behind thick cloud, bright and full.

Finally, they reached the corner. The moon reflected off the smooth stone ledge that jutted out just slightly like a bridge to nowhere. They turned off their engines and climbed out. He couldn't help but stand on the edge, looking down. There was nothing but the sheen of the water.

'Come away,' his father said.

He nodded and turned back to the Audi. His father squeezed his shoulder. Together, they hauled the driver from the back and strapped him behind the wheel.

'I'm not sure they're the type to wear seatbelts,' Tino said, 'we should at least undo the ones in the back.'

'No. We can't have any of them thrown from the vehicle on impact. They must burn in the car.'

'Why?'

His father stared at him incredulously. 'Because they've got bullet holes in their chests.'

Tino nodded. 'Of course.'

Gaspare started the Audi engine and released the handbrake. They walked to the rear.

'Wait,' Tino said.

'What?'

'Put it in second.'

Gaspare nodded. 'Good thinking.'

He put the car into second gear and then returned to Tino at the rear. They started to push.

'Wait!' Tino said again.

'What now?'

'Lights.'

Gaspare sighed, then nodded. He went the driver's door, opened it, turned on the headlights, full beam, then slammed the door shut.

'Anything else?' he asked.

Tino shook his head.

They pushed as hard as they could, and at the point Tino felt he might break his back they finally got it moving. They pushed and pushed and pushed, their feet scrabbling on stony ground, inching it forwards, and finally they felt the front wheels tip over the edge. Then it beached on its belly, the exhaust screeching. They turned their backs to it, took the weight on their shoulders, and heaved.

It got away from them quickly, they turned to see nothing. Then came the banging and smashing and crashing from below. The noises were deafening, echoing off the stone cliffs. They rushed to the edge and looked down, both holding each other steady. The Audi was rolling down the gorge, leaving a glittering trail of glass that caught the moonlight as it fell. Then it flipped and started to tumble end over end into the darkness. The exhaust pipe hung off the car's belly like the pin of a safety clip. A wheel flew off into the trees, cracking branches. Tino thought the sounds would never stop, they were as loud as cannon fire and would surely wake all of Tuscany. Then, with a final boom, the Audi crashed belly-up into the stream, its remaining front wheel spinning down to a stop.

The echoes died. This was the backcountry, there were no lights to come on, no people to shout. The only things woken were birds and bats. Silence returned to the darkness.

'It didn't explode,' Tino remarked.

'Of course not.'

Gaspare pulled a bottle of vodka from his jacket pocket and opened it.

Tino frowned.

'It was in their car.'

He then took a rolled-up handkerchief, dipped it into the bottle, took it out, and wedged the dry end in.

'All this needs is an accelerant.'

He lit the end with a cigar lighter and quickly, taking only a second to aim, tossed it into the ravine.

Father and son leant over to watch the tiny flame as it fluttered down into the darkness. It landed ten metres from the car, smashing into a puddle of fire. Where the Audi's fuel tank had ruptured on the way down it had left a trail. The trail burst into flame like a lightning bolt striking the upturned car. A fireball exploded from the carcass, and the tongues of flame did the rest.

FOURTEEN

The G-Wagen's headlights pierced the darkness. They had driven in silence, save for the woman's barked directions. Ribbons of tarmac turned to dirt, vines turned to bushes, dark curtains of trees. The roads were empty. The only signposts were village names that meant nothing to Cain. She had made him hide the satnav map that displayed on the centre console, but she couldn't hide the moon. They were still heading north. The petrol gauge crept down ever so slightly.

Every time Cain tried to start a conversation she would dig the end of her pistol into Dolly's ribs. He glanced in the rear-view mirror. No lights behind them. The man's eyes were closed, his head lolled back, but his chest continued to rise and fall. He was still alive.

'Here, on the left. Follow this track.'

There was a wooden gate blocking the way so Cain jumped out of the car and trudged through mud to open it. The world was completely black beyond the reach of the headlights, the tops of trees just silhouettes against the sky.

He returned to the G-Wagen and trundled it up the track.

'Stop the car!' the woman barked.

He slammed on the brakes. They all jolted in their seats. The man groaned.

The woman shot daggers at him. 'Shut the gate,' she hissed.

This time he gave it close examination. It was old and dry, almost flimsy. If you hit it going fast enough, with a big enough car like the G-Wagen, it would shatter.

'Don't get any ideas,' she said as he climbed back into the car, 'there's no way out of this for you.'

After a kilometre the track became an incline and black silhouettes of a farm peeked up against the sky like cut-outs. Moments later the headlights reached the buildings. It was a big place with several stone barns and a couple of new steel ones. Set further up the hill was a square farmhouse that loomed over them. The place was dark.

He pulled up in the little dirt courtyard.

'Turn off the engine,' the woman instructed, 'but leave the lights on. Then get out and put your hands on the side of the car.'

He did as he was told, his hands above the front wheel arch. The engine was warm. There was a cool breeze, and the night was silent save for a door or a window banging in the wind up at the farmhouse.

Dolly was ordered out of the car too and made to stand next to Cain.

'Stay here, Treasure,' the woman said, stroking the man's hair.

She climbed out of the car, took the keys from the ignition, and opened the G-Wagen's swinging rear door.

'Don't even think about running,' she told them. 'There's nothing but open fields in all directions, and with my rifle I could hit you from a mile away.'

They heard her rooting in one of the holdalls, then she appeared with black cloth bags, cable ties, and rope.

'This isn't necessary,' Cain said.

'I told you before,' she pointed her gun at Dolly's kneecap, 'shut up and she might survive the night in one piece.'

Cain sighed.

'Turn around,' she ordered.

They did.

The woman chucked Cain one of the bags. 'Put it on.'

He hesitated.

'Put it on!' the woman screamed, producing a thin sharp knife and turning to Dolly.

'Ok!' he shouted. Then calmer, 'ok.'

Gritting his teeth, he pulled the bag over his head. He could still make out the light from the headlamps, but nothing more.

'Tighten it.'

The bag had a drawstring, he pulled until it was snug around his neck.

'Hold out your wrists.'

He did. She chucked something to Dolly. 'Put them on him.'

He felt Dolly's hands on his wrists, then the sharp plastic of cable tie handcuffs.

'Tighter!' the woman barked.

She tightened them until they were just pinching his skin.

'Turn around,' she ordered Cain.

He obeyed.

He heard her holster her pistol. Then the second bag going over Dolly's head, and the angry insect clicking of the ties tightening. He heard her wince as they bit into her skin.

'Turn around.'

He did as he was told.

'Hands out, both of you.'

He held out his bound wrists, felt her tighten a rope around the cable ties. The same for Dolly. Then she led them like she was leading horses.

He stumbled forward, almost tripping on the uneven ground. They moved towards one of the buildings, the light changing. He and Dolly both bumped their shoulders on the doorframe and had to take turns to get through. The woman turned on a light, he could just make out the dark shape of her. He bumped into something metal, catching his hip. A hook or door bolt maybe. A second later, Dolly did the same. The woman didn't warn them of steps and once or twice he experienced that split-second of panic as he stepped into thin air. Eventually, she stopped tugging on the rope and ordered them to stand against a rough stone wall. There was a scraping of wood and then she slid something forward into his shins. He flinched. Then she slid something towards Dolly. She yelped.

'It's a chair, stand on it.'

They both obeyed, struggling to balance blind. Cain couldn't help picturing gallows. There came the whistling sounds of rope being fed through a loop and tied. Then the whoosh of rope being whipped through the air like a lasso. Cain could feel tension on his rope, and twice he heard the rope smack into the stone wall above his head and drop. Once it landed on his head. He didn't flinch. On the third attempt it seemed to catch on something high above his head and stayed there. His arms were jerked above his head as the rope was pulled tight.

The same process was repeated with Dolly.

There were footsteps, and then the woman pulled the chairs from under their feet. They fell into nothingness, all their weight forced through the cable ties. Cain groaned. It was like someone had taken a razor blade to his wrists. He could hear Dolly's feet scratching desperately against the wall.

'Stop kicking!' the woman barked.

Wood scraped across the stone floor. Dolly stopped kicking. Then his chair was put back too, but not upright, on its side, so that he had to stand on tiptoes to reach it.

'Struggle,' she told them, 'and you'll hang by your wrists until your hands drop off.'

The shape of her marched to the door. The lights went out. Total darkness. Her footsteps scratched on the stone, left the room, fading away.

'Cain?'

'Wait,' he said, listening.

The door of the G-Wagen opening. Then shut a minute later. The little electric yelp as she locked it. A light breeze was blowing the bag on his head, there had to be an open window in this room.

'It's just a little way, Treasure,' as faint as a whisper.

Footsteps on stone, heading away, with the occasional pause. *She's taking him up to the farmhouse.*

'Cain?' Dolly asked again.

'Yes?'

'What are they going to do with us?' She sounded quite calm.

'You'll be fine.'

'Are they going to kill us?'

'No, you'll be fine.'

'You don't know that.'

'Yes, I do. When he turned his gun on you, when she came running out of the vines, she said "not her".'

'That's just because she's wary of you. She's kept a gun on you the whole time.'

'No, that wasn't the way she said it. I've heard that tone a thousand times before. It means "*we need her alive*".'

'You're just saying that to make me feel better.'

'No. They were ready for us. Or she was, in her sniper's nest on the roof of the car. On an open stretch of road. That's why he followed us for so long without putting on his blues, he had to stop us in just the right place so she could cover him. They must have known about the trade in advance, probably got wind of it from the Croatian side. I thought at first they must have been after the money, but they never even searched the car.'

'And if they did know about the trade they would know the Croatians were the ones leaving with the money.'

He nodded, not that she could see it.

Dolly's voice was barely a whisper. 'Which means they're after me.'

'Yes.'

'Could the Croatians have hired them? Maybe they were going to take your money and then double-cross you, take me back, and sell me to someone else.'

'No, the Croatians tried to get more money out of

me. They threatened to shoot you.'

'There's seems to be a lot of that going on.'

'They wouldn't have done that if they were planning to double their money this way. And, no offense, hiring these two probably costs more than what we were paying for you. The gear these people have, the way she wields that rifle, they're high-class. Expensive. The Croatians were just smugglers. Small fry. They probably got sloppy, or blabbed about it to someone. But either way, whoever hired these two must think you're worth a lot more than fifty-thousand euros.'

'Wait a minute. They can't have got wind of it from the Croatians.'

'They must have.'

'They can't.'

'These two are professionals, you've seen the kind of gear they have. They're not pulling this scam every night. I agree anyone can dress as a motorcycle cop, pull someone over, and rob them, but very few people can plan a perfect ambush like that, or wield a weapon like that rifle. They had to know in advance. How else could they know you're worth stealing?'

'How did they know your route?' she asked.

'What?'

'*How did they know your route?* You said yourself it was an ambush, they had to know what route you would take. At the very least they had to know where you were going.'

Cain was silent for a minute. 'I should have spotted that. Thank you. That's very sharp of you.'

'I'm an NSA technician, Cain, I'm not an idiot.'

'Point taken.'

'So...' she continued, 'someone on your side either got sloppy, blabbed about it to someone, or...' she left it hanging.

'Don't sugar coat it, Doc, tell me,' he drawled.

'Someone set you up.'

He laughed. 'No, I don't think so.'

'It has to be.'

'There are a lot of other explanations.'

She scoffed. 'You'll draw your gun but you won't draw a conclusion.'

'Very witty. There must be a piece of the puzzle we don't have yet. Things don't add up.'

'Cain?'

'Yes.'

'I think it's time you levelled with me, don't you? We can't figure this out unless we both know what's going on.'

'That cuts both ways.'

'Fine,' she said, 'let's do this again: *quid pro quo*.'

FIFTEEN

The stone floor was sopping wet where Fortino had mopped all the blood. Now he was on his hands and knees with a big scrubbing brush. He swore he could still see specks of blood in the white mortar. They had washed down the walls, the table, the windows, the light fitting, even the bulbs. White cloths turned brown, grey, and pink. They were out the back in a plastic trug with all the sponges, mops, and brushes they had used. They would all have to be burnt.

Valentino patted him on the back. 'Come on,' he said, 'it's clean. We've got to pick the bullets out of the walls now. We need those tweezers you use for your eyebrows.'

Fortino smiled. The effort almost made him cry. He held it in, lip quivering. 'I'm sorry,' he whispered.

'For what?'

'For losing it with you earlier.'

'It's ok,' Valentino said, putting his arm around his brother. 'We all have our moments. We're here to help you through them, just as you're here to help us through ours.'

Fortino hugged him tight, giving his brother a proper squeeze.

'I'll go get my tweezers,' he said.

As he left the room, Cristino entered.

'How is he?' Valentino asked.

'Dead to the world.'

His brother frowned.

'Sorry, a poor choice of words.'

'Did he ask about the gunshots?'

'No, I think he's forgotten about them already. He probably thinks it was a nightmare.'

Valentino sighed. 'If only.'

'Do you think he ever had to deal with something like this?'

Valentino gave his brother a wary look. Fortino was upstairs now and Tino and their father hadn't returned yet. The two of them never spoke about their grandfather's history around the others. Their father forbade the subject, and their younger brothers didn't want to hear it either. So instead the two formed a secret club, sharing anything they learnt with the other. Their original source was a book Valentino had bought and still kept hidden in his office in the winery. A sensationalist history of notable Italian gangsters of the seventies and eighties. There was an entire chapter dedicated to "The Butcher of Matera". In lurid detail it told the story of his blood-drenched rise from poor cave-dwelling peasant to local crime boss at age seventeen. He had killed the old boss, a hated figure. Killed his six sons, all feared by the locals. And married his daughter against her will. It was medieval. After three years of institutionalised rape, the woman had died in a car "accident". He married their grandmother ten years later and Gaspare and his brother were born.

Of course, these days they could just Google him, not that they dared. It filled them with a perverse kind of terror to know that a man as bloodthirsty, as ruthless, was living in the same house as them and sometimes needed help to get up off the toilet.

'I'm sure he had people to do this *for* him,' Valentino said, answering his brother's question.

Their ears pricked up. They could hear the Alfa Romeo's engine approaching. Valentino rushed into the entrance hall just as the headlights and engine died. Two doors shut and then Gaspare and Tino marched in.

'Did it go ok?'

His father nodded. 'Perfectly. And here?'

'Fine. We still have to take the bullets out of the walls. Of course, the holes are still going to be there.'

'That's fine. I don't think there's any way to date a bullet hole, is there?'

He looked at Tino, who shrugged. 'I guess not.'

Fortino came down the stairs holding his tweezers. 'How did it go?' he asked.

'Perfectly. How's Nonnuccio?'

'Sleeping,' Valentino answered. 'Cristino checked on him just now.'

'Good. He is not to know about any of this. All of you, you understand that?'

The three of them nodded.

'You know how much he worries.'

'It's ok, Papà, we understand, but what if he notices the bullet holes?'

Gaspare thought for a moment, then shook his head. 'He won't. Where's Cristino?'

Valentino nodded to the room. Gaspare marched across the hall to the doorway, the three others in tow. Cristino was staring at the briefcase.

'Did you find those coins?' his father asked.

Cristino pointed to a muddy pile on the table.

'Thank God.'

'How did it go?' Cristino asked.

'Perfectly.' Gaspare was looking around the room, nodding his approval. 'Good,' he said, 'very good. What did you do with the cloths and brushes?'

'They're out the back. We'll have to burn them.'

'We'll have to burn our clothes too.'

'Why?'

'We all handled the bodies. Even if we can't see it, there will be blood, DNA, hairs, gunpowder residue, whatever it is, it's not worth the risk.'

'What do we do about the briefcase?' Cristino asked.

Gaspare thought. 'I guess we take out the money, put it in the safe, and then burn the case with everything else.'

Cristino was staring at the one open latch. 'It's a shame he hadn't opened it.'

'I take it none of them had the code written on a piece of paper or something?'

They all shook their heads.

'I'd better get a knife or a chisel or something,' Cristino said.

'Wait,' his father said, disappearing out of the room.

The older three looked at each other, then at Tino. He shrugged.

Gaspare returned with five wine glasses, placing them on the table and picking up the bottle that had sat there since the trade.

Fortino smiled in disbelief. 'Papà?'

His father didn't answer. He used the waiter's

friend that lived in his pocket to cut the foil off the bottle and uncork it. He poured five glasses and handed one to each of them. He held one out to Tino last. Tino looked into his father's eyes, trying to read his thoughts. After a moment he sighed and took it.

Gaspare held out his glass as if performing a toast. 'Tonight was the worst night of my life since your mother died.'

'Papà,' Valentino tried to interject.

Gaspare held up his hand to silence him. 'From the moment you were born, Valentino, I knew I would do anything to protect you. It wasn't a decision, it was... something I felt in my bones. And the feeling only got stronger as we had you Fortino, then Cristino, and finally, Santino.' He paused, clearly a little choked up. 'Tonight was the first night in a long time that I feared I might lose you. I hadn't felt that way since Tino, when you went into hospital with pneumonia because of the measles. My point is, it wasn't me who saved you tonight.'

'Papà,' Cristino tried.

'No, no. It's ok. Cain may have saved all of us, but with everything that we've had to do, with the way you've behaved, you have saved yourselves, and I'm very proud of all of you. You have become the men I always hoped you would be. I may never say it, but I love you.'

They all laughed. 'You say it all the time, Papà.'

Gaspare smiled, embarrassed. 'I'll shut up then.'

He raised his glass, then took a sip. They all copied him, except Tino, who just pressed the glass to his lips. They all put their glasses down on the table and Cristino went back to staring at the briefcase.

'Do we have a crowbar?' he asked.

'We don't need one,' Valentino said.

They all looked at him.

'Weren't any of you watching? The young one, whatever he was called, he already put in the code, he just didn't pop the latch.'

Valentino nudged Cristino out of the way, turning the briefcase towards him. The others gathered round.

'If I'm right...' he said, pulling the metal slide.

SIXTEEN

There was a distant rumble like thunder as Cain listened to Dolly's story, picturing it in the endless darkness of the bag on his head.

'I guess I'd been growing disillusioned ever since I properly read about Snowden, listened to the things he said. Disillusioned is a good word for it, because what you realise when you wake up to it all is that our moral superiority, our claim to be the good guys, is just a myth we tell ourselves. It stops us asking questions of our government. Of our colleagues. Even ourselves. There's just right and wrong, and a lot of what we do is wrong. Just plain wrong. So at first, of course, I began to sound out my colleagues, make comments, you know, but I realised pretty soon that people wouldn't talk. They thought it was dangerous. Inside the station, no one will talk. Maybe over a couple of drinks, but then they just start to suspect that you're one of the mole hunters, that you're trying to trap them, and they clam up. I couldn't blame them, I know that feeling, as soon as someone expressed any kind of criticism of the agency to me, I would be on my guard, like they were fishing. It's the atmosphere that working in surveillance foments. No one trusts anyone. Someone is always listening.'

She paused.

'So what did you do?' he asked.

'Your only option is to discuss these things online, where there's a degree of anonymity. There are all sorts of forums on the dark web, easy enough to find if you're good with that kind of stuff. There are groups, most of which claim to be only for agency staff, but you can tell from speaking to people that they're just pretending. They want you to give them operational information, details of ongoing programmes. And that puts you on guard, of course. Whether they're working for hostile governments or are just conspiracy nuts, who knows. And then there are people you talk to who you know are genuine. They have that same reluctance to mention any specifics, they never boast about anything. They listen, read, speak only when asked a direct question. I'm NSA, we're listeners, watchers, and you recognise your own. It's not so much what people say, anyone can pick up the language and copy it, it's how they behave, even online. In some ways they're the people you really have to be wary of. The nuts are harmless, but the genuine one's could be foreign agents, or they could be trappers, like Cabrera.'

'Who's Cabrera?' Cain asked.

'Solomon Cabrera is the agency's chief mole hunter. *Was.* There were all sorts of urban myths about him on the forums. He was their bogeyman. They said he could smell treason.'

She paused.

'I even applied for a job in his office once. How pathetic is that?'

Cain said nothing.

'There was this one person I met on the forums, his username was SãoPaulo1974, we took to just calling him Paulo. I assumed he was a man, we all did. He never said, but when you're a woman online you get a feel for that too. He was the one that introduced me to the Network.'

'What's the Network?'

'They're a group of staff inside the NSA, CIA, Department of Defence, who actively work to expose criminal activity to the public, passing information to a trusted ring of journalists. Proper journalists, *The Washington Post*, *The New York Times*, not hooligans like WikiLeaks. These aren't people who want to burn the agencies down, just reform them, to have them actually be as moral as they claim to be, you know?'

'What kind of criminal activity?'

'Illegal surveillance mostly, especially of American citizens or high-profile allies. I mean, that's the NSA's bread and butter. There were rumours we had a tap on the British Prime Minister's cell phone.'

'Yeah, I heard that. What else?'

'The rest was more in the realm of the CIA and DIA: black ops, rendition, torture, arms, any elements of our foreign policy that are not officially policy. But I'm NSA and didn't have access to any of that stuff anyway.'

'What was your job?'

She laughed. 'I worked in the furnace.'

'Furnace?'

'That's what they called it, you know, as a nickname. Basically, it was my job to wipe the hard drives of personal computers. How much do you know about computers?'

'I haven't used one for about ten years.'

'Well, speaking simply, there's something called a server which is a big computer, basically, and there are a bunch of them in the basement of every NSA station, and they are where most data is stored. They're networked in and out of the building, so that people can also access the data from other stations around the world, and obviously from Fort Meade. There's constant network traffic in and out of the station, data being sent and received by the servers. For that reason they don't keep the really dirty secrets on them, because they need to know that no one can access them. And encryption just isn't enough. They keep the really dirty secrets on their personal computers, locally. That means it's like having just one copy of a physical file, stored in your safe. You know no one else can get to it.'

'And it was your job to wipe these hard drives?'

'Along with other menial jobs. Anything soul-destroying. Punishment for the things I had said. A job of absolutely zero importance, a chimp could do it. Except it didn't take me long to realise that for a few minutes a week, each time they sent me a hard drive, I was in possession of the agency's deepest darkest secrets.' She sighed. 'But that was the joke.'

'What joke?'

'Cabrera was setting me up. He knew all about the Network, his team were probably all over the forums. He had sussed me out, sent me to the furnace where he knew I would be angry and presented with temptation. He knew that a deputy station chief's hard drive would be too good an opportunity for the Network to pass up. And we fell for it. I fell for it all.'

'But if it was a trap, how come you managed it?'

She chuckled. 'Because in one way he

underestimated me.'

Cain waited.

'He had my psychology nailed, that was for sure. He might have put me in exactly the place he wanted me. He might have understood and steered my disillusionment. But he couldn't think like me when it came to the practical side of actually stealing the data. The computer I use to wipe the hard drives has no network access, so there was no way I could send the files out of the building digitally, and he knew that. Everyone knew that. If he expected me to try and sneak a hard drive out in my panties he was wrong. They're all logged in and out, signed, monitored, delivered and collected by other technicians, if I didn't send one back and they didn't chase me up about it I'd be suspicious. He probably expected me to plug in another storage device and try and clone the drive, but I knew that wouldn't be possible. And if it was, again I'd be suspicious.'

She paused.

'So how did you do it?'

She hesitated. 'I haven't told anyone before. Not even the Network knew how I was going to do it. Cabrera had no idea, even when he cornered me afterwards, he had no idea how I did it.'

Cain said nothing. He just waited. She would tell if she wanted to, any attempt to persuade her would have the opposite effect.

'I took an analogue approach. That's what he couldn't predict. All I had to do was get the file up on the screen. You see, they liked to think of that furnace computer as just a paper shredder. They had stripped it down as much as they could, they hadn't installed any software except the formatting program, the only stuff on it was what came preloaded with Windows 10. But that was enough to view a PDF. Of course, I needed a decryption key, but the Network were able to get that.'

'What's a decryption key?'

'It's like a little USB that is loaded with an algorithm. You can't view the files without one. The idea is that if the server or a drive was hacked and files compromised, the thief couldn't view anything without physically stealing a key too. And if a key goes missing that code can be disabled.'

'Why didn't you have one already?'

'They're only for directorate-level staff.'

'Then the Network must have some pretty important members to get hold of one.'

'Not necessarily.'

'What do you mean?'

'How do you get into your apartment if you lose your key?'

'A locksmith.'

'Exactly: all they needed is one of the technicians who sets up the keys. Easy for them to set up a spare and send it out.'

'I guess. How did they get it to you?'

'In the mail.'

'Wasn't that risky for you?'

'They had to know I was in Hong Kong, that's true. I gave them the address of a hotel in the city. I picked it up from there. Actually, I paid a cab driver to go and pick it up for me, then meet me at a café.'

'Proper spy stuff.'

'I know you're mocking me.'

He smiled. 'If I am, I don't think I should. You're

the person who managed to steal a file from under the nose of the NSA's chief mole hunter, not me.'

She didn't respond.

He had to ask now. 'So, tell me. How did you do it?'

'How would you do it?'

'Me? I wouldn't even know how to work the computer.'

'Imagine it was a paper file. You couldn't take the original because they would know it was stolen, and you couldn't make another paper copy because you'd be searched on your way out. How would you do it?'

Cain thought. 'I suppose, if we're talking hypothetically, I would lay it out on a table and take a picture of each page with one of those aptly named "spy cameras" and sneak the film out in my shoe, or something.'

'Exactly. Except I didn't have a super-secret spy camera, I had a Kodak disposable I bought in a drugstore, you know, the type people leave on the tables at weddings. And I did exactly what you would do, I got each page up on the screen and took a photo of it.'

'But how did you sneak the film out? Or sneak the camera in, for that matter?'

'I used my coffee cup.'

'What? How?'

'I have this reusable coffee cup, a bamboo one, you know, and when I went in and out of the building I would have to put my bag through the X-ray and empty my pockets into a tray, like at an airport, but whilst I did that I would get the guard to hold my coffee cup. Then I would walk through the metal detector, nothing would go off, I'd get my things, put them back in my pockets, pick up my bag, and the guard would hand me back my coffee.'

'And that worked?'

'I practiced it a few times, got friendly with him. Then on the day I put the camera in a waterproof bag and filled the cup with hot coffee. That way it would feel warm and it would slosh about and it would smell right, there was nothing to make him suspicious.'

'And what did you do with the film afterwards?'

'When I got home I opened up the camera and put the film in the mail.'

She explained the story of how she and Cabrera were shot.

'Where did you mail it to?'

'Here.'

'Here?'

'Italy, I mean. I presume that's why they've brought me here, because they want to know where in Italy so they can grab Paulo too.'

Cain thought for a while, taking himself through her story again.

'So you stole just one file?'

'Just one file.'

'How did you know what to steal?'

'The Network were looking for something in particular. That's why the deputy station chief's hard drive was such a big deal. He was one of the few who would have clearance high enough.'

'High enough for what?'

'The Tourmaline Report.'

SEVENTEEN

Jolyon Maltby stood by the water's edge. Looking across the lake he could see the lights of Bellagio mirrored on the rippling surface. From this position he could imagine he was standing on the deck of a boat. *Free.*

The lake was quiet at this time, an empty sheet of black glass. The waves sloshed lazily against the stone wall below him. The only other sound was the wind that rushed through the valley, skating the surface of the water, bristling the trees on the hillsides, running like ribbons through his fingers, and coiling its way inside the shell of his ear.

He hated using the Germans and the decision rankled with him. As a taskforce leader he was used to total operational control. With the Germans he didn't have any contact beyond the initial phone call. There was no way to cancel an operation, no way of knowing the outcome until you saw it on the news. He didn't like it.

That was how they had maintained their anonymity, of course. No one knew their names, no one knew anything beyond the fact that sometimes a woman answered the phone and sometimes a man.

And, of course, they lived in Bonn. Or, at least, the phone number was a Bonn number, it was easy enough to route the call somewhere else. Maltby had heard all sorts of rumours on the circuit: ex-special forces, ex-BND, he may even have met them. The wildest rumour he had heard was that they were a suburban married couple, living their lives as pastiches of the decadent middle class: structural engineers, software developers, researchers for an environmental think tank, who knew? Any sort of job that your friends are unlikely to understand and where nosy parkers can be easily bamboozled with jargon.

Maltby knew that game himself. *British Army Liaison to the United States Department of State* were the words printed on his official identification. Whether that meant he was a military officer or civil servant was easily fudged, whether that meant he worked for Britain or America could be a matter of debate, and whether or not the nature of his work was military or diplomatic treated as something of an academic question. When pressed, Maltby would joke that his pension was held by the British government. Of course, there was no question he was British, you only had to look at him to see that.

The Germans were the best in the business, so he heard. If you hired them it was a cast iron guarantee that the target (or targets) would die. No need to follow up, no need to withhold half payment. The fact that they could command all their fee upfront was a clear demonstration of their reputation. And yet, it rankled with him. He knew why they had to hire someone "outside the family", the logic of that was obvious, but for the first time in his long career he felt like a criminal.

The Germans were only a backup plan anyway. It all came down to the briefcase. Would it go the way he planned? He gave a sick little half-smile at the thought. Nothing ever went *exactly* as planned.

He daren't look down at the lapping water for fear of his own reflection. If he went inside he would see the news, and he wasn't ready for that just yet. So he continued to stare at the lights across the water, wishing he were there.

EIGHTEEN

Cain's blood ran cold. 'What's the Tourmaline Report?'

'Exactly what it sounds like, a report.'

'Yeah, but about what?'

'I didn't know a huge amount of the detail.'

'But you read it, right? Whilst you were taking the photos.'

'Bits. But they just told me what I already knew.'

'Which was?'

'It was a report on an investigation that the NSA did into what they thought was a foreign operation, only they found out it was actually a CIA op. Deep, deep black. Completely off the books. But nonetheless, the NSA wasn't about to out the CIA, that would set a dangerous precedent. So they buried it.'

'So how come this deputy station chief had a copy?'

'It was circulated to a few people before they buried it. All copies were ordered to be destroyed, but the Network had a hunch this guy would keep his. He was that type. Of course, he wasn't interested in sharing it with anyone else. It was just insurance, like an ace up his sleeve, something to use if he was ever threatened.'

'And Cabrera used it as bait?'

'No, the hard drive itself was bait, but I don't think he had a clue what we were after. That was way above even his paygrade.'

'I see.' He tried to keep his voice casual. 'So, tell me, what were the CIA up to?'

'It's got nothing to do with tonight.'

'And? I'm hanging from my wrists with a bag on my head, I need something to distract me.'

'Like I said, I couldn't actually read the report.'

'But you must know enough? Something that convinced you to steal the file. What were the CIA doing that was so scandalous, that made the NSA so scared, that the top brass ordered this report burnt?'

'Well, I do know the gist.'

'So tell me.'

She was silent for a minute. He waited.

'It was a CIA taskforce, I don't know what their remit was. They seemed to operate all over the western half of the Mediterranean. South of Spain and France, all of Italy, west of Croatia, Albania, Montenegro, Greece. All the islands. And Morocco, Algeria, Tunisia—'

'I get the idea,' he interrupted.

'Fine. They used criminals.'

He waited for more, but nothing came.

'What?'

'They used organised crime networks to do a lot of... whatever they were doing. Whatever it was, they obviously didn't want any of it coming back on the agency so they would use outside contractors, private individuals, but also an awful lot of gangsters.'

'That's crazy.'

'Yeah. Directly or indirectly, by paying these

criminals for whatever services they provided, the CIA funded organised crime across a swathe of friendly nations.' She paused. 'Now you understand why the Network wanted to get their hands on this report so badly.'

Cain thought for a while before speaking.

'How did the NSA come to investigate a CIA operation in the first place? It doesn't wash.'

'They didn't. They were surveilling the crime networks.'

'The NSA were investigating European and North African gangsters?'

'Of course. Those organisations are responsible for trafficking IS fighters out of Syria and Iraq and into Europe. Our embassies are desirable targets for them, therefore it's national security. As I understand it, they were trying to find out how a certain group of Greek island smugglers were so much richer than others in the same game. They were looking for their benefactor, some big player. The answer was this CIA taskforce.'

'And the NSA were so scared because they found out the CIA paid some smugglers?'

'No, that's not what scared them. What scared them is that when they dug further, they found out that this same taskforce had at least one criminal organisation in their pocket in every country they operated in. What scared them is that they found out this taskforce had been operating for twenty years. What scared them is that they had near-definite proof that this CIA taskforce, and by extension the CIA itself, was the largest single private funder of organised crime across the Mediterranean.'

Cain was silent for some time. A door continued

to bang in the wind, far off.

'And what's Tourmaline got to do with all this?' he finally asked.

'Tourmaline was the codename of the commander who ran the taskforce. They never found out the taskforce's name. They never found out Tourmaline's identity, but if the report gets published someone will know. He, or she, won't be able to hide for long.'

They were both silent now. Another scops owl whistled in the night.

'Cain?'

'Yeah?'

'While I was talking I was thinking about what you said earlier.'

'That's a neat trick.'

'I think you're right. It would make no sense for the NSA to traffic me this way. Cabrera didn't know what I was after, he was just a loyal hound. But there's someone it would make perfect sense for.'

He didn't respond.

'Cain, this Maltby who you said hired you, he's CIA right?'

He stayed silent.

'His codename is Tourmaline, isn't it?'

'No.'

'It has to be him. He must have known what I was after, he must have had people in the forums too. His people snatched me from the ambulance, or they may even have been the ones who picked me up. He's trafficked me here using his networks, like the Croatians. These people you don't want to tell me about up at the big house on the hill, they're gangsters too, aren't they?'

'No,' he snapped. Then he sighed. 'At least, not anymore.'

Dolly waited. She was treading carefully.

'Maltby,' she finally ventured, 'Tourmaline is his codename, right?'

'No,' he drawled. Then he sighed. 'It's mine.'

NINETEEN

Baroffio climbed out of the taxi two hundred metres from the house, at the back of a queue of emergency vehicles.

'You can go home, Karim,' he said, 'I'll hitch a ride with someone.'

The taxi had to pull onto the grass to turn around properly. Baroffio sauntered up the road between the queue of vehicles and the cypress trees, taking a fresh pencil out of his pocket to chew on. He stepped over his first piece of rubble about fifty metres from the house. Between the cypress trees he could see the left half of the building, and as he reached the gravel courtyard he could see where the right half used to be. Around fifty people; carabinieri, firefighters, and paramedics; were trampling all over the place. Baroffio stood in the middle of it all, getting in the way.

'Can I help you, pal?' A carabinieri officer, young, goatee.

He showed his badge. 'Baroffio.'

'Oh,' the officer cooled, looking sheepish, 'you're the guy they called. How come you turned up in a taxi?'

'They offered to send one of your boys down to get me, but they said it was urgent, so I thought I'd wake up Karim, he's a friend of mine. Kid, do you know where I can find Major Marshal Li Fonti?'

'The Ispettore is over there.' He pointed to a huddle of men standing just outside the shell of the entrance hall.

'Which one?'

'The moustache.'

'Thanks, kid,' he said, patting the officer on the shoulder.

Baroffio marched up to the huddle. They ignored him.

'As soon as the medics say it's ok, I want a statement from the old man,' the inspector was saying. Moustache, *oiled*, buzzcut. He went on, but after a minute he couldn't ignore Baroffio anymore. 'Can I help you?'

Badge again. 'You're Major Marshal Li Fonti, pleasure to meet you.'

'Oh.' Li Fonti pouted. 'Everyone, this is Inspector Baroffio of the Polizia di Stato. Look, Baroffio, with all respect, this is our territory, I don't know why they called you, we can handle this.'

'I'm sure that's true, sir, and I don't want to step on any toes.'

Li Fonti turned away.

'The way I understand it, though,' Baroffio continued, 'your boss spoke to my boss, and my boss told me to come down here, and I have to do what he says. I'm sure it's no judgement on you, sir.'

Li Fonti sighed, exchanging looks with the others. They all looked unimpressed with this little man whose clothes were as creased as his face. He looked less like a detective and more like someone who had spent a night in the cells.

'Well,' Li Fonti patronised, opening up the huddle just slightly, 'as you can see, Inspector, we're all over it.'

'That's just the problem, sir.'

'Excuse me?'

'I stepped over rubble fifty metres from the house, about where that ambulance is. We've got, what, five dead? One injured? And this wasn't a gas explosion, so this could be a crime scene. If no part of the building is actually on fire, we need to get these firefighters off of here and back down the hill. Same with that ambulance if no one requires any further medical attention. And all your men need to back their cars up as far as those cottages and wait for my people to arrive and catalogue the scene.'

Li Fonti gritted his teeth. 'We have some of your men here already, Inspector.'

He gestured to a woman laying out evidence markers.

Baroffio's face lit up. 'Hey, Irene!' he called.

She looked up, startled, then returned his smile. 'Hey, boss!'

'I'll be damned. How are your twins doing?'

'Great. They started school last month.'

'No way!' He turned back to Li Fonti, still beaming. 'How about that, I'd swear they were only born last year.'

Li Fonti was not smiling. He turned to one of the other men in the huddle and sighed.

'Valery, get everyone down the hill. And get rid of that fire engine!'

He turned back to Baroffio with a wrinkled nose.

'I must say, *Ispettore Superiore*, that you don't look

145

like an inspector.'

Baroffio blushed. 'Well, I don't normally look like this, sir. It's three o'clock in the morning. I thought my days of being woken up in the middle of the night were over, you know. So did my wife.'

Li Fonti said nothing.

Baroffio scratched his unshaven chin as they walked over to where Irene was crouched. She was staring at the centre of the floor of what used to be one of the back rooms of the house.

'What have we got?'

'It looks like all five were crowded in this room when *something* exploded. Took most of this corner of the building with it and two of the internal walls. The blood spatter up and in a hundred-and-twenty-degree arc suggests they were all standing close to whatever it was.'

'Huddled over it?'

She nodded. 'If I had to bet.'

'High damage but minimal burns, we're looking at a bomb.'

'How can you possibly tell that?' Le Fonti asked.

'Have we got any shrapnel?'

'Fragments of casing,' Irene answered, 'and ball bearings.'

Baroffio nodded. Li Fonti frowned. *Definitely a bomb.*

'We haven't got anyone round here who can analyse that stuff properly,' she said, 'it'll have to go off to the lab.'

'I'll speak to the superintendent, tell him we're going to need experts. Even if he has to fly them up from Rome, we're going to need them.'

'You get to see a lot of bombsites in Montepulciano, do you?' Li Fonti asked.

'In Montepulciano?' Baroffio shook his head. 'No, no. Who are the victims?'

Li Fonti checked his notebook. 'Gaspare, Valentino, Fortino, Cristino, and Santino Di Matera.'

'Brothers?'

'Four brothers and father.'

Baroffio sighed. 'That's tough. Where was the old man who was injured?'

'Upstairs bedroom,' Irene answered.

'Grandfather?'

'Yeah.'

'Has he said anything?'

'He seems a bit confused,' Li Fonti answered, 'could be concussion, the paramedics are seeing to him now.'

'Any servants?'

'Two. They live down at the cottages, came running up when they heard the explosion. They're the ones that called us.'

'Has anyone spoken to them?'

'About what?' Li Fonti scoffed.

He shrugged. 'Well, the first thing I would ask them is if anyone else was at the house tonight. Where is the grandfather now?'

'There,' Irene pointed.

Baroffio looked behind him to the courtyard. A ninety-something man with a blanket wrapped around him was trying to get towards the house but carabinieri officers and paramedics were blocking his way. He was distressed, pulling his hair out. When Baroffio saw his face he felt a chill creep over him like cold fingers walking up his spine.

'What did you say their name was?' he asked.

'Di Matera.'

'And what do they do, these Di Materas?'

Li Fonti laughed. 'They make wine, Baroffio, look around you. I'm partial to their label myself, actually.'

Baroffio just nodded. He was lost in thought, chewing on his pencil.

'Those things will kill you, you know,' Irene joked.

He barely smiled.

He paced round the outside of the house, stopping when he got to the back garden. Li Fonti followed him reluctantly, Irene just looked on. Several carabinieri officers were mingling near them now, curious about this strange man who was leading their boss around.

Baroffio stared down at a piece of rubble. Then he crouched down on all fours, put on reading glasses, and hovered his face an inch above it.

Li Fonti sighed. 'It's a chunk of the rear wall.'

'It's got a bullet in it.'

'What? Where?'

'Here,' he pointed with his pencil.

Li Fonti also put on reading glasses to take a closer look. He frowned, then grumbled. 'That could have happened at any time, of course.'

Baroffio nodded. 'True.'

He stood back up, taking off his glasses and looking at where the manicured lawn was bruised and rough. 'Have your people been down here?'

'My men? No, why would they?'

'Those are drag marks.'

Li Fonti frowned again.

'A few sets by the looks of them. Someone has dragged bodies down from this room into the vines there.'

'You can't possibly tell that, anything could have made those marks.'

'These are deep prints. And look here, you can see where a pair of heels have been dragged across the grass. And here there's footprints over them, I think we're looking at three or four people in a line, all heading that way.'

Li Fonti didn't reply, he looked embarrassed.

'I'm going to follow these tracks,' Baroffio announced, 'if any polizia turn up, tell them to do whatever Irene says.'

He marched off down the garden, into the darkness of the vines.

Li Fonti left him to it and went back up to the house. He watched Irene laying out more evidence markers.

'He's a strange man, your boss,' he remarked. 'How can a little old cop from Montepulciano have any idea what a bombsite looks like?'

'First of all,' she said, 'he's not my boss anymore. I'm from Pisa, I was just down here lending some of your boys a hand when they got the call. Second of all, he used to work gang killings in Naples. He retired out here a couple of years ago, his wife made him. The compromise was that he didn't retire. He's seen just about every way to kill someone there is, and he's the best damn detective I've ever worked with. So, if I were you, I'd quit breathing down my neck and do whatever he told you to do.'

TWENTY

The darkness of the bag on Dolly Lightfoot's head was total darkness. And yet, somehow that darkness fizzed and swirled. It had layers, and endless depth. The mechanisms of her eyes were open wide like parched mouths to falling snow, but they were getting nothing. Devoid of any electromagnetic input with which to form images, the visual cortex still tries to do its job, and like a team of chefs deprived of fresh ingredients it went to the store cupboards, the memories and obsessions that buzzed away in the back of her mind. Sometimes, in her Hong Kong apartment, she would wake in the night to find the ends of thoughts still going. The same stresses, the same concerns, the same fears she had fallen asleep with, the voices still speaking, like a television left on. Her brain received all the channels at once, they were all jabbering, all squawking.

Her mind channel-hopped through the images, going down the numbers. Her and Cabrera on the bridge, the bullets bursting from his stomach into hers. Her first day in Hong Kong, feeling so lonely and homesick that she cried to *Gilmore Girls* clips on YouTube. Her first year at Fort Meade, abandoned in a submarine of office cubicles. Idaho State University, the graduation "march through the arch". Losing her virginity to a Psych graduate in his parents' summer house. Her last summer in town, helping her mother smoke out roaches at her grandma's old place. Junior High, that wisecracking spectator at the track meet who made fun of her height. Even younger, playing in the mountains of sewing her mother took in. And last of all, the base of her memories, the core of her existence: her mother sitting on the stoop of their apartment building, crying her eyes out the day her father left.

She had to focus now, she had to push it all away. Focus on the pain in her wrists. Cain was speaking. Cain was Tourmaline. Who *was* this stranger? What did she really know about him? *Nothing.*

'We all had worknames that were semi-precious stones,' he was explaining. 'Someone's idea of a joke, I guess.'

'And yours was Tourmaline?' she asked.

'Yeah,' he sighed, 'but I didn't run the taskforce.'

'Who were the others?'

'I didn't know them.'

'What were their codenames?'

'I didn't know that either.'

'Then how did you know they were all semi-precious stones?'

'I was told.'

She frowned. 'For an intelligence man you didn't seem to know a lot.'

'I wasn't CIA, I was just a...'

'Contractor?'

'Freelancer.'

'Doing what?'

'Things like tonight.'

'You said that before, but what does that actually

mean?'

He scoffed.

'Well?'

'It's difficult to say, no job was the same. Sometimes it would be an exchange like tonight, sometimes it would be finding someone, sometimes it would be protecting someone.'

'And like tonight, you gave money to criminals.'

'Most of my jobs didn't involve money.'

'But some did.'

'Anyone who pays a ransom is giving money to criminals.'

'What's your point?'

'My point is you don't like it, but you do it to save a life.'

'But you weren't paying ransoms.' She heard him grumble again. '*Tonight* you weren't paying a ransom, the Croatians hadn't kidnapped me, you were paying them for job well done.'

'I didn't know that.'

'Then why does the report say that you ran the taskforce?'

'*I don't know.*' He sounded angry. 'Someone has got their wires crossed.'

'Have they?'

'What does that mean?'

'Maltby ran the taskforce, didn't he?'

He didn't answer.

'I take it by your silence that I'm right.'

He still didn't answer.

'We've already established that Maltby set you up to get killed tonight.'

'Have we? I must have missed that.'

'You think this couple were just going to take me and send you on your merry way? If that was the plan, why not tell you about it?'

Still silence.

'He set you up to take the fall for all of it. And dead people don't argue. He must have been planning it for years. The only way the report could show that Tourmaline ran the taskforce would be if he had been submitting reports using that codename. Or if he communicated with other freelancers using that codename. You could have been Tourmaline to him, but he could have been Tourmaline to everyone else.'

A grumble.

'Are you still keeping an open mind!?' she shouted.

'I want answers, just like you. I've got a lot to process, lot to think about. There could be a thousand explanations. All I can tell you is that Tourmaline was my workname in communications with Maltby. And yes, Maltby was the one who offered me jobs.'

'Offered?'

'Yes.'

'How did it work?'

He hesitated. 'He would telephone me, sometimes meet me in person. Tell me the job, tell me the pay, I would say yes or no. If I said yes, I would pick up a prep file, or he would give it to me in person, containing all the information I needed to know. I would read it, and burn it.'

'And if you said no?'

'He would try and persuade me to say yes.'

'What was his codename?'

'Workname,' he corrected her. 'We say workname

in the CIA.'

'I thought you weren't in the CIA?'

He didn't respond to that.

'What was his "workname" then?'

He didn't answer.

'Let me guess,' she drawled, 'you were semi-precious, but he was precious. Right?'

Still no answer.

'What was he? Diamond? Ruby?'

'Sapphire.'

She chuckled to herself. Then she stopped. 'And yet he met you in person?'

'Sometimes.'

'That's unusual.'

'Well, there was no...' he trailed off.

'You knew him already.'

He hesitated, then sighed. 'Yeah. We knew each other.'

'How?'

'Special Forces. He was SAS, I was CAR.'

'CAR?'

'Canadian Airborne Regiment.'

Military guys. Dolly had met enough of them to know they placed too high a value on loyalty to each other. 'You really trust this guy, huh?'

'He's the *only* person I trust.'

She waited for him to explain that.

He sighed. 'We were part of a joint operation that ended in a mess. We were the only survivors out of a squad of eighteen. It was so secret we were forbidden even to go to their funerals. When we stepped out of that debriefing room I had no reason to think I would ever see him again. Seven years, four months, and twelve days later we ran into each other in a bar in Marseille. He remembered me, asked me to join his team of freelancers. He was working for the CIA now, of all people. He needed someone with a level head and a straight shot. I agreed, no questions asked. He told me later that it wasn't an accident, his running into me. He was honest about it. He was always honest, I thought. Or, at least, honestly dishonest.'

'How long did you work for him?'

'A long time. And nothing I did gave me any reason to question what we were doing.'

'That might say more about you than it does about him. You killed people, right?'

'Yes, when necessary.'

'When necessary?'

'When I deemed it the right thing to do.'

'The right thing to do?'

'Yes, just like tonight. Four men threatened your life. And the lives of the other five in the room. I knew that if I killed them, they would die, but you would live. Four lives for six. And me, seven.'

'But you didn't know that. All eleven could have lived. Your option was just a possibility, but by pulling your gun you made it reality.'

'So was all eleven living just a possibility. When the evening started, when the trade started, there were infinite possibilities, some more likely than others. A million different roads we could go down. The course of events closes off those roads at a terrifying rate. Over the course of just a few minutes they evaporated before our eyes until only two possibilities remained. I had the power to choose which. I used that power. Of course things could have gone wrong. I could have missed. I could have started a firefight that would have killed us all. But you can't allow yourself to be paralysed by the risk of the worst-case scenario, or by hope for the best. Not when lives are at stake. Doing nothing may frequently absolve you of legal responsibility, but I don't believe it absolves you of moral responsibility. I don't like it, but there are situations where you have to choose between lives. The reason I have killed people is because I've been in those situations more than most.'

She didn't respond, didn't know where to start.

That same door banged in the wind, up at the farmhouse. They had heard nothing of their captors for what must be two hours now. Her legs were shaking from the effort of balancing on tiptoes on her upturned chair, her calves burning like fire, her hands numb from the constriction of the cable ties around her wrists. If Cain asked her, she wouldn't even have been able to confirm she *had* hands.

'Let's focus on how you're going to escape,' he said.

'Why me?'

'I'm older, and fatter, and I think my gymnastic days are over.'

Something else she couldn't argue with.

'She lassoed the rope over some kind of hook or bar or something, it's not fastened,' he said. 'You should be able to hold your weight out on your wrists and walk backwards up the wall.'

'You make that sound ridiculously easy.'

'No, it's not easy. It's not easy at all. But it's necessary. The course of events has already closed off all but two possibilities. The first is that they kill me and take you wherever you're going. The second begins with you escaping.'

TWENTY-ONE

When Baroffio re-emerged from the vines, up to the house, there were four polizia officers taking photos of everything Irene had indicated with numbered evidence markers. The drag marks on the lawn were number 109.

Li Fonti's carabinieri were standing at the back of the house, three of them smoking, two looking at their phones. Li Fonti was standing with his hands on his hips. When he saw Baroffio, his hand darted up to smooth his moustache.

'Any luck, Inspector?' he asked sarcastically.

'Four bodies were dragged down to the winery car park. Two cars turned around and drove over the tracks, heading out. We need photos of those tracks, and we need them compared to the tyres of the cars they've got here.'

Irene had been listening, she nodded and instructed two of the polizia officers. Li Fonti stood open-mouthed.

'Did you speak to the servants?' Baroffio asked.

'One of your men did.'

A young polizia officer bounded up eagerly to Baroffio.

'You?'

'Yes, sir.'

'What did they say?'

'There was another man here tonight, sir, an American.'

'What was he doing here?'

'Just a dinner guest, they were told, but they reckon there was something big going on because the two of them were hurried out real quick like.'

'Did you get a description?'

The officer flicked back a page in his notebook. 'White, mid-to-late fifties, brown or red hair, light-coloured jacket. Broad build, you know, "portly". They both kept saying he was very polite. I couldn't get more, they only saw him briefly.'

'Did he bring anything with him?'

'The woman in the kitchen didn't see him arrive. The man, he says there was some talk of a briefcase, but he never saw it.'

'Ok.' Baroffio pulled a pencil from his jacket pocket and pressed the chewed end to his lips. 'Did he drive here?'

'Yes, sir, a silver Mercedes convertible. The man was very sure on that.'

'Soft top or hard top?'

'I don't know, sir.'

'It sounds like he paid more attention to the car than he did the man. Go ask him again. Get everything he remembers. Was it new? Was it old? How old? Clean? Dirty? Dented? Flat tyres? Bald tyres? Anything you can get. Otherwise, good work.'

The officer nodded and jogged away round the side of the house.

'Ok, we've got to find this man. Li Fonti, can you circulate that description to all your officers? Start with everyone in Tuscany. Say that we believe he's driving a silver Mercedes convertible, update it with any new details the kid gets. Obviously, he could be dangerous.'

Li Fonti nodded and turned to address his officers.

Baroffio marched over to Irene, who was categorising pieces of evidence laid out on plastic sheeting.

'So what's the story? This American drives here, delivers the bomb in a briefcase. He leaves. They gather round to open it, and... boom?'

'That's your job, boss, mine is evidence.'

'But what about these other bodies. Who were they? And how come the servants didn't see them arrive?'

'Not my job,' she repeated.

He grumbled, thinking and chewing on his pencil. He heard a zip being fastened and looked to his left just in time to see a set of blackened fingers disappear into a bag.

'That's the best limb we have,' Irene said. 'It's a left forearm, severed just below the elbow. Fingers all intact. Skin should help with the bomb composition. One of their motorcycle boys is getting ready to take it down to Rome rather than wait for the rest of this stuff to be sent down with our lot.'

'That's good of him. What have you got here?'

'Beyond all the stone dust, bits of the table. Some scraps of clothes. Glass.'

'Windows?'

'No, they were blown outwards, these were inside

the room.' With her gloved hands she picked up blackened beads. 'We've got some grains that look like clear glass, and some green.'

He nodded, crouching down next to her and putting on his reading glasses.

'We've got some coins. Small change.'

She picked up a blackened coin using a pair of tweezers and held it out for him whilst he pulled on a latex glove. Then she dropped it in his hand.

'Oh,' he said. The coin felt off somehow.

'Yeah, exactly. They're not euros. They look the same size but they're too light.'

The coin was black on both sides, a glance at the others showed the same.

'Too burnt for me to make out,' Irene said, 'but easy for the lab when they get there. There's another embedded in that forearm.'

Baroffio weighed it in his hand. 'You know, I used to have an uncle who was a jeweller. He'd hold a ring in his hand, feel the weight, and tell you how much gold was in it.'

He handed her back the coin and she put it neatly in its place.

'What else?' he asked.

'Bits of a watch. A ring.'

'Anything there?'

'No engravings. Expensive stuff though, especially the watch.'

'Anything more?'

'Bits of smartphone. Nothing out of the ordinary. The lab will find more mixed in with the rags and body parts.'

'Who needs the lab when we've got you? Keep

at it.' He stood up, putting his glasses away. 'Anything that will shed light on our mystery guest. Anything that looks like it entered the house today.'

'How will I know that?'

'I don't know. Maybe you'll know it when you see it.'

Baroffio wandered to the front of the house, where Li Fonti was still instructing his men. He nibbled on his pencil and stared out over the dark countryside.

'Four bodies,' he said to himself.

He turned back to the throng.

'What else is going on around here?'

'Excuse me?' Li Fonti asked.

'What other calls have you had? Anything out of the ordinary?'

'Err... I don't know.' He turned to his officers. 'Where's Rizzo? He always seems to know everything. Somebody find him.' He turned back to Baroffio. 'What are you thinking?'

'We've got four bodies unaccounted for.'

'We haven't found them, Inspector, I would've told you.'

Baroffio smiled.

The young officer who had first directed Baroffio to Li Fonti emerged from the shadows of the cypress trees with his hand raised. 'Here, sir. You wanted to see me?'

'Kid,' Baroffio said, 'what other calls have you got in this area tonight?'

'Sir?'

'Something out of the ordinary. Or anything. What's been going on?'

'I don't know, sir. We've all been worrying about

Russo.'

'Yes, of course,' Li Fonti said.

Baroffio raised his eyebrows.

'Motorcycle officer,' Li Fonti explained. 'Went AWOL this afternoon. Him, bike, both missing. We've checked at his apartment. Not at his mother's either.'

Baroffio frowned. 'Anything else?'

Rizzo thought. 'There was chatter about a car accident, that wasn't too far from here.'

'When?' Li Fonti asked.

'A couple of hours ago, I think. It was ours for five minutes, then it got taken by GdF.'

Guardia di Finanza? Fraud and smuggling.

'Why would they be interested in a car crash?' Li Fonti asked. 'Were there drugs in the car?'

'I don't know, sir, all I heard was that one of ours ran the plate through the database and before they could get a result she had the GdF on the phone telling them it was theirs now.'

Baroffio and Li Fonti shared a frown.

'How many were involved in the accident, kid?'

'Just the one car, I think, sir. Went off one of the hilltop roads.'

'How many people were in the car?'

'Four, I think.'

Baroffio only had to look at Li Fonti.

'I'll get on the phone,' he said, tugging at his moustache as he marched over to his car.

'Thanks, kid,' Baroffio said.

Rizzo beamed, turned, and marched back to his post by the cypress trees. Standing there smoking, also waiting for further orders, was a polizia officer.

'You've worked with the inspector before?' Rizzo

asked him.

'Baroffio? Yeah, once or twice.'

'He's smart.'

The officer grunted. 'He's a weird one.'

Copying Baroffio, Rizzo just raised his eyebrows.

'He eats tea leaves.'

'What?'

'Tea leaves, the perfumy ones, I can't remember what they're called.'

'He eats them?'

'Yeah. Other people eat pistachios, sunflower seeds, whatever, *he* eats tea leaves.'

Rizzo frowned.

* * *

Li Fonti returned from a heated phone call to find Baroffio smacking his lips as though he was sucking something, but his pencil was in his breast pocket.

'So,' he drawled, 'they don't want to tell me too much about it, but what I did learn is that the car that crashed down into a ravine, ten miles from here, belonged to the son of some big-shot Croatian smuggler. That's what set off the alarms and caused GdF to jump all over it.'

Something Li Fonti had said caused Baroffio to crunch whatever he was sucking on and speed over towards the evidence laid out on the plastic sheeting.

'*Where's that arm!?*' he shouted. 'Irene? Where's that arm?'

'What is it?' Li Fonti asked.

'Has he gone yet?' Baroffio asked Irene.

'Who gone? Where?'

'The bike cop. With the arm.'

'It's still here, I think.'

'Thank God!'

Li Fonti watched in horror as a carabinieri officer handed Baroffio a black bag, and the polizia inspector unzipped it to reveal a charred, severed forearm. Li Fonti's stomach did a flip, he had always hated bodies.

Baroffio extracted the arm from the bag and laid it on the plastic sheeting.

'I need your tweezers,' he said, whipping out his reading glasses.

Irene put them in his hand, he didn't even glance round to take them. He was staring at the perfect black circle of the coin embedded in the soft flesh of the inside forearm below the wrist. He teased at the edge of it with the tweezers.

'The force of the explosion pushes out a split second before the heat,' he was explaining, 'so if we're lucky...'

He managed to get the tweezers under the edge of the coin and peeled it from the skin with a sound like tearing paper.

He turned it over. The side that had been pressed into the flesh was bloody but unburnt, and the silver colour caught the light.

I'll know it when I see it, he said under his breath.

Li Fonti stood next to Irene and peered over Baroffio's shoulder, actively avoiding looking at the arm. The other officers, polizia and carabinieri, were gathered around him too.

Baroffio turned the coin to face the light. *Republika Hrvatska*, it said, *1 Kuna*.

Croatian.

Li Fonti thought he might faint. Then he regained control of himself and laughed merrily. He couldn't help but be impressed.

Hurried footsteps on the dirt. All three looked up to see Rizzo racing over.

'Sir! Sir!' he called.

'What?' Li Fonti barked.

'Sir, they've found Russo's bike.'

Mother of God. 'Where?'

'Halfway between here and Siena, on the old roads.'

'And Russo?'

The kid shook his head. 'They found it sitting on its kickstand, abandoned, key still in it.'

Li Fonti frowned. They all knew it didn't sound good.

'And, sir, a car, also abandoned.'

'What kind of car?' Baroffio asked.

'A Mercedes, sir. Convertible.'

TWENTY-TWO

'That's it, use the wall,' Cain said.

Dolly had tentatively brought one leg up behind her, putting her foot flat on the rough stone wall, balancing on the upturned chair with the other shaking leg. Cain could hear it rocking on the stone. He heard her sigh. A feeling of warm relief would be flooding through the bent leg. It's a joyous feeling to relax muscles you've been straining for hours, and to use muscles that have gone unused.

With a scrape and a swoosh, her foot slipped. There was a crash as her leg swung down from the wall and collided with the chair, kicking it away from her other foot. He heard her kicking, thrashing. She was hanging by her wrists.

'Cain!'

Then they heard it. A howl of pain. It carried on the wind that was banging that door. Drops of icy water trickled down Cain's spine. It was a woman's howl, but it didn't come from Dolly. A howl of anguish, Cain knew in his bones what it meant. It was the sound of two souls being wrenched apart by death. It was a sound containing madness, and murder.

'Cain?' A different note in her voice.

'Don't panic. It's not you she's coming for.'

'*What?*'

'You'll be ok.'

He listened desperately for the sounds of her approaching down the steps from the farmhouse. But he heard nothing. Nothing but that damn door and the wind, and Dolly's legs swishing in the air.

'*You!*' she hissed from the doorway.

Cain straightened up. Now he heard her footsteps moving towards him. They were so light, so nimble. She seemed to pay no attention to the thrashing Dolly other than to issue a derisive snort. Then a rope suddenly tightened around his ankles, slamming them together.

'Cain?' Dolly, scared.

His ankles bound, the woman released the slack on his wrists. He scraped his head on the wall and fell sprawled over the upturned chair, flopping like a fish slammed on a rock.

'Cain?' Dolly again.

'I'm ok.'

He felt a hook catch on the rope around his ankles. Then she was dragging him across the stone floor, hauling him in like a trawler net. She had tremendous strength.

He knew she was taking him to another room where she would kill him, probably torturing him to death. There was no reason to keep his dignity if it would cost him his life, so he thrashed as best he could. Now he really was like a fish on a line.

Dolly could hear the sounds and was calling out to him again, but he was too busy to reply. His jacket rode up and his shirt scraped on the coarse grains of sandstone. His hands were bound but as he was dragged through the doorway he was able to roll onto his side and clamp the frame in his armpit. It was enough, she pulled and pulled, but couldn't drag him any further. She dropped the rope, came over and kicked him twice in the stomach. The first time wasn't too hard. The second time she put everything she had into it, and it was a lot. He made a sound like the air being kicked out of a pillow, but still he wouldn't let go, and he could tell she was frustrated by his lack of reaction. Anyone else would smack him over the head with something, but she didn't.

He knew now. She didn't want him groggy. She wanted him awake and alert, able to feel whatever she had planned.

He listened. She seemed to have gone. Then he heard the G-Wagen engine start. He relaxed his grip, saving his strength. Then he heard the car crawling forward outside, getting a little closer to the building. Then it reversed. Then it crawled forward again. She was positioning it for something. He heard the car door slam shut and this time was attuned to her footsteps. The hook was removed from his ankles and chucked into a corner where it clanked on the stone, a heavy piece of iron. Then a steel carabiner was clipped to the ankle rope instead.

She stood back. 'I'm interested to see how you'll do this time.'

There was a piercing whine and Cain was ripped from the doorframe, skittering across the floor towards bright lights that cut through the bag on his head. The lights were the G-Wagen's headlamps, and the whine was the electric winch mounted to its bumper. He reached for the next door frame, finding only the door, pulling it shut on his fingers as he was dragged through. Blinding pain. He let go, sucking air through his teeth.

He could tell by the change in the light and temperature that he was outside now. The winch came to a stop and he knew he was out on the stone slabs between the barns. A courtyard, of sorts. It was cold, and he could sense dampness like mist or fine rain. She fiddled with his ankles again, there was another change of hooks. Then she walked away until her footsteps were imperceptible.

From her direction came the unmistakable rain-on-roof sound of a manual chain hoist, the woman running the chain quickly through the gears, slowly cranking the chain connected to his ankles. He pushed up onto his knees and tried to shimmy away, but the chain was taut a moment later and he was being dragged inexorably across the stone courtyard, one centimetre at a time. He kicked his legs, trying to shake the hook, but it was no use. He held his head against the ground, hoping to work the bag off, but the drawstring wouldn't loosen.

The light was changing ahead, he could tell through the blur of the bag that he was inching towards a pitched roof. As he entered its darkness his feet lifted off the ground. She was going to hang him from his ankles. He could hear her relentlessly pulling the chain, it spooling through her hands.

Soon his legs were straight up, and then his hips were off the ground. Then his shoulders, his weight on his neck. And then his head was off the ground, and he went higher still, until only his fingertips trailed on the ground.

She loosened the bag and ripped it off. He could

see her upside-down boots, the concrete floor beneath them. He looked up and around the building. The only light was a fluorescent tube. Corrugated steel roof above his feet. More hooks on a rail that stretched off into the dark. This was a meat locker, something like that.

The woman vanished. She left him hanging there for several minutes, the blood draining down from his feet and legs. It felt like someone was inflating a beach ball inside his head. His bandaged hand throbbed so hard it felt like he was holding his heart.

There was a loud metal clang that seemed to shake the frame of the building, and then she emerged from the darkness dragging what looked like an oxygen tank, but it was longer. It was some kind of gas canister, at least, and attached to it was a hose leading to something metal in her hand. She put the canister down a few feet from Cain and pulled from a sheath a curved knife. The knife she held in one hand, the metal hose-end in the other.

Cain studied her face. It was wracked with pain.

'He's dead, isn't he,' he said.

'Silence!'

She held the two items out from her body like Lady Justice with her sword and scales.

'I only know one way to slaughter an animal: cut the throat and bleed them. Farmers use a bolt gun like this to stun the animal first, so they can't feel any pain. Of course, some claim there is a humane way to bleed them without the bolt gun, but I've never believed that. Have you?'

He stared at her.

'*Have you!?*' she screamed. Apparently it wasn't rhetorical.

'No,' he replied, 'not really.'

'Tell me everything you know about the Englishman who hired us and you will get the bolt gun.'

Cain stared at her for some moments.

'Speak!' she barked.

'I'm thinking. I'm not sure who you're talking about.'

Her eyes narrowed. 'In my experience people tend to know the person who wants them dead, so speak.'

'There might be more than one Englishman who wants me dead. It would help if I knew exactly what he hired you to do. In relation to me and the girl, I mean.'

She laughed. 'If you don't speak, I'm going to stick this knife right in your stomach here, exactly where you shot Moritz, and watch the blood run down your shirt and over your face.'

'You should have taken him to a hospital.'

Her eyes flared with anger. 'I could cut you from neck to navel and watch as your guts spill onto the concrete.'

Cain sighed, staring down the pain in her eyes. 'Look, I know I'm going to die. I know that. This information you want is the only thing left I have to bargain with.'

She went to speak.

'*But I know it's not going to save my life.* I killed someone very close to you, I accept that. That's why I have to die, even if we disagree about whether or not you could have saved his life.'

She raised the knife at him.

'You're offering me the stun gun,' he continued, 'to be honest, I don't care how you kill me, it's all the same. The only thing I want is to know what's going to happen to the girl. And exactly what this Englishman hired you to do.'

'And then I'm supposed to trust that you'll tell me what I want to know?' she scoffed.

'You still have the threat of the knife. And you say this man wants me dead, so why would I protect him?'

She narrowed her eyes in contempt. 'We're both professionals. I think that means we have a certain insight into each other, don't you? It makes it very difficult to lie. You haven't accepted your death. I know that you're stalling. I know that you want this information from me because you're clinging to some slim hope of escape.'

He didn't reply.

She sighed. 'But I also know that as a professional, if I was in your situation, I would want to know what you're asking. I also know that if I tell you what you want to know, you'll *want* to tell me what I want to know.'

Cain said nothing.

'I took the call. The details came later, but he said six people lived in the house, another six would arrive over the evening. He had a plan to kill all twelve. We were just backup. If his plan failed then we were to kill as many as we could, but especially you and the girl.'

Cain winced.

'Then he changed his mind. Said that, if possible, we were to deliver the girl alive.'

'Deliver where?'

She shook her head.

'What was your plan?' he asked. 'How could you possibly kill all twelve?'

'The plan was only to kill the survivors of

the Englishman's plan. But...' She stopped, shrugged, weighing her head from side-to-side like a plumber calculating a quote for a new bathroom. 'If you hadn't shot Moritz, if things had gone to plan, we would have bundled you and the girl into the back of our car. Driven your car back to the villa, shot the six men who lived there, staging a firefight. The servants too, whom we would place in the courtyard, as though they were running from the building and were shot in the back. We would then shoot you in the stomach and drag your body around a bit until you died in a suitable spot. The other four, the ones who parked at the winery, would be the obvious culprits. If we could trace them, we would catch up to them, incapacitate them, shoot the driver, push the car off the road. It would look as though the driver had succumbed to his injuries and passed-out behind the wheel.'

Cain gulped. 'And the girl?'

'We'd deliver her as planned.'

'And now?'

'I could go back to the villa, kill the six there, dump your body, deliver the girl.'

'But...?'

'But Moritz is dead, so I don't care much about preserving our reputation. Tonight is the end of the line. We weren't briefed that you would be armed, or that you had training, clearly a history of violence. I blame him as much as you. So after I kill you, I will kill him.'

'And the girl?'

'She can stay hanging in that barn for all I care. She has no way to identify me. If you tell me what I want to know I'll make sure someone finds her. And your body. So, tell me his name.'

'Didn't he give you a name?'

'A fake one, yes.'

'What was it?'

'Tourmaline.'

Cain sighed. 'His name is Roberto Kearns.'

Her eyes narrowed. '*Roberto?*'

'Yeah, I know. His mother was Spanish. He goes by Rab. Rab Kearns.'

'What does he look like?'

'Tall. Kind of a scruffy dresser. Blonde. Beard last time I saw him, but that was ten years ago. Could be grey now, of course. My sort of age. Heavy-set, like me. But I can't tell you how to find him.'

'I know where to find him.'

Cain stared into her face. The pain and anguish had been smoothed out, she was cold now. She stared back, but what she saw in his face he didn't know.

'Thank you,' she said. 'You have earned the bolt gun.'

He gulped. He could hear a telephone bell ringing somewhere distant, probably up at the farmhouse. When was a phone call in the middle of the night ever good news? It rang out again, cold and clear on the night air like a whistle. The call was for him. *Your number is up.*

Cain had to close his eyes. For the first time in a very long time he felt the real fear of death. On a hundred different jobs he had fought for his life. He felt adrenaline every time, the focus that came with it, and the euphoria when he escaped yet again. This was entirely different. Twice before in his life he had been certain that he would die. The first time was on that fated SAS-CAR "special operation" with Maltby. The second time was on a job. And on both those occasions an ethereal calm had descended on him. He had accepted it in a way that seemed in logical opposition to his youth. On the SAS mission he hadn't really cared. Dying didn't seem like anything at all. He had often heard people express the view that you felt less as you got older, you became harder, calcified. But Cain thought the opposite was true. The reason children don't cry at funerals is because they don't understand them. How could they? But as you get older you have more context, you can remember your own pain when people express theirs. And as a result, you understand more. You *feel* more. Strange as it sounds, dying hadn't seemed like anything at all back then because he was still young.

The second time had been harder, but the calm had still come. It was the job. He had run the gauntlet a hundred times and survived, beating the odds. There was no cause for complaint.

But not this time. This time he felt a horrible, raging terror race through him. He didn't want to die here. He didn't want to die like this. He didn't want to die yet. Not yet. God could give him ten more years, couldn't he? Just ten?

None of this was visible to Mila as Cain closed his eyes. His face twitched, flinching ever so slightly, as he heard the squeaking tap of the canister and the hiss of the gas rushing up the hose to prime the bolt gun. He didn't struggle as she positioned the barrel at the top of his forehead. He could feel the vibrations of her fingers tapping on the trigger, then they rested. Positioned. *Ready.*

The telephone was ringing again. It wasn't going to stop until it was answered.

Then it came. Finally, mercifully, like an old friend, the calm descended. He listened to the world he was kissing goodbye. There was the hissing of the gas, the banging of that door in the wind, the far-off whistle of a scops owl. And then the sound of steel through skull.

TWENTY-THREE

Dolly gave up kicking. The pain in her wrists was ebbing away, along with all feeling. She had to think. What could she do? Hanging by her wrists, bag over her head, gently twisting this way and that, rope creaking above her, she didn't even know which direction the wall was anymore.

She could swing. It was the only thing she could do. So she started to sway her legs backwards and forwards, building up momentum until she was swinging like a pendulum. On the backswing she felt the bottom of her shoes brush against the wall. She swung harder, and this time, when she brought her legs up behind her, the slight heels on her shoes caught and lodged on the rough stone, latching her to the wall. Warm relief flooded into her legs as they rested bent for the first time in hours.

Think!

She lifted one foot. The second she took her weight off it the other one lost its grip. *Falling.* Stomach-in-throat panic. Then the rope snapped tight, hanging her by her wrists again. She felt the sensation, like someone tugging at them, but they were so lifeless by now that she didn't feel any pain. She kicked, but without the pain she could focus.

She might scream, she might flinch, she might cry, she couldn't hold it all in like these pathetic posturing men with their single "manly" tears and their gritted teeth, but she was not weak. She was just as strong. Just as capable of "dealing with it". Of course she screamed when things hurt, or when she was scared, she was human, what of it? She could deal with it. *So deal with it.*

She started swinging again. It had worked before. She kept swinging, legs up behind her, legs out in front, trying to catch her heels on the rough stone.

It took longer to do it deliberately than it had taken to do it by accident, but they did catch eventually, and she took a moment to breathe. She held the position, terrified of losing her footing again. Her legs began to shake. There was a tiny pool of fire in her stomach where the gunshot wounds were still raw.

Let's work out the science of this.

She thought about it. People scooch up chimneys by pushing their weight out against each wall. She could do the same, except she had to keep the rope taut and use that instead.

The way she saw it, there were a hundred things that could go wrong with this plan, but all she would do for now was try and get her feet higher and higher up the wall. Leaning forward until her weight was shared evenly by the rope, she lifted one foot off the wall and planted it just a centimetre higher. She waited until she was sure her weight was now shared between the rope and that foot, and repeated the process with the other. It worked. So she kept going.

Eventually, her feet were almost as high as her

hips, and this is when she realised she had a problem. Because her wrists were tied together she couldn't pull herself up the rope. The only thing she could do was walk her feet further up the wall and slowly turn herself upside down. Still, she thought, if that was the only thing she could do then she might as well do it, staying where she was wasn't going to help her.

So she did. Dolly Lightfoot walked up the wall. When her torso was at a forty-five-degree angle below her hips she could feel the rope running tight from her wrists, over one shoulder, down her spine. Then, shifting a foot another centimetre, she felt something against her heel. It was the hook. She actually had her foot on the hook in the wall that the rope was looped over. If she could somehow get the rope off the hook she would fall to the stone floor and then things would be a lot simpler. It would hurt, but she didn't care about that.

She thought about kicking it with her foot, but she couldn't lift her foot off the wall without falling. She tried to think through the science of it again: the rope was pulled down over the hook by her weight. All she had to do, in theory, was get the rope higher than the hook. The only way was to jump. She had to push off the wall, push up somehow, so that in the brief moment of slack the rope would rise off the hook and then drop without catching again. If she did it wrong she would drop until the rope snapped tight again, breaking her wrists, and slamming into the stone wall.

What was the alternative?

Her whole body was shaking from the stress of holding this upside-down acrobatic position. Without even planning, without counting down, with that immediate instinct that suddenly takes over, she launched off the wall with both legs, wildly throwing her wrists up as high as she could. She heard the slack rope smack on the wall, and then she was freefalling through darkness.

She landed on her feet, sending a tremor of furious power up her heel bones, through her knees and spine. She was squat on the ground, the rope draped over her head. Wrists still bound, she loosened the drawstring on the bag and ripped it off.

She gulped air, filling her lungs with cold and damp. Then she pulled at her bonds with her teeth. As much as she bit and gnarled at them, she couldn't loosen the knot. She couldn't even figure out how it was tied. She squinted around the room. It was a stone barn, clearly old and disused. The room was empty save for the hooks in the wall, the two upturned chairs, and the rope around her wrists. The other end of the rope was looped in a figure of eight around a metal cleat. She unlooped it and carried the bundle of rope in her bound hands as she scurried out of the room.

Through the stone archway was an antechamber, completely bare save for another discarded rope and hook in the corner. She ran to the double doors and peered out. The wind was raging, still slamming a door somewhere up at the farmhouse. There was a light on up there now, puncturing its dark cliff face.

The G-Wagen was in the courtyard, lifeless. Peering through it, over to the steel barn, she could just make out the figure of the woman. She ducked back behind the door, heart pounding. She still had no way of cutting her bonds. She could jump in the G-Wagen, but she would be dead before she started the engine. She could make a run for it across the fields, but if the woman spotted her she'd get a rifle bullet through the chest. She had to do *something* though, at some point the woman would come back to the barn and then what would she do?

That same door banged in the wind. *The farmhouse.* There would be a kitchen, there would be knives, something at least to cut her bonds, then she could figure out what to do next.

She tiptoed out into the courtyard, crouching behind the G-Wagen. A cold breeze tickled her neck. Damp mist hung in the air. To her left, stone steps led twenty metres up to the looming farmhouse. Its front door was the one banging in the wind.

She slipped off her shoes, peeled off her dirty socks. There was no way to stay out of sight if the woman turned to look, but she seemed occupied. She went for it, legs pumping, arms swinging, light feet almost silent. One set, heel turn, a slight skid, another set, another heel turn, final set. She reached the front door and leapt inside.

She breathed. No sounds. No pursuit.

She was in a dark entrance hall. The house was silent, but there was light coming from a doorway opposite. It was barely enough. She marched cautiously towards the light and tripped on what felt like a footstool, landing sprawled on the floor. Insensitive to pain now, she jumped back up and looked down to see what she had tripped on. She recoiled, looking away. It was the body of an old man, the whites of his unseeing eyes reflecting the feeble glow. Still not looking, she reached down to feel his wrist for a pulse, but she jumped back the moment she touched him. He was cold.

She crept towards the light. The door creaked as she eased it open. Again she jumped back. Sprawled on the dining table, in the feeble light of shaded bulbs, was the man Cain had shot. He didn't move, just staring up at the light with glassy eyes. His bandages were clean, but there was blood on his fingers and around his mouth. A fly crawled along his bottom lip, its proboscis pecking at the already tacky blood. She reached out to feel his pulse. His wrist was warm, but there was no life in it.

She moved into the kitchen beyond the dining room, cut her bonds with a mezzaluna on the counter. There was a back door. She could see a short path leading into dark woods. The perfect escape route. She would disappear into the woods and hike through the Tuscan countryside until morning.

As she opened the door the cold night air rushed over her face, drying her eyeballs. She stared down the path, wanting desperately to run, but she couldn't take a step and cursed herself for it.

Sighing, she returned to the body of the man, to what she had seen gleaming on one of the cracked wooden chairs: a silver semi-automatic, silencer attached. Carefully, and with one eye on the man, Dolly Lightfoot picked it up. It was much heavier than she had imagined. She held it out level, its weight making it wander all over the place. She tried to keep it aimed steadily at a framed lace flower that hung on the wall. It was tough. Really tough.

She lowered the pistol and cradled it in her hands, her finger dancing on the trigger. There was a red dot on the side next to a sort of switch or catch. Guns have safeties, she knew that, but did the red dot mean it was on or off?

She would have to fire it to find out.

Holding it carefully, she went back to the kitchen and aimed the gun out the open door. She went to pull the trigger. *Squeeze.* She had heard someone say that once in a movie, "squeeze it, don't pull it." She had no idea what that meant.

But what if the silencer didn't work? Or was louder than she expected. She had heard of a suppressor too. Was this a silencer or a suppressor? Or were all silencers actually suppressors? She didn't have a clue. Was the gun even loaded?

There was another button below the safety. She pushed it and the magazine shot out onto the tiled floor with a bang. She jumped round in terror, looking towards the front of the house, trembling with anticipation, but there was only the return to silence. She snatched up the magazine, noticing the copper jacket of the bullet that poked its nose out the top. It had a dent in the front, with score marks on it as though someone had hammered at it with a chisel or something. She hadn't imagined bullets looking like that.

She slipped the magazine firmly back into the grip. It clicked into place. There was one more thing she thought of: didn't people pull the top back, or something, to load a bullet into the "chamber"? It took much more strength than she thought practical, but once done she felt the spring-loaded mechanism slot a bullet into place. What she held in her hands was now a volatile, lethal weapon.

The phone rang like a sudden scream from the hallway. Dolly's arms snapped out, aiming the gun towards the sound. The old bell shrieked again. She begged it to stop. The woman would hear it. She crouched on the ground, aiming the pistol at the front door. Waiting. Waiting for the woman. Ready to fire the moment she saw the door move.

She rode out four more rings, then mercifully it stopped. She waited two minutes, the house silent. Standing back up, she stepped gingerly through the dining room, gun raised in front of her. Past the body of the man, into the dark hall, over the body of the man she presumed to be the farmer. To the front door, opening it, the wind almost ripping it from her grip. Laid out in front of her she could see the smooth stone steps descending their twenty or thirty metres to the courtyard with the G-Wagen parked haphazard, the stone barn over to the right, the steel one to the left. Beyond them both, dark countryside under deep blue sky.

She took the first step, her eyes darting down to her bare feet, then back up to the world beyond the gunsight. Then the next step. She took long, controlled breaths. In through the nose, out through the mouth. Another step.

The shrill bell of the telephone pierced the night air. She froze on the steps. What if the woman came out now, curious about the phone?

Ten rings this time, then it stopped. She started moving again. Halfway down now, she could hear a voice. *The woman's.* She was talking, still in the steel barn.

She could see them now, only silhouettes but she could make them out. Cain was hanging upside down by his ankles, the woman standing in front of him with a knife in her hand and a gas canister by her side. Her heart started beating so loudly she was afraid they would hear it. Her hands were shaking, her arms trembling, it was the weight of the pistol, but the adrenaline too.

She had reached the bottom of the steps, there was just the courtyard to cross. The woman was saying something to Cain, she didn't speak German but she knew what '*Danke*' meant. It sounded final. She crept as far as she could, now into the shadow of the barn, still unnoticed. The woman placed something against Cain's forehead, he closed his eyes. This was it. She had no choice. She stood where she was, held her arms as steady as she could, aimed with rapidly fading hope, and pulled the trigger.

TWENTY-FOUR

There was a rolling mist creeping down off the hills that clung to Baroffio's neck like cold fingers. Crouched in the dirt, chewing his pencil, he stared at the tyre tracks. Held temporarily suspended in the inverse of a Dunlop, Goodyear, or Pirelli, these grains of dirt wanted to speak to him. There was always something left behind, it was the core tenet of detective work. Even when there was nothing, there was something. And sometimes, like tonight, you were cut adrift in a sea of evidence. In every direction there was something to analyse, something to spend more time on. You had to know where to focus. In Baroffio's long career, the most unremarkable thing left at the crime scene had often cracked the case. A white rubber scuff mark. The smell of ground coffee. A dirty tidemark in a spotless bathroom. Every speck of evidence told part of a story, if only you knew how to understand it. What did these tyre tracks want to tell him?

Dusting down his trousers, he stepped back up onto the road and surveyed the scene that occupied it. To his left, one abandoned carabinieri Ducati motorcycle. To his right, one abandoned silver Mercedes soft-top. A quiet night road, slightly elevated, slicing through a vineyard, the direct route to nowhere, now swarmed at both ends of the scene by carabinieri

Fiats, Alfa Romeos, and a Suzuki.

'So Russo pulled over the American,' Li Fonti said, 'then what? My guys found blood by the side of the road, here. He kills him?'

Baroffio shook his head. 'Russo disappeared in the afternoon, right? I can't believe he reappeared almost twelve hours later to pull over the American.'

Li Fonti just shrugged.

'And I can't believe he pulled over the American in the afternoon either. That would mean the American killed him, dumped his body, drove to the villa to deliver the bomb, then drove his car back here to the scene of the crime, got out and... simply walked off into the vines?'

'What then?'

Baroffio smiled. It took effort. 'I don't know. I can tell you what didn't happen, what *couldn't* have happened, but I can't make sense of this, or how it fits in to everything.'

He stood with his hand over his mouth for some time, then he began to itch his unshaven cheek with the back of his fingers as he thought.

'So, let's not bother. Let's not make sense of it,' he decided. 'Let's just be bloodhounds and follow the evidence.'

'I thought you were smarter than the average bear.'

'Every tough case I've cracked has been because of hard work and lucky breaks, not because I was smart. Tell me again what was in the car.'

'All the items required by law, plus a roadmap, sunglasses, first aid kit, pen, notebook, torch. Everything you'd want, nothing you wouldn't expect.

We'll be able to pull prints, of course, possibly DNA.'

'And it's registered to a Donald Cramer?'

'Yes, address in Florence. Both my guys and your guys are there now, but it doesn't look like he's home. His landlady's description matches the servants' description of the American to a tee. They're searching the place now, taking prints and DNA. If they match what we take from the car then we'll know for sure.'

Baroffio nodded. 'Sounds like our guy. Although, if he's a professional I suppose it'll be an alias.'

'A professional?'

'You don't use a bomb to murder people. Not unless you want everyone to know it was murder. Which murderers normally don't. They make it look like an accident, robbery gone wrong, that kind of thing. This wasn't really a "murder" at all.'

'Up at the house you said it couldn't be an accident.'

'Oh no, I don't think it was an accident.'

'So if it wasn't an accident, and it wasn't a murder, what was it?'

'An assassination.'

'You mean a hit? Ordered by whom, rival winemakers?'

Baroffio shrugged. 'It has all the hallmarks of a mob hit. We know Croatian smugglers are involved. And I have other reasons to suspect mob involvement.'

'What reasons?'

'I'm not sure I should tell you.'

Li Fonti frowned.

'Nothing personal. Let's just say that the old man back at the house is not just an old man.'

'And what? You think the American, the man

registered as Donald Cramer, is a professional assassin?'

Baroffio shrugged. 'Could be.'

'Should we pull our men out of his apartment? Keep an officer on surveillance to see if he turns up?'

'Might as well keep them searching, I don't think he'll go back there.'

'Why not?'

'His car is here. He wouldn't leave it unless he had to, he'd know it would lead straight to Donald Cramer. If he is what I think he is, he'll know that identity is blown. Following those leads will just waste time. What else have we got?'

'Blood,' Li Fonti said. 'Parts of a revolver.'

'Add a rifle shell,' Irene said, stepping up onto the road out of the darkness of the vines.

A long bullet casing glinted inside an evidence bag.

'Where did you find it?'

'Where the third vehicle was parked. You can see where they left the road further back, parked among the vines, then rejoined further up.'

Baroffio traced the journey with his eyes.

'Come over here, I want your opinion on the revolver,' he told her, leading her to the bonnet of a carabinieri Fiat.

The pieces of the gun were laid out. She pored over them, her nose hovering centimetres above the shards. 'There are specks of blood here. Not much, but some.'

'What do you think happened to it?'

'I'd say it was hit by a bullet.'

'Really?'

'A rifle bullet like this would do it,' she said, still

holding the evidence bag. 'Look, you can see the point of impact here, just above the cylinder.'

'The specks of blood suggest someone was holding it. If the sniper fired from that direction, where you found the casing, then the driver of the Mercedes had to be pointing it this way, towards the motorcycle.'

Irene and Li Fonti nodded, it made sense.

'Getting a gun shot out of your hand like that, how big an injury would that cause, do you think?'

'You're thinking of the blood on the road?' she asked.

'Possibly.'

'Of course it could do a lot of damage, but I can't see enough blood on the grips here, not to be consistent with the amount we found on the road.'

He grunted. 'And we haven't found more casings?'

Irene shook her head. 'We'll search the area this side of the Mercedes for the bullet, if it's still in one piece we'll find it, but I don't think it'll tell us anything that this casing doesn't.'

He nodded. Irene returned to her work. He turned to Li Fonti.

'Obviously, we'll take DNA from the blood and run it through the system, but if you could ask Russo's mother for a DNA sample we should be able to rule out whether it's his or not pretty quickly.'

Li Fonti sighed, then nodded.

Baroffio turned back to the scene. 'So where are they both?'

'Russo and the American?'

'Let's just say the Mercedes driver and the motorcyclist.'

Li Fonti shrugged.

'The third vehicle came out of the vines,' Baroffio mused, 'onto the road, leaving dirt on the tarmac as it reversed up to these two, then drove off in that direction, where we lose them after two hundred metres. Footprints, we've one set of heavy boots, most likely a woman, heading from the third vehicle through the vines to here, and a set of trainers, also probably a woman, going the other way. No other prints leading anywhere outside of this area. That means, alive or dead, it's likely everyone left this scene in the third vehicle.'

His pencil snapped in his hands.

Li Fonti studied him with mild concern. 'Ok?'

'This is it. The end of the trail.'

'A dead end?'

Baroffio shrugged. 'Not necessarily. We've got three good crime scenes, that has to be enough.'

Other officers were gathering around him now, both polizia and carabinieri.

'We've got blood, which means we've got DNA to run. We've got a bullet casing, and the remains of a bullet somewhere, we need a full analysis from ballistics. We've got pieces of a revolver, if the serial number is intact we need to know when it was made, where it was sold, and who bought it. We've got a name, Donald Cramer, and we know his apartment in Florence. We need to know everything we can, starting with phone records. Talk again to his landlady. How does he pay his rent? Does he get much post? Does he go to confession? We know he drives a rare Mercedes so let's start talking to mechanics and find out where he gets his car serviced, what do *they* know about him? We need someone working every lead, one of them is going to get us to the people involved in this.'

The crowd broke into a flurry of action.

'Oh, and we've got tyre tracks from the third vehicle. I'll take those.'

'*Ispettore!*'

Baroffio and Li Fonti turned to see Rizzo, the young carabinieri officer, running towards them.

'What is it, kid?'

'Sir, a milkman called in after he heard our appeal about Russo on the radio, says he saw a motorcycle officer heading up towards old Bianchi's farm earlier today. We've tried calling the farm but there's no answer.'

'How many times did you call?' Li Fonti asked.

The kid shrugged. 'Twice.'

Baroffio shared a look with Li Fonti, then he turned to Rizzo.

'Do you know the way there, kid?'

'Sure, it's over there,' he pointed to the dark horizon, 'just where you can see the crest of those hills. When the sun comes up you'll be able to see it.'

The two inspectors shared another look, then they both started running for the nearest car.

'Come on, kid,' Baroffio shouted, 'you're driving!'

TWENTY-FIVE

C ain opened his eyes. Still hanging upside-down, and beginning to feel sick, he looked at the body of the woman now lying on the floor. He didn't know whether to trust his eyes as he watched the upside-down Dolly gingerly entering the barn, a suppressed pistol raised.

'Shoot her again,' he said.

'*What?*'

'Shoot. Her. Again.'

Now squeamish, Dolly half-closed her eyes and looked away as she emptied a bullet into the woman's torso. The body didn't move.

'She's dead,' he said. 'Take her knife, cut me down.'

When he landed on the concrete he barely had the strength to stand up. His legs had been strained for hours, then drained of blood. On top of all that there was the stress. He sat on the concrete, bringing his knees up to his chest.

Dolly was facing away, cradling the gun in her hands. She wasn't making any noise, and he couldn't see her face, but he could tell she was crying.

'You did the right thing.'

'Please, don't—' she snapped, not managing any more.

He left it, sat there just studying the back of her head and her slumped shoulders.

'Let's get out of here,' he said.

She sniffed, then nodded.

He crawled on his hands and knees to the woman's body and went through her pockets. He found the car keys quickly enough. He slid them across the floor and through Dolly's legs.

'Go get in the car, just don't leave without me.'

She put the pistol on the floor, snatched up the keys, and marched out of the barn.

Cain went through the rest of the woman's pockets, finding nothing but a scrap of paper. Pocketing it, he stood up on shaky legs and breathed in the misty air.

They had touched too much. There was no way to wipe everything down. Even if he wiped down the doorframes and the chairs in the barn, there was no way of knowing what Dolly had touched up at the farmhouse, and Cain had a strong, instinctive desire to get away from this place as soon as possible. But one thing he couldn't do was leave prints on a gun, so using his sleeve he picked up the pistol and wiped it clean.

Then he had an idea. If his instincts were right, it might just work. So, paying no attention to what Dolly was doing with the G-Wagen, he jogged up to the farmhouse and crept inside. He pressed the pistol into the dead man's hand, "Moritz", she had called him, and then let it drop to the floor. A simple country detective might conclude they had killed each other, and be happy with that.

When he returned down the steps to the G-Wagen, he found Dolly fiddling with the licence plate.

'What are you doing?'

'They've got different plates in the back.'

'What?'

'In the back, under the floor. There were different plates: German, Spanish, Belgian, Swiss. I went for Spanish. They spoke German so I assume they use either the German or Swiss plates most of the time, they must have changed to the Italian ones when they crossed the border.'

'Good thinking,' Cain replied. 'How are you feeling?'

'Don't worry about me.'

'Ok. Who's driving?'

'You. Keys are on the dash.'

Cain climbed up into the G-Wagen's driving seat, then he had another thought. He climbed back down and went over to a hose that was coiled by the stone steps. Turning on the tap, he walked back to the G-Wagen.

'What are you doing?' Dolly asked.

'Washing it down.'

'There's no blood on the car, I've already checked.'

'It doesn't hurt to be thorough.'

The Italian plates were still on the ground.

'Put those in the back. If the cops run them they'll know what to look for.'

She stepped away as Cain washed down the car. He turned off the hose and coiled it back up, wiping down the nozzle and tap.

As he turned back towards the car he glanced over the vast, dark countryside that was laid out in front of them from the hillside. Lights caught his attention. A string of headlights, a convoy, slicing their way through the darkness two, maybe three, miles away.

'Let's go!' Cain said, hurrying to the car and jumping up into the driver's seat.

She was already in the passenger seat, strapped in and ready to go. Cain fired up the engine and reversed out of the courtyard, wheels spinning on the dirt road as he quickly turned the car. He bombed it down the hill.

'Get ready,' he said as the lights caught the cracking wooden gate.

Dolly looked at him terrified, gripping the door to brace herself. He slammed his foot on the brake, skidding to a stop with just two metres to spare.

'Go!' he barked.

She undid her seatbelt and jumped out, opening the gate whilst Cain tapped the steering wheel impatiently. He drove through and she closed it behind them. He leant over and popped the door handle, she jumped back in.

'You didn't have to close it, you know.'

'Habit.'

He sped off down the dirt road, praying he would reach the turning before the convoy did. They made it, no sign of them. He turned without braking, almost throwing Dolly out of her seat.

'Do we have to go so fast!?'

'Yes.'

The road curved, they were out of sight, heading north now, away from the convoy, but he wouldn't relax until they had put more miles between them.

Ten minutes later, they joined a tarmac road,

then the autostrada.

'Slow down,' Dolly said, 'we'll get pulled over. For *real* this time.'

She was right. He eased the G-Wagen down to the speed limit. The roads were empty. There was no one behind them. They were safe now.

'What did you mean back there, about the plates? The cops knowing what to look for.'

'All the plates will be registered under the model and colour, so if they ran them they'd know to look for a silver Mercedes G-Class.'

'No, I got that bit, I meant, why don't we want the police to find us?'

He glanced at her, trying to understand why she was asking, but he couldn't get a read on her.

'I think we need to have a long conversation,' he said.

She sighed and closed her eyes, resting her head against the window.

He stared back out at the road. A sign hove out of the darkness: "AUTOGRILL 2km".

'Are you hungry? Because I'm starving.'

'I don't think I've eaten a thing for two days,' she replied, eyes still shut.

'Two days?' He gave a low whistle. 'Do we have any money? Did they have a stash in here somewhere?'

Eyes open now, her face lit up. *'Oh yeah.'*

TWENTY-SIX

The Autogrill was empty as Cain and Dolly pushed open the glass door and stepped up to the counter. There were no customers, and no staff he could see. There wasn't even music or radio playing. His eyes naturally darted to the empty buffet table and salad bar.

'Hello?' he called, taking a seat at the diner-style counter.

'Just coming,' a man replied, appearing from the kitchen out the back.

He considered them for a moment, drying his hands with a tea towel. They looked like they'd dived from a moving car and rolled their way up to the door, but they were so concerned with the menu that the man just shrugged.

'What can I do for you?'

'What can we get?' Cain asked.

Dolly was poring over the breakfast options, salivating. They were hungry like stray dogs.

'We stop serving hot food at midnight, I'm afraid. We've got sandwiches over there in the fridge, and I can do you a couple of hot coffees.'

'When do you start breakfast?'

'Seven,' he replied flatly.

Cain checked his watch. It was just approaching five.

'Do *you* make the breakfast when the time comes?'

'Yes.'

'Do you have everything you need for it?'

The man sighed. 'Yes.'

Cain reached into his pocket and pulled out a note. 'I'll give you five hundred euros to make us some breakfast.'

The man instinctively reached for the note, then hesitated. 'Look...'

Cain found another note. 'A thousand. Seriously.'

The man frowned.

'We're just really hungry,' Dolly pleaded.

He sighed, then rejected the second note. 'This is enough,' he said, pocketing the five hundred. 'Do you know what you want?'

'I think...' Cain said, taking one final look at the menu, straining without his reading glasses, 'we'll have one of everything. *Each.*'

The man sighed again.

Cain offered the other note and the man snatched it this time.

'It's going to take some time,' he said, 'I can't do them all at once.'

'That's fine, we'll have them as they come.'

The man disappeared out the back.

Cain looked at his bandaged hand. There were some brown spots where blood had seeped through the cloth.

'I'd better take a look at your wounds,' he said.

'What?'

'Where you were shot.'

'I understood what you meant. Why do you need to look at them?'

'You've been knocked around a lot. I'd better check you haven't ripped any stitches.'

'I haven't got stitches anymore.'

'They took them out?'

She raised her eyebrows as if to say, *Oh boy.* 'I remember that. They definitely took the bullets out.'

'I meant the stitches. They took the stitches out?'

'They must have.'

He frowned. 'If the stitches are out, it's been long enough if you were going to get an infection, and you're not feverish, so they obviously did a good enough job. How does it feel?'

'It's ok.'

'You didn't feel any sudden or sharp pain when you were hanging by your wrists.'

'Not in my stomach,' she said, rubbing her wrists.

'You may not be bleeding out of a hole in your stomach, but we need to check you haven't reopened any internal wounds.'

'How would we tell?'

'There would be bruising by now, and soreness.'

'*I'll* go check,' she said, getting up and heading to the toilets.

'All fine,' she said when she returned. 'I was lucky, the bullets went through Cabrera before they entered me, he must have slowed them down. All I got left with is a couple of cigarette burns. How's your hand?'

'It'll be fine, but I won't be firing a gun anytime soon.'

Dolly made no comment.

'I'm not a nut, you know,' she said.

'Excuse me?'

'I'm not crazy. I know you think I'm a conspiracy nut, the same as all the rest.'

'I think you're brave.'

'Excuse me?'

'You took a stand for what you thought was right. Even though you knew it would cost you. That's bravery in my book.'

He smiled, she didn't know what to say.

'What's right, what's wrong,' he continued, 'maybe that's a matter of opinion. But I don't think it's a matter of opinion that what you did was very brave.' He sighed. 'You say you're not a nut. Well, I'd like to say that I'm not in denial. I know what I did, for Maltby, for the taskforce, I'm clear-eyed about it. I did good things. Every time you mention what he's accused of in the report, I think of the times I saved someone's life. And what happened the times I wasn't there to do my job. Like what might have happened tonight.'

'We're both part of a system,' Dolly started.

But at that moment espressos and orange juice arrived, followed closely by bread with jam, marmalade, and Nutella. They downed the drinks, then consumed the plate in less than a minute, Dolly licking out the remains of the single-serve spread pots.

Cain studied her.

'What?' she asked.

'I was just wondering what comes next.'

'Am I your prisoner again now?'

'No,' he said with feeling. 'No.'

She sat up straight, dignified. 'Then I guess this is

goodbye.'

'What will you do?'

'Hitchhike, I guess. Disappear. Go anywhere they won't find me.'

Cain huffed.

'What?' she asked, offended.

'You're lying.'

'Whatever,' she grunted.

The man placed two sfogliatelle on the counter. At first they hesitated to touch them, the atmosphere still tense, but then Cain grabbed one and Dolly snatched the other, tearing into it. They were still warm and the buttery pastry melted in their mouths.

'What do you mean, I'm lying?' she finally asked, spraying pastry.

'You're going to go where you mailed the film to.'

'So what if I am?'

'I don't blame you, you want answers. So do I.'

'Yeah, well, I'm sorry, but I don't feel like letting you tag along.'

Cain said nothing.

Dolly looked away, maybe she felt mean. 'Anyway, I'm not even sure I can remember the address.'

'Villa Cardinale, Via Regina, Tremezzina, Como, Italy,' Cain rattled it off simply enough.

❊ ❊ ❊

Confusion mutated into horror, but it didn't sink into her stomach like a heavy weight, like it had in Hong Kong. It all sat on the surface. All her feelings were muffled somehow. Overriding them all was a towering, existential tiredness. She was so tired. So goddamn tired. *Who was Cain? How did he know that address? Had she got him wrong?* These questions and more passed over Dolly Lightfoot's mind like dark clouds.

'A difficult address to forget, I would think,' he said.

She went to say something but couldn't find the words. Eventually she breathed just one: 'How?'

He smiled, dropping a scrap of paper on the counter. The address was handwritten.

'It was in her pocket.'

She breathed a sigh of relief, the dark clouds cleared. But newer, lighter questions skated across her mind. 'Do you think she was going to kill Paulo too?'

Cain shook his head.

'Wait,' she said, 'how did you know that was where I sent the film?'

'I didn't, that was a guess. An educated guess. You see, I have a theory.'

The man brought them a selection of panini with different cheeses and salami in, plus some croissants. They were beyond the staple Italian breakfast now and onto the stuff they kept on the menu for German and French tourists. They wolfed them down. Even the most important conversation could wait for food.

'What's your theory?' she asked through a mouthful of provolone and fennel salami.

'You won't like it.'

'I promise I won't scream.'

'I don't think Paulo exists. Maybe the Network exist, maybe they're real. But Paulo...' He shook his head.

'What do you mean, he doesn't exist?'

'It's Maltby.' He paused for dramatic effect. 'We've

both been played, right from the beginning. That's why she had that address, it was where they were going to take you.'

He was right, she didn't like it. At least he was finally admitting the obvious truth about his friend.

'If that was the case, why didn't he just get *you* to take me?' she asked.

'We've already established I was supposed to die.' She frowned.

'Think about it. He persuades you to steal a report that conveniently accuses me of all his crimes. He gives you an address to send it to. Some base of his, I guess. It all goes to plan—' He stopped mid-sentence.

'What?'

'It all went to plan, so why do they need you? It's not to keep you quiet, you don't know anything about Maltby, you've never heard of him.'

She shrugged. 'Because of Cabrera?'

'No, why would they care if you're arrested? If anything, it neatly ties up their whole narrative. All you know is that you spoke to some guy on a forum, and Cabrera and the NSA just blame the Network. There's nothing tying any of this to Maltby, so why run the risk?'

'To get you involved?' she suggested. 'You need to be dead for his plan to work, if his plan involves releasing the report.'

'But there's a million ways he could kill me. Why involve you? And why would he ever release the report? What does he have to gain?'

'If he doesn't want the report released then I'm a liability because I know it exists.'

'That's not good enough,' he mumbled.

'Why not?'

'Because others know it exists too. The person who wrote it, for starters.'

They sat back in silence. The man turned on the big television that hovered over the empty tables. Italian breakfast news chattered out. He turned the volume down until it was a gentle murmur. Dolly found it easy to tune out. She had eaten too much and her stomach was starting to hurt. It groaned and grumbled, feeling like one of those machines that cubes cars, but she tuned that out too. She began to appreciate the logic of Cain's theory. So far, all roads led to Maltby. How else would "Paulo" know about the report, something so secret that only a handful of the NSA top brass had a copy? Why else would the assassin sent to kidnap her have Paulo's address? The woman told Cain she was instructed to take her to Maltby, and Villa Cardinale was the only address she had on her. It made a horrible kind of sense. Cain was right. And now she found herself at the same dead end: if they had the report, why did they need her?

She laughed.

Cain raised his eyebrows.

'They don't know they've got it,' she said. 'I'd say they didn't get it, but I saw it go in the mail. Sure, maybe they haven't got it, between Hong Kong and Italy there are a lot of places for the postal service to lose it, but I'll bet they simply don't know they've got it.'

'You're rambling.'

'They weren't expecting a roll of film. No one was. They were expecting a USB stick or a hard drive. They think I've stashed it somewhere, or sent it somewhere else. And they need to know where. They saw the news:

Cabrera was killed, I was in hospital. But they don't know what happened to the package.'

'Are you saying this thing that they're after could be sitting in a pile of unopened mail? Or they could have thrown it in the trash?'

'Have you got a better theory?'

He sighed. 'No, I haven't. What I know is that the answers we're both looking for are here.' He tapped the scribbled address.

'So... we're going together?'

'If you're happy with that.'

'Well, if we're both going we might as well go together.'

She looked away, embarrassed again. The truth was that she was glad they were going together because she had no idea what they were going to find. On balance, she trusted Cain. It wasn't so much the things he did or the things he said, it was the way he did them and the way he said them. He felt like your best friend's dad, the one that didn't leer at you. He reminded her of the good guys she had met in the NSA, and there were plenty of them. The ones who had seen everything and knew how to react. But as she looked at him now, he didn't seem to notice her. He was distracted by the television, his face pale.

She whipped her head round to look. It was the news, footage from a helicopter circling a villa on a hill. She had seen that villa in the Mercedes' mirror as they sped down the hill.

Behind the villa the sun had risen over the horizon, and leading up to it was a trail of police cars, ambulances, and fire trucks. As the helicopter circled around she saw what Cain had seen. One side was open like a dolls house, the rubble strewn across the hillside, a sprinkling of yellow evidence markers catching the morning sun. She understood the chyron well enough: "*5 MORTI*".

She looked back at Cain. He was standing now.

'Let's go,' was all he said.

PART III

You Are Cordially Invited…

TWENTY-SEVEN

Maltby ducked down one of the villa's covered porticos. He skipped down three steps through dappled shade towards the azure water. Fast moving, in and out of light, the classic technique to evade a sniper. But it was no use.

'Sir? Sir!?' Roberto called.

Caught, Maltby stopped in his tracks. *Damn.* He turned back, forcing a smile.

'Yes?' he asked.

Roberto had been running to keep up with him, his vast forehead glistened in the sun.

'We have some ribbon choices for you to look at,' he said.

'Ribbon?'

'Yes, we have red and we have cream.'

Maltby sighed. 'Well, we have some other red decorations, so let's go with red.'

'Yes, sir, but the red is edged with gold and the other decorations have silver in them.'

'Fine, let's go with the cream then.'

'But, sir, the cream is of a different thickness, it may not go with the rest.'

'Then the red.'

'Oh, but sir, the gold. Gold and silver, some people like it, but really, sir, you must come and see.'

His hairy hands waggled on the end of his sun-damaged arms, grey smudges of faded tattoos poking out from his sleeves. He was the sort of man Maltby loathed. He despised indecision. No decision should take longer than thirty seconds, most shouldn't even take one.

'We have some more silver ribbon,' he was rambling, 'but that is even wider, and we have used it in the centrepieces—'

'Look,' Maltby cut him off, 'use your judgement. I trust you.'

'But, sir, La Signora, she say that you are in charge. La Signora, she... er...' He flushed with embarrassment, he didn't want to say she scared him.

Maltby ground his teeth. Why did she have to tell Roberto that? Was it punishment? Of course it was. Everything she did was punishment. She knew it would drive him mad. She was putting him in his place by making him her party planner. Like a cuckolded husband or one of the household staff.

'What is your job, Roberto?'

He was taken aback by Maltby's tone. 'Sir?'

'What. Is. Your. Job?'

He shrugged. When that wasn't enough he gestured around to the garden, and the preparations that were going on.

'Come on, Roberto, use your words. What is your job?'

'I set up for parties, for events.'

'You've seen a lot of parties, a lot of events, right?'

He smiled, baffled. 'Of course.'

'How many?'

'Sir?' He frowned like a suspicious child.

'How many? Roughly.'

He shrugged again.

'Guess.'

'A thousand?'

'Don't ask me, tell me.'

'Yeah, a thousand, I guess. Maybe.'

'Good. A thousand parties. That's a lot more than I've ever seen, and I wasn't ever involved in setting them up or choosing the... the, er... ribbons. And everything else. I don't really do parties, you see, I don't like to be the centre of attention.'

He grinned. Roberto returned it, nervously.

'The point is: don't you worry about La Signora, you just make this party look like every other party you've worked on. Nothing too flashy, nothing too boring, just like every other party, ok?'

'But sir, they were all different.'

Maltby sighed. 'They were all different, eh?'

'Yes, sir.'

'Do you have a brochure?'

'Sir?'

'Like a flyer, an advert?'

'We have a website.'

'Great, and on that website is there a big picture that comes up first, that shows off what you can do. You know, to reel in the punters, to get them salivating, get them ringing that number of yours.'

'On the left there is a picture.'

'Well, I want this party to look like that picture on the left.'

'But that is a wedding.'

'I don't care. Just take out the lace and the signs saying bride and groom, and make the sodding party look like that.'

'But, sir-'

'I'm not looking at your damn ribbons, Roberto. You'll have to chase me, pin me down, and hold my eyes open. Are you prepared to do that?'

He hesitated. 'No, sir.'

'Then you're going to have to use your own judgement. I trust you.' He grinned. 'Don't worry about La Signora, I'll deal with her.'

Roberto nodded slowly, but he didn't move.

'Go, get on with it. We need it all done before tonight, don't we?'

'Yes, sir.' He nodded, then turned and hurried back up the steps.

When Roberto reached the top, he left the portico and rounded the corner to the front of the villa. He turned to face the hill that stretches up beyond the road. It rises steeply through trees, past the older, now modest villas. Above these, slopes of green grass, split only by the dirt roads that lead to clusters of three or four houses. As you get higher these houses disappear, and just as the ground takes on a vertiginous incline, you notice another three times what you have already climbed left still to go, and that this is not a hill at all, but Monte Crocione, a mountain, and you give up. A chapel perches on the rock shelf at this point of despair: Capella Angeli. It was to this that Roberto directed his gaze as he made the sign of the cross and begged God for his assistance.

❊ ❊ ❊

What Roberto couldn't know was that it was not just God to whom he looked when he made the sign of the cross. Capella Angeli sits at the end of a dirt track that winds its way back and forth across the green slopes, then cuts into the rock to claw up to the chapel, where the road stops and a hiking trail begins.

Parked at the end of the road, outside the empty chapel, the only car was a silver Mercedes G-Wagen. And at the edge of the rock precipice on which the chapel sits, two figures were lying on their bellies, looking down over Tremezzina and the blue water beyond. One, a young woman, held binoculars. The other, an older man, held a telescopic sight that had been removed from a high-powered rifle.

'It looks like they're setting up for some kind of party,' Cain said.

'You can see that from here?'

'This scope is pretty powerful. We're about half a mile away, straight line, maybe three quarters. Well within the range of that rifle. I believe the record is something like two miles.'

'You mean if you saw him you could pick him off right now from up here?'

'I definitely couldn't. She probably could've. Although it's very windy here. The snipers in the CAR had to take all that into account: wind, heat, the drop of the bullet, even the curvature of the earth. But that was never me, I was a close quarters kind of guy. Double-tap to the chest and keep moving.'

He sighed, put down the scope. Dolly put down the binoculars. They shared a look.

'We didn't come here to kill anyone,' he said.

'Of course not. I'm a little concerned you felt the need to say that.'

'You're the one who said about picking him off from up here.'

'I was just curious.'

'Good.' He sighed again. 'The way I see it, this party makes our job much easier.'

'It does?'

'We may not have come here to kill anyone, but we know Jo is very happy to kill us. He can't do that in front of a hundred guests in someone else's house.'

'Someone else's house?'

'It's not his style. It's too...' he thought for a moment. 'Obvious.'

'Too obvious?'

'If he was rich I'm sure he'd buy a big house, but it wouldn't be some grand villa. He'd buy one of those sprawling city apartments with a hidden door. And if he did retire to the countryside, he wouldn't buy something in a tourist hotspot, he'd buy a house in the middle of nowhere surrounded by a whole lot of land. He'd buy acres of it. His own private kingdom.'

She was watching his face. 'You know him pretty well.'

'Yeah,' he nodded. 'Yeah, I know him pretty well.'

She gave a sombre smile, then she moved the conversation on:

'What are you suggesting?'

'We drive over to Bellagio, check into a hotel, then we buy ourselves some nice clothes, get some sleep, and get something to eat. Not necessarily in that order.'

She nodded. 'Sounds good to me.'

TWENTY-EIGHT

As the orange sun dipped behind Monte Crocione, Como and its nestled towns, old farms, and villas, were suddenly plunged into darkness. For the last hour the hillside on the east slope of the lake had been brushed with gold. Bellagio, protruding out into the lake, was also washed with this light, and you could trace the minutes before sunset by watching the darkness creep up the bell tower of the Basilica until there was only a golden tip on the spire, then nothing.

But after the darkness came a light, if not *as* beautiful, that had a beauty all its own. A thousand pinpricks of silver light erupted across every bank like fairy lights strewn in wreaths. The brightest and most impressive were on the great hotels, perched on the waterfront, the lights rippling in their reflections.

With the night lights, the big cars started to arrive at Villa Cardinale; the big, long wheelbase cars that you don't drive yourself: Rolls Royces, Bentleys, Jaguars, Mercedes, BMWs, and a Lexus. All of them hoping to be the most fashionably late, and all of them blocking the road as the driver pulled up to the gates of Villa Cardinale to reveal their passengers like the stamens at the centre of an unfurling flower.

Watching from the shadows of the upstairs

balcony, Maltby stared at them with a rising hatred that surprised him. He wondered why it surprised him. He knew he hated them, he had always hated the super-rich, or even just the mildly rich. The officer class, that's what they were. Every single one of them was born rich, and had got richer by taking money out of other people's pockets. *Taking food out of other people's mouths.* And these were the people he killed for. They may not know it, just one more entry in a long list of things they didn't know, but they were the status quo. The status quo he had fought to preserve since the moment he signed-up. They could solve the world's problems with the resources they commanded, but they had to be given a shindig like tonight just to part with their small change. Maltby had long come to the revelation that the richest are the meanest. They are the only ones whose compassion you have to buy, because they can't simply see difficulty and hardship and feel empathy and give their money. How could they understand? They've never experienced it. But they can understand a free buffet, and they'll give a twenty-thousand-euro donation if you throw in live entertainment.

He turned from the window, starting a begrudging march towards the main stairs. Below him he could hear the rumble of guests moving through the lobby, spilling through the rooms into the gardens that sloped down to the water's edge. He had only made it three steps down before one of them recognised him.

'Jo!'

It was that harlequin-faced hag Marie Roussel. Wearing a silver dress and a diamond tiara, with silver glitter make-up, she looked like a fairy godmother from a Hallmark movie.

This evening, it took Maltby a second longer to turn on his fake smile. For a moment, she looked genuinely unnerved.

'Marie, you look enchanting,' he purred.

Then, of course, she was all smiles and blushes. 'You old flatterer!'

'Oi! Less of the old, thank you.'

'You wear it well. Men improve with age.'

'Tell that to my knees and back.'

'Whereas us women, we fall apart, I'm afraid.'

'You continue to buck that trend.'

'Stop it!' She batted him playfully. 'Anyway, where is our hostess?'

'You can guess, surely?'

'Not still working?' she gasped.

'You know her: when the work is done, she'll be down.'

'Looking fabulous, I hope.'

'No need to hope.'

She gave a treacle-sweet smile and wafted towards the next room.

As his foot hit the bottom step he was accosted by Scotty Singh, who had come to a black-tie event wearing a T-shirt under his dinner jacket.

'Jo! Good to see you. You're looking well.'

'Thanks, Scotty, you look healthy yourself.'

'Thank you. My nutritionist has me on this new diet, calls it the gladiator diet. It's a lot of wholegrains and a lot of beans, a lot of dark veg. It'll add thirteen and a half years to your life.'

'Tell that to the gladiators. I'll stick with steak Béarnaise and lobster thermidor.'

'That stuff will kill you eventually.'

No, Scotty, it's conversations like this that will kill me.

'I'm going to dive right in with something,' he said, 'because I don't know when I'll get another chance. I want to offer you a job, if the lady of the house will release you.'

Maltby was taken off-guard. 'Really? In the computing industry?'

'Tech.'

'Pardon?'

'We call it "tech".'

'Well, that's why you don't want me. I'm about as analogue as they come.'

'It's not that kind of job. We need someone who can put on events like this, show some of the more analogue investors a good time, speak to them in their own language. From the right generation, if you know what I mean.'

Maltby thought of all the ways he could kill Singh with his bare hands. He could snap his neck like a bundle of twigs. But if it was dealer's choice, he would take the Champagne flute in Singh's hand and push it through his eye socket.

'Thanks, Scotty, but you know what I'm going to say.'

Singh smiled. 'You're a loyal man, everyone admires that. But the offer is there.'

'Thank you.'

'Where is our hostess, anyway?'

'She'll be around, I'm sure. Go help yourself to some of the food. And get your chequebook out!'

'No one uses cheques anymore, Jo.'

'I know that, Scotty. It's a metaphor.'

He stepped off the stairs and into the throng, dropping his smile like a hot brick.

TWENTY-NINE

C ain and Dolly had no trouble finding the right clothes in Bellagio's designer shops. Cain was dressed in a midnight blue Valentino tuxedo with ivory shirt and black bowtie, and when he saw himself in the mirror he felt like James Bond. Dolly was dressed in a long black Dolce & Gabbana dress that cost more than she earned in a month, and she was now a brunette.

They were walking steadily along the lakeside promenade, road to their left, glowing lamps above them, railings to their right, dark water sloshing just below. A silhouetted promontory loomed ahead, growing larger as they approached, blotting out the lights of the opposite shore like a ship pulling between them.

Most of Como's villas are perched on the steep shore-side of the road, but Villa Cardinale rests on this jutting promontory, affording it the luxury of sitting directly on the lakeside. This means its grand balconies and stepped gardens are behind it, unmarred by a view of the road, and the only tourists who can see them are the ones on the, admittedly frequent, water taxis.

'I think maybe you should have gone for black,' Dolly said, 'it would have been more inconspicuous.'

'I'm not hiding.'

She adjusted her neckline. 'Are you nervous?'

'Why?'

'You're not sweating is all. I'm sweating like a pig.'

'I guess I am.'

'You guess?'

He smiled. 'Believe me, I'm feeling what you are. It's a biological reaction. My heart is racing, stomach churning, and yes, I am sweating. I'm just used to it.'

'How come you look so calm?'

'Experience, I guess. Sweat is the most difficult thing. Sticky armpits, beads of it in your hairline. I hate it, but you can't fidget or mop your brow, it makes you look nervous. I knew someone who got killed by sweaty balls.'

'Killed?'

'Yeah. Some Tunisian terrorists thought he had something to hide. He wouldn't stop fidgeting, itching his pants. They thought maybe he was nervous, maybe he was double-crossing them, maybe he had something down there that was irritating him, like a weapon or a wire. But I knew it was just the heat. They wouldn't believe me though, and he wouldn't stop. It put them on edge. Finally, when he undid his belt and reached into his pants, two of them shot him.'

'At least I won't have that problem.'

'When you find that control getting away from you just focus on your breathing.'

'I know how to deal with anxiety.'

'The real secret is to accept that you're terrified, but to pretend you're not.'

'Is that what men do? I thought you were all genuinely unafraid.'

'Pretend you're an actor on stage, playing someone fearless. Then just act the part. Really lean into it. Full Daniel Day-Lewis mode. Or Meryl Streep in your case. Live the part.'

She frowned. 'Dress for the job you want, basically? You sound like a self-help book.'

'Well,' he shrugged, 'I *am* trying to help.'

As they approached the gates, they could make out the two-hundred-metre drive that led to the front doors. It was flanked by trees, and more wooded pockets dotted the sides of the promontory. The land rose in the middle, where the villa was perched, then stepped down steadily towards the water. It gave the impression of a floating island, temporarily docked by the shore.

Either side of the gates there was a big guard in a black suit. One male, one female. They subtly scanned all approaching guests. The female guard stopped a young man in a blue blazer, carrying a satchel. She opened the satchel, saw something she didn't like, and thrust it back to him with orders to leave. He had the cheap, thick-soled shoes of a reporter. Across the road Cain could see a small crop of paparazzi.

Dolly slipped her arm through his.

'Good idea,' he whispered.

'I'm going to fall over otherwise, these damn heels,' she said, towering at least a foot over him.

'At least we look the part.'

He hid his bandaged hand in his pocket and put on a pompous expression. They strolled through the gates unmolested. They fit: just another rich, old, white guy and his much younger wife. They followed three identical couples down the long drive.

The villa glowed in the light of flickering oil

223

lamps. A creamy yellow façade with three curved stone steps leading up to modest double doors. Over the long walk, Cain had time to study the situation. The ground floor windows were small, barred with curved iron. Two guards stood either side of the main doors, scanning new arrivals. He had hoped to slip round the side and find another entrance, but that wasn't going to happen. They joined at the back of a small crowd that was funnelling inside.

Three broad, stone steps and they passed through the double doors. The entrance was a triple-height hall. Dominating the space, a great staircase rose to the floor above, merged with a balcony, then climbed to the second floor to reveal another, smaller balcony. It was like standing in the stalls of a theatre, looking up at the grand circle. Cain was reminded of Gaspare and his sons' house, but where that staircase had been wood, this one was pale stone. Where Gaspare's floor had been uneven stone slabs, this one was marble, different colours cut into geometric patterns. The walls were a sky blue, rising up to a painted frieze that covered the final metre before the ceiling. And the grandeur didn't stop there, the ceiling was covered in stone hexagons, each one containing a unique sculpted flower head. This house was a monument to the old rich. The craftsmanship, of course, done by the poor. And tonight the old rich and the new rich were mingling here, with the poor doing the catering.

The entrance hall was filled with enough guests for Cain to feel safe, but they needed to move somewhere quieter as soon as possible. Just inside the door were young women standing at tables draped in white linen, on them rows of flute glasses effervescing with sparkling wine. The scent of the bubbles filled the air.

'*Franciacorta, Signore?*'

'*Franciacorta, Signora?*'

They each accepted a glass. The guests were flowing towards the staircase where it split them into two streams like the prow of a steamer. The two streams coursing through doors that led further into the villa, towards the gardens. Her arm still through his, he broke from the crowd, leading her quickly through an open doorway and closing it behind them. They were alone in a green chamber with plaster scenes on three walls. Two tall windows looked out into dark trees.

'What do we do now?' she asked.

'If this villa is like any other big house there will be servants' areas, even their own corridors and staircases. Downstairs, as it were. I'll search those areas, you search upstairs.'

'Why me?'

'Because it's best if I stay out of sight. He's never met you, probably never heard your voice, just a photograph. If he sees you, with that hair, with that dress, you've got a good chance he won't be able to place you.'

She frowned. 'I thought you weren't hiding.'

'That doesn't mean I want to be found.'

'Whatever. How are we supposed to find a roll of film in this massive house? *If* they've still got it.'

He shrugged. 'We'll have to work fast.'

'And if we're caught?'

'Think of an excuse.'

'Like what?'

'You were looking for a lipstick.'

'A lipstick?'

'A chapstick or something. If it's a desk, a pen.'

'A pen?'

'Painkillers. Whatever it is, think of something specific, but don't rehearse what you're going to say. Stick to the item, don't change your story. And if they ask questions act casual and behave as though they're the weird one.'

'That really works?'

'And as soon as you've said your first thing to them, start walking.'

There was a small door in the corner of the chamber, plastered and painted to match the wall.

'That will be the servants' door,' he said, giving her his glass, 'I'll go that way. You'd best head back the way we came, try and find another staircase to get to the first floor. The bedrooms should be empty.'

He stepped up to the hidden door.

'Good luck,' she said.

With his hand on the knob he turned back and nodded. 'Let's find this film before they find us.'

THIRTY

Dolly Lightfoot flinched when the bolt on the servants' door shot back into place. It sounded like a cell door. She didn't want to admit it, but she felt vulnerable without Cain. In Hong Kong it had been everything or nothing. From the moment Cabrera showed up at her apartment she assumed she was going to die. Getting the package in the mail was the only thing that mattered, walking away with her life would be a bonus. But then, death was always the easy option. There are no hard choices when you're dead. If she was honest, she was far more afraid of prison. She assumed she would die to avoid thinking about what happened if she lived. *What next?* On the other side of this evening the same question lurked. But none of that mattered right now.

What now? In Hong Kong she understood the systems, she felt prepared. Tonight was far more complicated. Tonight was alien to her. She was paddling in a world she had never even glimpsed. The super-rich. Did they even walk and talk like she did? How could they not smell the poverty on her? She would just have to pretend, like Cain said. So she flicked her head back, put on her most imperious expression, and marched back into the entrance hall.

She was going to march straight up the main stairs, she didn't care what Cain said about that. She had to live the part, and this young, confident, super-rich woman had smeared her lipstick on her wine glass and was going to march into the first woman's bedroom she came to, and put on a new shade. No wait, that didn't make sense. What did she know about rich women? They were capricious. And mean. And vicious bitches. They were like the popular girls at school who had called her names and made fun of her height and braces. That was it: her rich, older husband (or fiancé?) had made some comment about how he was glad she hadn't gone for one of those godawful dark shades she normally wore. She had thrown her drink in his face and now she was going to barge into the first woman's bedroom she came to, and put on the deepest, darkest shade she could find. And if she couldn't find any, she'd use eye pencil.

When she was three paces from the stairs her arm was snatched and held by man's grip. She whipped round, too close to take in anything but details: desperate eyes and an even more desperate goatee.

He barked something in Italian.

'What?' she yelped, frozen to the spot.

He stared at her for twenty seconds, eyes narrowing. She tried to take in more of him. A suit, but skinny. He didn't look like security.

'You're from the agency...' he hissed.

Her heart lurched like an engine stalling.

'We're not paying you to stand around!'

He marched her to the nearest linen-clad table, shoving a tray into her hands. He snatched the two flutes from her and placed them on it, then two more.

She looked at the two women serving the drinks. They were also wearing black dresses. But *hers* was Dolce & Gabbana! *Maybe that's what the normal people wear around here?*

The man jabbered some more, pushing her towards the next room. Flabbergasted, she drifted through the doorway just to get out of his sight. The room was empty, but there were two glasses discarded on the mantelpiece, so she collected them, almost dropping her tray.

There was another servants' door, hidden in the corner just the same. She had the tray in her hand. She knew she could pass for one of the caterers. She made an executive decision.

Through the door was a downward-sloping passageway with no windows and bare bulbs that hummed. She marched with her head high until she came to a door on her left. The door was short, with a rounded top, and opening it revealed a small office that might once have belonged to a butler or housekeeper. Perhaps it still did.

She closed the door behind her and put the tray down on a small wooden desk that took up much of the room. On it, a cage in-tray housed a handful of letters and packages. She rifled through them. None of them were the one she had sent. She checked the drawers, nothing but stationery in the top two, the bottom one was locked. She gave it a hard tug, causing the desk to lurch. The glasses on the tray wobbled, tinkling like a wind chime. One toppled off the tray, over the edge of the desk. She caught it an inch from the floor. Her hands were shaking.

There was a letter opener on a scarred leather

blotting pad. She wedged it in the gap near the drawer lock and tried to turn the catch. No luck. The old desk was too solid to bow the wood.

She looked around. There was a plant on the windowsill. Nothing underneath. There was a tiny fireplace, nothing on the mantle. By the door there was a set of wooden shelves, the side of which would be obscured when the door was open. She remembered the duty officer's station back in Hong Kong, how the old timers kept the key to the beer safe behind the logbook cupboard.

There was a slight gap between the shelves and the wall. She felt inside it. There, hanging on a screw, was a small key. Running to the desk, she slipped it into the drawer lock. It fit! Trembling, she turned the key and wrenched open the draw. *Porn.* And what looked like some confiscated spliffs. This was the housekeeper's stash of contraband. Sighing, she locked it back up and returned the key.

Balancing the tray with her knee, she closed the door behind her and continued down the narrow servants' corridor. There was a different light ahead. Moonlight and moving shadows. A small window just below head height. *Her* head height, at least. It was thin, comprised of four leaded panes, and the moonlight was augmented by a lamp on the wall just outside. This was the side of the villa most closely guarded by trees and they were the only view. She could hear footsteps crunching on gravel though. She could hear voices too. *American voices!* She crouched out of sight.

'What are you doing?' A young woman's voice. 'The Nazi Postmistress told us explicitly we couldn't smoke on our breaks. The owner hates it.'

'So what? The agency is paying us minimum wage. Mrs Citizen Kane in her Xanadu ain't the boss of me, so I'm smoking in my smoke break.'

The first woman grumbled. 'Pass me one, at least.'

Dolly smiled. She liked the sound of these two.

There must be an outside door nearby, she thought. Holding the tray high she marched down the corridor and soon the cacophony of kitchen noises echoed off the walls. She reached a line of waitresses huddled in the narrow corridor. The one at the front was handed a tray of canapés and ushered through a door. Then the next in line, and so on.

'Empties, coming through!' Dolly shouted out as she barged past the line and into the kitchen. Spotting a back door, she put the tray down and was out the door before anyone had time to complain.

It swung shut behind her and she found herself on stone slabs, next to large bins, a short wall ahead, then trees beyond. She followed the stone slabs around the side of the villa and soon found the small nook where the two young women were smoking. Their eyes darted up to her, cigarettes frozen in the air.

'Thank God,' she said, 'there's somewhere to sit,' and plonked herself down on a bench.

On the opposite bench, the young women went back to their smoking.

'You're American,' the smaller of the two said.

'So are you.'

'Kansas,' the woman said.

'Idaho.'

The larger woman studied her. Her dress, her shoes. Dolly smiled but it wasn't returned. Then she smiled at the smaller woman. She was shy and would only return her look in fleeting glances.

They both had that small town look. *Main Street USA*, as Cabrera had put it. It was what he saw when he looked at her. Maybe everyone did.

'You both from Kansas?' she asked.

The small woman nodded.

'Travelling around Europe?'

'Just Italy,' the larger one said.

'I'm Faith, by the way,' Dolly said.

'I'm Madison. This is Abi.'

'Let me guess, you lost your money and now you're trying to earn enough for your flight home?'

'Just because we're all American doesn't mean you're entitled to our life story.'

'Ouch. I wasn't prying. You girls aren't on the run, are you?'

Abi eyes flashed.

'Whoa, I was joking. What did you do?'

'We didn't do anything!' Madison snapped, taking Abi's hand in a grip that was more than friendly. 'We had good reasons to leave.'

A wave of sympathy rushed over Dolly. 'I'm sorry, I didn't mean anything by it.' She sighed, bit her lip. 'To be honest, I was just chatting with you hoping to find out more about the people who own the house.'

'Didn't you get the briefing?' Abi asked.

'Briefing?'

'Yeah, we all got it. There was like a whole thing we had to read.'

'Oh, did they email that to you?'

'Yeah.'

'I was only drafted in last minute. The agency just called me up two hours ago, so I didn't get any of that.

It's just that everyone keeps talking like they're some big important person.'

Madison scoffed. 'I'd never heard of them.'

'Wait, what?' Abi turned to her. 'They didn't mention any name in the briefing.'

'No, I know, that quiet woman who works here said it.'

'What was it?' Dolly asked.

'I don't remember. I didn't recognise it. The rest all just call her *"La Signora"*.'

Dolly frowned. 'What was in the briefing?'

'Just loads of crap about her being very important and respect must be shown at all times, yadda, yadda, yadda.'

'No one is allowed to go upstairs,' Abi added.

'Yeah, that was in there. The other rules were just like what we had to wear, where we had to go when we got here, all that. I eavesdropped on the other girls talking though, apparently she's like some major rich person. The old kind who you never hear about. She probably owns all the banks, or something.'

'You speak Italian?' Dolly asked.

'No, one was German or Swiss or whatever, so they spoke English to each other.'

'What else did they say?'

'Nothing, just that she was like stupidly rich, like proper-big-houses-all-over-the-world rich, you know. Refined, civilised, European businesswoman. Only not a businesswoman, more like one of those people who are real rich because they own all the land and stuff. Feudal-like. What's that big Jew family that all the conspiracy nuts go on about?'

'The Rothschilds?'

233

'Yeah. Like them. Or the Gettys. Families who made their money two hundred years ago out of something boring but important and somehow still own everything. She's one of them.'

'You seem to know a lot about this stuff.'

She shrugged. 'I read *The Economist*.'

Dolly smirked. 'Who's the quiet woman you mentioned? The one who works here.'

'She's called Paula.'

'What does she do?'

'She's La Signora's maid, or whatever. The only person allowed within ten metres of her.'

Dolly smirked again.

'I'm not joking, that was in the rules too. Not that they'd ever put us rubes anywhere near her. No eye contact, don't speak to her, all that, like she's a gorilla or something.' Her eyes suddenly narrowed. 'What makes you so curious, anyhow?'

Dolly opened her mouth with absolutely no idea what she was going to say.

Just at that moment, a short, stocky woman marched round the corner. She wore an aggressively starched suit and had short black hair that looked like an oil slick. All this together made her look something like a communist dictator.

'Crap!' Madison said, throwing her cigarette on the floor and spitting out the smoke.

Abi threw hers behind her and tried to hold the smoke in.

The woman's eyes stabbed at them. Dolly knew instantly this was the woman they had nicknamed "the Nazi postmistress". It was a good nickname.

Her silent fury was tinged with a well-hidden

desperation that only her eyes betrayed. 'Where's Paula?' she snapped.

The girls shrugged.

Her eyes noticed Dolly. Appraised her designer dress. Statuesque figure. Makeup subtle and sophisticated.

'You, come with me,' she barked.

'What for?'

'You will deliver La Signora's evening drink.'

'Me?'

'Can't you do it yourself?' Madison asked. 'Or are you not allowed?'

The woman's eyes flared. 'I distinctly told the agency *"No Americans"*.'

'I'm American,' Dolly said.

The woman appraised her again. 'Yes, but you're different. You have the bearing and grace of a European.'

'You've barely seen me stand up.'

The woman sighed. 'But like most Americans you don't know when to be quiet. You will not say a word to La Signora. Now follow me.'

'*Good luck*,' Abi mouthed.

'And you two,' the woman started, turning back round to face them, 'are lucky there is a breeze tonight or you would have been dismissed without pay. La Signora despises the smell of cigarettes.'

She looked up the side of the house, just as Roberto had looked up the hillside to Capella Angeli. But she wasn't looking for salvation.

Dolly followed her gaze. The creamy yellow façade, clean and perfect like icing on a cake, started above the small window into the servants' corridor, rising up the path of a green drainpipe, to the tall ground floor windows. These windows were framed with the green leaves of a climbing plant, its tendrils extending up to the painted green shutters of the second story. The reach of the creeper did not extend to the modest peephole windows of the third floor, the servants' quarters. Above these small punctures, the terracotta tiles of the roof jutted out, and yet there was more. Three storeys above the four women, a room was built into the roof of the villa, in the style of a Renaissance castello tower. A yellow light burned in the window, and the window was open. *La Signora despises the smell of cigarettes.* Smoke travels. What else travels?

Dolly gulped.

THIRTY-ONE

When Cain closed the servants' door, leaving Dolly in the green chamber, he found himself in a narrow windowless passage, sealed in pitch black. He groped for a light switch with no luck. He had too much pride to open the door again. The good news was that no light meant no one was using this corridor tonight.

After a minute, his eyes adjusted, and he could make out a silvery glow. Soft moonlight from a small window. The corridor sloped down as he walked carefully towards it, his hand trailing along the wall for balance. He reached an odd, half-moon window and looked out. He was along the front wall of the villa, his head now at ground height. He could see down the long path, all the way to the gates, to the lights on the hillside opposite. Somewhere up in the vast dark wall of the mountain was the chapel they had used as a lookout post earlier today.

A few guests were still making the long walk, and he wondered again why guests weren't permitted to drive up to the main entrance. Was there a genuine reason, maybe the drive was too narrow for cars to turn? Was it just because a hundred limousines queueing and idling was ugly? Or was it something else? Maybe it wasn't a practical reason. The owner might choose to make all their guests endure the long walk so they admired the house and its grounds. Or was it a great leveller, so there was no competition to show up in the best car? Or was it, as Cain suspected most, a forced show of deference? Like the long walk to the altar. He could only speculate.

Feet crunched on the gravel outside the window. Guards patrolling. He slunk back into the shadows and continued walking, yellow light now bleeding down the passage. He reached a junction and glanced down a lit corridor. Bare bulbs above a queue of waitresses. At the front of the line, each one passed a tray of empty glasses into the kitchen and was given a loaded tray of canapés.

He stopped one of them. '*Aspetta!*'

She froze.

He took a canapé from her tray and made a show of eating it.

He nodded. '*Vai avanti.*' And let her go.

He made his way along the line of waitresses until there was the unmistakeable bark of someone in authority. The head of a short woman with shiny black hair bobbed into view. He ducked up a set of stairs to his right, hovering on the half-landing, hoping to head back down when she had gone, but her voice approached the stairs, so he quickly zipped up to the floor above. There was only a small door, and nowhere to hide, so he skipped up the next flight, waiting in the shadows by the next door. Still, she kept coming. He slipped through the door and pulled it not-quite-shut behind him.

Watching through the open crack, he saw the

short woman climb to the first floor and call up.

'Paula?'

She moved past the door and up to the next floor, out of Cain's sight. Distantly, he heard her call again.

'*Paula!?*'

So much for his plan to stay downstairs. Cain let the door shut and turned to assess the dark corridor he had found himself in. He was on the first floor, near the back of the house. To his left, a door was open to an unlit room. He could smell the sweet night air from the gardens. He could feel a draught and hear the ripple of conversation, shoes clacking on stone, and the lake licking the shore.

He padded into the room. With the moonlight streaming in through the tall windows, it only took him a moment to make out the shapes of the furniture. A bedroom. Sparse, impersonal. A *guest* bedroom. He stood to the side of the open window, making sure he wouldn't cast a silhouette, and looked down to survey the crowd of partygoers. There were long tables set out with mouth-watering displays of lobster tails, caviar, and other food he couldn't make out. There were three bars, one on the patio behind the house, two more in the middle of the gardens. At each a team of four were shaking cocktails and popping bottles of fizz to satisfy an eager throng. A flame erupted from a bartender as he used a blowtorch to char orange peel. Titters of laughter bubbled up from the crowd, and from all the plus-ones came the constant flash of selfies. Looming over them all, a huge moon turned the rippling lake into a sheet of silver glass.

There were two people directly below the window, an old European woman and a young

American man. Cain couldn't see their faces.

'Scotty Singh, nice to see you again.'

'Marie. I wondered if I'd see you here.'

'Where was it I saw you last, Monte Carlo?'

'I believe it was Kuala Lumpur.'

'I'm sure you're right. Everywhere is starting to look the same.'

There was something performed and insincere about the exchange. It reminded Cain of the old CIA codephrases used to identify yourself to a contact.

'What brings you to Como?' the woman asked.

'Is this party not reason enough?'

'I suppose it is.'

'And you?'

'We always spend the season at our place on Capri. When we received the invite, I naturally took the short hop up here. I'm staying in our Milan apartment for a few days. Yourself?'

'I'm flying back tonight.'

'To California?'

'Yeah, I'll sleep on the plane. We've got an expo tomorrow.'

'How is everything in the computer trade?'

He sighed. 'We call it tech. We don't make computers, you know.'

'I'm sorry, what do you make?'

'Everything from global network platforms to smart speakers and high-end peripherals.'

'I don't know what any of those things are. I've never got on with computers.'

'How are things in the being-incredibly-rich trade?' he teased.

'You could answer that question yourself, you're

worth ten times what Andrew and I are worth.'

'Touché.'

'What is it you need from her this time?'

'The same as always.'

She scoffed. 'You're one of the richest men in the world, Scotty, how can you possibly need money?'

He paused. Cain felt the tension. As much as he shifted though, he couldn't see them, they were still directly below the window.

'Here, come round the side of the house. I don't like talking in front of the staff, you never know how many she's paid to eavesdrop.'

They moved away. Cain quickly stepped from the window, through the room and back to the door. He peered out. The corridor was still empty. He skipped down it and slipped into a room on the side of the house. It was densely packed and in the darkness he had to squeeze past the furniture to reach the window. It was closed, so he opened it just a crack. He picked up their voices instantly.

'I can't believe you're finally going to tell me what hold she has over you,' Marie said.

Scotty sighed. 'I'm a victim of my own success, I guess. It's my fault for taking the company public.'

'But you kept fifty-one percent of it, Simon read it in the *Financial Times*.'

'Simon? I thought your husband's name was Andrew?'

'It is. Simon is our son. Adopted.'

'Well, I kept fifty-one percent of the *parent* company, she let me have that. And even that serves her purposes, you know how she likes to stay in the shadows.'

The woman grunted agreement.

'That's strictly confidential, you understand. The board would force me out it they knew I'd been so stupid.'

'Of course. I wouldn't betray our trust. We promised, remember.'

'I remember. Having someone to talk to about... *her*, is the only thing that has kept me sane, even if we do only run into each other a couple of times a year.' He paused.

Cain could start to make out the room now. It wasn't furniture he had squeezed past, they were glass cases, and more were mounted on the walls. There was something inside them he couldn't make out. Some metal pins. Needlework patches perhaps.

'What about you?' Scotty asked.

'Oh, it's been a huge help for me too. I can't tell you what it's been worth to me. I don't feel alone when I talk to you.'

'No, I meant *what is the hold she has over you?* You never told me.'

'Oh, she's had me for a long time. I'm one of the original cast of these parties. She beckons, I come running. I smile, I wave, I volunteer and donate, and I die inside a little more every time.'

'But what's the hold she has on you? It can't be money.'

A mechanical quality entered her voice. 'A long time ago, when we were both young, she took Andrew from me. He and I were always meant to be together, ever since we were children. Everyone in our circle knew it. She knew it too, and that's why she took him from me. She said she'd give him back to me, but at a price.'

'But it's done now, you and Andrew have been married for forty-five years, you've got Simon, why do you have to keep paying?'

'Oh, no, this wasn't the price. She made me go to a doctor, I didn't really understand what he was doing, I knew it hurt, but I was young and... *ignorant*.'

'Ignorant?'

'In the ways of sex and biology.'

'He raped you? And she made you see him?'

'Oh no. He sterilised me.'

Scotty Singh was silent. Cain was silent with him. He could make out the glass cases now, and he could make out what was inside them. They were butterflies, pinned to canvas. A collection of beautiful creatures, dead forever.

'I...' Scotty started.

'It's quite all right,' she said. 'She knew how much I wanted to be a mother. And it's not that we haven't been blessed with Simon, we have. But if Andrew ever found out, I don't think he'd understand. He says that he would have come to his senses eventually, even if she hadn't rejected his proposal. He says that, but he doesn't *know*. I do. If she'd said yes—'

'How is it all right?' Scotty demanded.

'Excuse me?'

'You said it was quite all right. It's the most horrific thing I've ever heard. Why didn't you go to the police? How can you stand the sight of her?'

Cain was right there with him. Was she mad?

'There's nothing that can be done. Especially now.'

'But how...?'

'How do I live with myself?' She sighed, but it was out of tiredness not shame. 'It's like an absence. A hole really, that I carry around with me. When it happened, it was like a great gaping hole, bigger than me. I thought it would swallow me up. But each day I teetered on the edge I managed to shrink it just a bit. And a bit more. Until today, when I can carry it around in my pocket, even if I can never get rid of it. Sometimes I take my eye off it and it grows bigger, but then I work on it again and —'

'Hello!' a voice boomed.

Cain could've sworn he heard them freeze solid. He froze solid too. *Jo!*

'What are you two doing round here?' Maltby asked. 'She's a naughty one, Scotty, I warn you.'

Cain tried to get a look at him but couldn't.

'I didn't realise you two knew each other so well.'

'Of course we do,' Marie said, recovering quickly, 'we're always at the same parties. Where was it last time, Kuala Lumpur?'

'Yes,' Scotty said, 'and Monte Carlo before that.'

'That's right, yes.'

'Well,' Maltby purred, 'come back and join the party, these bushes are probably full of old perverts trying to cop off with their plus-ones.'

'Don't be disgusting,' Marie mocked as they moved away.

'I'm not joking, you know what these randy old bastards are like, especially when they're drunk. I should know, I'm one of them.'

'Don't be silly.'

'You're lucky one of them hasn't gone after you, Marie, you look so ravishing in that dress.'

'Stop it,' she giggled, 'your wife will hear.'

Wife!? Cain gripped the windowsill.

'Where *is* she, anyway?'

'You know her...' he started.

'I know. *When the work is done...*'

THIRTY-TWO

'Y ou go up the stairs, all the way to the top, along the corridor to the room at the end, there will be a man outside, he will let you in. Put the ice in the glass before you go into the room, but only just before, understand?'

Dolly Lightfoot nodded.

'You put the glass down on the desk, you turn, and you leave. You do not look at anyone, you do not speak to anyone, you do not smile, understand?'

'I understand.'

Jabbering, the "Nazi Postmistress" had explained that La Signora always took a glass of exactly seventy millilitres of Dolin white vermouth, over ice, at nine o'clock in the evening. It was always taken to her by Paula, La Signora's most trusted servant, but Paula was nowhere to be found. Now, with the tray in her hand, Dolly was ushered in the direction of the backstairs with, to her immense surprise, a pat on the bum. She decided not to say anything, *this time*.

The door to the stairs creaked, then her heels clacked on the stone steps, despite a thin carpet runner. She concentrated on the tray, trying to balance it with one hand underneath like waitresses always did. It was frustratingly difficult and she was terrified it would tip, so she resorted to using two hands like a normal person. She trod on her dress and almost stumbled, so then she had to use one hand to hoick it up and go back to one underneath the tray. And she had no hand to hold the bannisters. She was a grown woman, for Pete's sake, she could walk up a flight of stairs without clinging to the banister! She breathed a sigh of relief when she reached the very top.

The cold iron doorknob throbbed with her heartbeat. Gingerly, she turned it. It squeaked like a mouse. The door scuffed open into a dimly lit corridor. The lights on the walls flickered, and to her amazement she realised they were not electric lights, they were candles in holders. A large man in a suit filled the entire end of the corridor and it was hard to see how he could move out of the way to let people through the door he was guarding.

She shuffled down the corridor, muffled voices ahead. As she passed the only other door, it opened into her face, into the tray. She whisked it to the side before it made contact. It tipped, the glass scooted across, hitting the rim. She levelled the tray in time, caught it. The weight of the ice bucket had stopped it going over.

An older man stepped up and out, as if from stairs. He didn't notice Dolly Lightfoot juggling the tray, but she noticed the way he walked silently. She hadn't heard him come up the stairs, and she couldn't hear him now, despite watching his feet hit the floor. The guard squashed himself into a corner to let the man in, and for a second she glimpsed a large desk and someone seated hunched over papers, then it was shut again.

She checked the tray, moving the glass back near

the centre. She hadn't spilt anything. Stopping in front of the guard, she tucked her hair behind her ears. He smiled at her.

'*Giacchio*,' he said.

She blinked. 'What?'

He smiled again. 'Ice.'

She tried to balance the tray with one hand, she was shaking.

The guard held it steady for her.

'Thank you.'

Whilst he held the tray, she used the silver tongs to transfer three ice cubes from the bucket to the glass. They clinked, then cracked with a gentle pop.

'Enough?' she asked.

'One more.' He winked at her.

She added one more and he handed her back the tray.

He gave her a reassuring nod and opened the door.

The room was smaller than she expected. Square, with a small fortress-like window in each wall. The ceiling was higher than the corridor, protruding up from the roof like the tip of a tower. Sitting at the desk was a slender woman in her late sixties, possibly early seventies. Her hair was cropped but layered, and as silver as moonlight. It framed a sharp, but not unattractive face. She was wearing a white dress with a shear top layer threaded with gold leaves. Beneath the desk two feet were crossed in gold sandals. And over the woman's shoulder, framed in the narrow window, the moon and its reflection on the water.

Dolly Lightfoot felt something rarer than rubies: admiration. This was the kind of woman she wanted to be when she was old. *Dignified, powerful, sophisticated.* In her mind she left out "rich".

There were three men in the room. Two of them wore grey suits the same colour as their skin, hovering near the desk, waiting for the woman to sign the document. She was taking her time, reading every word. The third man was the silent one who had entered just before her. He was dressed in a tuxedo, leaning against a bookcase, studying his fingernails as though he had just received a manicure.

There was only one empty space on the desk. Everything else became a blur. Paralysing fear, she hated herself for it. Her feet felt like buckets of water. The ice rattled in the glass as she placed it. She snapped back up straight and turned, she was going lightheaded.

'Leave the ice.'

She froze. The woman had a deep, authoritative voice which glued Dolly's feet to the floor.

The nonchalant man stood up off the bookcase and with a charming smile gently took the ice bucket from the tray.

'Where's Paula?' he whispered in a purring English accent.

Her nerves were like guitar strings, and he was playing them with a razor blade. The age, the charm, the English accent, it all matched Cain's description perfectly.

She went to answer him, *but her American accent would give her away!* He was looking right into her face. Could she fake an accent? Could she remember any Italian? She did French at school. She could just about answer in Cantonese. She opened her mouth but choked on her indecision.

Maltby smiled sympathetically. 'Of course you don't know. Off you go.'

She fled from the room, not looking back. By the time the guard closed the door, she was already halfway down the stairs.

* * *

Fifty-eight kilometres south of Villa Cardinale, Mirella Marino was performing the pre-flight checks on an AgustaWestland AW139 twin-engine helicopter. At the moment Dolly Lightfoot was fleeing down the servants' stairs, Marino was checking the radio was tuned to the correct frequency. Some cowboys liked to fiddle with the frequency. Sometimes she thought they did it just because they knew a woman would be flying it next and they resented her. They resented how good she was.

She dusted down the screens and gave the cyclic and collective lever a wipe. She loved the 139, it had the poise of a rescue chopper with the pulling power of a troop transport, and she was looking forward to when the call came. For once she wouldn't just be circling over the city, chasing cars. She would be zipping over the mountains, rippling the trees. She would have to resist the urge to buzz the small towns. She wanted to come in low, skating over the shimmering surface of the lake, then roar up over the villa. But this wasn't a war movie, this was her job. Right now, it was a clear night with a full moon and minimal winds, but the weather report showed a chance of fog. And they had chosen her. They had chosen her because she was the best. It was going to be a good night's work.

Fog. She had to check the thermal imaging system. They had been very clear about that. Diagnostic checks passed. Everything was in order. She was ready. One more espresso perhaps, she had nothing to do but wait for the call.

THIRTY-THREE

She definitely looked familiar, Maltby thought, but he couldn't think from where. Familiar, but different somehow. Maybe it was the hair. Or the dress. If only she had said something, maybe that would have jogged his memory. Did she recognise him too? Was that why she was so terrified? Was she a local girl? Or did she work in one of the bars in Bellagio? *No.* With a gut-punch of terror he flicked through his mental photo album of the prostitutes he had visited in the last few months. That didn't seem right, either. But... it would explain her reaction.

He would have to find her again.

'What are you thinking about?'

The other two were still waiting for her to finish reading the contract. She was asking *him*. He stood up off the bookshelf.

'Nothing exciting,' he replied. 'I had better go check on our guests.'

'Again? They'll get sick of you.'

'No one gets sick of being told how wonderful they are.' He smiled, adding, 'my beautiful goddess.'

He nodded to the others, who still looked like bait in a shark tank, and left.

Quickening his step down the narrow stairs,

through the hidden door into the second-floor corridor, he joined the main staircase and descended both flights to the ground floor. It was quieter now in the main entrance hall, most of the guests had arrived and filtered through to the gardens, making it easier for him to spot staff. She wasn't here. He walked round to the right, the route most guests took, checking the rooms on the way. Two waitresses. Still no sign of her. He stepped out into the gardens, onto the terrace. He was immediately accosted by guests, all congratulating him on a wonderful party, all asking where his wife was. He humoured them each. A few asked who he was looking for. Every time he replied, 'You, and now I've found you.'

He worked down the right-hand side of the gardens until he could see the boathouse silhouetted against the water. There were no staff this far from the house. He headed back up the other side. Still no sign of her. He tugged at his bow tie, trying to breathe. He moved back into the house and checked the back rooms again. Still empty. He opened the door to the servants' area and descended to the kitchen. He checked every waitress in the queue, but she wasn't there.

He found the housekeeper administering them.

'That girl you sent up with La Signora's drink, where is she?'

Her eyes widened. 'Nothing is wrong, I hope?'

'Nothing to worry about. Nothing at all. Where is she?'

'I don't know, she hasn't come back yet.'

'Let me know the minute she returns.'

'Yes, sir. I will hold her here and call for you immediately.'

He smiled. 'She's not in trouble.'

The housekeeper nodded in a way that reminded him of a keen sergeant he once knew. Always did everything his captain said. Got his head shot off planting a flag.

He worked his way back down the queue, double-checking the women, then he ascended the stairs and was standing back in the main entrance hall.

There was someone new, a guest he didn't recognise. Something about him put Maltby on alert. He didn't fit. Although he was wearing a dinner suit, it was so obviously a cheap one, the collar shiny and synthetic. A small man, perhaps Maltby's age, he was standing with his hands in his pockets, rocking back and forth on his heels. He was making no attempt to progress further into the house, so he couldn't be one of the tabloid hacks who always tried to sneak into the parties, although he had the same unkempt appearance, like an unmade bed. If anything, he looked like he was waiting for someone.

'Can I help you?' Maltby asked, startling the little man.

'Er... my English...' the man replied haltingly, '...not good.'

Maltby asked him again in Italian.

'No, thank you. I'm just waiting for the host.'

'I am the host.'

His face lit up. 'Wow, that's impressive, he went off to find you that way,' he pointed, 'and you appeared a second later this way.'

'Who went to find me?'

'Er, I don't know, he looked like he was in charge so I told him I needed to talk to the host, he went off that way. Tall guy, tuxedo, little moustache.'

This man was clearly a simpleton.

'Like I said, *I'm* the host. Who are you?'

'Oh, *you're* the host. Nice to meet you.' He held out his hand.

Maltby shook it. It was like sandpaper. 'And who are you?'

'You said you're the host, but I didn't catch your name, sir.'

'Maltby. Jolyon Maltby. J-O-L-Y-O-N M-A-L-T-B-Y. Good enough?'

'Joe-Leon? I've never heard that name before. Where's it from?'

'England.'

'Really?' The man beamed. 'I eat Earl Grey tea leaves.'

Maltby frowned. *What?* He was getting very frustrated very quickly.

'What's *your* name?' He said it loud and slow to try and get through the man's thick skull. 'And what do you want?'

The little man reached into his jacket pocket and tried to take out his wallet but it was too tightly wedged. He hadn't got a lot of wear out of that cheap suit. He got it out eventually, but it wasn't a wallet. It was a badge.

'Baroffio, I'm an *Ispettore Superiore* with the Polizia di Stato.'

Maltby's eyes narrowed, then he sighed. Now he recognised the air of a country policeman. He had even got all dressed-up in his off-the-peg policeman's ball costume in the hope he would be invited to help himself at the free buffet.

'Is this about noise?'

'Noise?'

'Have the neighbours complained?'

The inspector shook his head. 'No.'

'Is it about traffic then? We're not responsible for where people park. And there's no special permits needed for having a party, I take it?'

'No, no.'

'Then what is this about?'

'It's a security matter, sir.' He leant forward. 'Is there somewhere else we could talk?'

'We can talk right here.'

'Very well, sir. I'll talk quietly.'

He shuffled even closer.

'Are you aware of the explosion that occurred at a villa near Montepulciano last night?'

An injection of ice water into Maltby's veins. He had noticed the way this bumbling inspector's eyes flashed up to his on the word "explosion". He was inches from his face, he would have read even the tiniest reaction. He didn't believe he *had* reacted, but the body made so many involuntary micro-expressions it was impossible to be sure.

What the hell had happened? How the hell had anything been traced back to him? It was impossible. Inconceivable. *Unbelievable.* And yet here the inspector stood. Half a metre from his face.

'I, er... yes. I believe I did see something on the news.' He smiled, then stopped. What an idiot he was, blindsided by this little man.

'You think you saw something about the explosion?'

'Saw or heard, it might have been one of the decorators who were here today that mentioned it. But what could it possibly have to do with us? You said it was in Montepulciano, right?'

'Nearby.'

'So, I don't understand what it has to do with us.'

'That's a long story, sir.'

Maltby smiled through gritted teeth. 'Well, please... actually, do come through to a different room, I'm sure we can find somewhere private for us to speak.'

Baroffio nodded.

Maltby led him through the house. 'Have you eaten, Inspector?'

'Not, er, no, not properly. I could eat more.'

Maltby turned to a nearby waitress. 'Bring us a selection of, er, whatever we've got. We'll be in the downstairs study.' He pointed to a door near the back of the house.

He led Baroffio into the room. It was lined with those leather-bound books that look great, but nobody reads. They weren't Maltby's taste, too pompous, but they went with the house. There was a tantalus in the corner and an open box of cigars on the writing desk. This wasn't really a private room, just a pretend one to flatter guests. He invited Baroffio to take a seat in a deep armchair.

'Drink?' he asked.

'No, thank you, sir. I can't do that.'

Maltby nodded, poured himself a scotch, and perched on the desk a couple of metres away.

'So, Inspector, tell me your long story.'

'Well, I suppose I can shorten it a bit, I appreciate that you're very busy, this looks like a very important party. I can give you the short version. Although, of course, it doesn't contain all the facts.'

'Go ahead.'

Baroffio hesitated. 'With which, sir?'

'Which what?'

'The long version or the short version?'

'The short version, please.'

'Very well, I only ask because some people, they like the long version, they like to know every detail.'

'Fine, give me the long version.'

'That's very interesting. You see, sir, you're like me: I like to know every detail. Some people, a policeman comes round, they don't know why he's there, they think it's a mistake, he mentions a crime they say they're nothing to do with, they want the short version, they want to get it over with. But not you, sir, you want every detail. The long version.'

'Is it long because of all this preamble?'

'No.'

Just as Baroffio was about to speak more the waitress appeared.

'Oh, wow, look at this,' he said, taking one of the plates piled with cold meats, fish, and salad. 'This looks incredible.' He thanked the waitress first, then Maltby. 'What is this purple fish?'

'It's salmon.'

'I've never seen purple salmon before.'

'It's cured in beetroot.'

Baroffio nibbled a cautious bite, then nodded enthusiastically. 'It's delicious.'

'You were on the verge of telling me why you're here, Inspector.'

'Yes, absolutely,' he said with a full mouth, then took a minute to chew and swallow.

Maltby sighed. The little man was playing games again. He opened his mouth to snap at him, but Baroffio beat him to the punch.

'So, last night there was an explosion at a villa outside Montepulciano, as you heard from one of the decorators. A real tragedy, five people lost their lives, an entire family. Did they mention any other aspects of the story?'

'Who?'

'The decorators.'

'None that I can remember.'

'I just want to make sure I don't keep telling you things you already know.'

'Just assume I know nothing about it, Inspector.'

'I don't want to waste your time.'

'Please continue.'

Baroffio stuffed in another mouthful of food, taking his time chewing.

'An explosion,' he said when he had swallowed, 'is one of the most complicated scenes to process. There's bodies, they have to go for postmortems. There's residue to go to the lab. And then there's the regular forensic evidence, the DNA, blood, fibres, general debris, the works. There has to be a full investigation, like a plane crash or something.'

'Thank you, Inspector, I understand all that.

'Then, of course, there's interviewing the witnesses.'

'Witnesses?'

'Oh yeah, of course.'

When Maltby said nothing, Baroffio raised his eyebrows inquiringly.

'I guess, I just assumed... because of the number of deaths, that that was everybody in the house. That everyone died. The news didn't mention any survivors.'

'Oh, well, the witnesses weren't there at the time of the explosion, but they were at the house before and after. It was thanks to them that we knew what vehicle to look for.'

'Vehicle?'

'Yeah, er, hold on...' He checked his pockets with the hand that wasn't holding his plate. He then swapped the plate to the other hand and searched his other pockets. 'Not there either,' he mumbled. He then tried to put the plate down, but seemed unsure where to put it.

'Here,' Maltby said, snatching it.

'Thank you.'

The inspector then managed to extricate his notebook from his inside pocket (the first one he had checked, Maltby noticed) and took his plate back.

'A silver 1970 Mercedes-Benz 280 SL Pagoda,' he said, flipping through the pages. 'Someone visited the house that evening, driving that car, and naturally we want to speak to them.'

'Well, I don't own one of those, Inspector, I assure you.'

Baroffio smiled. 'Oh, no, sir, I know you don't. In fact, we already found the car last night.'

'You found it?'

'Oh, yeah.'

'Where?'

'What is this?' he asked, pointing with his fork. 'I don't know what this is.'

'It's caviar.'

'Really? I've never had caviar before. I've seen the little tins on sale before. I've wanted to try it. My wife says I should go ahead and buy it, but it's not something I can really afford on my salary, I tell her my shoes don't even cost that much. Do you know how much they cost?'

'Your shoes?'

'Those tins. A hundred euros, some of them. And we're not talking a big tin like tomatoes, or even capers. It's a little tin, like anchovies. Although it looks more like a little tin of boot polish.'

'Inspector—' Maltby tried to interrupt.

'This amount here, this must be like, what... twenty euros worth?'

'More like fifty.'

'Fifty? Wait until I tell my wife. You sure throw one hell of a party.'

'It's for charity.'

'Really, that's wonderful. What charity?'

'It's for the Numan Foundation, for children with spinal injuries.'

'Boy, those kids must be loving this party.'

'You were saying about the car, Inspector.'

'Which car?'

'The Mercedes. Where you found it.'

'Oh, right. Yeah, we found it a few miles from the crime scene. At another crime scene.'

'Crime scene? Then the explosion...?'

'Oh, yeah. I heard people on the radio speculating about a gas explosion, but there's no gas up there to those villas, they all run on generators and old furnaces. It wasn't an accident or anything, it was a bomb.'

'A bomb?'

'Oh yeah, no doubt.'

Maltby nodded. 'You mentioned a crime scene with the Mercedes though.'

'Yes, oh yes. We found some bullet casings and

some blood.'

'But no bodies?'

'Bodies, sir? No, no bodies.'

'It's just that you said you found bullet casings and blood. And a car. But no bodies?'

'No. There was evidence of a third vehicle though.'

'A *third* vehicle?'

'Yes, did I not say? With the Mercedes there was also a carabinieri motorcycle, I'm very sad to say. The officer hadn't reported in since the afternoon. Poor guy, you can imagine everyone is very upset. Everyone in the area, pretty much, seemed to know him. Me being polizia and him being carabinieri I don't believe our paths ever crossed, but it sounds like he was a real nice guy. Apparently, he still used to visit his mother every day for lunch. Someone had to tell her. That's a tough job.'

'I'm sorry to hear that.'

'Thank you, sir. His body has been recovered, along with the body of a local farmer. Both at a nearby farm. Along with the bodies of two unidentified persons, a man and a woman. The dust and dirt on their clothes matches that of the area where the Mercedes and motorcycle were found.'

Maltby's sigh of relief fogged his whisky glass. Cain and Lightfoot were dead: *no warm leftovers to deliver.* Thank heavens they were dead, that was all that mattered now. There couldn't be any evidence linking them to him, the Germans were too efficient for that. *And yet*, here the inspector sat.

'I'm sorry, I'm completely lost. I don't understand what any of this has to do with me.'

'Oh, no, sir, you misunderstand me entirely. This has nothing to do with you.' He waved his hand vigorously. 'I have absolutely no reason to suspect you of anything to do with any of this.'

'Then why are you here? Why did you want to speak to me?'

'Sorry, sir, I'm getting to that. We found evidence of a third vehicle, like I said, tyre tracks, so we have to assume that everyone who left that crime scene, alive or dead, left in that vehicle. Tyres are very interesting, it's wonderful if you're a detective and you find perfect tyre tracks because every tyre is unique. And not just every brand, every individual tyre wears in its own way. It's to do with the weight on the car, the routes driven every day, on tarmac, on dirt, on gravel, which brake pads are older than the others, it's really fascinating. It's like a fingerprint for a car. Luckily for us, these were official Mercedes tyres, not the cheap substitutes like you or I would buy.'

'Mercedes tyres? Then surely the tracks came from the Mercedes?'

'The convertible? Oh no, definitely not. No, they were too far apart, we're looking for a vehicle with a much wider and longer wheelbase. A much heavier car too, judging by the depth. We sent photos of the tracks over to a guy I know near Monza, he said unequivocally that those tracks belong to a Mercedes G-Wagen. Isn't that incredible? I don't know how he does it. Anyway, there aren't that many G-Wagens passing through Tuscany on any given day, so once we had enough kids scouring the autostrada cameras we found the vehicle and were able to trace its journey both backwards and forwards. It came over the border from Switzerland, so we got access to the Swiss cameras, traced it back over the border from Germany, we're still waiting for access to the German cameras.'

So they had to pass by here on their way, was that all it was? Could it be?

'And if they came from Germany,' he said, trying to sound like he was just realising it, 'they would have passed by Como.' He frowned. 'But the autostrada is at least twenty kilometres from here, Inspector, down by the southernmost point of the lake.'

'You're right, they came down from Germany, through Switzerland, past Como, to Tuscany, and did whatever they did. But as I said, we can trace their journey both backwards and forwards. Actually, they even changed the plates to try and avoid the automatic recognition, but G-Wagens are too rare in Italy, the kids found them pretty much instantly.'

'So...?'

'So, having done whatever they did, they headed back north again, towards Germany, heading back the way they came. Except this time they pulled off the autostrada around Como.'

'When?'

'The Monte Olimpino exit.'

'*What time*, Inspector?'

'7:38 this morning.'

Maltby sighed. 'They probably just wanted something to eat, or somewhere to park up and take a nap.'

'They didn't return to the autostrada.'

'Well, maybe they figured out that you'd be able to track them that way, took a different route. If they're professionals, changing the plates on their car, wouldn't they know that? There's no reason they would come up as far as Tremezzo. What are you suggesting?'

'Like I said, sir, I'm not suggesting anything. This is just a security issue. That's why I'm here.'

'What do you mean, a security issue?'

'We believe these people are dangerous. Killers. Twelve bodies last night alone.'

'And...?'

'Did I not say?' Baroffio looked down sheepishly for a moment, then his eyes flashed up to Maltby's. 'The Mercedes, the G-Wagen, it's parked a hundred metres from your front gate.'

THIRTY-FOUR

altby's head swam, the little man's words echoing in his ears: *"it's parked a hundred metres from your front gate."* He knew they must be here for him. Were they observing him now through a high-powered rifle? He felt comfortable expressing his obvious concern and confusion as he casually stepped away from the windows.

'But don't you worry,' Baroffio was saying, 'your safety is my number one priority, I'm going to stick to you like glue.'

Maltby managed a smile. 'I'm not going to let you ruin my evening. And I can't have you cramping my style, I've got to charm these people into parting with their hardly-earned cash.'

'I'm afraid I have to insist.'

'Inspector, who's house is this?'

Baroffio straightened his collar. 'It's yours, sir.'

'And you're a guest. As you can see, we have ample security. We always do, and it's tripled for events like tonight. Obviously, I share your concern. And I appreciate you coming here. You're welcome to seat yourself by the main stairs, or wander the gardens, but I will not permit you to "stick to me like glue". Is that understood?'

'Yes, sir.'

Maltby reached for the door.

'Just one more thing, sir,' the inspector called.

Maltby turned. 'Yes?'

'You mentioned your security, I'll need to speak to whoever's in charge.'

'Excuse me?'

'To make them aware of the situation.'

Maltby opened his mouth to object.

'So they can do their job,' Baroffio added.

Maltby sighed. 'Of course. I'll send them right over.'

'To the main stairs?'

'To the main stairs,' he confirmed, and left before the inspector could stop him again.

At least he was just one policeman, he thought, as he struggled to remember why he had been running around in the first place.

Oh, yes, that random woman. He chuckled to himself.

Oh, God!

He caught his foot on the edge of a half-closed door and smacked his head on the architrave. He rubbed his forehead, but the pain was nothing compared to the realisation he had just had.

He knew her face so well. He had studied it for hours, trying to read what was written there, but only ever in photographs. That was the strange sense of familiarity. Divorced from that context, his brain just hadn't made the connection. Distant continents of his brain, there were no neural links that spanned that reach, no pathways, no route from those photographs to his wife's study. And yet somehow she had made exactly that journey. *Dolly Lightfoot.*

In many ways he *did* know her. He had to get the measure of her as he tailored his lies, his steady drips of information to nudge her in the right direction. She was alive. And *here.* But the inspector had said a man and a woman were dead.

A ray of sunshine entered his heart: *Cain.* Cain was alive. *Good on him.*

Was Cain here?

No. He probably let her go. It would be his outdated idea of chivalry. Maybe she even saved his life? Then he would owe her.

And Dolly Lightfoot had tracked him here? She had taken the car. Changed the plates. *Clever girl.* But how had she tracked him here? He chuckled. Of course she hadn't. This was where she was supposed to send the hard drive. She was looking for Paulo. She knew nothing about him. She knew nothing at all. Which was why she was snooping around.

None of this matters.

She had escaped gangsters and assassins, only to deliver herself into his clutches. He had to find her. Where was Daveed?

It took Maltby two minutes to find him, his diamond earring glinting above the heads of the guests. He was keeping watch by one of the garden bars.

'I need you to find a girl for me,' he said, dragging Daveed nearer the trees.

'Anyone specific?'

'American. Thirties. Dark hair. Black dress.'

'One in particular?'

'She's sneaking around, pretending to be a

waitress. I don't care if you round them up one-by-one, she has to be found. Just... keep it as quiet as you can.'

Daveed nodded.

Maltby returned to the house to check on Baroffio, peering at him from the shadow of the main stairs. He was sitting there like a naughty child. Maltby nodded to himself. *Good boy.* But the little man had a sixth sense, turning his head before Maltby could duck away.

'Would you like a coffee?' he asked, styling it out.

'Sure, that would be great.'

'Ask these people,' he gestured to the staff, 'they will get you anything you want.'

'Excuse me, Mr Maltby,' Baroffio called to his back, stopping him before he could leave.

'Yes?'

'I'm still waiting for your head of security.'

'Has he not been round to you yet?'

'No. Maybe if you tell me his name, I'll be able to find him myself.'

'I'll send him another text,' Maltby said, disappearing towards the gardens. *Stay there, little man.*

His phone buzzed in his pocket. It was a message from Daveed:

"Found her"

That was quick. Too quick, he thought.

"How do you know?" he sent back.

"Lindhardt found her snooping around"

"Send photo"

It arrived half a minute later. Her face scowling like a cornered animal. It was her all right.

"Reception room" he messaged back, then slipped his phone into his pocket.

As he looked up, he collided with a man in a

midnight blue dinner jacket. They were both knocked backwards.

'I'm sorry,' he said.

The man grinned.

Maltby froze.

Cain.

THIRTY-FIVE

'That's the first apology I've ever got from you,' Cain joked.

He watched a genuine smile break over his old friend's face, then Maltby leapt forward and hugged him.

'It's great to see you, old sport,' he whispered in his ear.

'You too.'

'Look at you,' he said, releasing him and taking him in. '*Cain*. As I live and breathe. You've certainly weathered the last ten years better than I have. You've held onto your hair, and your stomach. How have you done that on your diet?'

'*Nine* years. And I may look better, but I feel twice as old.'

'And still a snappy dresser.'

'Well, we always had that in common.'

'Quickly,' Maltby said, grabbing him by the arm and leading him into a small room near the back of the house.

The silhouette of a plant's creeping tendrils danced in the moonlit panel of the window. Dim waist-level light was coming from a reading lamp on a desk. There was an armchair, a button-back sofa, bookshelves, tantalus, and a box of cigars. A clichéd "gentleman's study". It went with the clichéd English gentleman that Maltby played in polite company.

He shut the door behind them, and his voice was low when he asked, 'What happened?'

He decided to play it cool. 'How much do you really want to know?'

Maltby snorted. 'Enough to know what you're doing here.'

'The trade went awry, best I spare you the details. Then, when I was driving with the girl, we were jumped by a couple of pros with enough weaponry to start a small war. What have you got me into?'

'Where's the girl now?'

Was it worry Cain saw in Maltby's face?

'Tied up in the trunk of my car. Messy, but it's the only way I could be sure.'

Cain saw something change in his friend's face but didn't know what. He was having trouble reading him. He couldn't remember lying to him before, not seriously.

'Your car?' Maltby asked. 'Have you even got a boot in that grand tourer of yours?'

'No, I was forced to abandon mine, I'm driving the pros' SUV.'

'I see. Isn't that a risk?'

'I changed the plates, and there are no marks on it.'

'And when did you stop off for a tuxedo?'

He smiled. 'When I saw you were having a party. I didn't think you'd want me drawing attention.'

Maltby nodded. 'Good thinking. Well, you give me

the keys and I'll send you the money. Best if you sneak out one of the side doors, old sport.'

'There are three cocktail bars in the garden, you've got lobster platters on the patio, you're living in a mansion, and you're not going to have a drink with me for old times' sake?'

'I'd love to.'

'Great.'

'But not tonight.'

'Come on.'

'I'd love to. I really would.' He turned and rested his elbow on one of the bookcases, hiding his face. His other hand toyed with a book. 'Ever since I learnt you were in Florence, I've had this fantasy of driving down to visit you. We'd be in some backstreets bar, just like we were in Marseille. We'd laugh, we'd joke, we'd talk about all the scrapes we were in. Then, when they chucked us out, because we'd been talking for hours and hours, we'd wave goodbye to each other and know, as much as we hated to know it, that we'd never see each other again.' He adjusted the book until it sat at the same depth as its neighbours. 'Sentimental rubbish, I know.'

'I would have liked that. Except for the last part. Why didn't you?'

Maltby turned, smiling the way he always did when about to say something they both knew was untrue.

'Because then I would have nothing to look forward to.'

A vacuum of silence formed between them, like a sudden change in pressure, emphasised by the footsteps and snatches of laugher just outside the door.

'I'm really glad you came here. I really am. Two

minutes, barely a hundred words spoken. And I wish I could leave it at that. Perhaps I should just let you leave without asking the question...' His brow was wrinkled. '...but how did you know to come *here*?'

Their eyes locked. Electricity jumped between them like two exposed cables. It had been nice to live the fantasy for two minutes, Cain thought.

'I found this address scribbled on a piece of paper when I checked the pros' bodies. You tried to have me killed. And you tried to make double-sure of it too.'

Maltby's hand dived into his pocket.

Cain's jumped behind his back.

Maltby looked as though he had spat in his face as he slowly took out a hipflask. He perched on the arm of the sofa, his face half in shadow.

He took a swig. 'And yet I'm so glad you're alive.'

Cain marched towards him, trying to find his eyes. 'What the hell have you got into?'

'Get out of here whilst you can.'

Cain watched him.

'No one else knows you're here. You can walk out the front gate, disappear again.'

'I intend to...'

He paused, waiting for Maltby to look up.

'...but not yet.'

Maltby shook his head.

Cain continued: 'Because you want me to walk out, taking the blame for everything you did with me.'

'I don't know what you're talking about.'

'You know exactly what I'm talking about, *Tourmaline*.'

'Your workname?'

'And yet apparently a CIA taskforce leader,

workname Tourmaline, has been contracting out jobs to organised crime lords for the last twenty-five years. And that shit is about to hit the fan.'

'So the girl talked before you put her in the boot.'

Cain said nothing.

'And you think you can trust someone who is trying to convince you to set them free? She would have told you anything.'

'So, it's not true?'

'What is true, is that she stole classified information from the United States government. That information is a threat to national security. CIA, DIA, NSA, the entire Alphabet is after her.'

'Then why wasn't she taken into custody in Hong Kong? Why have her trafficked here by organised criminals, to you? Is that not a risk to national security?'

'I don't think it's your job to question the decisions of the democratically elected government of the United States of America.'

'You're saying the President and the Senate Intelligence Committee know about this operation?'

'I think it's a little bit below their pay grade, don't you? Nonetheless, the intelligence community are an arm of government.'

'Not an elected one.'

'Semantics.'

Cain sighed.

'Is that what you're saying though, Cain? That if the president and all the little congressmen-and-women knew about what I did and were just fine with it, then you'd be just fine with it too?'

'I thought you didn't do anything?'

'Because I get the distinct impression that you're

asking me to justify my entire career to you, personally, soldier.'

'Maybe I am.' Cain nodded to himself. *'Maybe I am.'*

'And how on earth am I meant to do that?'

'Just tell me it isn't true.'

'What isn't true?'

'That whilst I knew you as Sapphire, everyone else knew you as Tourmaline. That you were using me as a, er... a tethered goat, for when the wolves came.'

Maltby smiled and shook his head. 'No. You have it all wrong. I can understand how it looks, but it's not like that.'

'Which part?'

'All of it.'

'You haven't been using the workname Tourmaline?'

'No.'

'It's in the report.'

'Yes, but that was a decision I made twenty-five years ago. It was standard operating procedure.'

'Bullshit.'

Maltby held his hands out. 'It was insurance.'

'Yeah, insurance, exactly. For you. And with every policy there's that bit you have to part with to make a claim. *The excess.* I'm the excess.' He pointed with his bandaged hand, making it throb. 'Insurance indeed, for all your dirty deeds.'

'Dirty deeds? Come on. Are you a child?'

'You paid CIA money to gangsters, and who knows what you got in return.'

'Don't be so naïve!' Maltby snapped, rising out of the shadows. 'I know that's what it looks like to everyone else, to the officer class miles behind the line, but you're smarter than that. You know what spies do: break into apartments, bug phones, hack into bank accounts, smuggle people across borders, blackmail, kidnap, *murder*. All I did was pay the professionals to do it. I got done what Langley and Washington wanted done, and I kept their hands clean. And their consciences.'

'Nice speech.'

'It's the truth.'

'*I know*. It's not that I don't believe you.'

'What is it then?'

'It's that...' he struggled for the words. What was it that really stung him? 'I believed you were an honourable man.'

'None of us are. *None of us.* That's just a fantasy you never grew out of.'

Cain huffed.

'It's a luxury,' Maltby continued, 'to feel like you do. A luxury I granted you. And the rest of them.'

'How many more were there?'

'How many what?'

'Agents. Operatives. Taskforce members like me.'

'There were no other agents like you, Cain. The rest all knew what they were doing. I didn't have to treat them like children.'

Cain ran his tongue along his teeth, looking away from his friend's face. Exhaled. Then looking up, dived back in. 'You remember the debrief when we came back from Djibouti? When they told us we couldn't go to their funerals?'

'Of course I remember.'

'You were angrier than me. Your buddy, Hussain,

you knew his wife, his two boys. You signed-up together.'

'*I said I remember.*'

'Mission or no mission, you would have been at his funeral. Because he was your buddy. Not just a fellow squaddie, a friend. But you were told if you were seen there you'd lose your commission. Do you remember what you said to me?'

Maltby said nothing.

'"Toys, that's how they treat us. Like tin soldiers they can push around. And when they've finished playing they can just sweep us back in the box." But we weren't tin soldiers. We were real people. So we slept overnight in the church, up by the organ, because there was no way they were going to keep us out. You had to be there for Hussain. Even if all we could do was listen from the rafters.'

Maltby looked at his shoes.

'*And* I know what you did for those boys afterwards. Created a trust in their name, paid into it every year. Sent his widow a little money every month too.'

Maltby said nothing.

'You know, that night we slept in the church, we'd known each other for twenty-three days.'

'Why did you come here?'

'I came for the truth.'

'You seem to know everything.'

'I hoped I was wrong.'

Maltby smiled a sad, self-pitying smile. 'Every old spy is someone's loose end.'

The vacuum returned between them.

'Why did you come here?' Maltby asked again.

'I told you.'

'You lied. You're not that sentimental. It's how you've survived so long.' Maltby's eyes were darting now. 'You've come for the file. The report. You think we have it. Why would you think that?'

Cain took a step back.

Maltby's hand snapped round from behind his back. A small black semi-automatic glistened in the soft light.

'We have the girl.'

Cain's eyes narrowed.

'She's not in the boot of the G-Wagen, she's wearing a black dress, she's died her hair, and we have her.'

Cain said nothing.

'I'm going to put this gun away. We're going to go out there. You're going to follow my instructions. And we're going to go to her. And then she's going to tell me everything I want to know.'

THIRTY-SIX

Maltby tucked the gun back into his waistband and gestured to the door.

'Chop, chop,' he drawled.

Slowly, Cain turned his back on him and stepped to the door, opening it quickly. A flow people were passing, heading for the gardens. He waited for Maltby to reach his side.

'Through there, the door at the end.'

He stepped out into a long ballroom, which opened onto the gardens. A pianist was noodling away in the corner, every note crashing onto the hard marble floor. Small clusters of guests were laughing, champagne clutched in their talons. He crossed it swiftly, entering the hallway Maltby had indicated, striding to the door at the end.

'Do you want to do the honours?'

'After you, old sport.'

Cain gripped the handle and gently pushed the door open. Behind his ear, Maltby took a sharp breath.

The room was high-ceilinged and over-gilded, peppered with modern sculptures. A private collection. Through windows to the left the garden guests could be heard, but the view was blocked by thick curtains that looked like they'd stop a bullet. Dolly was in the centre, her arm clasped by a guard with a diamond earring, his other arm poised inside his jacket. There were two other guards.

None of this was what surprised Maltby, of course, and Cain could only deduce that it was the woman sitting in a gold chair on a small dais at the other end of the room. She was flanked by the two other security men, and Maltby must not have known she would be there. She was an attractive woman roughly ten years older than Cain and Maltby, and she was dressed in a white and gold dress of impeccable design. Elfin cheekbones, moonlight-coloured hair, and cold expression, she looked at home among the statues.

Maltby found his tongue. 'Hello...' he stammered.

'You can call her "darling" in front of me,' Cain said.

He didn't look for Maltby's reaction, instead he nodded at Dolly. Her hair was tousled and the man's grip on her was tight, but otherwise she looked unharmed.

'Are you ok?'

She nodded.

'He has a gun,' Maltby said.

The man with the earring nodded to one of the other two. The guard frisked Cain aggressively, ripping the stitching on his new suit. He held his empty hands out afterwards, having found nothing.

The woman spoke her first words, they were to Maltby: 'Close the door, you cretin.' She exhaled the frustration.

Smiling upon her throne, legs crossed, but leant slightly forward, she studied Cain. He returned her attention, trying to align her with the image he had formed overhearing the two guests whose life she seemed to own. It didn't take long. He saw in her face the same thing he had seen in Luka's the night before: this was a woman who could be very cruel.

'Cain,' she purred. 'I know so much about you, I feel like I'm meeting Jo's first wife.'

'You have me at a disadvantage.'

She grinned. 'Obviously.'

Maltby returned from closing the door. 'They think we have the file.'

'Why else would they be here?'

'I'm sorry I missed your wedding,' Cain said. 'I'm a little insulted I wasn't your best man.'

'Slap her,' she said.

The man with the earring raised his eyebrows.

'Slap her, Daveed. I want to see his reaction.'

Before Cain could say anything, the man crashed the back of his hand into Dolly's jaw. She would have hit the floor if he hadn't been holding her so tightly. Tears pricked the corners of her eyes as she glanced up at Cain, a red mark glowing across the side of her face.

'Let go of her,' the woman said.

She leapt to Cain's side, clearing her eyes with the back of her hand.

Daveed circled them until he was three steps behind Cain, covering the door, his gun out.

Cain turned back to the woman. 'What's next?'

'You're only in this room so I know where you are. My business is with Dolly. I want her to speak, not you.'

'What do you want?' Dolly croaked.

The woman smoothed flat the front of her dress. 'You have no doubt deduced that it was us who manipulated you into stealing the Tourmaline Report.'

She waited for a response. Dolly said nothing.

'An eight-month-long tactical operation,' the woman continued, 'involving a team of twenty researchers, analysts, and agents. The person you knew as Paulo was a work of fiction, designed by our team, tailored to your individual prejudices. This part of the operation was highly successful, you agreed to steal the file and deliver it to us. However, the Agency became aware of your intentions and thwarted, we thought, your attempt. And so, just as in all failed operations, a wrap-up plan was put into action. You would be captured, debriefed, and executed. And to avoid any opportunity for blowback, Tourmaline's former networks would be purged of anyone with the potential to compromise his identity.'

'You mean *Sapphire's* former networks,' Cain said.

Her eyes rolled over to him.

'*Cain.*' The word slithered out of her. She slipped her hand into a pocket hidden in the folds of her dress, turning something over with her fingers. 'I don't know what kind of upbringing you had, what Jo knows he never shared, and I was never interested enough to ask. I myself was very fortunate. But I did have to endure some of my father's games.'

She paused. He waited. Where was this going?

'We were very rich. In the town where we lived most of the year, my father owned the bank, the main street, a large number of the neighbourhoods. If someone couldn't pay their rates or their mortgage, they could transfer the property to him and he would settle any debts. They would then pay their rent to him. Even the local council sold the town hall to him and leased it back. He built up a nice collection that way. Of course, it was nothing compared to our family's assets.' She shrugged. 'Some men have train sets, he had the town. But his favourite game was to send me to the shops with less money than I needed to buy what he sent me for. He did it to teach me a valuable lesson. The first time was for a packet of drawing pins from the stationers, I was eight at the time, and I always carry a pack with me now to remind me.'

Cain could hear them shuffling in the packet as she turned it over in her pocket.

'Some of the shopkeepers were happy to be short-changed just to stay in my father's good graces. Some of them took pity on a young girl, terrified of going back home without the items her father had sent her for. Some got angry the second time, or the third, and had to be reminded of the power my father had. Others rolled over every time. I had to be able to tell, that was the lesson. Fear or pity, carrot or stick. If I failed, my father would play his other game with me. I understood why, of course, the stakes had to be real or I wouldn't learn. I learnt very well.'

She took the packet of pins from her pocket and threw them across the room to Daveed. He snatched them from the air.

'His other game he mostly played with the staff. If one of them stole something, broke something, or if he caught them out in a lie.'

Daveed dragged a small table from the corner of the room, then opened the packet on it, in front of Cain and Dolly. He laid out three of the brass pins, their points dancing to a stop.

'This game was much simpler. You could explain yourself, but every time you spoke you had to slam your hand down on one of the drawing pins.' She smiled sweetly. 'I'll make this simple for you, Cain. You *can* speak, but every time you do, you must slam your hand down on one of those pins. I can't abide wasting time. This game will teach you brevity.'

'And if I don't?'

She gave the tiniest twitch of her head. In a flash, Daveed snatched Dolly's hand and slammed it down on the first pin. She screamed, collapsing to the floor as he let go. Cain lurched at him, but the man's gun was already at his belly. The other two guards had drawn theirs the second he had moved, they pointed them across the room at his chest.

He looked at the woman on her throne. She was grinning. *Bitch.* He knelt down to Dolly. She was whimpering, drawing in sharp breaths. She was cradling her hand but she let him look at it. The brass pin was embedded in the pad of her palm below her thumb. It wasn't a serious injury, of course, but that was the point. It hurt enough, but would never leave a scar.

He pulled it out before she could protest, and pulled her to her feet. She sucked at the dot of blood that formed.

The woman raised her eyebrows, daring him to speak. He said nothing.

'And now...' She rolled her eyes over to Dolly. 'You being here can mean only one thing: that you succeeded in extracting the report from the NSA station in Hong Kong in a physical form. You've come here either to deliver it or, more likely, to recover it, having deduced from conversations with Cain the true nature of this enterprise. A search of the house is underway, but in order to expedite the search I am willing to make you an offer.'

'I don't want your money.'

'I'm not offering you money. I would never, ever trust an arrangement so insecure.' She paused, again smoothing flat the front of her dress. 'I have a house, a villa, you would call it, by Lake Lucerne, not too dissimilar to this one, although built in the Swiss style, of course. Rather gaudy, if I'm honest, looks like something Disney would build. It gets marked on tourist maps as a castle. But that's ridiculous, of course, because it's not a defensive structure and would function very poorly as one. It has over thirty rooms. Tennis courts. Ten acres of gardens. A boat house. Some dreary American owner installed a bowling alley in the sixties, if that's your sort of thing. I've no idea if the mechanism works.'

She brushed an errant wisp of hair from her forehead and continued:

'You would live there, on your own, for the rest of your life. You would have a household staff, and the house would be yours to do with as you wish, so long as you do not exceed an agreed annual budget. Your access to the outside world would, of course, be limited. Television would be fine, but no phones or internet. After some months, should you prove trustworthy, you would be allowed visits to nearby villages, to ramble over the mountains, to sail the boat out on the lake, all accompanied by security who will be there to supervise you, although for appearances sake they will appear to be your protection. Think of it as house arrest in one of the finest houses in Europe. Or think of it as the idyllic early retirement so many dream of. It will be a very comfortable life. A lonely one, perhaps, but that will be no change for you.'

Dolly said nothing. Cain was proud of her. She just stared at the woman, who slowly, subtly smiled.

'I know you play the revolutionary, Dolly, but it's not out of any great political desire to change the world. It comes from a disappointment in your life, Dolly's life, not the career of an NSA Officer. Your life is not all you dreamed it would be. It never will be. And I cannot offer you that, but I can offer you something deeper, more primal, that which you have been longing for since you first drew breath: safety, security, *no more worries.*'

Still Dolly said nothing.

'And I would be prepared, under the condition of an established fiction, perhaps you've been hired to look after the house when the owner is not living there, for you to have your mother visit you, shall we say... once a year? I would also be willing to provide the money to keep your mother in the greatest possible comfort as she ages. I know she's thinking about retirement, what with her recurring wrist problems, her arthritis.'

Cain heard Dolly's sharp intake of breath.

'She's been hoping to save up enough to finally leave her job at the textile mill, hasn't she? There's a wonderful retirement home just twenty miles from where she lives, close enough for all her friends to visit. Private room. They have games nights, movie nights, trips to the theatre. And the local rep group even come and perform Gilbert & Sullivan tunes every Christmas. Your mother does love musicals, doesn't she?'

Dolly gulped before speaking. 'How do you know all that stuff about my mom?'

'Intelligence was gathered as part of the operation.'

'Intelligence?' Cain scoffed. 'And what part of the Alphabet do you work for?'

She just looked at him. She gave him two seconds, then she twitched her head again. Cain slammed his bandaged hand on the table. There was the low, heavy heat of last night's wounds, and the sharp, cold pain of the pin. It was quite a package. He gripped the edge of the table with his left hand. He couldn't help the low groan that escaped him.

'Jo and I were CIA,' he continued, 'Dolly is NSA. Who do you represent?'

She didn't answer.

'Or are you just in this for yourself?'

'You can't be that naïve?'

'He isn't,' Maltby said, stepping forward, 'Cain knows the truth as well as I do. After all, we learnt it together, didn't we? *People* give orders, Cain. Some of those people are employed by the government. Some of them get paid with our taxes. That doesn't make their decisions right. Or moral. And I know you agree with me, whether you admit it or not. If they ordered you to drown a sack of kittens you wouldn't do it.' His smile dropped. 'You need to convince Dolly to take the offer.'

Cain said nothing, sucking air in through his teeth as he braced against a rolling aftershock of pain from his torn hand.

'I'm British,' Maltby continued, 'you're Canadian, and yet we both serve the interests of the government of the United States of America. We don't do it because we're proud American patriots, we do it because we know it's for the greater good. NATO, "the West", whatever you want to call it, represents the democratic way of life.'

'And that's what you're fighting for? Democracy?'

'That's another pin,' the woman called.

He looked at her. She gave him less than a second. He slammed his hand on the table. He felt it pop the skin of his palm. His legs went weak, but clinging to the table he stayed up. The pain dimmed fast enough for him to get his legs back. Daveed put out another.

'We're fighting for what we've always fought for,' Maltby said, 'but now we get to issue our own orders. I'd like to think we could do a damn sight better than the politicians.'

'The status quo,' Cain struggled through gritted teeth.

'If you like.'

'The establishment.'

'That's what I'm against,' Dolly said.

'And you, Cain?'

He didn't answer.

'Can't you see what we're doing? Can't you see it's all for the same cause? Don't make her kill you. We should be working together, once again.'

Cain said nothing. Sweat was dripping into his eyes. He looked at the woman.

'You can answer,' she said.

'Can't I see what you're doing?' he spat.

He held his bandaged hand up to Maltby's face, the round heads of two pins looking like brass blisters.

'You need to convince her to take the offer,' Maltby said.

'What happens to Cain?' Dolly asked.

The woman hesitated, almost sighing, before she answered. 'Cain will be executed whether you accept the offer or not. That is non-negotiable, and you have no power over his fate. And no responsibility either. He will die. You are only choosing for yourself.'

'No. I won't take your deal.'

Cain looked at her. 'You've got a way out. You should take it.'

Dolly ignored him, her eyes were fixed on the woman's. She raised an amused eyebrow.

'Tell him,' Maltby said. 'I think it will help him understand.'

'Very well,' she drawled, 'But he will still be executed, whether he convinces you or not.'

Maltby didn't argue.

'Have you heard of Robert Raskin?' she asked Cain.

He shook his head.

'He's Deputy Director of the NSA,' Dolly said.

'Correct. And he's also the man who inherited the results of the Tourmaline Report from his predecessor, who commissioned it. Robert Raskin did not approve of the report, or rather of the investigation. One does not mark the CIA's homework unless one wants the CIA to start marking theirs. Which Robert Raskin did not. And so he buried the Tourmaline Report within forty-eight hours of it arriving on his desk. It was the only sensible course of action. But it does open up an opportunity for us.'

'How?' Cain grunted.

'Like any sensible large enterprise with a great deal of capital at expense, my various trusts and funds have political forecasters. For the last two years those forecasters have predicted that Senator Landon Temple, the junior senator from Louisiana, will be named the Democratic Party nominee for President within the next two electoral cycles. Within that scenario there is a more than fifty percent chance that he will win the presidency. He would be the first president from the Deep South since Carter, although less of an intellectual. Due to the Duke University connection with his father, he would be expected to appoint the by-then Director of the NSA, Robert Raskin, as Secretary of State. The other scenario sees him appoint Raskin as National Security Advisor. That's if a particularly isolationist Republican Senate seem likely to deny his cabinet appointment.'

'And?'

'And at that point Robert Raskin ceases to be a member of the intelligence community and becomes a politician. In the intelligence community, suppressing the Tourmaline Report would win him plaudits with the few who knew about it, a sort of grudging respect. But a Secretary of State of the United States of America who saw fit in his former role as Deputy Director of the National Security Agency to suppress evidence of sustained criminal activity by the Central Intelligence Agency would present an outwardly liberal Democratic presidency with no small problem.'

'And you're basing all this on a forecast of what *might* happen in the next decade?'

'Yes,' she replied plainly, as though any other behaviour were ludicrous. 'Think of it like a stock option. One stock option in our vast portfolio.'

'But it was Jo who committed this "sustained criminal activity", you don't even think it was wrong.'

'That's quite beside the point.'

'Which is?'

'Robert Raskin is ambitious. Wherever he ends up, he will not want to lose that position. If we play him right, we will have sustained and considerable influence over him.'

'Blackmail.'

'I think that's another pin, don't you?'

He didn't hesitate. He didn't want to give her the satisfaction. After all, the fear and the pleading was where the real pleasure of game lay. He slammed his hand on the table, giving out a violent groan. The pain was everywhere now, rising like the tide, his whole skeleton wanted to leap out of his body. His legs quivered, betraying him. Sweat was pouring down his sides.

'Supervision,' she said. 'We're not doing it for our own interests.'

'A firm hand on the tiller?' He choked out the words.

'Precisely. Making sure it can't wander too far this way or that.'

'A righteous cause, Cain,' Maltby said. 'She keeps the politicians in check, whilst you and me go out to battle. Out in the provinces. Turning the natives against each other. All to protect the citadel, like the knights of old. Chivalry, and all that rubbish.'

'The citadel?' Cain smiled, masking the pain. 'The Belvedere is one of my favourite walks. I make sure to get up there a few times a year, to see the city change with the seasons, you know.'

'Sounds lovely.'

'It was built so the Medici could get into its walls from their palace if the city came under attack.'

'Fascinating,' Maltby drawled.

'You see, the citadel is already the most protected part, built to save the rich. Whilst all around it the ordinary people live their lives. And die on its steps.'

'Well, maybe I didn't choose exactly the right metaphor.'

'I think you did.'

'Steady on, old sport.'

'The knights of old were mercenaries, not old romantics. They fought only for themselves. And if they didn't get paid, they'd switch sides.'

'That's enough now,' the woman said. 'You will be executed. I only explained it to you to reassure Dolly that we're not bad people. We're the good guys.'

Dolly laughed.

The woman was not amused. 'Think about everything I've said. Your life in Lucerne, your mother. That is the carrot, there *is* a stick.'

THIRTY-SEVEN

M arie Roussel gave a long, withering sigh as she watched the hordes of rich and ignorant young people crowding the cocktail bars, taking selfies. The way the men slapped and punched each other, the way the women shrieked with laughter, so abrasive on the ear. They were not here to donate to the charity, they were here to be seen here. But not even by the people actually here, but by people on Instagram, whatever that was. *So unsophisticated.* What was wrong with young people these days? Then she remembered herself at that age. She must have seemed just the same to women of her mother's generation, let alone her grandmother, and that's the age she was to these kids after all. The cycle was beginning again, and soon many of them would be caged birds like Scotty and herself. Except that none of them looked important enough.

Whilst looking round she noticed a man standing near her, also observing. Although she knew he must be younger than her, she classed him as "older". He had the ingrained tan and hairy hands of a southern Italian. He was not exactly good-looking, but he had a face that a mother could love. He looked like a faithful old dog. Simple, sweet, loyal. He reminded her of her husband. He had the same awkward look, wore his dinner suit with the same discomfort, although it was noticeably cheaper than anything Andrew would buy.

He smiled warmly at her and she smiled back.

'I don't suppose you know if any of them serve coffee?' he asked.

She chuckled. 'No, I don't think they do. The closest you might get is an Espresso Martini.'

'That means they have an espresso machine though, right?'

'Unless they already have it chilled.'

He frowned. 'That's not really what I'm after.'

'I'd love a tea, myself.'

'They've got all these staff around, we must be able to find someone who can make tea and coffee. What do you say?'

She hesitated for a moment, but then he smiled again.

'Why not?'

They retreated inside through glass doors, entering the long ballroom where the pianist was noodling away. There were tables and chairs set out, most of them empty.

'Excuse me,' the man said, stopping a nearby waiter, 'I don't know if you remember me, I was sitting by the big stairs.'

'Of course, sir.'

'I don't suppose you would be able to get the lady a cup of tea?'

'Certainly.'

'And a macchiato for myself?'

'I'm sure we can do that for you, sir. Where will you be?'

'Oh, we'll wait right here. Or... is it ok if we sit at that table over there?'

'Certainly, sir, you may sit wherever you like.'

'Thank you.'

As they approached the little table, the man pulled out her chair for her. *Such a gentleman.*

'I'm Marie, by the way,' she said as he sat down opposite.

'Baroffio.'

'Is that a first name?'

'No, but it's what everyone calls me.'

She frowned, but he smiled again, and she couldn't help smiling back. His cheery demeanour was infectious. She envied him.

'So how do you know our hosts?'

'I don't actually.'

That explains it. No one who knows Liese is that happy.

'I just met him, Mr Maltby, tonight,' he said.

'Oh, you mean Jo. Charming man, the son of a lord they say.'

'Really?'

'So they say.'

'I don't really know anything about him.'

'You're not somebody's plus-one, are you?' she asked with a cheeky smile.

He smiled back. 'No, I'm here alone. Yourself?'

'Alone,' she replied, adding hastily, 'my husband hates this sort of thing.'

'See, my wife's the opposite, she's going to be jealous when I tell her about this.'

'Why didn't you bring her?'

He hesitated. 'Well, there wasn't really the opportunity.'

'You're a corporate guest, are you? Here on

business.'

'Yes... I'm here on business.'

Another caged bird? She wondered. Didn't want to get his wife involved, the same way she hated whoring herself in front of Andrew. *But he said he didn't know them. And he's so cheerful.*

'You said you hadn't met Jo before tonight?'

'No, well, this isn't really my area, you see.'

'Yes, I can tell,' she said kindly, taking another look at his shiny tuxedo.

'Tell me about him.'

'Oh, well, he's British, *English*, you know that. The son of a lord, like I said. At least, that's what people say. He's er...' She trailed off, thinking. *What else is there?* 'You know, I don't actually know that much about him. Not in that way. They've only been married five years, or not even that.'

'What does he do?'

'Well, I don't know what his official job title is, I'm sure there's some arrangement, but he basically assists her with everything she does, whatever it is she has to do, with her companies, her assets, whatever you want to call it. I'm sorry, I never had much of a head for business. He comes across a bit like...' She tried to find the right description. 'You know how the president has a Chief of Staff, a bit like that. I guess he's part-advisor, part-bodyguard, part-secretary. This is only from what I see, of course.'

He nodded, looking quite happy with her feeble explanations. 'And before he married her?'

'You know, I haven't a clue.' She considered for a moment. 'Although I've always got the impression he was in the military. A lot of Andrew's family, that's my husband, were in the military, not Andrew, God rest him, and you could always tell which ones. I think it's in the way they stand so straight.'

Baroffio nodded.

'Just like how you can always tell a policeman, don't you think?'

He was about to speak but was interrupted by a waitress arriving with their tea and coffee. He thanked her and asked if he should tip. She said no.

Her turned back to Marie. 'I didn't know what the rules were, you know. I didn't want to be rude by just assuming.'

She chuckled. He really was sweet.

He took a sweetener dispenser from his pocket and popped one in his coffee. 'You mentioned her companies, what business is she in?'

'You mean...?'

He said nothing, just raised his eyebrows as he stirred the sweetener into his coffee, waiting for her to finish the thought.

'You really don't know who she is?'

He shook his head.

'But you're here, how could you not?'

He showed no signs of understanding.

'You've heard of Vermuth?'

'Like Cinzano?'

'No, not vermouth, *Vermuth*. It's the family name.'

'Should I have?'

She was shocked for a moment, but then shrugged. 'No, I suppose not. I just assumed that because you were here you...' she trailed off again. *Not a caged bird.*

'Is it the name of the company?'

'Well, yes, and no, it's...'

He raised a quizzical eyebrow.

'They own the bank of Lichtenstein. Or at least they used to.'

'Jo and his wife?'

'The family, Vermuth. But that was a hundred and fifty years ago. They used the money to form a trust, or fund, or whatever it's called, to invest in a range of companies. Obviously, each generation of the family had children and marriages and divorces and the Vermuth trust was divided amongst more and more people. Some family members sold their shares, some of them sold them to hundreds of small buyers, or to other trusts or funds, its value having risen so much over the generations. It was officially broken up in...' she thought, 'the seventies it was, I believe, into five or six smaller trusts, or funds, or whatever. It's like a cell dividing and dividing and dividing. Constantly growing and splitting.'

'Like a cancer.'

That made her smile. 'Liese got to keep the name, I believe. Her trust remains intact. She doesn't sell shares. She doesn't sell at all. She just buys. She's rich beyond imagination. Beyond comprehension. *Not that you'd always know it,*' she added under her breath.

'What do you mean by that?'

She backtracked. 'I didn't mean anything specific.'

'It kinda sounded like you did.'

She looked up into his faithful old dog face. It was so innocent, so trustworthy, she couldn't resist it.

'It's just... sometimes the richest can be the meanest, can't they? Her father, I was just thinking of. When he couldn't look after himself anymore, she put him in a home. She could have afforded any care he needed, or any home he wanted, but instead she put him in the local charity run home in the town they grew up in. It was a very spit-and-sawdust kind of place, especially after he had stopped donating to them.' She used the back of her spoon to pin the slice of lemon floating in her tea and bleed it. 'He didn't last long.'

THIRTY-EIGHT

Dolly Lightfoot stared at the monster on the throne, repulsed by her previous admiration for her. Cain, Maltby, Daveed, the two guards, they were nothing more than blurs on the edge of her vision. She was so focussed they were starting to grey out. Only the centre was in colour. Her focus. *La Signora.* Dolly was waiting for her to speak.

'Do you know what the biggest lie in the world is?' The old woman said at last. 'It is that there are things money can't buy. It's a lie invented by poor people to make themselves feel better. And there is nothing that I do not have enough money to buy.'

La Signora's eyes were now locked on her, like a tiger in the grass. It made the hairs on the back of her neck prickle.

'As part of the intelligence gathered on any subject, we compile what is known as a "fear file". Fear is an incredibly strong motivator, and when you need to press someone, like a torturer, you need to know which tool to use. I have all the tools I need to use on you. And I'm not talking about the pathetic fears: rats and snakes and spiders. I'm talking about the horrors that keep you awake at night. The news stories that make you shudder. The greatest horror. Not death, death is... easy. Death is not a universal fear, not for those without children. But you share the great fear that all us women share: to be some man's victim.'

Tiny bugs were crawling under Dolly's skin.

'You're walking down the street, a van pulls up, the door rolls open, you're bundled in, the van speeds off, you're never heard from again. But for you the nightmare is just beginning. Most are never found. Except perhaps, charred bone fragments found a decade later in the base of someone's wood stove. Sometimes they do survive. You read about women who have escaped from basements after ten years. And they were just there the whole time, next door, in a suburban neighbourhood. And what good did all their screaming and shouting do them? When you see the stories on the news your brain shuts down because you don't want to imagine it. Then, in the middle of the night, when you're tossing and turning, unable to sleep, that thought enters your mind, that deep fear: *what if it happens to me?* So you reconcile yourself with the thought that *I would just kill myself.* But you wouldn't be able to, it's not so easy as that. And they don't give you the opportunity.'

She paused for effect. No one said anything. She knew she had their attention and Dolly hated it.

'You see, our deepest fears are not animals, or items, or people, they're scenarios. And I know what your scenario is. The one that keeps you awake at night.'

There *was* something. One thing. It had terrified her since she was a teenager. Images flooded her mind, but she shook them away. She couldn't know.

'Oh, I but I *do* know.'

Dolly let out a whimper. *So pathetic.*

'I know the details of it.'

How?

'I know the detail that makes you turn on all the lights, check your apartment door is locked, and watch clips of *Gilmore Girls* on YouTube to comfort you. That scenario will be your life. What's left of it.'

Cain lurched forward. 'And you'd do that to a fellow woman?'

The woman sniggered. 'It won't stop there.'

No!

'Oh yes, your mother too. But not the same scenario. Her fears are simpler. She's afraid of dying alone, but who isn't. She's afraid of being old and poor, but who isn't. She'd suffer all of those, and just about anything else, so long as she knew you were happy and healthy. She worries about you, she always has. She can't help it, you're her baby girl. What would destroy her would be to know what that man did to you. To read about it. To see it when she closes her eyes. To hear it in the quiet still of the night.' Her voice was almost a whisper now. 'I think that would be the worst horror of all.' Then suddenly, she perked up with a smile. 'Which does make things, logistically-speaking, much simpler for us.'

THIRTY-NINE

'So, you don't really know anything about Jo's life before he married Liese,' Baroffio remarked, trying not to sound too interested.

'No, I guess we've never really asked him. Why look a gift horse in the mouth?'

Marie looked embarrassed. He said nothing.

'I probably shouldn't speak like that, but it has made it much easier, her having someone approachable to speak to, rather than having to go through one of the security guards or some timid staff member of who's even more scared of her than we are.'

'Who's "we"?'

Marie blinked. Twice. 'Excuse me?'

'You said "we".'

'Did I?'

'Yes, you said it twice.'

'It must have been a slip of the tongue.'

'I see. I thought you might have been referring to your husband, Andrew.'

'That's right.'

'But you said he hates this kind of thing.'

She looked terrified for a split-second, and then relief flooded her face as she spotted someone over his shoulder.

'Scotty!' she called. 'Come meet my new friend.'

A lanky young man approached. He was lean and looked artificially healthy. He shook Baroffio's hand with a relaxed smile, but then he read something in Marie's face and quickly sat down between the two of them.

'What's the matter?' Baroffio heard him whisper in American-accented English.

'You don't work for her?' Marie asked Baroffio, ignoring the man.

'No.'

'You promise?' There was a note of desperation in her voice.

He nodded. 'I promise.'

'And you don't work for *him*, either?'

'What's going on?' Scotty asked.

'He's been asking me lots of questions about Jo and Liese. I didn't realise it until just now.'

'Who are you?' Scotty demanded.

'I'm a police officer,' he answered calmly, switching to English.

He took out his badge and casually handed it to the American like it was a new wallet he'd asked to see. 'Baroffio, Polizia di Stato. That's a lovely accent you've got, by the way. Texan?'

'California,' Scotty corrected him as he handed back the badge. Then he lowered his voice. 'Why are you interested in Jo and Liese?'

'I'm not. If I asked too many questions, that's just force of habit. I apologise for upsetting you, ma'am.'

Scotty was studying him. Baroffio knew the type, used to being the boss everywhere they went. They never respond well to police.

'You're not a guest then?' Scotty asked. He spoke slowly, warily.

'No, I'm here on business.'

'And what business is that?'

'Police business.'

'What are you investigating? Surely you're allowed to tell us.'

Baroffio shrugged. 'Well, there's what I'm allowed to do and there's what would be a good idea. They're rarely the same thing.'

'Something financial, I'm guessing.'

'He was asking about Vermuth,' Marie said.

'No,' Baroffio replied, 'it's nothing financial, they leave that to much smarter people. It's murder.'

'Murder?' Marie gasped.

'But I have no reason to suspect the involvement of our hosts. No reason whatsoever.'

'Then why are you here?' Scotty asked.

'I'm here for their protection.'

Marie leant forward. 'What have they got to do with a murder?'

'Nothing at all.'

They both sighed.

'But...'

They tensed up again.

'...certain enquiries have led us to this address.'

They frowned.

'Like I said, I'm just here for their protection. I was just curious who I was protecting.'

'What would you like to know?' Scotty asked.

'I was just curious what Mr Maltby did for a living. He's the one I've spoken to.'

'I told you he works for the trust.'

'That's not true actually,' Scotty said. 'Technically he works for himself. Liese's charitable foundation employs him as a consultant, he's not involved with the investment fund.'

Scotty stopped. Baroffio wanted to know more, so he said and did absolutely nothing.

'I'm hoping to poach him for my own company,' Scotty explained. 'Obviously, we did some background work.'

'What did he do before that?'

Scotty smiled. 'He was British Army Liaison with the State Department.'

Baroffio raised an eyebrow.

'Pretty impressive, huh?'

Baroffio nodded agreement. 'Which side did he work for?'

'What do you mean?'

'Well, was he employed by the British to liaise with the Americans, or was he employed by the Americans to liaise with the British?'

Scotty frowned. 'Well... I don't know. I didn't read it off his LinkedIn page, we had investigators, they... they had to investigate. I mean, he's British, isn't he?'

Baroffio nodded. He saw a tingle of fear in Scotty now.

'Is that everything you wanted to know?'

Baroffio rocked his head from side to side as though considering the question. 'Just one more thing.'

'Yes?'

'A hypothetical.'

Scotty's eyes narrowed.

'If two people were afraid of Liese Vermuth.

Really terrified. Hypothetically, what would they be afraid of?'

Marie was trembling.

Scotty smiled as though it were an amusing, purely academic question. 'She's a very rich woman. That kind of money can mean life or death for a company, I don't think you'll find anyone here who wants to get on her bad side.'

'I see.' Baroffio nodded to himself. 'Well, does anyone know where I can find her?'

'I'm afraid we can't help you there. No one has seen her all night. Come on, Marie...' he said.

She leapt out of her chair.

'...let's go get a real drink.'

FORTY

Liese Vermuth adjusted her engagement ring. The sapphire had worked its way round to the inside of her hand.

'I have made the choice as easy for you as I can,' she said, looking down at the stubborn American girl. 'You can reconcile yourself to the knowledge that there was only one sane, reasonable choice you could make. No one could possibly expect you to act differently. For your sake, or your mother's.'

The girl said nothing. Liese could see the fear in her, why hadn't she cracked?

As the silence drew on, she ran her tongue over her teeth in frustration. *Stupid American woman.* She found herself really hating her. She was dispassionate with most of her victims, they were just cattle to be led. But this insignificant woman with an inflated sense of herself was like a stubborn mare. The mares couldn't understand that all their mothers were glue. She needed the whip.

'Perhaps you don't believe me?'

'I believe you,' Dolly hissed.

'Don't flatter yourself that you have it in you to resist me.'

'When they came for me in Hong Kong I was willing to jump off a bridge.'

'As I said, death is easy.'

Dolly shook her head. 'You haven't understood me. None of you have understood me.'

'Dolly—'

'It's Agent Lightfoot, actually. I am an agent of the National Security Agency, and whilst I may have burned that bridge, I still have the nation's security at heart. It's people.'

Ha! 'Funny—'

'Shut up and listen for once!' she snapped back.

Vermuth choked on her tongue. *Tread carefully, little girl.*

'You all think I stole the report because you made me do it.'

We did.

'Sure, you may have pushed me over the edge, and Cabrera gave me the opportunity, but I did it because it was the right thing to do. It's the principle that convinced me, it wasn't anything you said, or any of the lies you told. It was the truths you told. What Maltby did as Tourmaline was wrong. What the NSA did by covering it up was wrong. The choice I had was clear: lose my job, my freedom, maybe even my life, to do the right thing. And you convinced me to do the right thing. To make the hard choice. And now you put me in exactly the same situation, and you expect me to take the easy option?'

Dolly wasn't shy now, wasn't looking down, afraid of her. Her eyes were blazing, matching everything she gave her.

'*No!*' she bellowed. 'I won't do it!'

Cain was smiling like a proud uncle.

Vermuth seethed. *You won't smile like that when I kill you, old man.*

* * *

Silence descended over the room, but Dolly's words still echoed. Cain watched the acceptance slowly settle into the woman's face as she realised Dolly was committed to her decision. There was a roar of laughter just outside the window, and in Cain's mind the logistics of exactly how they were going to kill them began to dominate. They had to do it here, in the room, because the second they opened the door they could scream and shout, and there couldn't be any witnesses.

'So be it,' the woman hissed. 'You're only slowing us down, we'll find it within twenty-four hours. You've achieved nothing.'

'Then why are you still trying to convince me? Do it now.'

The woman nodded at Daveed.

He pulled a suppressor from his pocket and casually screwed it onto the end of his pistol. Cain watched Maltby retreat towards the window, out of the firing line.

The calm descended on him once again. This was ok. They had kept their dignity. He could go out like this.

Dolly's hand brushed against his and he took it, trying to share the calm with her.

* * *

Dolly took his hand, trying to give him some of her strength. The poor man had been through an ordeal with the drawing pins. He had been cut down, and now there was nothing he could do to save them. *So what?* They had fought the good fight.

Like a gunshot, the door opened, flooding the sounds of the party into the room. Everyone span. A bumbling man was standing in the doorway with a look of embarrassed shock. *Drunk, no doubt*, she thought.

'John!' Cain called to him, 'How are you!?' advancing on the stranger and dragging her with him. 'You remember Dolly. Dolly, you remember John.'

Cain grabbed the man's hand and shook it violently, gritting his teeth through the pain. The man's other hand was still on the doorknob. She took it in hers, not letting go until Cain had forced the man backwards into the corridor and all three of them were in view of other partygoers.

'You must have me mistaken,' the man said in Italian-accented English.

Still holding him tight, Cain smiled. 'You know, you're right. My mistake.'

'*Sta' senza pensieri*,' the man said, smiling at them both.

Cain released the stranger's hand and she saw there were spots of blood on his dressing.

'Say, that's a hell of an accent,' the man said. 'Texan?'

'Canadian,' Cain replied offhand.

Dolly felt someone's breath next to her ear. It was Maltby.

'My dear,' he said, grasping her wrist behind her

back. Her other arm was stretched out in front of her, still held by Cain as he tried to lead her into the party.

'You think you want the same thing,' he whispered in her ear, 'but you're wrong. You want to publish it. He wants to destroy it.'

Then he let her go, and Cain dragged her off into the party.

❋ ❋ ❋

Maltby turned his attention to Baroffio. The little man's show of embarrassment at bumbling in had vanished, he was busy watching Cain and Dolly disappear into the gardens.

Maltby heard his wife's steps approaching behind him and felt a twinge of fear.

'Inspector,' he said loudly enough that she would hear, providing her with a vital briefing in one word. 'You've been sneaky.'

Baroffio's eyebrows shot up.

'Pretending you don't speak English.'

'I said my English was not good, and it isn't. Not as good as your Italian, I mean,' he replied in perfect English.

Maltby's electric smile flickered across his face.

'Who are you?' Vermuth shot.

'Inspector,' Maltby purred, 'may I introduce my wife, Liese Vermuth.'

'A pleasure to meet you, ma'am.'

'Who are you?' she repeated.

He produced his badge. 'Baroffio, Polizia di Stato.'

'What do you want?'

'I don't know if your husband has mentioned—'

'That a Mercedes believed to be driven by two suspected assassins is parked on the street outside? No, he hasn't. What do you want?'

'Excuse me, ma'am?'

'It's not a difficult question, is it?'

'No, ma'am.'

'Well then?'

Baroffio straightened his bow tie. He looked like a child asking the scary lady next door for his ball back.

'Well, ma'am, I would like to stay here at the party for your protection.'

'I think my security team can handle it, thank you.'

'If I'm here I can also call for backup if an emergency occurs.'

'We can use a telephone.'

'I understand, but I won't get in your way, I promise. I'll just sit quietly in a corner and be on hand if you need me.'

'How gallant,' she drawled.

'Excuse me?'

'No.' She said it low and slow. 'You are an uninvited guest. As a police officer you have no right to enter private property without an invitation, and any invitation my husband may have given you is now rescinded. You are disinvited.'

'That's not strictly true, ma'am, there are a number of situations when a police officer can enter private property without invitation.'

'To arrest someone, to pursue a criminal, to break-up a disturbance. Are any of those situations happening now?'

Baroffio shrugged. 'No, I guess not.'

'In this situation, do you have any legal basis to stay if I simply ask you to leave?'

He thought for some time before answering. 'No.'

'Well, I believe I have already asked you to leave.' Gesturing to one of her guards, she added, 'This man will make sure you do.'

* * *

The RIB rocked gently beneath Polizia Locale Officer Abramo Ricci as he stared through the night-vision headset. Laying low in the boat, on his belly, with his vision restricted by the goggles, was strangely disconnecting, as though he were floating on the water himself. The water was still tonight, the lake was quiet of traffic, the sky was clear, and the moon was bright. All made their job much easier. He and his colleague were tasked with tracking any boats that tried to leave the villa. No one was going escape the net, not tonight.

His eyes were trained through the headset into the green world of infrared-vision. After the first hour they had started to sting from staring at the LCD for so long, but now they had adjusted, and the weird thing was that the world didn't look green at all. Just black and white.

He stared across the rippling glass surface of the lake, to the boathouse, and the shore of the promontory around it. There were no boats to be seen, but the boat house was on the shadowed side and there were enough secluded places for a small launch to hide. This guy was dangerous. And he was a pro. Tracking him this far was a lucky break. If he got away, they might never catch him again.

In the last few minutes he had felt the cold hand of damp on his neck. His years on boat patrol told him fog was coming. It would be here within the hour, and it would make their job much harder. If the guy was smart, he would wait for the fog.

There was a flash, then a flickering light in the window. It glowed in the infrared display, far warmer than anything else in his vision. His colleague piloting the RIB had spotted it too. Should they report it?

It kept flickering. A candle, nothing more. But it meant one thing for sure: *someone* was in the boathouse.

FORTY-ONE

Cain kept his grip on Dolly tight as they moved through the crowd in the gardens, only releasing her when they reached the first bar. He ordered them both a Ramos fizz.

'What's in it?' she asked, rubbing her arm.

'I don't know, I just know it takes a long time to make.'

One-by-one, he picked the drawing pins out of his bandaged hand. When he looked up he saw bodies slicing through the crowd at an angle. Security officers slowly flanking them, like white blood cells swarming towards an infection.

They stopped on the periphery, not yet attacking, their eyes on them at all times.

'We'll be safe as long as we stay among people,' he said.

'But the film isn't among people.'

'We don't know where it is. Our best bet is to hover near the main entrance and leave with a big crowd.'

'I just told that woman I was willing to die to expose the report.'

'What difference do you think your death will

317

make?'

'The point is to try.'

'And what about exposing the report? What difference will that make?'

Her eyes burned into his. 'Very little, probably. But we have to chip away at that mountain. Every time corruption and hypocrisy are exposed it turns one, or ten, or ten thousand people's heads, and makes them see the world the way it is, even if just for a moment.'

'Is that really worth your life?'

'My life isn't worth that much, Cain.'

'Everyone's life is valuable.'

'Says the person who's killed six in the last twenty-four hours.'

He looked away into the crowd.

She sighed. 'I'm sorry. Actually, no, I'm not sorry. We're both willing to spend lives fighting for what we think is important, the difference is that I'm only paying with my own.'

'I didn't kill the woman, you did, and you're gambling with my life too.'

'You're free to go, sneak out like you said.'

'I didn't mean it like that. I intend to see this thing through to the end.'

'Why?'

He felt like laughing, but it wasn't funny. *Chivalry, and all that rubbish?* 'Because they're bad people. And despite your irritating personality you're a good person. And I may be able to help.'

'This isn't a bar fight.'

'No, it's an assault.'

'And you're the type that crosses the street to help?'

He turned back to her. 'Always.'

She was watching the circling security guards. 'And what'll happen when you get too old to take them on?'

'I'll lose. But it hasn't happened yet.'

She sighed, then smiled. 'It looks like there's no getting rid of you.'

A hand slapped onto Cain's shoulder. 'I'ma have to see what we can do 'bout that.'

It was Daveed, head of security, with his flashy earring and even flashier grin. Cain could feel the man's strength in the hand that gripped his shoulder.

'I don't know what it is y'all hoping to do, but you ain't going to be able to do it, friend.'

'What are you going to do,' Cain asked, 'shoot us before we even get our drinks? Might be a bit messy, don't you think?'

'Oh, I got ways, don't you worry 'bout that. I got ways. But for now, I'ma stay here and enjoy your company. You can tell me all about how you plan to stay right here, with your elbow on this bar, until the last guest has gone home. And I don't care if the two of you pee your pants in the meantime, for real.'

'And if we were to wander off?'

'You'd hit the ground before anyone knew what happened. They'd hear the sound of a glass breaking, a thump, and there would be you on the floor, face down, and I would be trying to help you back up saying something like, "Hey, friend, I think ya had a bit too much, let's get you somewhere cooler," and then I'd drag your corpse down to the boat house.'

Cain nodded. He could probably do it.

'Your drinks, sir,' the barman announced, placing

two foaming Ramos fizzes next to Cain's elbow.

He gave the barman a fifty euro note and told him to keep the change. Then he took a sip, placing his broad frame between Daveed and Dolly. Smacking his lips, he nodded his approval.

'This one's for you,' he said, and pretending to slip, threw the other one down Daveed's front.

The big man jumped back. A foaming mixture of gin, lemon juice, lime juice, sugar syrup, orange flower water, vanilla extract, egg white, cream, and soda water dripping down his suit from stomach to groin. Cain could hear it fizzing. It slopped onto the stone terrace. Daveed looked like he wanted to kill him right there and then, but the nearby guests were staring, there had been a great gasp when it happened. Instead, a big, shit-eating grin cracked Daveed's face.

'You're a child, you know that, for real.'

The barman passed him a cloth.

'I'ma stand here wet,' he declared, wiping himself down, 'I don't give a shit!'

Then Cain saw the panic flash into his eyes. Daveed flattened him against the bar as he ran past, scanning the crowd and signalling to the other security men.

She had taken the initiative just as Cain trusted she would. The few seconds distraction had been all she needed. What she would do now though, he had no idea. What hope did they have of finding the film?

He merrily took another two sips of his drink whilst those around him continued to throw scowls. Daveed was ten metres away, barking into the microphone in his cuff, then he marched back to the bar.

'Just so you know,' he said, jabbing a finger at

Cain's chest, 'I'm the one that's gonna kill you.'

FORTY-TWO

Dolly leant her weight on the tree trunk. Her legs were burning, adrenaline coursing through her body. She had run from the bar, through the crowds, straight into the dark world of trees and bushes beyond the edge of the manicured lawn. She'd been crouching there now for twelve minutes. Time to make a move.

Keeping low, she circled round towards the house. Her stupid heels were sinking into the soft earth and she had to walk on tiptoes. Every time she snapped a dead branch she froze like a deer in a hunter's gunsight, but there were no footsteps, no searchlights. Finally, she made it to the side where she had sat with Madison and Abi. They were still there!

She burst out of the trees, startling them.

'Thank God you're still here.'

'We're not *still* here,' Madison huffed. 'We've been working, we're just on another break. *Jesus Christ*, you look terrible, what happened to you up there?'

'What?'

'The last we saw of you the Nazi Postmistress was stealing you away to deliver La Signora her nightly blood of virgins, or whatever she drinks.'

'I need some different clothes.'

'You wanna swap?' Abi asked.

'They're too similar, are there any uniforms or anything?'

'I think there's a changing room for some of the male staff, for the chefs and stuff.'

'Can you grab me some of their clothes? I don't care what they look like, I just need to look different.'

'What did you do?' Madison asked.

She thought for a moment. 'I threw her drink all down her.'

'By accident?'

'Not really.'

'Damn!'

'She was rude. Look, I need those clothes.'

Madison shook her head. 'I applaud you for sticking it to that old witch, but if they catch us we won't get paid.'

'Please.'

'Sorry, no.'

She looked at Abi, but she shook her head. If Madison said no then it wasn't happening.

'I'll give you this dress once I've changed.'

Madison frowned. 'I don't think we're the same size. Plus you're about six inches taller than either of us, more like eight, it won't look the same.'

'What do you care? It's Dolce & Gabbana, you can sell it.'

'It's Dolce & Gabbana?'

'Yes.'

'Like genuine? Not a knock-off?'

'Genuine.'

Madison rocked her head from side to side,

weighing up the options. 'You drive a hard bargain,' she answered at last.

Five minutes later she returned with a bundle of clothes. Black men's trousers, a black men's shirt, and black men's shoes. Dolly had to change in the cold night air. Abi shielded her eyes, but Madison sat back and watched. Her eyes bulged when she saw the bullet scars.

Everything fitted except the shoes.

'These are way too big,' she complained.

Madison shrugged, taking a drag on her cigarette. 'I thought you'd have big feet.'

'I'm not an ogre.'

'Hand over the dress.'

Dolly handed her the folded bundle.

'Good luck,' Abi mumbled.

'Thank you.'

Madison held the dress up against herself, checking the length. 'How did you enjoy being Paula for five minutes?'

'Being what?'

'*Paul-a,*' Madison enunciated.

'Who's Paula?'

'*Paula.*'

Dolly just stared at her.

'The woman you stood in for. Although I'm sure she never threw the woman's drink over her, timid little mouse by all accounts. She's all anyone can talk about tonight: Where's Paula? She's not here. She's not in her room. She's not downstairs. She's not upstairs. Paula, Paula, Paula.'

Paula. She had addressed the envelope to "Paulo", their nickname for SãoPaulo1974. If a package arrived here addressed to Paulo, what would they assume? They might not even notice the one-letter difference.

Dolly's instincts were tingling.

'Is that unusual, Paula not being around?'

'Well, I don't know, but people are talking like it's pretty darn unheard of.'

When someone breaks their routine, analysts pay attention. Just like when she gave away her fish. That let Cabrera know she was planning something. And now Paula. She was La Signora's most trusted servant, "the only person allowed within ten metres of her," and tonight was the night no one could find her. Who was this "timid little mouse"? Someone else beaten down by La Signora? Someone looking for an opportunity to get one over on her boss?

A snatch of something Daveed had said to Cain echoed in her ear: *"...drag your corpse down to the boat house."*

'Where's the boat house?' she blurted.

'My guess is down by the water.'

'Is there a map?'

'Do you have a map of your house?'

'My house isn't on an island.'

'It's not an island, it's a promontory.'

'Whatever. I'll find it myself.'

She turned, heading for the trees.

'You're welcome,' Madison said.

She looked back. 'Thank you. Really.' She paused. 'Obviously, don't tell anyone.'

'Obviously,' they replied in unison.

She stepped down through the treeline and was absorbed into darkness, holding onto branches to avoid slipping. When she turned to look back the gradient was steep enough to hide all but the roof of the villa and the single tower room. The light was off, *she* was not in residence. Dolly stared at the black square of window, mesmerised, just as she would sometimes peer into the darkness of her neighbours' apartments.

The light came on. She threw herself on the ground. Had the woman sensed her? Did she know she was being watched?

She peered up at the yellow glow through the treetops. It was like the searchlight of a prison watchtower. *You can do this, Dolly Lightfoot. You can do this.* She scrabbled backwards down the slope, heading for the water's edge, until enough layers of trees shielded the glow.

FORTY-THREE

Cain had reached the bottom of his Ramos fizz. Daveed was still staring at him. Cain could tell he was picturing all the ways he could kill him, but he didn't care, he just smiled. She was gone now, he thought. Whether she found the film or just escaped, he would never see her again. *Good for her.*

Some of the partygoers were still wary of him, having witnessed the drink-tossing, but most had moved on, replaced by only slightly different people. There was a ripple of backslapping and enthusiastic greeting that made its way through the crowds towards him like a torpedo just below the surface of the water. When the crowds parted, Maltby emerged.

They said nothing to each other.

'Whiskey sour,' he said to barman, adding, 'use the Reserve.'

'You always had expensive tastes,' Cain said. 'At least now you can afford them.'

Daveed stepped close to Maltby, whispered something in his ear.

'You can go change your shirt,' Maltby replied, 'I'll take over the babysitting.'

The security chief frowned. 'I'ma take over the

search for *her.*'

'Marvellous idea.'

With a glare at Cain, Daveed left.

'Can I get you another...' he looked at Cain's foamy glass, 'whatever-that-is?'

'No, thank you.'

'Hey, Jo!' another guest interjected, 'Great party!'

'Thank you! Have you had enough to eat? Don't forget to write a big fat cheque.'

'I already have!'

'Then don't waste your time thanking me, you keep enjoying yourself,' he said, patting the man on the back and sending him off into the crowd.

The barman handed Maltby his whiskey sour and he nodded his thanks.

His smile dropped. 'You should have left when I told you to, old sport.'

'You shouldn't have tried to kill me.'

Maltby huffed.

He downed his sour in one, then grumbled, 'Follow me.'

They left the bar, approached the trees, and descended stone steps worn down over the centuries. The crowds were out of sight. To their left Cain could hear the lake licking the shore. After thirty seconds of deepening darkness the steps plateaued, and he heard Maltby strike a match. He lit an oil lamp in a great glass orb. It was fixed into a stone wall by a curving wrought iron arm. Cain guessed this path was the route to a boat launch, or something similar. The sounds of the party had vanished entirely, there was only the sound of the water.

Maltby rounded on him. 'Are you totally stupid?'

Cain said nothing.

'Can't you see what's going on!?'

'Tell me again how it's all for the greater good.'

'Not that claptrap! Do you think I believe any of that!?'

Cain circled him, moving so the lamp was behind him and he could see Maltby's face.

'She collects people.'

'What does that mean?'

The lamplight burned in Maltby's eyes. 'Liese. She collects people. Whether it's through blackmail or money or fear, she gets her claws into them and turns them into marionettes.'

'That's quite a mixed metaphor.'

'I'm serious!'

'You tried to have me killed.'

'She made me! Don't you get it yet?' He looked away, over the lake.

Cain said nothing, watching the back of his head and his tight shoulders.

'I met her when I was still with the Agency. I'd been invited to the ambassador's New Year's shindig in Rome. I was honoured, you know. After so many years in the shadows, living like a monk, operating as a dirty secret, here I was being invited into the light. That was a joke, the station chief didn't even know I was inside the tent. Pudgy man with bulging eyes, he believed the cover, thought I was British Military. They thought I'd muscled my way in from our embassy, some of whom were there, and I had to spend the whole evening avoiding them in case it became too obvious they didn't know me either.'

His frame stiffened. Was he remembering the

awkwardness of the party?

'She was the only person keen to talk to me. I didn't know who she was, but it was obvious she was the guest of honour. The ambassador was put out because she was more interested in me than him. So, being the vain old bird I am, I stuck to her like glue. Then, whilst the fireworks went off and everyone's heads were turned, she laid it out for me straight. She knew who I was, she knew about the taskforce, and she knew what we got up to. She knew it all. I've no idea how.'

'Old sins...' Cain said.

'She had enough evidence to make things sticky for me, and I had to know that the Agency would drop me in ten seconds flat. That was the whole point of us. Then she said she could make it all go away if I gave in my resignation and came to work for her for a massive pay rise.' He chuckled. 'She made it sound quite good, old sport. Private security, nothing more. I was under no illusions that I knew what I was getting into, but I knew for certain what I was getting out of.'

He paused.

Cain said nothing.

'At first, she just wanted to use me for her dirty jobs, the same thing we did for the Agency. None of it was worse than anything we'd done before, if anything it felt cleaner. And the operating budget was higher. Then she saw... "greater opportunities".'

'You married her.'

He turned. 'She trapped me. You can't say no to her. She's always been bothered by men looking to marry her money, she saw an opportunity with a man of a close enough age. It would shut down that nuisance forever. And people don't like her. Socially, I mean. It can be a surprising barrier for even the most powerful, but if people liked *me* it would make things that much easier for her. Easier to lure people into her web, easier to hide her scheming. So there were a lot of reasons, and as I said, you can't say no to her.'

'Do you...?' Cain left the question unasked but hanging in the air.

Maltby's jaw tightened. 'I have... marital jobs to perform, yes...' he bit his lip, 'when I'm the one she wants.'

Cain raised an eyebrow.

'The same goes for me, although for appearances sake I'm not allowed...' he paused, corrected course, 'she arranges women.' He didn't seem to like the look on Cain's face. 'Oh, come on! It's better than you and your occasional fumble with an aging waitress.'

Cain blinked. 'Wow. Somehow I'm still the one being insulted.'

Maltby sighed. 'I'm sorry. It's a defence mechanism. Survival instinct or whatever.'

'You can say that again.'

'You don't understand. I've seen her do it to others. Christ, half the people at this party will be in her collection. You just witnessed her do it to the girl.'

'*Try*. She *tried* to do it to Dolly.'

'The night isn't over yet. She gets her hooks into them—'

'I thought they were claws.'

'Whatever. She gets her claws into them, pierces them, and she has them like a scrap of paper on a thread. The girl will be one of them too. That's what getting this report is all about, it's about getting another person on that thread, not just Robert Raskin, but Dolly. And me too.'

'I thought she already had you.'

Maltby didn't seem to have heard this comment. 'I'm with you, we have to destroy it. Tonight, before it's too late.'

'Why? She said she was going to sit on it. You said it yourself, it's leverage. It's not in her interest to expose what you did.'

'You don't understand, *this is our only chance.* She doesn't keep things here. Once she has it, she'll send it away. It gets sent to her secret repository, even I don't know where that is. Christ, she may even have several, dotted around the globe like server farms. Somewhere there's a great store of people's secrets, gathered and catalogued like all the teeth taken by the tooth fairy, just waiting to be exposed if you step out of line. If you say no to her.'

Cain said nothing.

Maltby stepped closer. 'You and me together, we have to find the report. We have to destroy it for both our sakes. And then we have to kill her.'

FORTY-FOUR

Dolly saw the silhouette as a giant sitting perched on the rocks. The great stone arches that supported its weight were bent legs ankle deep in the moonlit water, its tall windows a pair of eyes looking mournfully over the lake. Now, as she rounded a rocky crag, she saw the boathouse up close. The upper floor was built in the same style as the house, painted the same colour, the roof the same terracotta, a perfect model of the villa. But the boat launch and supporting arches were stained green by lapping waves, like the rotting root of an exposed tooth. Through the leaded windowpanes, she could just make out a flickering glow. A single candle. Somebody was in there.

Dolly clambered off the rocky crag onto the grass, joining the stone path leading to the boathouse door. The door was just a wall of darkness, shadowed in its archway, but she could smell the inside. It must be ajar. She reached out, managing to feel her way through the dark slit without making a sound.

Lapping waves echoed off the bare stone walls, assaulting her ears. This was not a boathouse that had been converted into a summer house or guest chalet, this was still just a boathouse. It was humid inside and the heavy smell of damp and mould imposed itself on her, like wearing someone else's wet coat.

The boathouse was one large space. The furthest third of the floor was open, with steps leading down to the water. Along the walls there were racks of twisting ropes, life jackets, and other paraphernalia. Just before the open steps a single candle was flickering on the ground, and kneeling next to it was a young woman. Even from this distance, Dolly could tell from the red and puffy skin around her eyes that she had been crying.

Not wishing to startle her, she called out gently: 'Hello?'

The woman shot up to her feet, her short heels scrabbling on the stone floor. She swiped quickly at her eyes and picked up the candle.

'I'm sorry, I didn't mean to scare you. Do you speak English?'

'Yes,' she whispered.

Dolly doubted her chosen strategy for a moment, but there was simply no lie she could think of that sounded less ridiculous than the truth.

'It's Paula, right?'

The woman's eyes widened, their glassy surface flickering with the candle.

'My name is Dolly Lightfoot. I work for the American government.'

Paula took a step back.

'There's no need for you to be afraid, I just need to speak to you. Is it alright if we both sit down?'

The woman hesitated for a moment, then nodded. Dolly approached. They sat down cross-legged on the stone, the candle between them, looking like two girls at a sleepover.

Dolly smiled at her, unsure how to start.

'How did you look for me?' Paula asked in bad English.

'Instinct.'

Paula frowned, confused.

'That's not as much of a bad joke as you might think.'

'La Signora, she knows I'm here?'

'No.' She paused. 'Are you hiding from her?'

'No...' Paula wiped her wet cheek, 'I just needed somewhere to... think.'

Dolly nodded, studying her for a moment before speaking. The red puffy eyes. A permanent crevice between her eyebrows, carved by years of frowns.

'Are you ok?'

'I apologise.'

'Don't apologise, it's fine. We all have bad days.'

Paula nodded.

Dolly followed her instinct: 'Bad news?'

'Yes.'

'Something you don't want to tell La Signora?'

She frowned. 'Oh, no. My mother, she's very sick. She will not alive long.'

God. 'That's horrible, I'm sorry. Is she being looked after?'

She didn't understand.

'Is she in hospital? Or with nurses?'

She shook her head.

Maybe she needs money.

'She is too stubborn,' Paula explained, 'the hospital, they say they cannot be ok with her.'

'That's very difficult. Is she ok with you?'

'I cannot visit her, she is in Lucca. It is far away.'

'I understand that. I hate living away from my mom. It cuts me up that I can't just swing by and have a chat. I call her every day. *Used to.* Will you go look after her yourself?'

She shook her head. 'I cannot leave La Signora.'

'She won't let you?'

'I would not ask her. She needs me.'

'Does your mother not need you?'

The suggestion seemed almost absurd to Paula. 'I owe La Signora.'

'In what way?'

She didn't understand the question.

'You owe her, yes? How? What hold does she have over you?'

'Hold?'

'*What* do you owe her?' Dolly pressed.

'This job. She has done a lot for me.'

Not out of charity, I'm sure. 'It's just a job.'

'It is a good job.'

'*Is it?*'

Paula nodded enthusiastically. 'Oh yes. My mother also worked in a big house. Except for Sundays, she only had one Wednesday and Saturday off a month. I get every Saturday.'

'But surely La Signora can do without you for a time? For your mother's sake.'

'She gets very angry.'

'You shouldn't be afraid of her.'

'No, not at me. She gets angry at others when I am not around because they do not do things properly. I cannot leave her.'

Huh? This was not at all what Dolly had expected.

'You're very loyal to her,' she said.

Paula just nodded.

'You think a lot of her.'

'I don't understand.'

'You like her?'

'Oh, yes. She is...' unsure of the English she reverted to Italian: *'forbidabile.'*

Dolly smiled. 'She is that.'

'I wish I could be like her. Whatever problem your government has with her, she will win.'

She looked certain of it. Dolly kept smiling.

'Oh, it's nothing like that,' she said nonchalantly. 'I do work for the American government but it's a personal problem I need to speak to you about. Although it does concern La Signora tangentially. You probably don't know what that word means.'

Paula's eyes narrowed. Dolly thought for a moment.

'Have you ever said something you shouldn't have and wished you could take it back?'

Paula shrugged, then nodded. 'Yes, of course.'

'You see, I sent something here, to the villa, and I shouldn't have. It was a mistake. I meant to send it to my friend, Paulo, and I was in the process of sending stuff here to La Signora too, and I got the addresses mixed up. I know from talking with her this evening that she hasn't seen it, even though I know this is where I sent it. It would be better for me, better for everyone, if she didn't see it. I really need it back. And, of course, Paulo... Paula... I thought maybe it had been given to you by mistake.'

Paula thought hard, then shrugged. 'I don't remember anything like that. I get very little packages.'

'It would have been an envelope,' she pressed, 'a

brown one, not too big. One item in it, not very heavy.'

Paula shrugged again. 'What was in it?'

She hesitated, but she had no choice. 'A roll of film. In a little black pot, like in an old camera.'

Paula shook her head. 'Oh, no, I've not been sent anything like that.'

Dolly sighed. *Damn.* She thought hard.

After a minute Paula began to fidget.

'It was definitely sent here,' Dolly grumbled.

Paula had nothing to say to this.

'As the person most trusted in the household, you still might know where it might be.'

'I don't understand. What is it you want?'

'I sent something here. It would have arrived probably last week. But it didn't have anyone who lives here's name on it, so I guess it just got chucked in a drawer somewhere. I need it back, but I don't know where to look.'

'La Signora?' the woman asked, confused.

Why had she even mentioned her? She could have pretended to be a guest at the party, some American idiot looking for the nude photos she had meant to mail her boyfriend.

She had to run with it: 'If she sees it, I could get into a lot of trouble with her. And that would be bad for everybody involved. It might even get La Signora in trouble. So, for her sake, and for mine, I just need your help finding it.'

'I... I don't deal with anything like that.'

'You don't deal with her mail? Take it up to her, or anything?'

'Yes, of course, but if it didn't have her name on it, it would not have gone to her.'

'Who would have dealt with it?'

Paula shrugged like it was obvious. 'Jana.'

'Who's Jana?'

'The... she keeps the house.'

Housekeeper. 'What does she look like?'

Paula thought. 'She is quite short. Wears men's clothes, like you. She colours her hair with the black pomade like the men used to do in the movies.'

The Nazi Postmistress. Damn! She thought the nickname was just because of the way she looked. She had been so stupid!

'Thank you,' she said to Paula, standing up.

'If I see La Signora, I will tell her about you. I cannot lie to her.'

Part of her wanted to laugh defiantly, another part wanted to kick the candle against the wall and threaten her. By the time she had decided either way, she had already left the boathouse.

FORTY-FIVE

'I can't help you look for it if I don't know what we're looking for,' Maltby said. 'How the hell did Dolly do it?'

Cain said nothing. Behind his old friend, the opposite shore of the lake had faded into mist. The visible stretch of the lake was shrinking. There was no escape, no outside world to dwell on, or dream of. There was only the immediate situation.

'You still don't believe me, do you?' Maltby asked.

'No.'

'You think I'm lying.'

Cain sighed. 'No.'

Maltby just stared.

'I've given up thinking either way, I'm just going to wait to find out.'

Maltby frowned, but ploughed on: 'She sent it in the post, right? If it came in with the name Paulo on it then it could have—'

He stopped at the sound of footsteps.

They were descending through the haze that had formed around the oil lamp. Cain could tell from the figure coalescing in the vapour that it was a man, shorter than average, with an upright walk. Someone who had spent their working life on their feet. When they finally emerged from the mist, Cain could see it was the same man who had burst in and inadvertently saved him and Dolly. Then, he had looked drunk. Here, he looked like the soberest man in the world.

Maltby flared with anger. 'Mr Baroffio, I believe my wife told you to leave!'

The little man smiled as though Maltby had asked him a polite question.

'I was leaving. A guard was escorting me to the main entrance when he received a security flash and had to rush back to the house. I just wanted to check everything was ok.'

'Everything is fine, thank you.'

'What happened?'

'Nothing. *Really.* A bit of an overreaction by our security staff.'

The man had the wisdom, and the self-control, not to say anything. He waited. Cain noticed the cheapness of his tuxedo, the thick soles of his shoes. *Law enforcement, in whatever form.*

'A guest threw a drink over one of their colleagues, they were concerned it might escalate.' Maltby couldn't help giving Cain a pointed glance.

The man followed it.

'Canadian,' he said with a smile. 'We didn't get a chance to be properly introduced.' He marched down the last few steps and held his hand out to shake. 'My name is Baroffio.'

Maltby stepped closer as though preparing to throw himself between them.

'*Piacere,*' Cain replied, holding up his bandaged hand to show why he couldn't shake.

Baroffio frowned sympathetically. 'I'm sorry, I didn't catch your name earlier.'

'Cain.'

'Inspector Baroffio is with the Polizia di Stato,' Maltby announced, 'he's investigating a suspicious car that's been dumped out on the street.'

'A suspicious car?'

'Yes, didn't you say it was a Mercedes of some kind?'

'That's right,' the policeman replied, 'but I didn't say it was "dumped". They might have business here.'

'Who's "they"?'

Baroffio looked down at Cain's bandaged hand. 'That does look bad. How did you do it?'

He smiled. 'Karma.'

Baroffio's eyebrows raised.

'I stole an apple off a tree. Cut myself peeling it with a knife.'

'It looks nasty.'

'It's not that bad.'

Baroffio went silent again. Cain knew he was waiting for him to ask about the Mercedes. He just smiled. It was like a staring contest. Eventually, Baroffio blinked:

'The car was involved in a triple homicide last night. And that triple homicide is linked to another five murders earlier in the evening. And they in turn may be linked to four more bodies.'

'That's alarming. Jo, what kind of guests are you inviting to your parties?'

'Very funny,' Maltby said, 'but the inspector assures me he's just here for our protection.'

'I'm not sure I find that reassuring.'

'He didn't say "reassure",' Baroffio remarked, 'he said "assures", they're different.'

Cain smiled. 'Your English is very good. Far better than my Italian.'

The inspector looked sheepish, his eyes glancing to Maltby and back. 'Well, you know, I watch a lot of American movies. I like to watch them in the original version, you know, not the dubbed version. My mother, she can't speak a word of English, she always watches the dubbed version. I remember one Christmas I insisted we put on the subtitled version of *It's a Wonderful Life*, she couldn't stop complaining, she said Jimmy Stewart didn't sound like Jimmy Stewart. I said, "How can that be possible? *That's* Jimmy Stewart." Do you know how?'

'I suppose because she's used to hearing the dubbed version.'

'Exactly. You might not know, but with dubbed actors they tend to use the same Italian actor every time they need to dub a particular star? So, George Clooney, Tom Hanks, Meryl Streep, the same person dubs them in all their films. Not the same person for the three of them obviously, that would be silly. But if you're a young actor and you get chosen to dub a small part in a Hollywood film and the actor playing that small part turns out to be the next Marlon Brando, then you could have yourself a job for life.'

Cain could see what he was doing. The energy of the conversation dipped for just a moment as his foot came off the accelerator to change gear, then his eyes flashed back up to Cain's:

'Where in Canada are you from, Mr Cain?'

'Montreal.'

'You flew over here just for this party?'

'No, I live in Florence.'

'Ah, *Bella Firenze*, lovely city. My wife and I honeymooned there, a long time ago now. What do you do there?'

'Nothing. I'm retired.'

'Ah, what *did* you do there then?'

'Nothing. I just retired there.'

Cain knew for certain now, he was here for him. They traced his car, the convertible. He knew it wouldn't take them long, but he didn't expect them to trace the G-Wagen here. Policework was all technology now, and it was terrifying how fast it moved. By now they must have spoken to his landlady, to his neighbours. But they wouldn't have photos. Of course, they would all say he was American, but this guy wasn't stupid enough to be put off by that. They had traced the car all the way to the street outside. And now the detective was here, talking to the two men at the centre of it all. Did he know that? Or did he only suspect?

'The five murders, is that the explosion I've heard about?'

'Yes,' the inspector replied, 'yes, it is.'

'What's it all about? The news wasn't very clear about that.'

'What is it all about?'

'Yeah. The news talked about the bomb, talked about how many died, but they said they were winemakers. Why would anyone want to kill a family of winemakers?'

'Well, that may or may not be the case, I can't answer questions about what they said on the news.'

'But do you know?' Cain pressed.

'Well, how much can you ever know about why anyone did what they did? You can ask them once you catch them, sure, but even then...' He shrugged.

'But you must have an idea.'

Baroffio hesitated for a moment. He was watching Cain's eyes carefully. 'Yeah, I've an idea.'

Cain waited, but Baroffio said nothing more. 'Please,' he pressed.

The inspector hesitated, tugging at his earlobe. 'Whilst there's no stigma attached to the people that died, and this is purely theoretical, you understand, I have reason to suspect the murders are connected with organised crime.'

'Organised crime?'

Baroffio nodded.

'In what way? Revenge?'

The inspector shrugged. 'Possibly.' He looked from Cain to Maltby, then back. 'In organised crime there is generally only one good reason to kill someone.'

'What's that?'

He itched his stubbly chin. 'Obviously, I'm discounting the kind of pointless murders that anyone with a gun might commit. And of course people do kill people for revenge. But the kinds of murders that get *ordered* in organised crime? Sure, there's the kind of murder that is purely a business decision. Killing the competition. But that's rare.'

Cain nodded.

'Sometimes people say, "they killed them to send a message". I think they get it from the movies. Sure, they might want people to know they did it, that's not why they killed them. They still had to have a reason to kill them, they just wanted people to know about it.'

'So?'

'Most bosses are intelligent. At least, they know their own business. They are... "savvy", I think the word is. And the only good reason to kill someone is to stop them talking. Because that's really the biggest threat to them.'

'I see. And they'd kill a whole family of innocent people to do that?'

Baroffio nodded. 'That's how these people operate.'

'*These people*,' Cain repeated. 'The person who did this must be pretty serious. Dangerous, I mean.'

'All criminals are serious. All of them are dangerous.'

'But to kill innocent people...?'

The inspector rocked his head from side to side as though weighing up Cain's words. His performance had slipped slightly, he had been bounced into giving honest answers because Cain really wanted them.

'Yes, I guess you're right. Maybe it's simplistic, but as a humble policeman I believe there are really just two types of criminals.'

'Oh, yeah?'

'There are those who are desperate, just looking out for number one.'

'And the other type?'

'They're the ones who just don't care.'

'Don't care?'

'Yes.'

'About what?'

Baroffio shrugged. 'Life. Their fellow men and women.'

Cain nodded. 'The tricky thing is telling the

difference, I guess.'

'Actually, no. I tend to know the moment I meet them.'

'Really?'

'It's my job.'

The look that passed between them was like an electric shock.

'The ones who don't care, they're the ones who are beyond redemption, I guess?' Cain asked.

'I'm a catholic, I don't believe anyone is beyond redemption.'

'And as a cop?'

'I don't believe anyone is beyond redemption.'

The engines of the conversation had stopped and they were now gliding silently through the misty air.

'As you can see, Inspector,' Maltby said, breaking the silence, 'we are all quite safe, everything is under control, and I think now you had better leave.'

Baroffio nodded absently. Then looking up, nodded directly to Maltby, and to Cain.

'Good evening, gentlemen,' he said, and turned to march back up the steps.

'Your English really is very good,' Cain said to his back. 'You understand all the nuances. I don't even know the Italian *for* nuance.'

There was a grin on the inspector's face as he spoke over his shoulder. 'We say "*sfumatura*". It means the "shades".'

* * *

Cain stood in silent thought for several minutes after

Baroffio disappeared into the mist. It closed off the world around them, just as his options had evaporated in front of him. His patronising words to Dolly came back to haunt him:

When the evening started... there were infinite possibilities... a million different roads we could go down. The course of events closes off those roads at a terrifying rate. Over the course of just a few minutes they evaporated before our eyes until only two possibilities remained. I had the power to choose which. I used that power.

Maltby didn't interrupt him. Maybe his old friend already knew what he was thinking and was just waiting for him to announce it.

'I'll help you stop her,' Cain said. 'Because she's evil. Because I want to end the suffering she's causing. But after that, we're through. I never want to see or hear from you again.'

He could see Maltby fight an instinct to smile. 'One last mission, old sport? One last hurrah for Cain and Maltby?'

He said nothing.

'This could be the end of a beautiful friendship.'

He rubbed his bandaged gun hand. 'And this time, it really will be the end.'

FORTY-SIX

A knock at the window made Jana jump. *What the devil!?* Her head snapped round. Who would dare knock on her office window? Surely not a member of staff, it must be some drunk guest, lost in the dark. Her stomach dropped an inch when she saw a pale face floating at the top of the window. Then she recognised the tall American.

It had been almost two hours since she sent her off with La Signora's nightly Dolin, and not long afterwards Mr Maltby had come downstairs looking for her. And then, an hour ago, members of Daveed's staff had come pacing down the corridors, violently searching every room and corner. And here she was now. *Well, well, well.* Satisfied, she smirked her most sinister of smirks.

But the American's facial expression didn't change. She knocked again, and Jana felt a cold chill run down her spine. The American's face was pale and wet. And she wasn't wearing her elegant dress but was robed in dark cloth that hung limply off her frame. As a girl, Jana had been told the superstition of a Jewish dybbuk, the lost soul of a dead person, looking for help.

She shook away such foolish thoughts and

unfastened the window.

✳ ✳ ✳

Dolly pulled the window wide and with her long legs was able to step right over the sill, into the tiny office. If her memory and spatial awareness were correct, this was the tiny office she had searched first. She had thought then that it was the housekeeper's office, and she had been right. If the envelope had been in here all along she would kick herself, it was the first place she looked!

'It's Jana, right?' she asked.

'Yes,' the woman replied cautiously.

She went for it: 'I know what you did.'

Jana turned to pick up the phone. With one swipe of a long arm, Dolly knocked it onto the floor. The old Bakelite cracked and the bell jingled. Jana leapt for the door.

Dolly leant over her and held it shut. Jana clung to the handle. Head and shoulders above the woman, Dolly hissed down into her ear:

'I know what you did. The envelope addressed to Paulo. It arrived here, there's no Paulo, so you opened it, you found a reel of film, and you saw an opportunity to get your revenge on La Signora.'

Jana was pale. A bead of sweat crept from her hairline and dived down her forehead.

'Wha—?' she breathed.

'Don't lie to me.'

'It didn't happen like that.'

Dolly just waited.

'I didn't know who it was for. It was just a roll of film, how was I to know what it contained?'

'You had it developed?'

'Who are you?'

'I work for the National Security Agency of the United States of America.'

Jana looked up at her with gaping eyes.

'You've read the report, yes?'

Jana gulped. 'Yes. Well, not all of it. It's quite difficult to read because the writing is so small, and there are two pages to every photograph. I had to use a magnifying glass. I don't think I could remember any of it.'

'But you know it's watermarked with the NSA seal.'

Jana nodded.

Dolly sighed. 'Are we cool now?'

'What?'

'Do I have to keep holding this door shut?'

Jana shook her head.

'Good.' She relaxed off the door. 'Tell me what happened.'

Jana retreated behind her little desk, staring down at the broken phone as she spoke.

'It arrived in an envelope. It was addressed here, but to a Paulo. There is no Paulo here, so I opened it like I always would. It was just the roll of film, no note or anything. So, I put it in a drawer and didn't think about it. But a few days later I had to go over to Bellagio, and when I grabbed my things, I saw the roll of film and I just... was curious, you know. So, I took it to the one-hour photo place and collected it after my shopping.'

She stopped.

'Go on,' Dolly pressed.

'I didn't look at them until I got back here, and even then, I was so busy that I forgot about them until the evening.'

'And then?'

'I saw that they were photos from a computer screen, and I used a magnifying glass to read what I could, my eyesight is not very good, and I saw that they were American government files, and I knew that they must have been meant for La Signora or Mr Maltby, and then I was very scared. She would be very angry if I had developed the film when I was not meant to, or if she knew I had read some of the files.'

Please, no! 'What did you do?'

'I destroyed it.'

'The film?'

Jana nodded.

'And the photos?'

'Yes. All of it.'

Dolly was stunned, struggling for words. 'Wh… what did you do, throw them in the trash?' She was looking around for the bin in the room.

'I burned them.'

She couldn't move her feet. She slumped back against the wall.

'Were they important?'

She couldn't answer, every time she opened her mouth to speak she needed to breathe.

Jana watched her keenly.

She swallowed enough air to ask: 'Why didn't you just destroy the photos and give the film to La Signora?'

'It was out of the canister. They cut up the film and give you the developed negatives. I couldn't give it to her without telling her I had it developed.'

She was right, Dolly knew that.

And so it was: she had panicked. La Signora commanded too much fear for her to own up to what she had done. Far easier to destroy the film and pretend it had never happened.

Dolly held down a sudden spike of vomit. All that struggle, all that pain, and this was the end of it. *Destroyed.* She had stolen from the NSA, *committed treason*, for nothing. When they caught her, she would go to prison for a decade. Tears pricked the corners of her eyes. But not tears of sadness, tears of frustration. *Exhaustion.* She had given everything to this, she felt like a car running on fumes. And now, she might just lie down on the floor and wait to be found. What was the point of anything else?

'But it's good news for you, right?' Jana asked, eyeing her suspiciously.

'What?'

'You work for the NSA. You already have the files. And now this stolen film is destroyed.'

Dolly said nothing.

'Unless you're lying to me.'

Her silence said enough.

Jana sat down on her little throne. Her hand instinctively coiled within reach of where the phone had been. Her voice was cool, her position of authority restored:

'If you try and block that door again, I will scream until they bring La Signora down here, and I will turn you over to her.'

'If you do that, I'll tell her what you did,' Dolly shot back. 'You'll be a liability to her, and she wouldn't stand for that. She'd have Daveed kill you with his silenced pistol before the last guests have even left the party.'

Jana's lips pressed tightly together, her jaw clenched. '*Zugswang*,' she hissed.

'What did you call me?'

'It's a German word.'

'What does it mean?'

'It's from chess. It's when you're in a situation where the fact that you have to make a move is a disadvantage.'

'A stalemate.'

'Not quite. That is a different thing. That is where you *can't* make a move.'

'Whatever.'

Jana seethed. 'Leave by the window. Go far away. I will never mention this to anyone. You must do the same. It would not be good for either of us.'

The barbed wire of horror was coiling itself around Dolly's stomach. She was going to vomit, she could feel it. Best to leave quickly and maintain her dignity. She turned to the window, then froze.

She span back.

'You're lying!'

Jana frowned, she couldn't find the words to defend herself against this sudden accusation.

'You're lying. You destroyed the film, but you kept the photographs. If you were so scared of La Signora you wouldn't take that film to be developed. The moment it arrived with a strange man's name on the envelope you would run it past Maltby to be safe. No, you were curious, like you said. You were curious and when the photos came back you sensed an opportunity to screw over La Signora because you hate her.'

'I don't hate her.'

'You hate her. I know that because *I* hate her and I only met her for the first time tonight. She tried to pull a fast number on me, she probably did something more subtle on you. What hold does she have over you?'

Jana shook her head. An involuntary response, it betrayed her.

'Fine, don't tell me. You have the photos, but you don't know what to do with them. You can't threaten her directly, you can't extort money from her, she'd kill you. You've worked in this house long enough, you know what happens.'

Still Jana said nothing.

'But you don't care about money. You just want to hurt her. You don't even care if she knows it was you, you just want the pleasure of hurting her. *I am your opportunity to hurt her.*'

'How?'

Dolly couldn't help smiling. 'Because she will have lost.'

FORTY-SEVEN

The stairs were cramped and twisted like a small intestine, leading up into the roof, to the dreaded room. Every step gave out a screech like she was stepping on a cat's tail.

Marie reached the narrow corridor, lit with flickering candles that over decades had left black smudges on the walls. There was no guard outside the door, that was odd. She knocked timidly.

'*Enter.*'

The study's three windows gave a panorama in triptych. To the left, hillside dotted with the lights of lonely houses. Opposite, winding shoreline with its necklace of hotels and villas. And to the right, the rippling silver glass of the lake.

Liese was alone, sitting at her desk, her attention focussed as always on a ream of paperwork. The tip of her pen hovered over the words like a conductor's baton. Every few lines she would stop, underline or circle something, then carry on.

Marie stood in silence for ten minutes until Liese finished a section of whatever it was and put down the pen. Then she looked up at Marie and gave the satisfied smile of someone pleased to find a child exactly where they left them.

Liese said nothing, staring at her for two minutes, watching Marie avoid her gaze, until finally the woman could take no more and spoke:

'You sent for me.'

'I know.'

'Well, what do you want?'

Liese bristled. 'What's that tone? Do I sense some fight in you tonight?'

Marie's eyes burned at her, then looked at the floor.

'No,' she whispered.

'Good.'

She paused. Another show of power.

'Simon works for the WMO still, correct?'

'What?' Marie asked, startled.

'Simon, your son. He continues to work for the World Meteorological Organisation in Geneva. I am correct?'

'Yes,' she said, adding, 'as far as I know,' for no reason.

'As far as you know? What kind of mother are you?'

Marie opened her mouth to speak.

'That's a rhetorical question, don't answer. I need to see him.'

'What?'

'Have you gone deaf?'

'Why would you need to see Simon?'

'I don't see how that's any of your business.'

'I'm his mother.'

'No you're not! Besides, does he run the rest of his WMO business past you? Do you approve his other meetings?'

'No, but—'

'Do you approve my meetings, Marie?'

She shook her head. 'But why Simon? Can't you meet someone else from the WMO?'

'I don't know anyone else at the WMO.'

'You don't know Simon either.'

Liese reached into her pocket, but the pack of drawing pins wasn't there. She picked up her pen instead, drumming it on the edge of the desk.

'I don't understand your reluctance. You know the cost of saying no.'

Marie said nothing.

'I need to see him next week. Wednesday morning, here.'

'You can't, he's going to New York next week.'

'I need to see him next week.'

'He's going to New York.'

'I heard you. Did you hear me?'

Not wanting to say it a third time, Marie shrugged. 'I don't understand what you want me to do?'

'Talk him out of it. Make him come here instead. I'll pay for all the travel, he can stay in the Grand Tremezzo.'

'You don't understand, he's been looking forward to this trip for months. He's going to speak at the UN.'

'To the General Assembly?'

'No, of course not.'

'Good. Then he can skip it.'

'What am I meant to say to him?'

'You're his mother, legally speaking, you'll think of something.'

Marie stood there in stunned silence. Liese

stopped tapping her pen and went back to combing through her paperwork.

'Please.'

Marie said it so quietly that Liese didn't register it at first.

'What did you say?'

'*Please.*'

Liese stifled a laugh.

'Please, not my son. I'll do whatever you want, but not him.'

'Do you think this sudden show of motherly love is going to persuade me? Don't be so pathetic.'

'I am this pathetic. You've made me this pathetic. Liese, I will do anything you want, but leave Simon alone.'

'You *will* do anything, and everything, I want. Do you understand that? You will call your son, you will lie to him, beg him, threaten him, guilt him, you will do whatever it takes to get him here next week. Because you don't have the ability to say "no". I have removed that word from your vocabulary. When you are in my company that word chokes in your throat like an allergy. You would do well to forget that word ever existed. That's the way it's always been, and you can stand there crying, but that's the way it will always be. Until the day I die.'

FORTY-EIGHT

J ana checked the corridor for searching guards. All clear. They dashed through the darkness, then up the same servants' stairs Dolly had used to take La Signora her drink. For a terrifying moment she thought they were heading all the way to the top again. But no, they stopped at the floor below and entered a different narrow corridor.

There were six small doors leading to the original servants' bedrooms. Jana's was opposite the stairs, the traditional place for the housekeeper so they could catch anyone who tried to sneak out at night. With a heavy brass key, she unlocked the door, ushered Dolly inside, and locked the door behind them.

The sting of dust prickled the hairs in Dolly's nostrils. The room was under the eaves of the house, the ceiling slanted over one small window. The walls were plain stone, the floor plain boards. Cobwebs hung from the exposed beams like dream catchers. Under the window was a modest single bed covered with a sheet and blanket. There was no photo on the nightstand, just tubes of hand and face cream. Against one wall was a small chest of drawers, hiding in the shadows, and next to it some laundry hung over the back of a beaten-up chair. On the other wall was a shallow fireplace, a bookcase with a laptop perched on top, a small armchair in the corner. Dolly could picture Jana spending her lonely evenings here. There was a connecting bathroom through an open door, and she could see a sink in the corner. Sitting in one of the soap holders was the tin of black pomade. There were smears of it on the taps, and above the sink there was a rusting, cloudy mirror in whose untrustworthy reflection the housekeeper would sculpt her hair.

Jana turned on a sickly yellow lamp and moved to the chest of drawers. She laid down flat on the floor, reaching her hand underneath it. Dolly moved to look out the window, her heels clacking on the wood. She peered down into the darkness, but there was nothing to see. There was a scraping sound as Jana lifted a loose floorboard and slid it out from under the chest of drawers. Then, still on her front, her head disappeared under the heavy piece of furniture and Dolly could hear her rooting around in the cavity underneath. A minute later, one of her hands appeared and something slid across the floor.

Dolly bent down to pick it up, but Jana barked, 'That's not it! Leave it alone.'

She didn't pick it up, but she couldn't help looking at it. It was a notebook, possibly a diary. Then there was another swoosh of Jana's hand and another item skittered across the floor. This time it was a photograph in a silver frame. A bashful young woman posed with a parakeet on her shoulder. The clothes looked at least twenty years old and the picture was fading.

'Is this you?'

'Mind your own business.'

The next item was heavy, making a racket as it skated across the floor, coming to rest against Dolly's foot. A steel revolver glinted up at her. Then a box of bullets scooched across the boards, clinking together at her feet. The next thing in Jana's hand was a wad of euros. She didn't slide them across the floor. Then, she placed something else on top of the wad and pulled her head out from under to stand up. Picking up the final item, she turned to face her.

In the lamplight, Dolly could just make out the coloured card folder from the photo shop.

'If I give them to you, what will you do with them?' Jana asked.

'I've got an old college friend whose dad writes for *The Washington Post*.'

'Why not WikiLeaks?'

'Because I want them taken seriously.'

'WikiLeaks is very serious.'

Dolly smiled. 'Leave the media strategy to me.'

Jana frowned. 'How will sending them to a journalist hurt La Signora?'

'Because that's not what she wants. She wants to hold on to them, use them as blackmail material. She always gets what she wants, right? Well not this time, not if you give them to me.'

Jana hesitated.

Dolly held out her hand.

'No,' Jana said, 'I've changed my mind.'

'What?'

'I don't know you, how do I know what you'll do with them? I will send them to WikiLeaks myself.'

She turned back to the chest of drawers. Dolly glanced down at the gun but pushed the thought away.

'Wait!' she said.

'No, sorry.'

'We can both have them.'

Jana turned to study her, her scepticism deepened into a heavy frown, but she said nothing.

'You must have a phone.'

Jana hesitated to answer, but finally grunted, 'Yes.'

'And it takes photos?'

'And?'

'So take a picture of each photo. You can send them to whoever you want, I don't care, I want them out in the world.'

'A photograph of a photograph?'

'Of a computer screen, yeah, I know, but none of that matters as long as you can read what's on them. Here,' she moved to the bed, 'under this lamp, lay them out on the white sheet, one at a time. I'll help you.'

Jana moved slowly towards her.

'Come on, hurry up, if anyone catches us we're both toast.'

'Ok, crazy American,' Jana said, 'you take the photos on your phone, I'll keep these.'

'I don't have a phone.'

Jana frowned.

'Search me if you want.'

Jana grumbled as she set to work laying the first picture on the bedsheet. She adjusted the lamp, then played with the height and angle of her phone. Dolly leant over her shoulder, keen to get her first glimpse of the photos she had taken a lifetime ago. They weren't as clear as she had pictured in her mind, by they would do. You could read the report, that was all that mattered.

'You're blocking the light,' Jana told her. 'Go over by the door and listen for anyone coming.'

Almost tripping over them, Dolly picked up the revolver and box of bullets, and at that moment she heard the unmistakeable creak of footsteps on the stairs.

Jana froze. Dolly fumbled with the bullets, ripping the box. They spilled out onto the floor in a deafening clatter, rolling in every direction. Panicking now, she got down on all fours to pick them up. The footsteps were getting closer. She grabbed one pesky bullet, loaded it into the cylinder. Then another. The door to the corridor opened and the footsteps stepped onto the creaking boards. A third bullet, that was enough. She dropped it in the cylinder, slammed it back in line with the barrel and levelled it at the locked door. There were two pools of shadow in the crack of light underneath. Then the light in the corridor went out.

Dolly pulled the hammer back, cocking the revolver.

There was silence for an agonising second. Then the footsteps moved down the corridor. They heard another heavy brass key unlock a creaky door, then the thump of it closing.

'Just Paula,' Jana whispered.

The same Paula who said, "If I see La Signora, I will tell her about you," Dolly thought.

Time was running out. Dolly pictured the sand in an egg timer, it had formed a well as the last grains shuffled towards their doom. Those million different roads Cain talked about were closing off. Did one of them still lead to her escape?

'Hurry up,' she hissed.

'I need to do them right.'

Dolly huffed, relaxing her grip on the pistol. The door was locked, the floor was too creaky for anyone to surprise them, but still she kept the gun in her lap.

'What did she do to you?' she asked almost casually.

'Mind your own business,' Jana replied, not breaking from her task.

Dolly looked down at the dated picture in its silver oval frame. 'Who's in the photo?'

Jana was silent for a moment. Dolly didn't hear her huff or complain. When she had finished with the photo she was arranging, she spoke:

'She catches people, you know that.'

Dolly nodded, then realised Jana still hadn't broken from her job even to glance at her.

'Yes.'

'She caught both of us.' She said it matter-of-factly, like it was nothing devastating or heartbreaking. 'Then she made us choose which one of us she would set free and which one she would keep. I very bravely let Marta go free.'

Dolly frowned. 'She actually let her go free? Really destroyed whatever hold she had on her? Evidence, whatever it was?'

'Yes.'

'That's surprising.'

'It was a way of being twice as cruel. Forcing the two of us to fight for survival. To tear us apart. But she didn't know, because she's never been in love. She didn't understand. There is always the stronger one of you, isn't there? The one who can take it. The one who walks home when there's only room for one more in the taxi. The one who has to sit next to the weird looking stranger in the cinema. The one who answers the door on the days you're both feeling depressed. I remember the moment as we looked into each other's eyes, it probably only lasted a second. *We* knew. If she expected us to fight, she was wrong, we knew it would be me. I could take it.' She paused. 'I think she did it for fun.'

'What did she have on you?'

For the first time she broke to look at Dolly, and her eyes were cold.

'Seriously, learn to mind your own business,' she said.

Dolly nodded.

FORTY-NINE

F og licked the tops of the trees as Baroffio made his way down the long drive, heading for the gates. It had been misty last night at the farm too, when they found the three bodies. A woman shot through the head in the barn. A man who had slowly bled to death on the dining room table from a rudimentarily patched stomach shot. And finally, carabinieri motorcycle officer Emilio Russo, whose body had been broken and packed into a plastic barrel. That one was especially tough for Li Fonti and his men.

And now the mist was enveloping this place. They seemed polar opposites, the poor rural farm perched high on a hilltop, surrounded by darkness, and the grand villa by the lakeside, haloed by lights, but the mist knew no difference. It settled on them both. It seemed emblematic to Baroffio, despite his prosaic mind. The mist obscured, and you had to get up close to see what was really there.

The guards ignored him as he passed out of the gates and wandered down the road. He passed by the G-Wagen, sitting just as they had left it, took a right, and wandered up a short, steep road. Ahead was a narrow three-story house with salmon-coloured render and wooden shutters. He stepped right in through the front door.

The array of officers looked up at him. One was in the process of cleaning and checking his Beretta M12 submachine gun. Others were chatting quietly. Another was scrolling through his phone. The local police chief, who had obtained this staging post for them, was dozing in the corner. His wife, who had insisted on coming with him, was passing round another tray of coffee. Everyone stopped when he entered.

'Well?' Li Fonti asked, sipping from a tin mug.

Baroffio nodded. 'He's in there.'

'So we go?'

He shook his head. 'Not yet. Too many civilians. If he's as dangerous as he appears, I'd feel a hell of a lot better if we waited until the guests have left.'

He turned to a bored Polizia Locale officer, who was slumped against the chimney breast, absently twanging the aerial of the radio he was clutching.

'Have the guys on the boat reported anything?'

The officer stood up off the wall. 'Ricci says there's very little activity on the water tonight. Two kids messing around on jet skis, a couple of pleasure boats, the restaurant boat doing its usual route, a few water taxis, the water buses.'

'That doesn't sound very quiet.'

'Quiet for Como.'

'And the boathouse?'

'There was someone in there, but they think they've left now.'

Baroffio frowned. 'What about guests who arrived by boat?'

The officer shook his head. 'They had to moor down here and go in by the main gate.'

'This fog is going to make things much harder,' Li Fonti chipped in.

'Tell them they can move in closer if they have to, but just night-vision, no lights yet, we don't want to spook him.'

The officer nodded and relayed the order over the radio.

'What's his plan for getting out?' Li Fonti asked.

'I'm not sure he has one. He changed the plates, he thought that was enough. He wouldn't have hung around here so long if he thought we were on his tail. I say we wait until the guests leave. We've got eyes on the gate and we've got eyes on the water, he can't get past us. They've got armed guards, probably as many guns as we've got, and about two-hundred guests. The odds of a stray shot from them or us are just too high. That's the last thing any of us want.'

Li Fonti nodded. 'I'm happy with that. We can wait.'

The officer checking his M12 had taken the bullets out of the magazine and was now loading them back in.

'Son,' Baroffio said, 'how many times have you checked that gun?'

The officer hesitated, then said with a smile, 'I won't do it again, sir.'

'Thank you.'

Baroffio gratefully accepted a coffee from the chief's wife and went to stand by a window, staring down the steep tarmac. The end of the narrow street, where it met the main lakeside road, was now just a wall of mist. Occasionally the silhouette of a young man or woman would cross through it. Without knowing he was doing it, Baroffio took a pencil from his pocket and started chewing on the end.

* * *

Baroffio had been staring and nibbling for some minutes when Li Fonti joined him by the window. In the twenty-one hours he had known him, Li Fonti had picked up on the polizia inspector's obvious tick.

'What's bothering you?' he asked.

Alerted to the pencil in his mouth, Baroffio quickly tucked it back in his pocket. Then he itched his stubbled chin and smiled, but for the first time there was no mirth in it.

'A ghost from my past,' he said.

Li Fonti just waited.

'I'm sure you can tell by my accent I'm not a Tuscan.'

'Your officer, Irene, said you're from Naples.'

'That's right. Born and raised.'

'She said you worked the Camorra killings.'

Baroffio looked a little embarrassed. 'I'm sure she was trying to make it sound impressive, but the truth is that if you're a cop for long enough, in Naples I mean, you're going to work gang murders. It's part of life. Half the kids I grew up with had fathers or uncles who worked for one of the clans. Half of them probably work for them now. Everyone knew a shopkeeper or street-seller who had been roughed up or turned over by them. It's the reason I became a cop. Of course, back then I didn't know that half the cops worked for them too. That's how I recognised Giuseppe Gallo, obviously.'

'Obviously,' Li Fonti replied, teasing only slightly. '"The Butcher of Matera", they called him. Matera wasn't our patch by a long stretch, but he had shared interests with a couple of the Naples clans, and he would visit them once in a while, so his picture was on our wall. *Financial* interests, I mean. Gallo, along with these two Naples clans, had access to an income the GdF couldn't pin down. They were making a decent chunk of money, which ruled out extortion, but the money wasn't regular, so that ruled out drugs. Which really only left trafficking. Naples being a busy port, with Salerno next door too, it's common enough. Sex workers, slavery, illegal immigration.'

He was still looking down the road into the mist, and the reflection in his eyes turned them milky. It was creeping towards them now.

'Drugs, trafficking, even the clans themselves, that was all in the hands of the GdF. But we got the murders. And we had managed to turn some informants inside the clans, separate to the GdF's. Young kids, mostly. The ones we could lean on. It was a dirty business.'

'Policework,' Li Fonti said.

'As I said, it was all the GdF's business, but their reputation was not so great. Not with us anyway. We knew that any money they had to bribe our officers with was left over from bribing the GdF's first. Hence us running our own informants. It was from them that we got our only real intelligence on this cashflow. From what we could tell there was no standing arrangement, simply an outside element who often employed the clans to smuggle cargo in using the Tunis to Salerno route, sometimes even the long route from Tel Aviv to Salerno. Gallo had made the introduction, vouched for the client, evidently the client employed Gallo with certain other activities. In the end, that kind of money for one-off imports raised the spectre of terrorism, and so we couldn't hold on to it ourselves any longer. By that time the political situation was different and we were happy to pass it on to the GdF and Interpol and count it as one less headache for us. The most important thing we learned was the client's alias: Tourmaline.'

'Tourmaline?'

He glanced at Li Fonti. 'Yeah, it's English for *tormalina,* like the stone.'

He looked back out the window and the pencil came out again.

'A year passed, maybe more, I didn't think about it again. We went back to solving murders and rolling over informants.'

He noticed the pencil and put it away again.

'There was this one kid, Miko. Black. Said he was eighteen, which got around the paperwork, but he was probably something more like fourteen. He gave it away to anyone who would pay. Us, GdF, your lot. It was a miracle he had got in with them, the clans are not known for their inclusive hiring processes. They had a name for him I won't repeat. Pretty soon some of the officers started using that name for him too.'

Baroffio turned his nose up at the memory.

'Then one day he starts telling everybody he's got some big information to sell. He wants proper money, not the twenties and fifties we were giving him. Most of us would have written it off as what it always was, just more of the same information we got five times a day from different sources. But clearly someone else thought otherwise because of what he told me.'

He paused.

Li Fonti pressed him: 'What did he tell you?'

Baroffio's body language changed, relaxing as his voice became that of a street punk:

'I'll tell you what I told that other officer, but no more, not until I get my money. So I told him: Come on, Miko, you know how this works. You've got to give me something to give my boss so he'll sign off me drawing out the money. I can't help you otherwise, and I want to help you. *The butcher's coming to town,* he said. So what? I said. He comes to town all the time. *Not like this,* he said, *'cause he's meeting Tom O'Lean.'*

'Tom O'Lean?'

'He thought it was an Irish name, he must have overheard it. All he knew was it was important, and it was hush-hush. Of course, it meant something to me. He said he knew where they were going to meet. Where they were going to be. Where *Tourmaline* was going to be. Miko was going to watch it all and afterwards he would tell me everything about them. Alright, I said, I'll pay the money, I'll pay the money right now, let *me* watch them. But he wouldn't tell me. Maybe I was too excited, maybe it put him off, maybe it made him think it was worth even more. I gave him everything I had in my wallet, but it wasn't enough, said he had a better offer. I thought he was lying. I promised him the most I thought I could get out of my boss. All he said was he'd think about it.'

He paused for a moment. Li Fonti said nothing.

'I thought about following him, but I couldn't follow him into those neighbourhoods, they knew me too well. That would be signing Miko's death warrant, I thought. But it turned out I'd already done that.'

His milky eyes moved to Li Fonti.

'That evening they dumped him on the steps of the station. Threw him from a moving van. The nerve of it. Two officers got him inside, we all rushed downstairs because of the commotion. I recognised him immediately, of course, despite what they'd done to his face. They'd cut out his tongue. Then, in case the point wasn't obvious enough, they'd cut off his lips. He'd already lost a lot of blood. Before he died he managed to scribble four letters on a charge sheet that was lying by the desk sergeant's window: I N G L. We could never say for sure what it meant, but I had an idea.'

'What was your idea?'

'*Inglese.*'

Li Fonti frowned. 'And why is that bothering you tonight?'

Baroffio gave an uncertain smile. 'Because I think I just met him.'

He went back to staring out the window. The pencil came out once again, but he didn't chew on it, he was clutching it. Li Fonti glanced around at his men, they were bored, but they were ready.

There was a sharp crack. He looked round at Baroffio, who was staring down with shock at the broken pencil in his hand.

'Damn it,' he said. 'Damn this fog. Damn the past. And damn sitting around. Radio Marino, tell her to get in the air. We go in twelve minutes.'

FIFTY

Cain followed behind Maltby, back up the stone steps and into the gardens. The crowd was thinner now, guests were trickling out like grains of sand dropping out of an egg timer. There would come a point when there were enough quiet corners for Daveed and his men to give Cain a swift syringe to the neck, catch him like he was drunk, and drag him down to the boathouse. Now he thought about it, he wondered why they hadn't done it already. A syringe went in the leg just as well, and no one would spot that in a crowd. Maybe he'd been safe with Maltby, maybe they would try it now.

Standing just a few meters away was a blond guard with a haircut you could use to sharpen a pencil. He spoke two words into his shirt cuff as they appeared. Cain clocked him, expecting to receive the same hard stare Daveed had given him, but instead the guard's eyes were focussed on Maltby. The guard did nothing more than stare though, and they stepped unimpeded through the glass doors into the villa.

'Paula's room is on the second floor,' Maltby said. 'You can only get there by the servants' stairs, we can get to them from the first floor. *Why do you keep walking behind me?*' he suddenly snapped.

'In case it's a trap.'

Maltby huffed. 'What can I do to convince you?'

Cain didn't answer.

'Well?'

'Maybe you can't.'

They reached the main stairs of the house. In the entrance hall, a group of four guests were leaving. They called to Maltby, who put on a smile and beseeched them to stay longer, there were still bottles of Champagne they hadn't opened. The guests laughed, waved goodbye, and left.

They climbed the stairs to the first floor and approached the hidden door to the servants' stairs.

'As soon as we have the file, we'll burn it,' Maltby said. 'Then you and I will go up to her office. I'll do the deed whilst you cover the door.'

'How are you planning to do it?'

'Silently.'

'And then?'

'Then, when the guests are gone, and the caterers have packed up, Daveed and his men will do their work like they always do. If we leave the body intact, they might just be able to make it look like heart failure. If not, I'm sure an accident can be arranged. Falling down the stairs or over the balcony would account for any broken or crushed bones in the neck.'

Cain must have made a noise, or something, not that he noticed it.

Maltby rounded on him. 'What does that mean? You and I have both had to kill people, and we've both wondered, every time, if they deserved it.'

'I didn't say anything.'

'There's a line, isn't there? Over that line, they

deserve it. Some of the people we've killed were closer to that line than others. Some, with the benefit of hindsight, or perhaps just old-age sentimentality, were just inside the line, and we wish things could have gone differently. Actions I regret.' He raised a single, stabbing finger. 'She is nowhere near that line.'

'And what happens tomorrow, you take over her empire?'

'Marriage has to have some benefits. Think what we could do with her money.'

'I'm not interested.'

'For good, I mean, not for ourselves.'

Cain said nothing.

Maltby sighed, turned ahead.

They reached the servants' stairs and crept their way up to the next floor. The corridor was silent. The lights were off. Maltby moved like a cat, silent on the creaky boards, his SAS experience evident in this simple skill that would have been invisible to anyone but Cain. Cain walked after him, and the boards did creak beneath his feet. He had never had that skill.

Gently, but with a precision that punctured the silence, Maltby knocked on a door at the end of the corridor.

'Paula?' he asked just loudly enough.

No answer came.

He held up crossed fingers to Cain and smiled, then he tried the door. It swung open with a creak, and Maltby took two steps into the darkness.

'She has a lamp by the bed,' he said.

As he said it the lamp came on.

❋ ❋ ❋

Maltby froze. Perched on the edge of the bed, with one hand on the dangling switch of the lamp, sat Daveed. In his other hand, a suppressed pistol pointed at Maltby's belly. He was wearing clear plastic coveralls from top to bottom that squeaked as he uncrossed his legs and stood up. Little elasticated covers protected his shoes.

'You've lost your edge, old man.'

'I don't know what you think you're doing—'

'Check your left jacket pocket, old man.'

Bristling from the repeated "old man" jibe, Maltby reached into his pocket and felt around. There was nothing there. Relief flooded over him. *Wait a minute.* Something brushed against his fingers. He felt a wave of disappointment. He wasn't angry or afraid, *just disappointed* with himself. He pulled out what looked like an ordinary silver dollar, but anyone holding it would know something was wrong. The weight was a little too light, and the thickness a little too wide. It was an old CIA combined tracker and listening device. It must be more than fifteen years old, Maltby thought, the new ones were indistinguishable from the real thing.

'I've heard everythin y'all said since you ordered me away from the bar. And I got it on tape.'

Damn him.

'Ok,' Maltby said, staying cool, 'what do you want?'

'What do I want? Your job.'

'That's a stroke of luck, because I want Liese's job. And *I* won't make you marry me.'

Daveed didn't say anything. Didn't pull the trigger either. Maltby couldn't hear Cain behind him, but he knew he was there.

'Come on,' he purred. 'You know we were just on our way to kill her. You heard it all. Why not join us?'

''cause I don't need to. I ain't afraid of her like you are. She ain't got no hold over me.'

'That's why she'll never give you the job. She'll kill you the second you play her the recording. She doesn't trust people she hasn't bought, and that recording is dangerous to her. She'll assume you've made a copy as insurance and she'll get the next Daveed to garrotte you right there. Probably that blond twerp, Lindhardt.'

'I'ma take my chances. And Lindhardt is loyal to me.'

'As loyal as you are to me?'

'As loyal as I am to *her*,' Daveed retorted.

His grip tightened on the pistol.

Maltby heard the boards creak as Cain took a step forward. 'You're both foolish for thinking you can kill anyone tonight.'

Daveed's eyes flicked to him and then back to Maltby.

'You listened in to our conversations,' Cain said, 'there's a police inspector here.'

'He just left.'

'And you think he's here alone? That you can kill someone and clean up before they search the place?'

'They ain't gotta warrant.'

'They don't need one.'

Daveed's eyes flashed over Maltby's shoulder, to Cain again.

'Explain that shit!' he barked.

'They're here for me. They think I'm the one who delivered the bomb to the Di Materas. Which I guess I am. And that I killed the Croatians. Which I guess I did. They also think I killed three others. I'm a wanted criminal. Presumed extremely dangerous. And he knows I'm here, he spoke to me. They don't need a warrant to enter private property in pursuit of a suspect, or to make an arrest.'

Shit. Cain was right.

'So we'll kill him too,' Daveed said. 'I ain't no gangbanger, I ain't gotta be scared of killin a cop. I've done it before.'

'Do you really think he's here alone?' Cain asked. 'Do you think he traced the car driven by a man who's killed twelve people in the last twenty-four hours and didn't bring armed backup? Where do you think he's just gone? He's gone to get his team.'

'That's truth, huh? Then what they waitin for?'

Cain said nothing.

Daveed smiled. 'I'ma guessin they ain't too hot on startin a firefight when there's still over a hundred guests out here. Cops hate it when a stray shot takes down an innocent white person. And these guests here, they like to hang around, drink up all La Signora's Cristal. That being truth, it sounds to me like if I kill you silently, I got me some time to clean up.'

Daveed was right. It also meant they could still take care of Liese.

'Work with me, Daveed,' Maltby said, 'and you can have the job you want. You've made your point.'

He took a step forward, buttoning his dinner jacket.

'*You've made your point*: you're a big player in all this. I shouldn't have left you out of my plans. And you didn't expect an offer from me, I understand that, but now you have a decision to make.'

'Nah, I already made my decision. D'you think I get all dressed up like this just to threaten people?'

Maltby seethed. *How dare he?*

'You're making a terrible mistake!' he screamed, stabbing a finger at him. 'Now, you listen to me, Dav—'

※ ※ ※

A puff of pink mist exploded from the back of Maltby's head. His body collapsed like a puppet with the strings cut, falling back hard against the open door and slumping to the floor. Even with the suppressor the shot was deafening in the tight, hard room, and it took Cain several seconds before he could hear anything else.

He looked down at Maltby's limp frame, the entry wound just a neat black circle below his left eye. He memorialised him with a few seconds of silence before he spoke.

'Someone will have heard that. Why don't you jump out that window?'

The suppressor was now pointed squarely at Cain's chest.

'I don't hear no panic, do you? No footsteps. No screams.'

A trickle of laughter through the window. The continued hum of the guests in the gardens. They hadn't missed a beat.

'You ruined my suit,' Daveed drawled, 'now I'ma ruin yours.'

Cain spun and fell. He hadn't meant to fall, he had meant to turn and run, but his foot caught on Maltby's arm and tripped him. Daveed's suppressed shot rang out, clipping Cain's jacket and puncturing the door of the room opposite. Cain landed hard on his shoulder, his hair swinging over his face. Looking up through it, he saw Daveed snarl, adjusting his aim to point down at him. There was a deafening roar and another hole ripped through the opposite door. Something hit Daveed in the middle of the chest, bursting a hole in his coveralls and fluttering his tie. There was a second deafening roar and this time Cain recognised it as the boom of an unsilenced, old-fashioned revolver. Another bullet ripped through the opposite door and this time struck Daveed in the shoulder. Whoever was in the other room was firing blind through the closed door. A third boom announced a third bullet, but this one struck the door frame of Paula's room, exploding splinters into the air.

Daveed was still standing. There was a heavy thud as his pistol hit the floor. He clutched his chest, remaining conscious long enough to see the blood on his hands. Then he fell backwards, smashing into the bedside lamp and toppling its little table as he fell. His knuckles rapped on the wood as his gun hand struck the floor. He was dead.

* * *

'Shots!' the officer clutching the radio repeated. 'Definite shots!'

Baroffio shared a split-second glance with Li Fonti, then they ran for the door. In a flurry of spilt coffee and squeaking boots, the carabinieri team snatched up their weapons.

FIFTY-ONE

S prawled on the floor, Cain pushed open the door to the room opposite. There was Dolly, also lying on the floor, having fallen backwards as she fired the revolver. Startled, she aimed at him.

'Woah!' He raised his hands.

She relaxed her arms.

Craning his neck, he could see the open door to a bathroom that connected to another room opposite the top of the stairs.

Dolly aimed at Daveed's body.

'He's dead,' Cain said. 'That's twice. Now I owe you.'

He pushed himself up onto his knees, brushed dust off his shoulders, and stood up. As she was doing the same he noticed a card folder on the floor. She must have dropped it in the action. He picked it up.

'What's this?' he asked, flicking through it.

He saw the photos.

She raised the gun to his chest.

He just raised his eyebrow.

She dropped the gun down to her side.

He passed her the folder.

'You did it,' he said.

She was looking at Maltby's body now. 'Sorry about your friend.'

'Thank you.'

'We have to stop her.'

'Sorry?'

She looked down into his eyes. Hers were steel. 'We have to stop her.'

He said nothing.

'You didn't hear, you don't know.'

'How are we going to stop her?'

She wouldn't say it. The revolver twitched in her hand.

'Don't end up like one of them. No one deserves to die.'

'You said yourself, sometimes it's necessary.'

'When there's no other option. It's not the same thing.' He looked at the folder in her hands. 'You got what you came for.'

She nodded. 'Yes.' She paused. 'Did you?'

He smiled, but he could hear footsteps now. And screams.

'Give me the gun. You'd better get out of here in the commotion.'

He took the revolver from her hand.

'Join the crowd, go wherever they go until you get out of the gates, then choose the quietest street and just keep walking until morning.'

'You're coming too?'

He shook his head. 'They're looking for me, if you stick with me you'll get caught. Quickly. Go. *Now!*'

He gave her a push and she started to run down the corridor. But she stopped halfway, turned.

'Cain?' she said.

He looked up.
Their eyes met.
She didn't say anything.
'I know,' he replied.
She smiled.
He smiled back.
She nodded.
He bowed theatrically.
She laughed.
He smiled again.
Then she turned, and left.

* * *

Baroffio reached the gates. The guards had abandoned their posts, rushing towards the house. The officers who had been watching the G-Wagen were now at the gates and looked to Baroffio for orders. Li Fonti and the armed team arrived seconds behind him.

'What do we do?'

'Form a line. *Form a line*, the three of you. Block this gate! You've all got his description. Don't be fooled by his age, I reckon he's fitter than any of us. No one gets past you without being checked. Not a guard, not a waitress, not if you think someone else has checked them, not one of us, *no one!* Understood?'

'Yes, boss!'

'The rest of you follow me.'

He passed through the gates and started running up the long driveway to the villa.

* * *

When the shots rang out, Liese Vermuth was still sitting at her desk. She hadn't noticed Marie leave, but she didn't care either. When she was done with people they might as well vanish, it made no impact on her whether they were still physically in her presence.

But the shots shattered the walls that separated her from her surroundings. They had erupted directly beneath her, from the servants' bedrooms. Her instinct was to investigate, to run towards them, not away. There was no danger that could touch *her*. Her legs pulled her up out of her chair, across the room, into the corridor. It would be logical to use the servants' stairs to investigate, but she never used the servants' stairs, so habit led her down the main staircase, *away from danger.*

❋ ❋ ❋

Marie was standing in the shadows of the second-floor corridor. Ten minutes ago, she'd had awareness enough to leave Liese's office, but when she reached the bottom of the study stairs she almost crumpled to the floor. She couldn't see because of the tears, and the thought of Simon was yanking on her chest like an anchor chain, pulling her down into a black well. One all too familiar to her lately. Suicidal thoughts swirled down there.

The gunshots brought her back to the surface. And she brought up with her a vain hope that Liese had taken her own life. It vanished as quickly as it arrived. No suicide ever shot themselves three times.

❊ ❊ ❊

Jana had been the closest to the action. She heard footsteps climb the stairs, and the tall American snatched up the revolver. When the footsteps moved down the corridor to Paula's room, Jana shoved the photos into the woman's hand so she could make a run for it. But she didn't. She just listened. It was Mr Maltby, and Daveed, and another man's voice she didn't recognise. Silently, the crazy bitch tiptoed through the connecting bathroom, into the empty room opposite Paula's.

What happened next, Jana barely registered. The moment Dolly started firing she ran for the stairs.

She joined the other two women at the bannisters of the main staircase, overlooking the great atrium of the entrance hall. They stood there, Jana, Marie, and Liese in the middle, the three of them peering over and down.

Guests were hurrying towards the doors, screaming, panicking, pushing, tripping. Her hands on the handrail, Liese leant forward to get a better look, taking one foot off the carpet.

'—the devil?' she muttered.

Jana looked at the lifted foot, and at the other perched on tiptoes. Electricity surged through her. Feeling suddenly naked, she looked up at the other woman, afraid she could see what she was thinking.

It was like looking in a mirror.

The other woman was poised in the same stance, her hands twitching just like Jana's. Written on her face was the same guilty excitement, the same terrified focus, like two cats about to pounce. Their gaze seemed to crackle with the same electricity, the same terrifying power arcing between them.

Then they both did it. They both put two hands on her back and pushed. She did nothing more than gasp as she toppled over the handrail, her hands pinwheeling out in front of her with nothing to grab on to. Her gold and white dress fluttered behind her as she fell the two stories headfirst like a brick wrapped in a binbag. Her skull hit the marble with the sound of a vase breaking.

A few guests hurrying towards the main door were caught in the "spatter" and the screams were horrific. At that point a full stampede started.

Jana vanished into the servants' stairs. Marie ran down the main stairs towards the body.

FIFTY-TWO

C ain wiped down the revolver and placed it on the floor next to Maltby. It wouldn't convince anyone he fired the shots, but it looked neater. Then he took a quick glance at Daveed's body. Nothing needed doing.

He wiped down the door opposite. He didn't remember touching anything else, it was Maltby who had touched the doorknob. He wiped the knob of the bathroom door, both sides, then the other bathroom door which connected to the housekeeper's bedroom, tracing backwards what he imagined was Dolly's route. Now in the room, he quickly wiped down the bed frame, door handle, bedside lamp, anything he thought Dolly might have touched.

Then he used his foot to open the bathroom door and went back in. He used his elbow to turn on the light. Above the sink there was a rusting, cloudy mirror. He stared into its untrustworthy reflection. An old man stared back at him.

Baroffio and his team were halfway up the long drive when the stampede started. The main doors overflowed with guests, spilling down the three steps onto the gravel. Some picked themselves up, treading over the rest, and kept running. Baroffio saw one old, bald man crunch his Cuban heel onto a woman's hand. She yelped with pain.

They were all heading for the main gates, a wall of them. The three officers he had posted there weren't going to be enough.

Baroffio stopped.

'Back!' he shouted. 'Back to the gates!'

Li Fonti stopped, stared at him wide-eyed.

'We can't let anyone leave unchecked!' Baroffio shouted. 'Quickly!'

He turned and ran.

Li Fonti looked up to the villa. In the five seconds they had stood still, indecisive, the crowd had made ground on them and were just seconds away.

'Quickly!' Li Fonti echoed.

The armed team swivelled on their heels.

* * *

There was blood on the marble when Dolly reached the main entrance hall. She slipped and skidded on it in her heels. She didn't look closely at the body, she knew who it was from the dress. At that time she didn't feel anything. She was too busy.

Madison and Abi were clustered in the corner with three other waitresses and a couple of chefs.

'What happened?' she asked them.

'There were shots,' Madison answered.

'She fell,' Abi said at the same time.

More guests pushed towards the main doors.

'Let's get out of here!'

They ran. Dolly had to elbow past a young woman who was live-streaming the panic to her Instagram followers. She sent her phone flying.

The folder of photos was tucked neatly down the back of her trousers, half in her knickers, half sitting against the small of her back. A bald man in a purple tuxedo grabbed her by the shoulder and pulled her out of his way. He toppled out of the main door and down the steps. As he got up he trod on a woman's hand, but didn't seem to care.

Dolly hesitated. There were armed officers heading towards them. She decided to rush them, there was only one way out. The officers stopped, turned, and started running from them. With her long legs she could probably catch them, but her heels were slowing her down.

Dolly and the waitresses kept the pressure on them. They were young and fit, unlike the chefs, who were lagging behind with the guests. They caught up with the armed officers, hampered by their heavy bulletproof vests, and they all reached the main gates together.

An officer at the gate took a cursory look at them, but made sure to check Dolly, probably because she was so tall and wearing men's clothes. He waved them through and pointed them over to a cluster of police cars forming a temporary cordon whilst another officer put out barriers. On the other side, the barriers had already been erected and an officer was guarding them. The siren of an ambulance was wailing on the wind, speeding down the road. The officers at the cordon turned to flag it down.

She took her opportunity, melting into a line of bystanders who had gathered by some bollards on the pavement opposite the gates. She crouched slightly, hiding her height. Then the officers began to corral the waitresses. She watched Madison and Abi forced into a group with the others. As they did so, another officer walked along the line of bystanders, pushing them further back onto the pavement and stringing tape across the bollards. He ignored her. She waited five seconds, then she turned and walked down the pavement away from the action. *Not too fast*, she told herself. She passed an opticians, then a bakery, up next was a café. Just before it there was an alley that led to some stone steps that cut through the block.

She turned into the darkness, reached the steps and hurried up them. She cursed her heels again and the racket they made on the stone. She checked behind her, but there was no one there.

This was it. She had really done it. She looked back towards the lights of the villa, just visible reflecting on the water. Beyond them was the sweeping searchlight of a police boat, and for a moment she felt melancholy. But then the real chill of the night air caught her, and she knew she had to keep moving.

※ ※ ※

When he reached the gates, Baroffio took charge. No one got out except past him. He made the guests form an orderly queue just inside the gates, watched over by the armed team, and one by one he checked them off.

The security staff gathered, led by an efficient

looking blond man. Baroffio made a place for them to stand, *inside the gates*. He wasn't letting them out. They were armed, and at the moment he couldn't think of a good reason to take their guns from them. They weren't currently showing any signs of misbehaviour, but he posted an officer to stand with them so that they couldn't come up with any agreed stories, or anything like that. He would be having a very long chat with them soon.

Another crowd of stragglers made it out the front door. The drunkest lot so far, they had probably been woken up by the shots. Either that or dragged from the gardens. They were the last, this group of eight, no more followed behind them as they made their way up the drive, laughing and joking.

Baroffio shook his head as the officers presented each guest to him. He had already scanned the queue and not seen Cain amongst them, but he was going to check thoroughly anyway. He wanted zero chance of a mistake.

His attention kept drifting to the final group making their way down the drive. This was Cain's final opportunity as he saw it. But they looked too young. That was, except for the old man at the back walking with a stick. Whether he knew the young people or not, Baroffio couldn't tell. If so, the young people had forgotten about him. With every laboured step he was left further behind, until he was separated entirely, shuffling down the long drive like a snail crawling over pavement.

Baroffio was concerned. So far there had been no Cain, no Maltby, and no Liese Vermuth either. Although the latter two might be reluctant to flee their own home.

He checked the last of the queue with a sigh. He was apprehensive about entering the house, even with Li Fonti's armed team. He didn't want to get into a firefight. It just didn't need to happen. He was disappointed with the Canadian, he hadn't seemed the type. He seemed too classy for that. But, he thought, he also hadn't seemed the type to surrender.

The young group arrived and Baroffio waved them through without bothering to check them. *Let the others do it*, he thought, frustratedly kicking a pebble into the bushes. Then he watched the old man, bent double, make his way up to the gate. He had a ring of white hair below a bald scalp, and a gut that sagged over his belt, straining at his shirt. *Not with a bang, but a whimper,* Baroffio thought, remembering a poem from his English classes all that time ago.

The officers stopped the old man at the gate and looked to Baroffio. The inspector shook his head and kicked another pebble. The officers directed him to wait with the other guests. He didn't seem to hear properly, so they repeated the instruction. He nodded and shuffled away.

No Cain. And no Maltby or Liese Vermuth either.

The drive was empty. And although the lights were on, there was no sign of movement in any of the windows. The place looked welcoming, but Baroffio was wary. He listened for the distant hum of the police boat but couldn't pick it out. *They must not be moving.*

'On the water?' he called to his officer clutching the radio.

The officer checked in with the boat squad, then he shook his head. 'Nothing,' he shouted.

Baroffio looked to Li Fonti and his team. 'Ok, let's go in.'

He led them down the drive in an open formation, there was no cover to be had. The armed team kept their eyes on the windows at the front of the villa in case Cain decided to take a pot shot at them.

Halfway up the drive the low rumble of an engine and the steady thump of rotor blades echoed off the steep hills. *Marino.* With a swoosh, the police helicopter was above them and its powerful searchlight was scanning the trees and gardens for any signs of movement.

Baroffio took out his own radio. 'Anything on thermal?' he asked.

'She's scanning the gardens now,' came the crackled reply.

Baroffio watched the helicopter as it flew in a circle around the little promontory, checking the gardens, trees, and bushes for any hotspots that might suggest a human.

The radio crackled again: *'Negative.'*

He's still in the house. For the first time in ten years, the old inspector pulled his gun.

They reached the three steps to the main doors, and at this point Li Fonti insisted that Baroffio take a step back. This is what the armed team did, it was the reason they were here.

The two inspectors stayed outside as the team of eight burst through the main doors into the entrance hall. Two minutes later, the team leader spoke over the radio:

'Ground floor clear, but we've got a body in here.'

The two inspectors hurried into the villa. A

woman's body was lying crumpled on the marble where she had fallen over the handrail of the large atrium. Baroffio recognised her.

'A guest?' Li Fonti asked as they crouched over the body.

'The homeowner.'

'Pushed in the stampede, I guess. What a tragedy.'

Baroffio looked up the height of the large atrium. 'Do you think there were many guests up on the second floor?'

'What do you mean?'

Baroffio stood back up.

'Make sure to check the servants' area downstairs,' he called to the armed team leader.

'I've got two already down there, the rest of us are heading up.'

Baroffio watched the six heavily-armed officers march up the stairs in standard two-by-two cover formation. They split at the top of the stairs, three going left, three going right. One after another they heard the thump of a door kicked open and then, '*Clear!*'

A minute later they regrouped on the landing. They marched up to the second floor, out of Baroffio's sight. Once again, only slightly quieter, he heard the doors being kicked open and the shouts of '*Clear!*' Then he heard the armed team ascend to the top floor. He couldn't pick up much more than that.

He wandered to the bottom of the stairs, fiddling with a china pot of ornamental canes. Each had an elaborate silver handle in the shape of an animal's head: an eagle, a falcon, a wolf, a hare, a dog, a duck, and a horse. Which one was he? They were probably worth a few hundred euros each, and anyone could just pick one up and take it.

Something didn't feel right. He couldn't believe the Canadian was hiding in some cupboard or basement. He had expected him to make a run for it, head to the boathouse, hoping there was a pleasure craft of some kind, maybe a jet ski.

And here, in the house, what he feared had already come true: someone was dead.

The radio crackled again. *'All clear, sir. The house is empty, but there are bodies up here.'*

Bodies. Plural.

'Where?' he barked into the radio.

'Servant's quarters, top floor.'

'On our way.'

The two inspectors ran up the main staircase to the second floor but couldn't see any officers. A hidden door opened and an officer directed them into the servants' stairs.

The team leader was standing at the end of the corridor, looking into a room. Baroffio could see blood and a sprawled hand. As he got closer he recognised the body.

'Jolyon Maltby,' he said. 'The homeowner's husband.'

'What about this guy?'

Baroffio peered at Daveed's body. 'I don't think I met him. He looks like he was dressed for an execution.'

'Yeah,' the team leader chuckled dryly, 'his own.'

'Baroffio, in here!' It was Li Fonti's voice, coming from a room across the hall.

He ran into the room opposite the bodies and could see Li Fonti standing in a connecting bathroom, staring in abject confusion.

'What is it?'

'See for yourself.'

He stepped into the bathroom.

First, Li Fonti held up a piece of black fabric with hooks and eyes. He and the others didn't know what it was. Baroffio hadn't seen one for almost thirty years, not since he helped his father clear out his uncle's possessions. His uncle had always looked in great shape, and they could never understand how such a healthy-looking man could die of a heart attack at fifty-nine. It was a men's girdle, he explained, for holding in the stomach.

Then, Li Fonti pointed to a rag of fur in the sink. Except, it wasn't a rag, or fur, it was a toupée of slightly curly chestnut-brown hair. Just like the Canadian's hair, except for the white at his temples.

It was as though Cain had vanished, and this was all he had left behind.

The truth crashed over him like a cold wave.

'I need to sit down,' he announced.

An armed officer grabbed the beaten-up chair from Jana's room and quickly put it under him. Baroffio collapsed onto it. He sat there for some time whilst Li Fonti ordered his officers about their business. The pencil came out of Baroffio's pocket and he nibbled on it pensively. Soon though, he began to smile, and even gave the occasional distracted chuckle.

EPILOGUE

The Nice Guy

C ain swirled the Burgundy, breathing in the aroma. Deep notes of leather and oak, a hint of berry sharpness. He sampled a taste, letting it swish around his mouth before he swallowed. A jammy fruitiness was foremost on his palate, which surprised him, but it soon gave way to a mellow tannin texture and a hint of spice. It was not Casa Di Matera, but it was good. He nodded to the waiter, who poured him a sensible lunchtime glass.

As he waited for his salade lyonnaise, he continued to stare over the Promenade des Anglais, drumming his fingers on his silver fox-headed cane. He watched the sandy beach below, and the calm Mediterranean. There were no tourists this time of year, and very few pleasure crafts, just the rippling blue expanse.

His eyes on the horizon, his mind turned to the problem at hand. He was down to his last thousand euros, and soon he was going to have to make some money.

'Monsieur Byers!' came a call from the other side of the patio. It was Marcel from the Hotel Matisse.

Some of the other diners turned their heads. What was that name? Ah, it was *him.* The well dressed older gentleman with the flat stomach and the wavy blond hair. Except, of course, for the white around his temples. He was the one the Niçoise café and bar owners referred to simply as *"L'Américain".*

'It just came in.'

Marcel handed him a copy of yesterday's *Washington Post.* Cain got it every day. Always a day late, of course. But today it hadn't arrived in time and he'd eaten his breakfast without it.

Cain paid Marcel for the paper, telling him to keep the change.

'Merci, Monsieur.'

It had been three months now. *Slightly more,* it was the beginning of February. Every day Cain got the paper, hoping to read the story and know she made it out safe. That she had done it, and it had all been worth it. Every day the story failed to appear, and he felt a pang of concern. He knew big stories took time to write, they required investigation, confirmation, legal consultations, but three months felt like a very long time.

Liese Vermuth's death hadn't even made the news outside Italy. And the story was just that a glamourous charity soiree ended in gunshots, murder, and a siege. Vermuth wasn't famous, just rich, so nobody cared. Maltby's name hadn't featured in any of the stories, he was only the husband of someone who wasn't famous. And there had been no mention of the police inspector either, Cain was glad the press had gone easy on him.

He unfolded the paper. The headline stared back at him in block capitals: *CIA PAID MONEY TO*

GANGSTERS. Underneath it: *Supressed NSA report details quarter-century of payments to European, North African crime syndicates.*

Seventeen pages of coverage. Dolly's name wasn't in any of it. Neither was his. Or Maltby's. But this was just the first story, there would be more. Tomorrow all the US papers would lead with it. There would be congressional hearings, resignations, the president would have to say something. It was all Washington would be talking about today. And Langley. Dolly had dictated their week, possibly the next few months. She had turned heads. Some people would pay attention. *Good on her.*

What would happen to her now? He wondered. Had she known what she was getting into? *Maybe.* Maybe she hadn't planned that far ahead, but that was no great sin. Life was to be lived in the moment, one day at a time, because you never knew which day would be your last.

He looked to the horizon again. Pondered the same question as before. He was down to his last thousand euros. He was going to have to make some money soon.

Just as before, no immediate solution presented itself. But he trusted that fate would provide one when the time came.

Champagne, he thought. The day called for Champagne.

BOOKS BY THIS AUTHOR

You Can't Make Old Friends

Blacklisted by the police, private detective Joe Grabarz is in no shape to take on a new case. But when his estranged best friend's body washes up on a beach, Joe will have to navigate roadblocks, personal demons, and deadly complications to solve the crime.

Choose Your Parents Wisely

A missing girl sends a community into hysterics — and street-smart detective Joe Grabarz can't help but be reminded of his very first case. Can Joe face the painful lessons of his past as he attempts to solve the disappearance?

It Never Goes Away

When Joe Grabarz discovers his friend's corpse in an abandoned farmhouse, he's the prime suspect in the case. As he fights to prove his innocence, he uncovers a strange connection to three notorious murders that happened ten years ago.

The Benevolent Dictator

A young man fresh out of university and desperate to get into politics accepts a job with the prince of a Middle Eastern emirate. It should be a golden opportunity, but when he arrives in the kingdom he finds it on the verge of revolution, and soon learns that the prince has enemies everywhere.

The Forbidden Zone

Tommy has vivid memories of the summer he spent at Boys Club Camp, where counselors were strangely obsessed with the camp's long-dead founder — and something evil was waiting in the woods. Now an adult, he's drawn back to the camp in this spine-tingling chiller that will have readers transfixed.

WANT MORE?

Subscribe for updates at tomtrott.com

ABOUT THE AUTHOR

Tom Trott

Known affectionately as "Supreme Leader" and "Tom the Unconquerable", he lives in Brighton with his wife and daughter. As a boy he collected all the James Bond films on VHS, and as an adult he enjoys changing nappies and desperately trying to get his daughter to sleep.

Tom has a day job but dreams of being a writer full-time, you can help make that happen by doing one or more of the following:

1. Leave a review on Amazon (this is the most helpful thing you can do)
2. Buy a print copy and put it aside for a birthday or Christmas present
3. Recommend the book to family, friends, colleagues, and on social media
4. Contact Tom on social media and offer him lots of free money (this would really help) or a publishing deal

If you've actually read this page, tweet with the hashtag #TheFlorentine

Printed in Great Britain
by Amazon

85577733R00235